WITH
A LITTLE
LUCK

WITH
A LITTLE
LUCK

Marissa Meyer

FEIWEL AND FRIENDS
New York

A Feiwel and Friends Book
An imprint of Macmillan Publishing Group, LLC
120 Broadway, New York, NY 10271
fiercereads.com

Library of Congress Cataloging-in-Publication Data is available.

First edition, 2024
Book design by Michelle Gengaro-Kokmen
Printed in the United States of America
Feiwel and Friends logo designed by Filomena Tuosto

ISBN 978-1-250-61893-1 (hardcover)
ISBN 978-1-250-34557-8 (international edition)
ISBN 978-1-250-35968-1 (special edition)
1   3   5   7   9   10   8   6   4   2

For Jesse, Sloane, and Delaney
(I know how lucky I am.)

Chapter One

Writ upon these hallowed pages is the epic tale of the great wizard Jude. His power was rivaled only by his immeasurable charm. His life was a series of grand adventures—battles won and battles lost, evil vanquished and goodness restored. He was a true hero of legend. His story, as penned on this brittle parchment, is a worthy one—a quest for the ages. A destiny built on fortune and misfortune, blessings and curses . . . and a love that has inspired the music of bards across the centuries.

Or, depending on your interpretation, it could also be the story of a sixteen-year-old boy, halfway through his junior year at Fortuna Beach High School, who works four days a week at his parents' vinyl records store. The sort of boy who draws comics when he's supposed to be taking notes on the Industrial Revolution. The sort of boy who isn't sure he'll ever be able to afford college . . . or a car, for that matter. The sort of boy who would rather take a lightsaber to his non-drawing hand than risk the rejection that comes with asking out a girl he likes and, thus, has never asked out a girl, no matter how many times he's imagined how it might go if he did. The possible good . . . and the far more likely, almost inevitable, bad.

But it's fine. I've got a decent imagination, which is almost as good as epic quests and true love. Imagination surpasses real life . . . what? Ninety percent of the time? Tell me I'm wrong. You're the one with your nose in a book right now, so I know you agree with me, on some level.

"The Temple of Torna Gorthit?" says Ari, startling me from my targeted destruction of the fourth wall. (Theater joke—don't worry about it.) She's reading tonight's open mic night flyer over my shoulder, the flyer I've been doodling on for the past ten minutes. "Sounds ominous, Jude."

"It is rife with danger," I say. The ballpoint pen scratches across the white paper, transforming the clip art of a vinyl record into a black sun hanging over a tree-studded horizon. I've altered the letters in OPEN MIC to look like an ancient temple, crumbling from time. "I'm still working on the name. Naming things is hard."

Ari leans closer. She has her hair pulled back in a loose, messy bun, but one strand falls out, brushing across my forearm before she reaches up to tuck it behind her ear. "Is that supposed to be me?"

I pause and study the flyer. Ventures Vinyl presents . . . Open Mic Night! 6 p.m., the first Sunday of every month. All musical styles welcome. The bottom half of the page used to be taken up with a line art sketch of a girl playing a guitar, but I've changed the guitar to look more like a medieval lute, lengthened the girl's hair, and given her a cloak and riding boots. Very medieval chic.

"Um, no," I say, tapping the drawing. "This is Araceli the Magnificent—most renowned bard in all the land. Obviously."

Ari widens her eyes knowingly and whispers, "I'm pretty sure that's me."

I lift up the page and turn it to face her. "This is a lute, Ari. Do you play a lute? Do you?"

"No," she says, studying the drawing before adding, "But I bet I could."

"Yeah. Araceli the Magnificent likes to show off, too."

Ari laughs. "So what happens in this creepy temple?"

"A group of bards compete in a music competition. To the death."

"Yikes." She hops up onto the counter. She's short, but somehow she makes it look easy. "Do lots of bards sign up for that?"

"It's either compete in the tournament or have your video go viral on YouTube and be subjected to the comments of a hundred thousand trolls. Literal trolls. The smelly kind."

"I see," says Ari, legs swinging. "Death sounds preferable."

"I thought so, too." I pick up my pen again, adding vines and foliage around the base of the temple. "I'm actually still figuring out the magic of this temple. I know there's going to be a statue in the last chamber, and I've got this idea that maybe there was a maiden who was cursed and turned to stone, and only someone deemed worthy can break the spell. If they succeed, they'll get bonus points on future skill checks. Like—magic that gives you uncanny good luck. But if they fail . . . I'm not sure yet. Something bad happens."

"Humiliation by smelly internet trolls?"

I nod earnestly. "It's a slow, painful death."

The record player clicks off. I'd forgotten it was playing, but I start at the sudden absence of music.

"You're a really good artist, Jude." Ari reaches for the beat-up guitar case leaning against the counter. "Thought any more about art school?"

I scoff. "I'm not lucky enough to get into art school."

"Oh, please," she says, unclipping the latches on the side of the case. "You have to at least try."

I don't respond. We've had this discussion half a dozen times over the last year, and I have nothing new to add to it. The people who get into art school on full-ride scholarships are incredible. Like, the sort of people that BeDazzle their own bodies with Swarovski crystals, call them blood diamonds, and host a faux human auction in the middle of Times Square in order to make a point about immoral mining practices. They are *artistes*—French pronunciation.

Whereas I mostly draw dragons and ogres and elves in kickass battle armor.

Ari pulls out the acoustic guitar and settles it on her lap. Like most of the clothes Ari wears, the guitar is vintage, inherited from a grandfather who passed away when Ari was little. I'm no expert, but even I can see that it's a beautiful instrument, with a pattern of dark wood inlays around the edges of the body and a neck that looks black until the light hits it in just the right way to give it a reddish sheen. The glossy finish has been rubbed away in places from so many years of play, and there are a few dings in the wood here and there, but Ari always says that its historic patina is her favorite thing about it.

While she tunes the strings, I lift the lid on the turntable and slide the record back into its protective sleeve. The store has been slow all day, with just a few regulars stopping in and one tourist family, who didn't buy anything. But Dad insists that we always have music playing, because we *are* a record store. I'm reaching for the next record on the stack—some '70s funk band—when Dad emerges from the back room.

"Whoa, whoa, not that one," he says, snatching the record from my hand. "I've got something special picked out for our inaugural open mic night."

I step back and let Dad take over, especially since choosing our music selection on any given day is one of his greatest joys.

It's not actually our inaugural open mic night. Ari had the idea last summer, and with Dad's okay, she officially started hosting them sometime around Thanksgiving. But this *is* the first open mic night since my parents finished signing the paperwork to officially buy Ventures Vinyl. The business itself was always theirs, but as of six days ago, they are now also the proud owners of the building, too. A twelve-hundred-square-foot brick structure in the heart of Fortuna Beach, with old plumbing, old wiring, old *everything*, and an exorbitantly high mortgage payment.

Proof that dreams do come true.

"Should be a good crowd tonight," Dad says. He says this every time, and while we've progressively become more popular over the months, it's considered a "good crowd" if we top more than twenty people.

It's been pretty fun, though, and Ari loves it. She and I both started working here last summer, but we were friends for years before that, and she used to spend so much of her free time here that Dad often refers to her as his sixth child. I think she would work here even if he wasn't paying her, especially on open mic nights.

4

Ari tells people these shindigs are a team effort, but no. It's all her. Her passion, her planning, her effort. I just drew some flyers and helped assemble the platform in the corner of the store. I guess it *was* my idea to frame our makeshift stage with floor-to-ceiling curtains and paint a mural on the wall behind it to look like a night sky. Dad says it's the best-looking part of the store, and he might be right. It certainly has the freshest coat of paint.

"Here we go," says Dad, flipping through the bin of records beneath the counter. The special or sentimental ones that he keeps for the store but aren't really for sale. He pulls out a record with a black-and-white image of two men and a woman standing in front of the London Bridge. It takes me a second to recognize Paul McCartney from his post-Beatles days. "All we need is love," Dad goes on, pulling out the album and flipping it to side B before setting it tenderly on the turntable, "and a little luck."

"Don't let Mom hear you say that," I say quietly. Dad has always been the superstitious one, and Mom loves to tease him about it. We've all heard it from her a million times, and I parrot now: "Luck is all about perspective . . ."

"And what you do with the opportunities you're given," Dad says. "Yes, yes, fine. But you know what? Even your mom believes in luck when Sir Paul is singing about it."

He lowers the needle. The record pops a few times before some deep, mechanical-sounding notes start to play over the store speakers.

I cringe. "Really, Dad?"

"Watch it," he says, jutting a finger in my direction. "We love Wings in this family. Don't criticize."

"You don't like Wings?" Ari says, shooting me a surprised look as her feet kick against the side of the counter.

"I don't like . . ." I consider for a moment. In my family, we're pretty much required to have a healthy respect for the Beatles, and that includes the Fab Four's solo careers. I think my parents might *actually* disown me or my sisters if we were to ever say something outright critical of John,

Paul, George, or Ringo. "I don't like synthesizers," I finally say. "But to each their own."

"I'm going to start setting up the chairs," says Dad. "Let me know if you need help with anything else." He wanders toward the front of the store, humming along with the music.

I glance at Ari. She has one ear tilted toward the closest speaker as she plays along to the song. I can't tell if this is a song she already knows, or if she's figuring out the chords by ear. It wouldn't surprise me if it's the latter. Pretty much all I remember from my brief stint taking guitar lessons years ago is how to make an A major chord, and how much my fingers used to hurt after pressing on those brutal strings for an hour. But Ari speaks the language of notes and chords as fluently as the Spanish she speaks with her family at home.

"So," I say, folding my arms on the counter, "are you going to start the night off with an Ari original?"

"Not tonight," she says dreamily. "There's a really beautiful cover song I want to do first."

"But you will play at least one of your songs, right? That's kind of the point of open mic night. To play original stuff while your captive audience can't escape."

"That's rather a pessimistic view. Here I thought the point was to support artists in our community."

"That's what I said." My grin widens. "I like it when you do originals. I stan you, Ari. You know that."

She starts to smile, but then diverts her attention back down to her guitar strings. "You don't even like music that much."

"Hey, only psychopaths and Pru don't like music. You can't put me in that group."

Ari gives me a side-eye, but it's true. I like music as much as the next guy. My appreciation just pales in comparison to the absolute obsession my parents have—and Ari, too, for that matter. My fourteen-year-old sister, Lucy, has pretty eclectic tastes and has been to more concerts than I have. My ten-year-old sister, Penny, practices her violin for forty-five minutes every night without fail. And my littlest sister, Eleanor—a.k.a. Ellie—sings a mean rendition of "Baby Shark."

Only Prudence, my twin sister, missed the music gene. She does like the Beatles, though. Like, really, really likes the Beatles. Though again, this could just be her attempt to not get disowned. See Exhibit A, above.

"Okay," says Ari, "then tell me your favorite song of all time."

"'Hey Jude,'" I say, no hesitation. "Obviously. It's, like, the song that made me famous."

She shakes her head. "I'm serious. What's your favorite song?"

I tap my fingers against the countertop glass, under which is sandwiched an assortment of collected memorabilia. Ticket stubs. Guitar picks. The first dollar this store ever made.

"'Sea Glass,'" I say finally.

Ari blinks. "*My* 'Sea Glass'?"

"I'm telling you. I am your biggest fan. Pru likes to claim that *she's* your biggest fan, but we both know she would pick a Beatles song as her favorite."

For a second I swear I just made Ari blush, which is not something I can say about many girls. I almost laugh, but I hold it back, because I don't want her to think I'm making fun of her. But then, since I don't laugh, the moment starts to feel awkward.

Over the speakers, Sir Paul is singing about how everything is going to work out, with just a little luck.

Ari clears her throat and tucks that same strand of hair behind her ear again. "I've been working on something new lately. I thought of playing it tonight, but . . . I don't think it's ready."

"Oh, come on. It'd be like . . . workshopping it."

"No. I don't know. Not tonight."

"Fine. Keep your groupies in suspense. But I'm just saying"—I hold up the doodled flyer again—"Araceli the Magnificent would never pass up an opportunity to mesmerize a crowd with her newest masterpiece."

"Araceli the Magnificent plays to taverns full of drunken hobbits."

"Halflings," I correct.

7

Ari smirks and jumps down off the counter. "How about this?" she says, setting her guitar back into its case. "I will play my new song if *you* submit one of your drawings for publication somewhere."

"What? Who would want to publish one of my drawings?"

"Uh—lots of places? How about that fan magazine you like?"

I try to remember if I ever told her my deeply buried dream of having an illustration printed in the *Dungeon*, a fanzine that covers everything from the Avengers to Zelda.

"Just submit something," she says, before I've had a chance to respond. "What's the worst that could happen?"

"They reject me," I say.

"You don't die from rejection."

"You don't know that."

She sighs. "It doesn't hurt to try."

"It might, actually," I counter. "It might hurt very much to try."

Her frown is disapproving—but I can deal with Ari's disapproval. Or Prudence's. Or my parents'. It's the possible disapproval of the world at large that grips me in agonized terror.

"Rejection is part of the life of an artist," she says, tracing a sticker of a daisy on her guitar case. "The only way to know what you're capable of is to put yourself out there, and keep putting yourself out there, again and again, and refusing to give up—"

"Oh god. Stop. Please. Fine, I'll consider submitting something. Just—no more pep talks. You know they stress me out."

Ari claps her hands together. "Then my work here is done."

Chapter Two

It takes us most of the hour to reconfigure the store to make enough space around the stage. The store isn't huge, but once we roll the record bins and shelves off to the sides, it's roomier than it seems. We bring a dozen folding chairs out from the back room, setting them up in a half circle around the raised platform.

People start showing up around five thirty. Two people. Then four. Then *seven*. Pru and her boyfriend, Quint, arrive at a quarter till, holding hands as they stroll through the door.

We add another row of seats after the first dozen are filled up. It's the most crowded I've seen in a while, maybe the most crowded the store has been since last year's Record Store Day—a nationwide promotion that happens every spring and always brings in a bunch of customers.

My mom walks in a second later with my two youngest sisters, Penny and Eleanor, in tow. No Lucy—which isn't all that surprising. She has a busier social life than either Pru or I had when *we* were freshmen, and she has other plans most weekends. Plans that do not include hanging out in a musty old record store with her parents.

Ellie runs to Dad and throws herself into his arms. She immediately starts telling him about the macaroni craft project they made in kindergarten that day.

I walk over to Penny and drape an arm over her shoulders. "Did you bring your violin?" I ask, nodding toward the stage. "This could be the night you wow us all."

Penny frowns at me. I've been urging her to sign up for open mic night since the beginning, but she always says the same thing. "I am not playing in front of all these strangers."

"You play in front of strangers all the time at your recitals."

"Yeah, but with the stage lights on, I can't even see the people in the auditorium, so it's easy to pretend they're not there. Plus, I'm with the rest of the orchestra." She shudders. "I could never perform alone at something like this."

I know I'm not one to talk—it's not like *I'm* ever going to get up on that stage. We do keep my old acoustic guitar around, just in case anyone gets inspired to perform and didn't bring their own instrument. But that's never going to be me. "For what it's worth, I think you'd do awesome."

Penny flashes me an appreciative smile, before Mom pulls her away to claim the last two seats in the back row. Ellie plops down on Mom's lap. I head behind the counter to ring up a sale—a guy with a mean sunburn buying two Broadway musical soundtracks. As he walks away, I spy Pru making her way around the crowd with Ari's clipboard in hand, reminding everyone about the store's open mic night discounts. That's our Pru—always with a sales pitch.

"Ari!" I stage-whisper. She glances over at me, and I tap an imaginary watch on my wrist.

Ari grabs her guitar and bounds up to the stage. She taps the mic. "Hello, hello! Thank you all so much for coming tonight." She beams at the crowd, waving to some of the familiar faces.

When she first started hosting these, months ago, she always started the evening a little nervous and unsure, but that initial stage fright has ebbed with time. Now she seems like a natural, completely in her element. I've always been a little jealous of Ari for the way she isn't afraid to embrace her own quirks, all her charming eccentricities—whether that's talking out loud to herself when she's trying to figure out a new lyric, or showing Ellie how to do cartwheels down the store aisles on days when we're slow, or dancing unabashedly along the boardwalk, never caring who might be watching. Ari doesn't mind it when people notice her—something that I find utterly remarkable.

Ari sits down on the provided stool and pulls a clip from her hair, releasing the bun. A waterfall of wavy dark hair tumbles over one shoulder. "I'm Araceli, and I'm the host of our open mic nights here at Ventures Vinyl. To get us warmed up, I'm going to sing a cover of one of my favorite romantic ballads. This is 'Romeo and Juliet' by Dire Straits."

The hair clip, it turns out, is actually a guitar capo. Ari clasps it to the neck of her guitar and starts to play, her fingers plucking at the strings to create a soft, almost hypnotic melody. Even though I've heard Ari sing a thousand times, there's something about her voice that always makes me smile. She doesn't have a *powerful* voice, exactly, but there's something comforting about the way she sings. It's like . . . like that feeling you get when you've spent the whole day at the beach, and you're wiped out and sunburned and hungry, but then you lie down on your sun-warmed beach towel and the whole world fades away and you feel every muscle in your body relax and you can't remember ever feeling more content.

"Great turnout tonight," Pru whispers, sidling up to the counter, Quint beside her. Quint offers me a fist bump, the action a lot less awkward now than it was when they first started dating eight months ago.

While most people are listening raptly to Ari, Pru is studying the crowd like a scientist studies a specimen. "If we kill it on Record Store Day, then pull crowds like this through tourist season, we'll be in a good place come the fall."

Quint and I trade a look.

I know I shouldn't tease her for her business acumen, though. Pru has done as much for the record store as anyone these last few months, and she's not even on the payroll. In between school work and volunteering with Quint at the sea animal rescue center, which is owned and run by Quint's mom, Pru has been on a mission to revitalize Ventures Vinyl, a mission that she completely doubled down on once our parents announced their plan to buy the building. It was Pru's idea to transform the exterior storefront with a fresh music-themed mural, and the week I spent planning and painting it was easily the most fun I've had since I started working here. Pru also spearheaded our new social media accounts, which are now full of curated photos of the store and its merchandise—mostly taken by Quint, who has an eye for that sort of thing. Pru has spent whole afternoons passing out promotional coupons on the boardwalk, ordering specialty Ventures Vinyl merchandise to sell, and even inviting journalists from as far as L.A. to do write-ups on how the store is a landmark business in Fortuna Beach. One travel magazine called us "a refreshing blend of hipster cool and nostalgic comfort—a necessary stop for any music lover traveling the coastal freeway." Pru had the article framed and hung up behind the counter.

All her efforts have made a big difference. Combined with a growth in local tourism and a resurgence in the popularity of vinyl records (which have started outselling CDs for the first time in decades), the store has seen some of its biggest profits lately. Which is good, because—again, exorbitant mortgage payment.

"Ari sounds great," says Quint. "As per usual."

Ari's eyes are closed as she sings, lost in the serenade of a lovestruck Romeo. I know Ari doesn't want to be a *singer*—her dream has always been to be behind the scenes. The songwriter who creates the music and hands it off to the performers to do what they do best. But that doesn't change the fact that she's mesmerizing to watch when she plays, her hair shining under our hastily constructed stage lights, her fingers at one with the guitar.

And—okay, I know I shouldn't say this. I know I shouldn't *feel* this. But there is something about watching Ari in her element that always gives me this constricted, almost painful feeling in my chest. Like I never want to look away.

But don't get the wrong idea. I don't feel *that way* about Ari. Those feelings—those intense, all-encompassing, romantic-type feelings—are reserved wholly and completely for another girl.

A man in a suit comes up to the counter to buy a Nirvana album, and Pru and Quint step aside. Just as I've finished ringing him up, Ari's song ends to avid applause. I give her a loud whistle, and she meets my gaze, a grin on her face.

"Thank you," she says. "We've got a great list tonight, and I can't wait to hear you all. I might be back later to play one of my original songs. But for now, let me call to the stage our first performer . . ."

As soon as Ari has summoned the next act, she comes back to join us at the counter, her cheeks a little flushed.

"You were fantastic!" says Pru.

"Thanks?" says Ari, in that way she has of making every thank-you sound like a question.

We fall quiet, listening to the guy onstage as he covers an Ed Sheeran song. He's really into it, singing from his heart. Or diaphragm, or whatever people sing from that makes them sound really good.

A handful of performers follow him. A guy in board shorts comes up to buy a Ventures Vinyl T-shirt, but no actual vinyl. After he walks away, I take in the store. Two women are performing a song they wrote together—one plays ukulele, the other is on bongo drums. People are tapping their feet along to the music. A handful of guests are browsing the shelves while they listen.

I grab my pencil and start mindlessly doodling on the flyer again. I'm annoyed that I haven't been able to think of a good name for this temple yet, when the entire campaign is built around it. I look around, searching for inspiration, tapping the eraser against the paper.

The Temple of . . . Vinylia?

The Temple of . . . Escalante?

The Temple of . . . Fortuna?

Looking up, I notice Ellie squirming in Mom's lap, reaching the end of her short attention span. I call quietly to her, and she immediately rushes back to join me. I swing her up and place her on the counter, in the same spot Ari sat earlier, tuning her guitar. I hand Ellie a Ventures Vinyl–branded coffee mug full of guitar picks in all different colors, and she happily begins sorting them into piles. Mom shoots me a look of gratitude.

The duet finishes, and Ari returns to the stage, the clipboard tucked under one arm. She waits for the performers to clear away their instruments before taking the mic.

"I'm not sure I would want to follow that," she says, to a chuckle of agreement throughout the audience, "but it looks like I might have to, since we have reached the end of our sign-up sheet! While I play, Pru is going to pass this around again, and I hope we get a few more performers. Otherwise you'll be stuck with me for the rest of the night." She shrugs apologetically, even though that's hardly the punishment she implies it would be.

Ellie looks up from her arrangement of guitar picks. "Are you going to sing?"

"Me? No way. This is Ari's show."

"All those other people were singing," says Ellie.

"Yeah, but . . . they're, like, good at it." I shake my head. "I don't like singing." Better to tell her that, I think, than to try to explain why I would rather throw myself into a Sarlacc pit.

I'm sort of allergic to being the center of attention. It makes me break out in hives.

I wish I could say I'm joking.

Ellie's expression grows increasingly confused. "You sing to *me*."

It takes me a second to realize she's talking about the lullabies I'll occasionally stumble through to try to get her to go to sleep, when Mom and Dad aren't home to put her to bed. I can never remember any *actual* lullabies, so I mostly just sing whatever slow-ish songs come to mind. "Hey Jude" is one of her favorites, but she hates "Eleanor Rigby." I might, too, if I was named after such a depressing song. Sometimes I even sing Ari's songs to her, the ones that I've heard enough times to memorize.

Regardless, I'm not about to get up on that stage and sing *anything*. But I also don't want to plant the idea into Ellie's impressionable little brain that things like singing in public are horrific and mortifying and to be avoided at all costs, not when she's still at an age where she regularly—and shamelessly—belts out the ABCs in the middle of the grocery store. So I just put my finger to my lips and tell her, "Shh. That's our secret."

Ellie gives me a solemn nod, always glad to be in on a secret.

Onstage, Ari plays a few chords on her guitar, then leans toward the microphone again. "I thought I might play something I've been working on for the past couple of weeks. It's brand-new, and I haven't really tested it out on anyone yet. So I guess you're my guinea pigs." A few people applaud encouragingly. Ari's eyes dart in my direction, and I give her two thumbs up.

She looks away.

"This is called 'Downpour.'"

She plays through the chords one more time, strumming a melody that strikes me as more melancholic than a lot of her other songs.

She closes her eyes and starts to sing.

> *Never could say when it started*
> *Crept up like a storm in the night*
> *Not sure when I got so brokenhearted*
> *This love, a crash of thunder*
> *This love, a flash of light*

I lean against the counter and listen. Ari has written plenty of songs about love. First love, hopeful love, longing for love. But something feels different about this one. More emotional, maybe. More vulnerable.

> *Yeah, my love, it isn't a sunrise*
> *Was never the day shining through*
> *Here comes the rain, and I'm crying again*
> *Caught up in the downpour of me loving you*

Her voice wavers the tiniest bit, the only hint that she's baring her soul to a roomful of strangers. She opens her eyes as she starts in on the second verse. Her gaze drifts over the crowd.

We used to be sunshine and ice cream,
Kicking sand at the sun going down.
Oh, you and me, how easy it seemed.
But now I can't be wanting
'Cause this wanting is dragging me—

Ari's eyes land on mine again.

And she stops.

Just . . . stops.

Her voice catches. Her fingers stall.

She gasps and looks down at the strings. "Uh—sorry," she stammers, laughing uncomfortably. "I, um. I forgot the next part."

The audience chuckles along with her, but not in a mean way. We wait for her to gather herself. To continue on. But Ari doesn't continue on. She just stares down at her guitar, pink tinging her cheeks. She's quiet for long enough that people begin to stir.

I glance at Pru, wondering if we should do something. I've never seen Ari freeze up like this before.

Pru, closer to the stage than I am, whispers, "You okay?"

Ari's head snaps up, a wide-eyed smile plastered to her face. "Wow, I'm so sorry about that. I think that song is not quite ready, after all. You know what? Let me start over. I'll do a cover instead. How about, um . . ." I can almost see the wheels spinning in her mind, flipping through the internal jukebox of the songs she knows by heart. "You know what? I heard this one earlier today, for the first time in a while. Maybe it can bring us all a little luck tonight."

Cheeks still flushed, she launches into "With a Little Luck" by Paul McCartney and Wings.

Was that weird? That definitely seemed weird. Very un-Ari, anyway. I've never seen her clam up like that in the middle of a performance.

The new song choice reminds me that the *London Town* album is still on the turntable, still spinning from when Dad played it before, though the music ended a long time ago. We try not to let the albums spin and spin—the needle can wear grooves into the vinyl and ruin them over time—but the night has been so busy I forgot all about it.

I turn away from Ellie, who has arranged the guitar picks into a flower, and open the lid of the record player.

I freeze.

There's something on the record. A ball . . . or stone . . . or *something*. Spinning, spinning, spinning, just inside the needle.

I lift the needle and stop the record. It rotates a second longer before going still, the mystery object coming into focus.

"What the . . ." I pick it up and hold it in my fingers.

It's a twenty-sided dice, exactly like the ones my friends and I use when we play Dungeons & Dragons.

Well—not exactly. The dice we use are mostly made of resin or acrylic . . . except Russell, who shelled out for an expensive stone set that the rest of us are still drooling over.

But *this*. This is something different. It's heavy, like stone, but glints deep red and slightly opaque. Like a ruby or garnet. The numbers on each plane glimmer in delicate gold, their angular shapes looking more like runes than standard numerals.

In a word, it's *exquisite*. I've never seen anything like it before.

But where did it come from?

I look around the store, from Ellie to Pru to my parents. Everyone is watching Ari. If this was left as some gift for me to find, then whoever left it isn't watching to see my reaction.

But no, it couldn't be a gift from my family. This dice must cost a hundred dollars or more, and my family doesn't produce frivolous spenders. And yet it has to be a gift for me, right? Who else would be so excited to receive a dice like this?

I'll ask around once Ari is done singing, I decide, dropping the dice into my pocket while I slide the Wings album back into its protective sleeve, and then into the jacket. I tilt my head to one side, squinting down at the cover art. The temple I've drawn on the flyer sort of looks like one of the towers of the London Bridge that you can see in the background.

I set the album on the counter, where Ellie has changed her guitar-pick flower into the rough shape of a girl in a dress. At least, I think that's what it is. Guitar-pick art is pretty abstract.

I grab the flyer where I was sketching out the temple for my upcoming campaign.

The Temple of . . . McCartney?

The Temple of . . . Sir Paul?

The Temple of . . . Wings?

My pencil thumps in time with the music. Then, an idea.

I write it down at the top of the flyer.

The Temple of London Town.

I stare at it for a second, then erase *London Town* and replace it to read:

The Temple of Lundyn Toune.

It isn't awful. At least, I haven't managed to come up with anything better. But I don't need to make the final decision. I can let fate decide.

I fish the fancy dice from my pocket, turning it in my fingers to let it catch the overhead lights. I went through a phase a couple of years ago where I carried a dice around with me constantly, and would use it to help make decisions. It proved more effective than one would think. Can't decide what to order off a menu? Roll the dice and pick the entree number it lands on. Don't know which book on your TBR pile to read next? Roll the dice and count down that many books in the stack. Having trouble deciding just how many boxes of Girl Scout cookies you should order? Let the dice be your guide.

It takes a lot of anxiety out of decision making, is what I'm saying.

Onstage, Ari is finishing up the last chorus of the song. The crowd is into it. Mom is singing along, and a few other people join in. *With a little love we could shake it up. Don't you feel the comet exploding?*

I rub my thumb over the crisp edges of the dice, deciding that anything above a ten will officially consecrate the new name of the temple. Less than that, and I'll go back to the drawing board.

I toss the dice as Ari sings the last line. *With a little luck* . . .

The dice rolls across my drawing, across the counter, and comes to a stop right on top of the album.

A golden twenty glimmers up at me.

"Hey," I murmur. "Critical hit."

Guess that confirms it. *The Temple of Lundyn Toune* it is.

The last chords from the guitar fade away, met with applause from the audience, as I grab the dice again.

"What's that?" asks Ellie.

"A twenty-sided dice. I just found it."

"Not that. This," says Ellie, pointing at a piece of paper sticking out from the *London Town* record.

"No idea." I grasp the corner of the page and pull it out, while onstage Ari takes the clipboard back from Pru and calls up the next performer.

I examine the paper in my hand. It's a small poster with the same image as on the cover, including the London Bridge in the background.

With one notable difference.

It has a signature, scrawled in blue ink right beneath the album's title. It's messy, but if I didn't know better, I'd say that was a *P*, and an *M*, and . . .

"Holy . . ." I look up at Ellie, who is watching me curiously. "I think this is signed by Paul McCartney."

Her eyes widen. In our family, even the five-year-old knows who Paul McCartney is.

Is it authentic? Do my parents know? Surely if they did, they would have it framed or something, right?

"We'll show this to Mom and Dad after everyone leaves," I say, carefully tucking the poster back into the album. "I'm going to go put it in the back."

Pocketing the dice again, I take the album into the back room, which is a small, crowded space full of shelves overflowing with records that still need to be cataloged and priced, boxes of new merch, and my dad's very small and eternally cluttered desk.

I set the record on top of a stack of mail and am turning away when my hand bumps my dad's favorite travel mug balanced precariously on a stack of books.

I see it in slow motion. The tumbler tipping forward. The coffee sloshing over the rim. The album with the signed poster, just discovered, only inches away.

My body reacts on instinct. Like an out-of-body experience, I watch as one hand slides the album away while the other grabs a dustrag from a nearby shelf and throws it beneath the falling tumbler. The last remnants of cold coffee spill across the rag, sparing me a fraction of a second to get the album out from underneath.

I exhale in a sharp, startled breath, gaping at the little towel soaked through with coffee. A few tiny droplets spilled onto the pile of mail, but a quick inspection of the album confirms that it is untouched.

I laugh, a little bewildered. "Well. *That* was lucky."

Actually, it was borderline miraculous. I didn't even know that dustrag was there. How did I . . . ?

Shaking my head, I set the album aside, safely up on a shelf this time, right the travel mug, and wipe up the last bits of spilled coffee.

As my heart rate returns to normal, I slip my hands into my pockets and head back out to listen to the rest of open mic night. It's probably just the adrenaline, but I swear the dice pulses against my palm.

Chapter Three

The store is closed, but Ari and my family are still here, along with Quint, who is holding a half-asleep Ellie. (When he and Pru started dating, Ellie was the first one to extend the Honorary Big Brother title to him.) Everyone is crammed into the small back room, watching me as I gently pull the poster that Ellie and I discovered out of the *London Town* jacket. I hand it to my dad, who holds it with reverence, turning the autograph toward the light.

"Sir Paul," Ari breathes, as everyone leans forward at once to see it better. The scrawl of blue ink, a looping *P* and *l*, the sharp rises of the *M*, the drooping *y* that looks a bit like an afterthought.

Pru pulls her phone out and a second later is nodding thoughtfully. "Yeah, that looks like it," she says, showing a screen full of Paul McCartney signatures. Sometimes he just signs *Paul*, sometimes he adds the *M*, sometimes it's his full name, but in any rendition, the handwriting looks similar.

"I feel like I should be wearing gloves," says Dad. He lays the autograph gently on top of an unopened box so we can all peer at it.

"You didn't know it was signed?" I ask.

"No idea," says Dad. "I've owned this record for years. I didn't even think it had the original poster with it anymore, much less . . . *this*."

"This was the first record we ever played when we opened the store," says Mom. "Remember? You used to call it your lucky album."

"I guess you were right about that," says Penny.

Dad laughs, shaking his head. "This is an incredible find, Jude."

"Ellie spotted it first," I say. "It just slipped out of the case."

"It could still be a forgery," Pru interjects. "Is there a way to get it authenticated?" She's still looking things up on her phone, and now she shows us a website selling signed Beatles memorabilia. "It could be worth thousands of dollars if it's real."

Dad gasps, horrified. "We can't *sell* it!"

Pru rolls her eyes. "Of course we're not going to sell it. We'll frame it and display it nicely in the store. But don't you think it would be good to know what it's worth? And if ever we do get in another financial pinch, well . . ." She shrugs. "It's nice to have options."

"It wouldn't hurt to have a professional take a look," says Mom.

"Can we go home now?" says Ellie, her voice muffled against Quint's chest. "I'm *tired*."

"Yes, yes. We're going," says Mom. She gives Ari a hug. "You were wonderful tonight, hon." Then she hitches her purse up on her shoulder before taking Ellie from Quint.

"I should be heading home, too," says Ari. "I'll see you Tuesday."

"Wait, one more thing." I reach into my pocket and pull out the red dice.

Penny's eyes widen. "That's *pretty*."

"Yeah. I just wanted to say thank you to . . . whoever it's from." I look around. Mom and Dad. Penny and Eleanor. Pru and Quint. Ari. They all stare blankly at me, then trade looks with one another. Finally, there's a round of shrugs. "Really?" I say. "None of you left this for me? It was on the record player, under the lid. It couldn't have been put there by accident."

"I've never seen it before," says Pru, and everyone else is shaking their heads, too.

"Finders keepers," Penny says brightly.

"Right." I slip the dice back into my pocket. "I guess it's just my lucky day."

———————

Pru, Lucy, and Penny are sitting in our breakfast nook eating blueberry muffins from Costco when I come up the stairs from my basement-converted bedroom the next morning. Lucy's got one earbud in, the other dangling around her neck, but she pulls it out when she sees me.

"Let me get this straight," she says, before I've even had a chance to sit down. "You just *found* a record signed by Paul McCartney? Just . . . by chance?"

"A poster, actually. It was pretty weird." I dump my backpack on the bench and slide in next to Pru.

"And Mom and Dad didn't know about it?" says Lucy. "How is that possible?"

Penny shoves another bite into her mouth, crumbs littering the table. "Dad said he's had that record for a long time."

"Don't speak with your mouth full," Lucy chastises, but her look of disbelief stays on me. "How did you find it?"

"It was in the album jacket. It slipped out when I went to put the record back in."

"Huh. Do you think there could be more hidden treasures in that store?"

"I don't know. We always inspect used albums when people bring them in to sell. I think this was a bit of a fluke. I also found this last night." I show her the dice, which I slipped into my pocket on a whim when I was getting dressed.

Lucy's eyes start to brighten, but then quickly dim. "Oh. I thought it was a gemstone, not one of your gamer dice."

Clearly not from her, then, not that I expected it to be.

I tuck the dice away and start to reach for the last muffin, but a tiny hand beats me to it. Ellie, still in the Teenage Mutant Ninja Turtles pajamas I gave her for her birthday, clutches the muffin to her chest and glares at me. "Mine!"

I glare back, less intensely. "Flip me for it?"

She considers the proposal, then says, "Fine," and spins around to dig a quarter out of the jar by the stove.

I'm convinced that *it's not fair* must have been Ellie's first spoken words. For the first few years of her life, they were a constant mantra. Penny got a bigger piece of pizza? *It's not fair!* Lucy got to choose two songs during the drive to school, and she only got to pick one? *It's not fair!* Some random kid on YouTube has the newest set of My Little Pony dolls, and she doesn't? *It's! Not! Fair!*

So, sick of hearing those words, a few months ago Pru introduced her to the remarkable strategy of using a coin flip when fairness was in question, leaving the ultimate decision up to the universe. Ellie has been obsessed with coin flips ever since, using them to dictate everything from who gets to pick what board game we play, to whether or not she can watch one more episode of *Glitter Force* before getting ready for bed. It makes for a peaceful compromise . . . usually.

"All right," I say, taking the quarter from her. "You call it."

"Tails!"

She always picks tails.

I flip the coin. Grab it. Slap it onto my forearm, and show it to her.

"Heads."

Her nose crinkles in annoyance, but she doesn't argue. The will of the universe is the will of the universe, after all. Pouting, she sets the muffin back down on the table.

"Here," I say, grabbing a butter knife. "I'll give you half. But you have to go get dressed and ready for school first."

She makes a sour face, but turns on her heels and heads back up the stairs.

"And don't dawdle!" Pru shouts after her. "We're taking you to school and don't want to be late!"

"We're taking her today?" I ask as I saw the muffin in half.

"Mom asked us to. She's got a pile of bookkeeping stuff to get through," Pru explains.

Pru and I both got our licenses a week after our birthday, but neither of us can afford a car of our own, so we're pretty much only allowed to drive ourselves and our sisters to and from school in our mom's minivan.

The rest of the time we either take our bikes or rely on Ari to drive us around in her much cooler, though questionably reliable, sixties-era station wagon.

Mom strolls in a minute later and heads straight for the coffeemaker. "Morning, sweet children of mine," she says, pouring herself a cup. "Do you have your homework? Penny, did you get your lunch packed?"

We go through the usual morning routine—Mom's built-in checklist of things we're supposed to handle on our own but she has to follow up on anyway. Lunches, homework, signed permission slips, teeth brushed, hair combed, everyone wearing socks. (Penny has had an aversion to socks since she was a baby and will do just about anything to sneak out of the house without them.)

Once we've all passed inspection, Mom nods at me and Pru. "Thanks for taking Ellie to school today."

"No problem." I finish the last bite of my muffin and put Ellie's half in a bowl so she can eat it during the drive. We're all sliding out of the breakfast nook just as Ellie thunders back down the steps in a striped dress, leopard print leggings, and cowboy boots, her Hello Kitty backpack bouncing on her shoulders. She's also wearing fuzzy mittens, even though it's going to be eighty degrees today. I don't even know why she owns mittens. It's never cold enough around here to justify them. But we're all accustomed to Ellie's five-year-old fashion choices, so no one says anything.

"Shotgun," says Penny.

"Didn't you ride shotgun on Friday?" I say, handing the muffin to Ellie. "Pretty sure it's my turn."

"Flip for it?"

We do. Penny calls heads. I win.

This is followed by an argument over who gets to pick what we listen to during the ride. Another coin flip goes to Lucy. As the five of us pile into my parents' minivan, she connects her phone to the Bluetooth and puts on one of her favorite podcasts, something about space exploration. Ellie groans.

As Pru is pulling out onto the street, my phone chimes.

Ari: I was thinking about your magical mystery dice. Do you think it could have been a gift from the record store elves?
Jude: Oh yeah probably. I love those guys.
Ari: They're the best.
Jude: Or maybe you summoned it with your Level 5 bard magic.

It takes her a while to respond, the three dots coming and going a few times.

Ari: I am only beginning to discover my power.

I laugh, and Pru shoots me a curious look. "Who are you texting with?"

"Just Ari. She was wondering if I figured out who left the dice."

Her gaze darts from my phone to her own blank phone screen. She looks mildly suspicious, but not *everything* has to be in a group text.

I set the phone down and turn to the window, watching the familiar houses and palm trees go by, bright yellow buttercups sprouting up along the edges of the sidewalks. I listen to the podcast host energetically try to explain some of her favorite mind-warping facts about our galaxy. Evidently, our precise physical location in the universe has moved more than two hundred thousand miles since we started listening to this podcast episode, given how fast the Milky Way is turning. And there's a supermassive black hole at the center of our galaxy that contains the mass of more than four million suns. And every star we can see in the night sky is actually bigger than our sun. And scientists estimate there are one hundred billion planets in our galaxy alone.

Which means at least one of them has to have Ewoks. That's just statistics.

My phone dings again.

Ari: I'm pretty sure you owe me an art submission.

It's followed by a link to the online submission form for the *Dungeon*. I cringe.

Jude: You didn't finish your new song. Should I submit half a drawing?
Ari: Half would still be better than nothing...

She sends a photo she took of last night's flyer with the sketch of the bard, Araceli the Magnificent. In the photo I can see that it has creases from being folded. Ari must have slipped it into her pocket at some point.

Ari: This is a masterpiece, Jude. You're a modern day Da Vinci! You can't hide your talent from the world forever.
Jude: Challenge accepted.

"You sure are smiling a lot over there," Pru says.

I roll my eyes and tuck my phone away. "Ari's being ridiculous."

Pru side-eyes me in a way that seems more meaningful than it should. "And what ridiculous thing is Ari saying this morning?"

"She thinks I should submit one of my drawings to the *Dungeon*."

Penny gasps from the back seat. "That magazine? You should! You could be published!"

I shake my head. "They wouldn't take it. I'm not that good."

"Doesn't hurt to try," says Pru.

"Ari keeps saying that, too, and I'm just not sure I agree. Rejection sucks."

Pru raspberries her lips. "You'll never get what you want if you don't ask for it. Or better yet—*demand* that the world give you what you deserve."

I shoot Pru an annoyed look. "All I want from the world is a reboot of *Firefly*."

"I want world peace," pipes in Ellie.

"Oh yeah, that too," I say. "*Firefly* first, but world peace is a close second."

"Excuse me," says Lucy. "Why is everyone talking over my show?"

"Pause it," says Pru. No, *demands* Pru. (She makes it look so simple.) Lucy makes an aggravated noise in her throat, but she does pause the podcast.

"I'm with Ari," says Pru, pulling up to a red light. "You should be submitting your art to publications. The worst that can happen is they don't take it." Pru grabs a lipstick tube from the van's center console and starts to apply it in the rearview mirror.

"I know!" says Ellie, bouncing in her car seat. "Flip a coin to decide if you should submit something!"

Pru and I exchange looks as she snaps the lipstick lid back on. The light changes, and Pru pulls onto the street in front of Ellie's elementary school.

"Fine," I say. "We'll flip a coin."

"I'll do it," says Lucy, taking the quarter that Ellie fishes from her backpack.

"Heads," I call as she flips the coin. It hits the ceiling of the van, and she barely catches it before flipping it over onto her arm. Lucy shows Ellie first, who gives a loud cheer.

"Heads!" She beams and points at me. "You have to submit something!"

My brow furrows. "But I called heads. I won."

"Yeah, so now you submit something."

I open my mouth to protest, but Pru is laughing. "Guess you should clarify the terms next time."

I slump back in my seat. "I've been conned by a five-year-old."

Ellie's arms slither around the seat, hugging me from behind. I pat her on the wrist.

"Have a good day, Els. Mom or Dad will pick you up."

Lucy opens the door and Ellie scrambles out. As Pru pulls back onto the street, I open Ari's text. I click the link to the art submission form and fill it out, trying not to think too hard. Then I open my photos and scan through the art I've saved over the last few months, mostly things I posted to the forum I share with my Dungeons & Dragons group. I can't look at any of these drawings without criticism invading my thoughts. This arm placement is weird. The eyes didn't turn out right. No one's neck is that skinny. Why are hands so difficult?

I pick one before my doubts turn into nausea.

It's classic fantasy meets the real world. A group of adventurers—elves and warlocks decked out in cloaks and weaponry—stand battle-ready at the entrance to a chaotic high school cafeteria, where paper airplanes are zooming overhead, drama kids are practicing monologues on the tables, a food fight has broken out among the jocks, and lunch ladies are serving up mystery meat at the counter. The caption reads: *One does not simply walk into a high school cafeteria*, a play on the classic Mordor line from *Lord of the Rings*.

Is it funny? Is it good? I have no idea.

Attach.

Send.

Breathe.

"There." I hold up the screen so Pru can see the *Thank you for your submission* page. "Done." Then I take a screenshot and text it to Ari.

She responds almost immediately—a reaction image of Minions cheering.

It very slightly alleviates the momentary panic that strikes when I realize what I just did. I sent my art out into the world. To a real publication. To the *Dungeon*.

What if they hate it?

I swallow hard and shove my phone into my pocket. "Not that it matters. They won't take it."

To which Pru replies, in a singsong voice, "I guess we'll see."

Chapter Four

Five minutes later, we drop Penny off at the middle school, then drive around the corner to pull into the parking lot of Fortuna Beach High. Lucy is out of the van before Pru has yanked up the emergency brake, hurrying to meet up with her friends, who always hang out under a giant sycamore tree before school starts.

Pru and I head into the central courtyard. Quint and Ezra are loitering on a bench near the main office. This is something else that changed when Pru and Quint started dating. Pru and I used to make a beeline for the school library during downtime, where I could read or draw in peace and she could work on extra credit projects or whatever random thing had caught her single-minded focus that week. She used to treat the library like her own private office. One time I even heard her shush the librarian.

It's not that we don't have other friends. I have my D&D group—César, Matt, and Russell, plus Kyle, who joined up in the fall—but we almost never hang out before or after school. Plus there's Noah, Matt's cousin, who's a senior at Orange Bay Academy of Science and Mathematics, a.k.a. the school where the smart, techy kids go.

We also have Ari, of course, but she goes to St. Agnes, a prestigious private school.

So for a long time it was just sort of me and Pru. Not lonely, not alone, but not exactly social butterflies, either.

But with Quint in the picture, Pru was naturally drawn into the Fortuna

Beach social sphere, in which Ezra Kent is an unavoidable fixture. He was a bit of a package deal with Quint, I guess just like Ari and I were a package deal with Pru. Quint and Ezra have been best friends since, like, preschool or something, and while I have nothing against Ezra, per se, he is loud and unfiltered and the sort of guy who loves to be the center of attention. In essence, he is my opposite in every way.

"Yo, Pru the Foo and Jude the Dude!" Ezra calls when Pru and I are still halfway across the commons.

I grimace. "He really needs to come up with new nicknames."

"I've told him so a thousand times," Pru mutters back. "He does not seem to be open to constructive feedback."

We reach them, and Quint puts an arm around Pru, giving her a quick kiss.

I look the other way . . . and my gaze lands on *her*.

I stand straighter, my palms growing hot. Maya Livingstone is making her way across the commons. She's got her denim bookbag slung over one shoulder, the front flap decorated with a rainbow LOVE IS LOVE patch next to the iconic *Hamilton* star, plus a bunch of K-pop pins. (I know that Jimin is her bias . . . though I'm not entirely sure what that means.) Her hair is down today, thick black curls bouncing with every step. Jeans faded at the knees. Flip-flops. A purple zip-up hoodie. The morning sunshine lights up a smattering of freckles on her dark skin in a way that makes my mouth go dry.

I'm so distracted by Maya's sudden appearance that Pru and Quint could be doing headstands on the bench right now and I wouldn't notice. All my energy is divided between following Maya's movements as she greets her friends, her smile like a beacon in the courtyard—while also trying to appear utterly nonchalant.

Don't stare for too long.

Don't make eye contact.

Don't respond to that teasing smirk I can feel Pru sending in my direction.

"Shut up," I mutter under my breath.

31

"Dude," says Quint, leaning toward me, "we've been in the same classes together for forever. Just go talk to her."

Great. Even my sister's boyfriend can tell how pathetic I am.

I don't justify his suggestion with a response. Because if it was that easy, I obviously would have *just gone and talked to her* a long time ago.

———————————

So, okay. Let's take a pause here.

You and I have been getting along pretty well these last thirty or so pages, right? Getting to know each other. Enjoying some good tunes at open mic night. Marveling over the couture fashion choices of the world's five-year-olds. I hope it isn't too forward of me to say that I feel like we've kind of hit it off.

But there's one thing I haven't told you yet. One thing you should probably know about me before we go any further.

I am hopelessly in love with Maya Livingstone.

It's not, like, a secret or anything. In fact, I'm fairly certain that *everyone* knows . . . including Maya herself. I guess I just felt like the whole unrequited-love conversation isn't one that should come up in the first chapter. I wasn't trying to withhold anything from you, it's just not the sort of thing you lead with, especially when the case is as hopeless as mine.

Here's the thing about being hopelessly in love with a girl who is unequivocally out of your league: It's pointless. The chances of me ever being brave enough to ask her out are exactly zero. The chances of her saying *yes* are even less, which is both a mathematical impossibility and yet also somehow accurate. It's not that Maya is some teen movie cheerleader stereotype who only dates jocks or anything like that. Nope, Maya is smart and gorgeous and nice to everyone, and I'm not exactly special for having an unrequited crush on her. In fact, I'm amazed on a daily basis that she's single, and has been since she broke up with Leo Fuentes over winter break of our sophomore year.

So Quint's breezy suggestion that I *just go talk to her*?

Please. I would rather be buried alive under a pile of tribbles.

Here's the full story, since I guess it's relevant.

I have been in love with Maya since the fifth grade, from the day that Pru was out sick with chicken pox (I'd recovered from mine a month before) and missed out on the field trip to the aquarium, leaving me to fend for myself on the bus. Or so I thought, until Maya dropped down into the seat next to me and spent the hour-long ride talking about seals and jellyfish and how she was convinced that mermaids were totally real, because her grandma had told her lots of fairy tales from all over the world that had half-human, half-fish creatures in them, and what were the chances of that unless there was some truth to it?

I didn't have to say much during that ride. I just listened and smiled, absolutely in awe at how this girl was sitting next to me, talking to *me*. If I'm shy and awkward now, I was ten times worse in elementary school, but it was like Maya hadn't even noticed.

She was the nicest, prettiest, most interesting girl that had ever spoken to me, and . . . well, she still is.

She's been living rent free in my head ever since.

Not that we've talked much in the years since that fateful field trip. Maya sometimes smiles at me in the halls, just like she smiles at everyone. She stops by the record store on occasion and even tries to make small talk, but I usually clam up, and if I can think of anything to say to her at all, it's usually something weird or random or . . . I don't know. *Me.*

And yeah, I get a little jealous when I see Maya trading some goofy handshake with Quint or laughing at whatever inane thing Ezra said. It's so easy for people like them. They're comfortable in their own skin, and don't seem to worry about whether or not people like them.

How great would it be to just . . . be yourself, and know that society or the universe or the Force or whatever has deemed you worthy?

And yeah, I know how I sound. But I can't help it. I can't stop feeling this way. I can't take Maya down from that pedestal she so rightly belongs on.

The bell rings, and the crowded courtyard starts to clear out as everyone heads toward their classrooms. Pru, Quint, and I take off toward the science hall.

I linger a few steps behind my sister and her boyfriend, hands in my pockets as we're jostled down the halls, my new dice brushing against my knuckles. I share three classes with Maya this semester. First-period astronomy, second-period English lit, and sixth-period political science. I do not sit next to her in any of them, but in our first two classes I sit a few rows behind her, which is its own torture. The sort of torture where I *could* focus on her for fifty straight minutes, but I know better not to. The sort of torture where I could sketch out the curve of her neck, the curls of her hair, the slope of her nose and fullness of her lips, all in perfect, statuesque profile—but to attempt to draw her in the middle of class would risk someone noticing, and that could be disastrous in myriad ways.

It's the sort of torture that feeds into fantasies of Maya needing to borrow a pencil, to compare notes, to ask about an assignment, and me being right there with the answers. Maya, seeking *me* out, rather than any of our other twenty-six classmates. Maya, making up an excuse to talk to *me*. Maya, just . . . noticing me, really.

Noticing would be good. Noticing would be a start.

We arrive at the classroom, and I take my seat in the fourth row and try not to make a big deal out of it when Maya comes in a minute later. I pull out my sketch pad and start doodling on the edges.

I've had this idea lately of turning our next D&D campaign into a comic book—not to publish, but just something fun for me and the group—so I've been trying to get better at drawing scenery. One of my favorite things about being the Dungeon Master and creating campaigns is coming up with cool settings to explore. For our last campaign I created an entire fantasy island called the Isle of Gwendahayr, which I set up like an escape room, with puzzles upon puzzles, which the group had to solve in order to put together the spell that would either allow them to escape or drop them into a pit of lava if they got it wrong. It was a *ton* of work to create, and with finals coming this semester, I haven't had time to compile something quite as elaborate for this new campaign, but I still have some ideas I'm pretty excited about.

The drawing does the trick. In the two minutes before the bell rings again, I manage to not glance up at Maya even once. That's, like, a super-human feat.

Mr. Singh takes roll call and has us pass up our homework assignments from the weekend before launching straight into his lecture on the Milky Way.

"This should sound familiar from your reading assignment," he says, jotting a few notes on the board. I'm distracted, though, and my notebook page is quickly filling up, not with notes, but with a dense forest, a crumbling wall, an imposing door covered in runes.

"Jude?"

My head snaps up. "Yeah?"

Mr. Singh's smile is tight. He knows I wasn't paying attention. "Could you tell the class what Andromeda is? It was in your reading from the weekend."

Heat rushes up my neck. My ears start to burn. My heart thumps faster. This happens every time I'm called on to speak in class, whether I know the answer or not.

And this time, I definitely do not. I meant to finish the reading after open mic night, but in all the excitement at the store, I completely forgot.

I can feel Prudence in the seat behind me, doing her best to telepathically send me the answer. Sometimes that twin psychic thing works for us, but right now, I am not picking up any signals.

Andromeda. *Andromeda.* All I can think of is that Gene Roddenberry space opera that Matt, César, and I binge-watched over a three-week period during our freshman year.

But then, that name does ring a bell.

Andromeda.

Lucy's podcast. Wasn't the host saying something about Andromeda? What *was* it?

Mr. Singh frowns. "Can anyone else tell us—"

"It's another galaxy," I blurt out. "One that's on a direct collision course with the Milky Way. Scientists estimate that the two galaxies will crash into each other in about five billion years."

Mr. Singh stills. The moment is brief, this shock passing over his face. I don't blame him. I'm not sure I've ever voluntarily said so many words in his class at one time.

I'm a little shocked myself.

"That's right," says Mr. Singh. "Very good. Lucky for us, five billion years is a long time away, so we don't have to be too concerned with the inevitable destruction of the world."

He moves on with his lecture, and I exhale in relief. Pru reaches forward and gives my shoulder a congratulatory shove from behind.

For just a second, I even catch Maya's eye. A small smile before she turns away. A dip of eyelashes that almost certainly means nothing, nothing at all.

My pride lasts until next period, when Mrs. Andrews announces that we're having a pop quiz on the chapters of *The Great Gatsby* we were supposed to read over the weekend. I groan with the rest of the class. Pru shoots me a look, and only now do I remember that moment on Saturday when she reminded me about the extra chapters Mrs. Andrews added to our weekend reading.

"Relax," says Mrs. Andrews, handing out the tests. "It's multiple choice, so statistically speaking, most of you stand a chance of not failing."

I think she's joking, but no one laughs.

The test lands on my desk, and I click the lead down in my mechanical pencil. I start to read the questions, and . . .

Oh, crap. I don't know any of this.

Out of the corner of my eye, I can hear Pru's pencil scratching against the paper, circling answers with confidence.

Shaking my head, I get started. I do my best to make educated guesses based on what I've read so far. I'm one of the first to finish, but I don't want to be the only one standing up, so I pretend to be going over my answers until a handful of kids get up to turn their tests in. I avoid meeting our teacher's eye as I hand in my test then slink back to my seat.

"These will just take me a minute to get through," says Mrs. Andrews. "Consider this free study until I'm done. This would be a great opportunity to get started on this week's reading, or catch up if you're behind."

I'm tempted to ignore that not-so-subtle hint and keep working on the campaign map I started over the weekend, but I force myself to reach for *Gatsby* instead.

"Not bad, not bad," says Mrs. Andrews, ten minutes later. She starts wandering down the aisles, passing back the tests. "Nice work, Jude," she says, dropping my paper facedown onto my desk. My stomach twists, the sarcasm sticking me in the gut, and for a second I'm actually tempted to apologize, to promise I'll catch up on the reading for next time.

But then I flip over the paper and go still.

100.

Written in green ink.

Circled.

One hundred *percent*?

It must be a mistake. But there's my name, in my handwriting, at the top. And every question checked off—correct, correct, correct.

I glance around, wondering if Mrs. Andrews is pulling a practical joke on us, but Robyn in the next seat has an *80* circled at the top of her page, and I spy a *95* written at the top of Pru's, which she is scowling at.

I look back down at my quiz. All twenty guesses. Lucky guess after lucky guess after lucky guess.

My statistics teacher would have a field day with that.

Speaking of my statistics teacher—third period gets even weirder. Like, *really* weird.

Mr. Robles launches into a discussion on sample size and the difference between theoretical and experimental probability. He goes on to talk about an experiment in which a hundred people all started out standing. They each flipped a coin, and anyone who got tails sat down, while everyone who got heads flipped again. And again and again, until no one was left standing.

"There is no luck," he says. "It's all just probabilities, and in theory, things that seem impossible can occur with a large enough sample size. For example, with a group of one hundred people, after six coin flips, there will be one person left standing, who will have landed on heads six times in a row. Now, is it always going to happen exactly like that? No— because of . . . ?"

He waits for the class to respond, but only Pru shouts out, "Anomalies."

"That's right, anomalies. While unlikely, they do occur, because this is *probabilities* we are talking about, not *certainties*. Remember that discussion from last week? Keeping in mind that every coin flip has a fifty-fifty chance of landing on heads, it may not seem too out there for someone to flip heads six times in a row. But this experiment has been conducted using computer simulation with *ten billion* imaginary subjects, and guess what? The statistics held. In every round, roughly fifty percent of the subjects were eliminated, and in the end, one imaginary subject had flipped heads thirty-four times . . . *in a row*. Sounds impossible, but . . ." He shrugs. "Probabilities. So, based on that, we are going to run a much smaller simulation today. Janine, would you pass out these quarters?"

As Janine hands everyone a quarter, Mr. Robles puts up a chart on the board, determining that, with twenty-eight students, we should get through five rounds before we're all seated. I'm trying to figure out how we can replicate this experiment with Ellie at home, and whether or not it would ruin for her the magic of the universe making her life's decisions, when we're split up into pairs—in order to keep everyone honest, says Mr. Robles.

We all flip at once. Coins go everywhere—hitting the ceiling, clattering to the floor, rolling off under the desks. But after a few minutes of chaos, our results are in. Pru and I both flipped heads, so we both stay standing, but exactly fourteen kids sit down.

Some people look impressed that Mr. Robles's prediction was spot-on. The fourteen of us who are still standing flip again.

I get heads, but Pru sits down with tails, along with seven others.

This time, only six of us are left standing.

Flip.

Heads.

Only Carina, Jackson, and I are left.

Flip.

Heads.

I look around, and the moment I realize I'm the only one still standing, I immediately want to sink onto my seat and hand my quarter to Pru.

I refrain.

"Now, what do we think will happen when Jude flips again?" asks Mr. Robles. "Keeping in mind that every flip comes with a fifty-fifty chance of landing on heads."

My peers shout out their guesses. Most are saying tails, but a lot of people are rooting for heads to reign supreme.

It's harder to flip now that all eyes are on me, and I'm grateful that Ellie's obsession has given me lots of practice at catching it so I don't drop the quarter and look like an uncoordinated buffoon.

Heads.

Mr. Robles nods, and he starts to draw hash marks on the whiteboard so we can keep track of how many flips I've done.

Heads.

Heads.

Heads.

People are getting excited now. I even see Mr. Robles's eyebrows inching upward in surprise. This is unexpected, for all of us. *Possible*, of course. But still, unexpected. Highly improbable.

I keep going.

And going. And going. And going . . .

By the time class ends, the whole class is in an uproar. I've been handed a number of different quarters to try, and even some nickels, to make sure I'm not using a faulty, weighted coin. People are chanting my name with every flip. *Jude! Jude! Jude!* I don't know if I'm elated by this sudden rise in coin-flip heroism or horrified to be caught in the center of all this attention. My chest is itching under my shirt, and I'm pretty sure there are hives popping up on my skin, but no one can see them, so I try to play it cool, and just keep flipping.

All I know is that by the time the bell rings, dismissing us, Mr. Robles is counting the hash marks on the whiteboard and massaging his brow in disbelief. In *awe*.

Fifty-seven.

I flipped heads fifty-seven times in a row.

I didn't just beat the odds, I pulverized them.

Chapter Five

"What just happened?" Pru asks as we make our way out of the class. "That was . . ." She struggles for a word. "*Impossible.*"

"Improbable," I counter.

My whole body is vibrating from the energy of the coin-flip experiment. The sound of my name being chanted still echoes in my ears. People I barely know are slapping me on the back as they pass me in the hall, making comments about wanting some of that luck to wear off on them, asking me what numbers they should pick for this week's lottery. I don't respond, just smile tightly and laugh along.

Pru isn't laughing. She's looking at me like I'm a Rubik's Cube that she is determined to solve.

"Are you sure you haven't picked up some coin-flip strategy, all those times you've flipped with Ellie?" she asks. "Like . . . some specific . . . thumb . . . flick . . ." She mimics flipping an invisible coin, and I know she's wondering if it's possible, for someone to learn to flip a coin in the same manner so that they get the same result every time. I suspect Mr. Robles is wondering the same thing right about now.

We come to a fork in the hall, and I pause, shoving my hands into my pockets so people don't notice that they're kind of shaking with adrenaline. My left hand finds the dice deep in my pocket, and I instinctively wrap my fingers around it.

"I don't know what to tell you, Sis. It was super weird. But anomalies happen, right?"

She huffs, unsatisfied.

"I'll see you in poli-sci," I tell her, doing my best to seem nonchalant about the whole thing as I turn and head off to the cafeteria. Pru and Quint both have second lunch this semester, so I usually eat with Matt and César, and sometimes Russell, though he prefers to spend most of his lunch breaks in the library working on his novel, the third installment of an epic fantasy series he calls the Hidden Gates of Khiarin. Or, sometimes, the Khiarin Chronicles. Or, lately, the Keys to Khiarin. He struggles with titles more than adding words. Last I heard, this third book was already more than five hundred pages long.

Two members of our student government are on ladders on either side of the cafeteria doors as I pass by, hanging up a butcher-paper banner hand-painted with hearts and stars and music notes—a reminder to purchase tickets for this year's prom and junior prom dances.

I stop at the vending machine just inside the door and release my grip on the dice to fish a couple dollars from my wallet.

"Oh, man, don't!" a voice cries the moment the machine sucks in my second dollar. I turn to see César groaning and shaking his head at me. "Sorry, dude. This machine's busted. It's been eating people's money all morning."

"Really?" I turn back to the keypad. The blue screen is blinking at me, asking for my selection.

"I mean, give it a shot," says César, thumping his fist on the door, right in front of a bag of Funyuns. "But it took four dollars from me before I wised up, and didn't give them back."

"Sorry," I say, not sure what I'm apologizing for. Still, I punch in the code for the Cool Ranch Doritos.

For a second, nothing happens. But then the bar holding back the chips starts to rotate.

"Oh, come *on*," says César, thumping the door again as my Doritos drop down into the lower bin. "This thing hates me."

I start to apologize again, when I realize that the bar is still spinning.

We both go still, watching as a second bag of Doritos is released. Then a third.

"Whoa, *score*." As the bags keep falling, César reaches through the flap and gathers up the first three. The machine doesn't stop until the whole row of Doritos have dropped down into the bin—all eleven of them. "Guess that makes up for stealing my money," he says.

Our arms are full with crinkling, crunching bags as we head through the cafeteria. We dump the chips onto the table where both Matt and Russell are waiting for us, their trays full of pizza slices and milk cartons.

"Craving Doritos?" Matt asks speculatively.

"Machine's broken," says César. "It hates me, but Jude lucked out."

I slide into the table and pop open a bag. "You guys won't believe what I found at the store last night." I pull the twenty-sided dice from my pocket and hold it out on my open palm.

"Whoa," says Matt, plucking it out of my hand. For some reason, my gut twists, and I feel a Gollum-like urge to snatch it back from him, but I resist. I've been dying to show the dice to them all day, after all, knowing that my D&D group will appreciate it way more than my family did.

"It looks like it could be from one of those limited-edition sets they were giving out at Comic-Con a few years ago," Matt says, holding it up to the sunshine pouring in through the cafeteria windows. The refracted crimson light sparkles across our table. "What do you think it's made out of?"

He passes the dice to Russell, who frowns deeply as he studies it.

"No idea," I say. "Glass maybe?"

"Too heavy for glass," says Russell, handing it to César. "Feels like some sort of stone."

"Maybe it's a real ruby," says César. "Picture this. Some D&D group planned an elaborate heist to steal this from the crown jewels and then had it cut into a D20 as, like, a big FU to the monarchy." He excitedly slaps his free hand on the table, then points at Russell. "Now, that's a good story. You need to write that."

Russell looks less impressed. "Why does this mystery group hate the monarchy?"

"Dude, how should I know? You're the writer."

The dice makes its way back to me, with no more answers than before. I return it to my pocket. "We're still on for Saturday, right? Or are you all going to spend the rest of the semester drinking ale in Bork's Tavern?"

"That," says César. "Definitely that. Goren the Gruesome votes to hang out in the pub and get smashed."

"Please," says Russell. "Goren is always the first one to run off and get us all into trouble."

"Which is even more fun to do when Goren is drunk," says César.

"True as that may be," I say, "I'm going to have lightning strike the pub and burn everything down if you all won't leave on your own."

Russell grunts. "Deus ex machina. Shoddy craftsmanship, Dungeon Master."

"I'm just saying. Last time you all spent an entire session betting on that illegal dragon fight. I'm not putting up with that again."

Matt sets down his half-eaten slice of pizza, looking uncomfortable, and I realize he hasn't said much since I sat down. "Actually," he says, picking off a green pepper. "I've got some bad news."

We all fall quiet.

"I think Brawndo is going to have to sit this campaign out." He meets my eye, his face pinched apologetically. "I asked my boss to start putting me on the schedule for Saturdays."

I frown. Matt works at a fish and chips stand off the boardwalk. It's not exactly a dream job.

"Why?" César asks.

"It's our busiest day," says Matt. "You can get twice as many tips as working weekdays. I need that money to feed my gaming addiction, you know that."

"You need *time* to feed a gaming addiction," I say.

"Yeah. Maybe. But I'd also like to get a car at some point? Anyway . . . it just seemed like the right call."

44

"We could move D&D to a different night," suggests Russell.

We exchange doubtful looks. It isn't easy to coordinate the schedules of six high school students. I've got work at the record store, César's on the wrestling team, Kyle (who has second lunch) does track, and Noah is juggling their senior year, college applications, a math tutoring gig, plus being the president of their school's anime club.

And Russell—well, Russell just mostly works on his novel. But that takes up a *lot* of his time.

"It won't be the same without you," grumbles César. "Who is going to encourage all of Goren's stupid ideas now?"

"I'm sorry," says Matt. "I know it sucks, but you can do the campaign without me, right?"

My mind does cartwheels, running over the details of the campaign. Matt's character, Brawndo, is a barbarian, giving him the most brute strength of the group. It comes in handy, a lot, but . . . there aren't any specific challenges I've put into the campaign that will *need* him . . .

"Yeah," I say. "We'll make it work."

Chapter Six

Despite how our D&D group is losing a member right when we're about to start our new campaign, the rest of the day is . . . kind of awesome. I'm not sure I can remember having a better day, at least not during my high school career. There's almost a mystical quality to it, like Mercury's in retrograde and the stars have aligned in my favor or whatever.

In gym class, I make the best basketball shot of my life, a three-pointer that I'm not entirely sure should have been physically possible outside of the NBA.

In political science, Ms. Spencer pairs me up with Maya to discuss the role of the media in our most recent local elections, and normally this would leave me petrified, except Maya is in her element and has plenty to say on the subject, making it pretty easy for me to nod along in agreement and try not to make it obvious when I catch the occasional scent of her shampoo and nearly implode from olfactory overload.

I mean that in a good way. A *very* good way.

And then, miracle of miracles, Mr. Cross announces in my last period of the day, visual arts, that we're going to spend the next week drawing the human form, something I'm already decent at, but also would like to do better.

As soon as it's announced, Ezra throws his arms into the air and jubilantly proclaims—"Bring on the nude models!"

To which Quint shoves him on the shoulder and says, "You're up first, EZ."

And did Ezra jump out of his seat and start stripping off his T-shirt to a chorus of whistles and hollers from our classmates?

Of course he did.

It took the teacher ten minutes to get everyone settled down again— and Ezra fully clothed—and the rest of the period was spent looking at slides of artworks depicting the human body in various forms. Male, female, curvy, slender, short, tall, everything in between. Mr. Cross points out a lot of details I wouldn't have noticed on my own—how the arrangement of the figures alters their apparent relationships to one another. How the vibe of the piece changes in intensity when the figures are directly facing the viewer versus being turned into a profile view. How much the direction of the figure's own eyes and attention can impact the interpretation of the piece.

I sketch the whole time, trying to soak in as much information as possible, eager to see if this new information translates to my pencil.

My teachers don't even assign any homework. Not a single one. On a Monday.

That *never* happens.

Not that I'm complaining.

The house is quiet for a weekday afternoon. Well . . . quiet-ish. Pru left as soon as we got home from school, off for her volunteer gig at the animal rescue center. Lucy is at soccer practice. Mom and Dad took Ellie with them to the record store. That just leaves me and Penny, and Penny is upstairs practicing her violin.

Hence, quiet-*ish*.

I don't mind her practicing, though. She's improved a lot this last year, and after a while, the repetition of her recital songs becomes somewhat soothing background noise.

I'm at the kitchen table, munching through a second bowl of Lucky Charms and reading through my notes for the upcoming campaign, trying to figure out if I need to change anything now that we've lost Matt. I don't really *want* to change anything. I've put a lot of work into this campaign, and I'm tempted to just continue on with how I've designed it and make adjustments while we play, if necessary. That's the hallmark of a good Dungeon Master, isn't it? That we can be flexible and adapt the story as we go?

It also crosses my mind to try to find a new player, but I don't know who I would ask. None of my sisters are interested. Well, Ellie would probably love to, but I don't think bringing a kindergartner into the mix would fly with the others. I consider Ari. We've never had anyone play a bard in the group before, but she usually works at the store on Saturdays.

I look down at the blank page in front of me, tapping my pencil against my thumb. I think of the upcoming campaign. Lost ruins and hordes of goblins and a powerful curse . . .

The lead of my pencil brushes against the paper, and I start to draw.

The great wizard Jude, he had journeyed afar,
Slaying many a monster and foe—
'Til he came to the Temple of Lundyn Toune,
Where few souls had ventured to go.

Would his quest produce
treasures of
mysteries old?
Would his reward be
fortune and fame?

Or like so many paths he had wandered
before...Would this foolish crusade be in
vain?

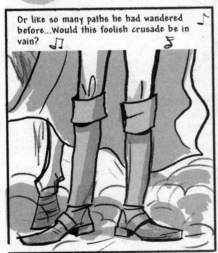

One could not know the fate that awaited
Our brave and intrepid knight...

It's oft been said that luck was never
his friend,
And let's be frank...things aren't
really looking too bright.

The chiming notification of a text message startles me from my focus. I peel my attention away from the page. My fingers are smudged with pencil lead. There's a crick in my neck from being bent over the table for so long. I blink around in a daze, wondering when the sound of Penny's violin fell silent. I have a vague memory of Lucy getting home and dropping her cleats in the entryway before dashing upstairs, but I was oblivious to the bright daylight dimming into purple dusk. My stomach growls—the two bowls of cereal more than used up in my rush of inspiration.

It's after our usual dinnertime. I pick up my phone and see that the text was from my mom, saying that they're going to be working late at the store, unpacking a bunch of new merch that came in, and asking if I can get dinner for myself, Lucy, and Penny. She's included a photo of Ellie, fast asleep on the old couch we keep in the back room, her favorite pony toys piled on her chest.

I respond with a thumbs-up emoji, and Mom sends a hug emoji back.

I roll my shoulder a few times, then get up and flip through the cabinets, finding a package of spaghetti and jarred tomato sauce.

I let Lucy and Penny know that dinner will be ready in ten minutes, and check my inbox while the pasta cooks.

One new email.

Subject: Art Submission for the Dungeon

I just about drop the phone into the pot of boiling water. I don't, thank Cthulhu, but also—it might be better if I did. It would probably be best to never open this email. To never read the rejection that's coming. It's like that Schrödinger's Cat experiment. Until you open the box, the cat is both alive and dead.

Until I open this email, my hopes are both alive and dead.

I know. I never really got the logic of that experiment, either. I'm just stalling.

Give me a moment.

One more.

Okay.

I'm ready.

I take in a stabilizing breath and open the email.

> Dear Jude Barnett, thank you for your submission.
> We like your artistic style and find the point of view
> refreshing. We are pleased to accept this for our
> July edition of the *Dungeon*—

It goes on, but I stop reading. I stare at those words until they blur together.

Pleased to accept.

Pleased to *accept*.

No. Way.

I feel the pull of a tentative, disbelieving smile on my lips. Am I imagining this?

I take a screenshot and text it to Ari and Pru. Pru's response comes back immediately.

> **Pru:** NICE. What are they paying?

I roll my eyes.

> **Jude:** Who cares??

When Pru doesn't respond, I sigh and check the *Dungeon*'s submission guidelines on their website.

> **Jude:** $50
> **Pru:** Not bad, but we'll renegotiate for the next
> one. You're free to accept.

Jude: When did you become my manager?

Pru: Since the womb, Jude!

Pru: You, Quint, and Ari might be the talent, but you'd be lost without me.

Pru: Okay, maybe not lost. But definitely starving artists.

Jude: That's artistes to you.

Pru replies with the artist emoji, beret and all.

Ari's text comes in a few minutes later.

Ari: I told you so!!!

My heart lifts as it starts to sink in. This is real. I submitted a drawing to the *Dungeon*, and they are actually going to publish it. I'm even getting paid. For *drawing* something!

Jude: Now you owe me a song.

Ari starts to type a response, the three little dots appearing next to her name.

But then the dots go away.

I wait.

After a long while, she starts to type again.

Ari: Araceli the Magnificent is on it!

My smile returns. I glance down at my sketchbook. Of the bard and the wizard—two characters who had no place in my new campaign yesterday, but now I sort of like where the story is heading. I wasn't sure before how I was going to start the group off on this new quest, but I can use the bard as an NPC to tell them about the mysterious temple and the wizard and the curse. Maybe she'll give them the Scarlet Diamond and—

My whole body goes still.

The Scarlet Diamond was a piece of treasure from the one campaign I tried to run with Quint, Pru, and Ari—a campaign that never really got off the ground because, even though they all said they were having fun, it was never a priority for anyone to keep playing and the story kind of just fizzled away. I hadn't thought much about it until now.

I pull the red dice out of my pocket and hold it up toward my drawing. I think about the story I've been concocting, the mythology of the temple that I was telling Ari about during open mic night.

A maiden turned to stone, a curse that can only be broken by someone deemed worthy. And for that adventurer who succeeds in breaking the spell? A gift. A spell that gives you uncanny good luck with every roll of the dice.

These things that have been happening to me. All these strange, happy coincidences. This isn't the Force. This isn't the universe. This isn't a series of statistical anomalies.

This is the magic of Lundyn Toune.

My breaths are coming in quick gasps, but . . . this is nuts. Am I actually considering the possibility that this might be . . . ? That the dice could be giving me . . . ?

That my life might actually have been touched by . . .

Magic?

I mean, I want to believe in sorcery and unicorns as much as the next guy, but . . . I don't actually believe in those things. I don't believe in *this*.

But then—where did this dice come from? And now that I'm thinking about it, things did start to get weird as soon as I found it. Weird in a good way. The Paul McCartney signature and how I miraculously saved it from that coffee tumbler, when my real-life dexterity score would usually be pretty dismal. Then I had all those lucky guesses on the literature quiz, and the vending machine score, not to mention the outrageous improbability of flipping heads fifty-seven times in a row.

The timer goes off, startling me. I glance over in time to see the water foaming up, and manage to pull the pot off the burner seconds before it boils over. I feel dazed as I go through the motions of getting out a colander and draining the pasta. Throwing it back into the pot and adding the sauce. Getting out bowls and forks.

I don't call my sisters yet, just stand there, the wooden spoon in one hand and the dice in the other. Thinking about lost temples and magic and luck.

The gold rune-like numbers glint up at me.

"If this is real," I whisper, "give me a sign."

Taking in a deep breath, I roll the dice.

There's the familiar, comforting sound as it clatters across the counter, hits one of the bowls, and bounces right off the edge. I jump back as it lands on the floor and rolls past my feet, disappearing beneath one of the breakfast nook benches.

I ponder the spot where it vanished. Legitimately surprised at first. I actually thought for a second that would work. I don't know what I expected, but . . . *something* cool. Something lucky.

So much for magic.

Vowing to never mention this to anyone, I crouch and stick my hand under the bench, feeling around for the dice. My hand lands on something long and narrow instead, and I pull out a mechanical pencil. I sigh and reach back under, this time finding the dice. I slide it out into the light, my eye catching on the number twenty shining on top.

"Cute," I say, grabbing the dice and the pencil and standing up.

Only then do I recognize it. The mechanical pencil. Dark blue and dusty. My lips part as I pluck the strands of a dust bunny off its eraser.

It isn't just any pencil. It's my *favorite* pencil, that I used to draw with all the time until I lost it. It's been missing for years, and now—here it is.

I turn my attention back to the dice, full of wonder. That twenty shimmers, and if I didn't know better, I'd think the dice just winked at me.

Chapter Seven

"Flip a coin for it!" yells Ellie, her mouth full of Eggo waffle.

"Don't talk with your mouth full," says Lucy. Followed by, "Heads."

She and I are standing at the kitchen counter, the last package of Pop-Tarts between us.

"Let's just each take one," I suggest.

But Ellie has already grabbed her coin. She flips it as well as she can, but misses the catch. The coin falls to the floor and rolls beneath the table. Ellie dives after it.

"Tails!" she calls out, reappearing on her hands and knees, coin in hand.

Lucy huffs.

"It's fine, you take them," I say. "I'll have cereal." I turn away and grab a bowl from the cupboard.

"You've been *really* lucky lately," says Ellie.

I pause and look at her. I haven't let the dice out of my sight since last night, even sleeping with it under my pillow, and putting it back into my pocket as soon as I got dressed this morning.

"You think?" I say, trying not to sound suspicious. Even though I'm now 99 percent convinced that I hold a magical luck-giving dice in my pocket . . . I'm not about to tell my sisters that.

"You've won, like, every coin flip," Ellie explains.

"I guess I have." I tuck the bowl into the crook of my elbow as I yank open the refrigerator and grab the milk.

When I turn back, Ellie's eyes are narrowed at me in suspicion. "Are you *cheating*?"

This, I know, would be an unparalleled betrayal of the sanctity of the coin flip.

"If I was cheating," I say, "I probably wouldn't give up my earnings so easily, would I?" I gesture at the toaster, where Lucy has dropped in the Pop-Tarts. But my hands are full, and in the next second, the bowl is slipping out of its tenuous position. I gasp and instinctively lift my foot.

To everyone's surprise—mine most of all—I catch the bowl on the toe of my shoe, an inch before it smashes onto the floor.

"Whoa," says Lucy, amazed. "You *are* lucky these days. You should go buy some scratch tickets. Or a lotto ticket or something."

I let out a nervous chuckle, my heart thumping as I set the milk down and grab the bowl. "You have to be eighteen to buy lottery tickets."

"Too bad," she muses, and I can tell she thinks I should go buy some anyway.

Pru strolls into the kitchen, grabbing a banana from the counter. "We got the best news at the center yesterday."

"That awful woman who stole all that money is going to jail?" Lucy asks.

This comment turns Pru's expression sour. She huffs, rolling her eyes upward. "*No.* Rosa decided not to press criminal charges. But their lawyers have been in negotiations, and it sounds like Shauna is going to have to pay restitution. So that's something. But—" Her eyes brighten again. "This is even better! The zoo that's taking Lennon and Luna *finally* finished construction on their new enclosure. They can be relocated in a few weeks!"

"Awesome," I say, raising my spoon in a mock toast. Ellie claps—happy to see Pru so happy—but Lucy looks confused.

"I thought you didn't want your sea lions to go to a new zoo," she says.

"Won't you miss them?" Penny asks. We've all been to the rescue center a handful of times since Pru started working there, and Pru is always ecstatic to introduce anyone to her two favorite sea lions, especially Lennon, the sea lion that we all had a part in saving when he washed up on the beach during the Freedom Festival. It's a sad story with a happy ending—Luna has a cognitive disorder, and Lennon lost his eyesight to an infection. Neither would be able to survive in the wild, so the center can't release them back to the ocean. But on the plus side, the two sea lions have become best friends (maybe more than friends? I'm not really up on the marine mammal romances happening at the center), and a zoo located just a few hours north of us agreed to take them both, so they won't have to be separated.

"Of course I'm going to miss them," says Pru, "but the enclosure at the zoo is going to be bigger and nicer than what they have at the center. It's time for them to move on. *And*, since it's not that far away, once Quint gets his own car, we'll be able to go visit them on weekends."

"Oh!" says Ellie, bouncing in her seat. "Can we go see them together?"

"Of course," says Pru. "Once they're all settled in, we'll plan a family trip."

"It sounds like things have been going good at the center?" I say between bites.

"Good, but busy," says Pru. "This is the time of year when a lot of pinnipeds are being weaned from their mothers, and not all of them are able to hunt well enough to feed themselves yet. We took in five new patients just last week. But at least the center is doing much better financially this year than in the past. Our fundraising initiatives have been taking off, we've gotten tons of new donors, and perhaps most importantly, we no longer have a skeezy bookkeeper skimming money off the top. So . . . yeah." She nods, satisfied. "Things are going pretty great, actually." She checks her watch and tosses her banana peel in the garbage. "Everyone ready?"

As we're heading to the car, we flip Ellie's coin three more times. First to see who has to drive, because even though driving is supposed to be this big rite of passage, Pru and I both hate driving the minivan monstrosity. I win the coin flip (obviously), and Prudence takes the wheel, complaining that she drove yesterday, but *what the coin sayeth* . . . We flip again to determine shotgun. I win again but let Penny have it because she claims that she didn't get shotgun *at all* last week. And the last flip is to see who has to sit in the middle of the back seat. I win a third time and keep my window seat, ruffling Ellie's hair when she glares daggers at me and mutters, "*Cheater*."

The radio is still on from when my mom last drove the van. The morning DJ is gushing about an upcoming sold-out concert, promising to give away a pair of highly coveted tickets before the morning is over. She's just gone to commercial when a figure outside Java Jive catches my eye. Electricity zips down my spine. "Pru, stop. Pull over!"

"What? Why?" she says, startled as she flips on her blinker. "What's wrong?"

"Nothing, I just . . . That was Maya back there."

Pru pulls over to the curb. The car has barely stopped rolling when I throw open my door and jump out, absently tucking my phone into my pocket.

"What are you doing?" cries Penny. "We're going to be late!"

I look back at her, then gesture down the street. "We're less than two blocks from Ellie's school. Can one of you walk with her the rest of the way, and we'll pick you up at the corner?"

"*Walk?*" says Ellie, like I've just suggested she go climb Mount Everest.

"Don't whine," says Pru. "Jude is right. Lucy, can you go with her?"

"Why me?"

I don't stick around to hear the ensuing argument. I jog down the sidewalk, all the while wondering if I was seeing things. Wishful thinking? A mirage?

But no. There she is, pacing back and forth in the parking lot, a cell phone held between her ear and shoulder. A small Toyota Camry sits in the next parking space, its hood propped open. Maya looks frazzled, her free hand scrunching some of her hair into a fist—and that look, more than anything, is what made me stop.

"Maya?"

She swivels toward me, startled, then wilts with relief. She holds up a finger, then looks back at the car. "It just won't start," she says to the person on the phone. "It was fine. I just stopped for a second, ran in to get a coffee, and when I came back out . . ." She doesn't speak for a while, nodding along to whatever the person on the other end of the line is saying. "Uh . . . the battery looks like . . ." She frowns, staring at a black box in the corner of the engine. "A battery? How should I know?" She sighs. "I know, I know. It's just that I'm going to be late . . ."

While she talks, I lean over the engine. I can feel heat radiating off it.

"What's going on?" asks Pru. I glance over to see her and Penny walking toward us.

"One second," Maya says to whoever she's talking to. She lowers the phone, looking flustered. "My car won't start. My dad thinks it could be the battery, but I don't have jumper cables or really any idea what I'm doing." She laughs wryly. "I'm kind of stranded."

"We can give you a ride," I say hastily.

Too hastily? Do I sound eager? Desperate? Just the right amount of helpful?

But Maya's smile is grateful, if still pinched with worry. "Thanks, but I might have to wait for AAA. I don't want to make you late, too. So—it's okay. I just . . . It's probably something stupid, you know?" She heaves a heavy sigh, then lifts the phone back to her ear. "Sorry, Dad. Some of my friends were driving by and stopped to see if I needed help . . ."

While she talks to her dad, I study the engine. Metal and plastic, nuts and bolts. What would Ezra do? Admittedly, this is not a question I ever thought I'd ask myself, yet here we are. Ezra works at Marcus's Garage, fixing cars and doing . . . mechanic-y things. (That's a technical term.) He would have jumper cables, for starters. Probably an entire toolbox, just in case. If Ezra was here, he could probably take one look at this engine and know exactly what to do to fix it, whereas I might as well be trying to translate a sheet of hieroglyphs. I'm not even sure it *is* an engine. Could it be a motor instead? I can never remember what the difference is.

Right now, I would give up my prized Gimli Funko to be able to fix this problem for Maya. I picture what that would be like. Sleeves rolled up, grease smeared on my palms, a wrench in my back pocket. (Where did he get the wrench, you ask? Well, don't.)

I press my hand briefly to the outside of my jeans pocket, where I can feel the dice snugly inside.

I can do this. I can fix this. If this was a D&D campaign, I would roll for perception to see what was wrong, then a survival skill check to see if I knew how to fix it. And with a magic dice, the answer would be yes, of course. I can do anything. Right?

I imagine the way Maya would look at me as I diagnosed the problem. What she would say if I told her I could fix this for her, no sweat. She would look at me like a freaking hero as I tinkered away with this . . . thing. Whatever this is, that looks a little bit like a metal bolt next to the battery. It budges the tiniest bit as I reach over and give it a twist. Some white powdery dust flakes off.

"What are you doing?" Pru hisses at me.

"Hold on, Dad." Maya lowers the phone again and looks at me, then down at the engine-motor-thing. "What did you do?"

"Uh—I'm not sure," I say, heat creeping into my cheeks. "But that seemed . . . loose?"

Maya stares at me.

I clear my throat. "You could try turning it over?"

That sounds like something Ezra would say.

Maya opens her mouth, but hesitates a long moment. Then she nods, hope flickering in her eyes.

What am I thinking?

Which is exactly the question Pru hisses at me as Maya slips into the driver's seat.

I flash my sister a panicked look. "I don't know. I just thought—"

I'm cut off by the sound of the engine roaring to life, so loud that Pru and I both jump back from it.

"What? That was *it*?" blurts Maya. "Jude! You did it!" She jumps out of the car again, and before I realize what's happening, her arms are around me. The hug is short but overwhelming, and as she pulls away I feel like my heart is going to burst out of my chest. "You are my *hero*," she says, punching me lightly on the shoulder. "How did you know to do that?"

I can't speak. This is the greatest moment of my life.

"Jude is full of surprises," says Pru, jabbing me between the ribs. I recoil.

"Bloody brilliant." Maya slams the hood shut. "Thank you! I can't even. I'm so glad you stopped." She exhales a loud breath. "Okay, we are all going to be so late. I'll see you at school?" She turns away and starts talking into the phone again, explaining to her dad what happened.

I stand there gaping another second, until Pru grabs my arm and drags me back down the sidewalk.

"How *did* you do that?" Penny asks. I'd forgotten she was there, but now she and Pru are both staring at me like I just went Super Saiyan.

"You know as much about cars as I do," says Pru. "Which is *nothing*."

I try to appear equally confounded, even though . . . I know it wasn't me. It was the dice. "I can't explain it. I just saw it and took a guess. I just . . . I got lucky."

"These lucky coincidences seem to be happening to you a lot lately," Pru mutters. She studies me a long moment, then gets an odd, faraway look in her eye. She turns away, sighing, "Enjoy it while it lasts."

Chapter Eight

We should be late, but we're not. After picking up Lucy in front of the elementary school, we make every green light and even score a parking spot right by the main entrance, even though the lot is otherwise full. Now that I'm looking for the signs, I can't help but think this is the magic helping me out yet again.

Pru and I are slightly out of breath when we hurry into Mr. Singh's classroom just as the bell is ringing.

Maya comes in three minutes later, and despite the annoyed look she gets from the teacher, she beams at me as she makes her way to her seat.

Did you catch that? No? Let me say it again.

She *beams* at *me*.

In fact, Maya is looking at me like I just saved her drowning cat, and it sets every nerve on fire. I know I should smile back. I know that a normal guy like Ezra (is Ezra a normal guy? let's not dwell on that) would smile back. He'd act all suave and carefree and like, *No big deal, I fix things and stuff*. But evidently I've got all the game of pre-Spider-Man Peter Parker, because I start riffling through my backpack until I'm sure Maya is no longer looking at me.

Mr. Singh starts in on a lecture, but within seconds I notice Maya passing notes with Katie, who sits behind her. I chew on the cap of my pen, wondering if they're talking about me. That seems presumptuous, though, and at some point I catch Maya whispering, *I forgot!*

Katie looks aghast. What did Maya forget? Her birthday? With a look like that, I'd half expect her to say that Maya forgot to stop by the hospital and donate a kidney.

Maya glances up at the clock, then surreptitiously reaches for her backpack and pulls out her phone. She's hiding it under her desk, but I crane my neck to see the screen. She opens up her web browser. A site pops up, bold letters and numbers at the top. KSMT 101.3.

A radio station?

"I'll take that, Miss Livingstone," says Mr. Singh, swooping in out of nowhere and grabbing Maya's phone away. She gasps, reaching for it, but he's already turned off the screen and spun back toward the front of the room.

"Wait! I just need to do something real quick!"

"It will have to wait until after class."

Maya and Katie exchange distraught looks, before Katie shoots her hand into the air. "Can I use the restroom?"

Mr. Singh glares at her. "Five minutes into first period? You should have gone before class started. Let me get through this explanation, then you can go."

"But—" Katie clenches her jaw and looks up at the clock.

"You'll survive," says Mr. Singh. He deposits Maya's phone on top of his desk and sorts a stack of papers. "Ah, but before I forget . . ." He glances up, scanning the class. His gaze lands on me. "Jude, could you run this up to the office?"

"Me?" I ask, perplexed.

When a teacher needs an errand run, they almost always ask Pru. Stalwart, dependable Pru. It's not like I'm a troublemaker or anything. I'm not really *anything*. I skate by unnoticed as often as possible. That's how I like it.

Why is he asking me?

But Mr. Singh just gives me an impatient look, so I take in a breath and get out of my seat. I can feel Katie scowling at me as I take the envelope and step out into the hall.

When I reach the office, our receptionist is humming along to a song on the radio while she sorts papers into a filing cabinet. It's an old standard—Frank Sinatra, maybe? But as I'm waiting for her to notice me, I realize it's one of the new covers sung by Sadashiv, a British Indian singer who's broken a bunch of records *and* been called the world's handsomest man. I only know this because Lucy and Penny both stan him big-time, and because Maya came into the store last year asking about his new release, so now I notice whenever one of his songs comes up on my sisters' playlists.

The song finishes, and I clear my throat. Mrs. Zaluski turns toward me. "Sorry, hon, I didn't hear you come in."

"From Mr. Singh," I say, holding out the envelope.

"Oh yes, thank you." She's reaching across the counter when our vice-principal, Mr. Hart, pokes his head out of the office.

"This is it!" he says.

Mrs. Zaluski gasps and misses the envelope just as I'm letting go. It flutters down onto her desk, landing on her keyboard, but she ignores it and turns toward the small speaker behind her computer monitor. She reaches for the dial, turning up the volume.

It's the same radio DJ we heard in the car this morning, a lady with a bright, chipper voice. "Thank you for being with me today! I'm Vanessa Hsu, and you're listening to KSMT 101.3, and *yes*, it is the moment you have been waiting all morning for! We are about to give away VIP tickets to this Thursday's sold-out Sadashiv concert. I've got our last pair of tickets sitting right next to me, and I am going to give them to caller number *one hundred*."

Mrs. Zaluski and Mr. Hart both reach for their phones while the DJ gives the phone number to call.

With no one paying attention to me, I back slowly out of the office, letting the door swing shut behind me.

I usually keep my phone in my backpack when I'm at school, but now I can feel it heavy in my back pocket, still there from when I hopped out of the car this morning in my hurry to help Maya.

The hall is empty as I pull out my phone in one hand, my dice in the other.

There's no way, of course. The odds have got to be . . . I have no idea. Ten thousand to one? Maybe not that much, but still. Like—a really big number to one.

But I punch in the phone number anyway. My finger hesitates as I struggle to recall the final digit. I rack my brain. I can almost hear the DJ saying it, but . . .

The dice jumps out of my hand.

I gasp as it clatters for a second on the hallway floor, before stopping right between my feet.

Not twenty this time. Rather, the number four shines up at me.

I don't think. I just punch in the final digit—four.

This is impossible.

Obviously.

But . . .

With a little luck.

I don't even hear it ring before there's a voice on the other end.

A bright, chipper voice.

"Congratulations! You are caller one hundred, and you are going to the Sadashiv concert!"

I walk back to the classroom in a daze. After announcing my win, the DJ passed me off to a producer at the radio station, and I gave them my information. They're even going to send a limousine.

For me and a friend.

Me and a plus one.

Me and a date.

I'm still clutching my phone when I walk back through the classroom door. Mr. Singh gives me a disappointed look, like I've been gone way too long and therefore betrayed his trust. But I hardly notice. My nerves are humming to the point of being jittery as I pause at the front of the classroom.

I look at Maya in the front row, vaguely aware that people are staring at me. *Everyone* is staring at me. My heart drums so hard I imagine they can all hear it.

I was never going to do this. I was never, ever going to ask Maya out. Because there would be no point. Because she would never say yes. Because I would be rejected and devastated, and it was just safer to not even try.

And to even consider asking her out *in front of people*?

No way.

But here I am, standing up in front of the whole class, whispers floating around me and Maya's expression turning into a concerned frown. Mr. Singh asks me what's going on, then tells me to take my seat. Pru and Quint and all my classmates are shifting uncomfortably, whispering among themselves.

I'm terrified, but it's a vague, distant sort of terror. Because there's also magic crackling in the air around me, even if I'm the only one who can feel it. I have the strange sensation that I'm watching the scene unfold from afar. Like I'm not a player in this scenario at all, but rather, I'm the Dungeon Master, waiting to see what will happen next.

Charisma check. Roll for performance.

"I . . . um . . ." My voice breaks. Someone laughs awkwardly in the back.

I clear my throat and hold up my phone, as if that explains everything. "I just won two tickets to the Sadashiv concert. It's this Thursday."

Maya's eyes widen. Katie lets out a small shriek of disbelief. Something passes through the classroom—whispers and glances and someone in the front row murmuring, "What are you doing, man?"

I ignore them all. I have eyes only for Maya.

"Maya. Would you . . . want to go? With me?"

The room erupts into hoots. Guffaws. Incredulity. Without looking around, I know the consensus from our peers. Jude Barnett is asking out Maya Livingstone?

Right. No chance. Nice try.

But I don't care what they think. Right now, I feel lucky. I feel like a wizard, with magic up my sleeve.

Because Maya is smiling again. Stunned and glowing and smiling *at me*, again.

I see her mouth form the word more than I hear it. One word. That's all it takes.

Yes.

Chapter Nine

When I get to the record store that evening, I all but run inside. Or skip. I might be skipping. I've felt like this all day, like I could literally float off the ground. I have no idea what was covered in any of my classes, but despite my obvious distraction, no one called on me to answer any questions or discuss any assignments. There were no pop quizzes, and the sculpture I turned in for visual arts last week came back with glowing remarks, even though I hardly understood the assignment.

I feel invincible.

I find Ari in the hip-hop section, checking for any records that have been misshelved.

"Ari! You won't believe what happened."

She jumps as I barrel toward her. I'm breathless as I try to tell her, the words all pouring out of me at once. The radio station, the phone call, the tickets. Two tickets—me. A plus one. A *date*.

I know I'm rambling. I keep forgetting important details and having to backtrack, and twice I almost slip up and mention the dice and have to work to try to cover it up, and Ari is frowning in confusion through most of it, but then her eyes start to widen.

"A . . . date?" she says, a squeak in her voice.

My grin widens further. "I asked Maya." The words don't feel real coming out of my mouth. "And she said *yes*."

Ari's expression falls, but the look is brief.

"Wow," she says, picking up a record from the bin and setting it on a stack beside her. "That's . . . wow."

I wait while Ari flips through the rest of the bin. There's a beat-heavy reggaeton song playing through the speakers—likely Ari's choice, not my dad's—but she's not humming along to it like she usually is. Like she was when I first came in. I'm pretty sure I'm not imagining the strange vibe coming off of Ari, but I don't know what to do. I feel like there should be *more*. I want to press her for more of a reaction to my news. She knows that asking out a girl—asking out *Maya*—is a huge deal for me. I never would have had the confidence to do it if it wasn't for this magic dice.

I wonder what Ari would say if I told her that part of the story. Would she believe me?

"Yeah, so," I say, deflating, "the radio station is pulling out all the stops. Sending us a limo and everything. What am I supposed to wear? Should I get her flowers or something?"

Ari inhales a deep breath and looks over at me again. Her expression is tight at first, but then it softens. "Flowers are a nice idea. Do you know what her favorite flower is?"

I snort. "I don't know what her favorite anything is. But you like daisies, right? I could get those."

Ari holds my gaze, expressionless, for a long moment, before she returns to flipping through records. "Just try to be yourself, Jude. You don't have to do anything special to impress her."

"I beg to differ. I've been in love with her for *six years*, and just being myself hasn't exactly gotten me anywhere. This is my chance."

"That's what I'm saying. You've known each other since elementary school, but you haven't really *known* each other. How many conversations have you had with her? If she could get to know you the way I do . . ." She stops herself, then gives a small smile. "You'll be fine. Trust me."

It will be impossible to relax, to just be *me*. But Ari's words give me some small encouragement, anyway. "You make it sound easy."

"It's supposed to be."

I turn to the bins on the other side of the aisle. "Have you been through these yet?"

"Not yet."

I start flipping through, searching for anything out of place. But I'll admit, my mind is elsewhere, and I'm hardly paying attention.

After a few quiet minutes, Ari clears her throat. "I have news, too. Not nearly as exciting as yours, but . . . it's something."

"Yeah?" I glance over my shoulder. "Tell me."

"The Condor Music Festival is coming up in a few weeks, and they host an annual songwriting competition." She takes in a long breath, as if bracing herself. "This year, ten finalists will get to perform their songs at the festival, and . . . the grand prize winner will get five thousand dollars *and* three days at a recording studio to make an album."

"What? Ari! That would be amazing. You're entering, right?"

"I was thinking about it. That new song I started at open mic night? I've been working on it, and . . . I think it's decent. I mean, it still needs work. The chances of winning—"

"Stop it. You sound like me," I say, giving her a gentle shove. "You have to enter. What I heard of that song was incredible, and even if that one isn't ready, you've got other great songs, too. Can you imagine if you won? To record a whole album? Something you could send to record labels and artists? That could launch your whole career."

She crinkles her nose. "I probably won't win."

"That's what I said about getting published in the *Dungeon*, and yet . . ."

She beams. "You're right. I need to be optimistic." She lifts her face toward the ceiling, extending her arms upward like a cheerleader striking her final pose. "I've totally got this!" But then she just as quickly lowers her arms, cringing nervously. "Unless I don't."

I shake my head at her. "If the festival is only a few weeks away, the deadline to enter is probably coming up soon, isn't it?"

"That's the thing. Entries need to be submitted by midnight this Sunday. And I can't just send an audio file. They want a link to a video, something posted online, so they can share it on their socials." She shrugs. "Part of their publicity campaign, I guess."

"That doesn't give us much time."

Ari's eyes meet mine. "Us?"

"You need a cameraman, don't you? And Pru already told me she's vying for your manager position, so you know she'll want to help."

"I'm sure she's busy at the center. And you've got your big date now . . ."

My big date. The words hit me with a jolt of euphoria.

I am going on a date with Maya.

Of course, the reminder also brings a strong undercurrent of panic, because . . .

I am going on a date with Maya.

"We'll make it work," I tell Ari. "We can record after school on Friday, then edit it over the weekend and submit it on Sunday, *hours* before the deadline."

"Okay. Let's make it happen!" She squeals and claps her hands to her cheeks. "Oh my gosh, I can't believe I'm going to do this! What if . . . No. I can't think about it. I'll just freak myself out."

"Believe me, I know the feeling."

The door opens, and Pru and Quint come in, Ezra slouching in behind them.

Ezra's face lights up like a pinball machine when he sees me. "There he is!" he howls, spreading his arms wide as he makes his way down the store's center aisle. "The man of the hour. I've heard the stories, but I'm still not sure I believe it. Asking out Maya Livingstone in the middle of class like that? *Damn*, that is *bold*. Give me some of that rizz, my dude."

He holds his hand out, which I slap, lamely. Undeterred, Ezra takes his hands and pretends to smear my "rizz" all over his chest. "Yeah, I was needing some of that! *Speaking of* . . ." He swivels toward Ari and wraps an arm around her shoulders. "Escalante, I heard you killed it at open mic night. You just say the word when you need me to come in and hold back the mob of screaming fans."

Ari rolls her eyes, though there's a hint of a blush rising in her cheeks.

I loudly clear my throat. "Ari has news."

Ari flashes me a grateful smile, then tells everyone what she told me about the music festival and songwriting competition. As expected, Pru, Quint, and even Ezra are immediately on board to help film her video.

"We could do it here," says Quint. "In front of the mural Jude painted for open mic night. It would make a cool background, if we framed it just right." Then he does that thing that photographers do, where they make a pretend lens with their thumbs and forefingers, peering through the frame to see how it would look on film.

"Really? I don't want to be in the way . . ."

"You won't be in the way," says Pru.

"I agree," I say. "If the acoustics work?"

"I'd use a mic," says Ari, peering at the mural. "Channel the sound directly into the software. I mean . . . yeah. It could work."

"Plus, if you win," says Pru, "it would be free publicity for the store."

"I'm probably not going to win. There could be thousands of entries."

"But there's only one Araceli the Magnificent," I say. *And maybe my luck will rub off on you*, I think, but know better than to say it out loud.

Ezra folds his arms. "Can I be in the video? I could be a backup dancer. And I play a mean tambourine." His eyes light up. "Oh, you should make that into a song! 'Mean Tambourine'! There's your hit single right there. Write that down."

Ari nods at him earnestly. "I will get right on that."

Chapter Ten

I check the time on my phone. I still have twenty-seven minutes before the limo is supposed to arrive. How can twenty-seven minutes seem like an eternity, and also like no time at all? It's like I've been stuck in a time warp all day, time speeding so that thirty minutes passes in a blink, then slowing down so that two hours go by in a snail's crawl.

And all the while, a ticking clock in my mind.

When I woke up: T minus twelve hours until my date with Maya.

Heading to first period: T minus ten hours and forty minutes until my date with Maya.

Breaking for lunch: T minus seven hours and thirty minutes . . .

You get the idea.

Of course, the weird thing is, I *saw* Maya at school. But that's normal. I see Maya every day. I listen, enraptured, when she speaks in class, every day. I generally do my best to avoid making meaningful contact with her, *every* day.

But a date? That's new. That's horrifying.

Wait—no. I mean awesome. And amazing. And . . . yeah, it's possible that I'm going to be sick.

One might think that, with such a momentous evening approaching, Maya and I would have acted differently toward each other yesterday and today. We could have talked in the halls before class. Made plans to get dinner before the concert. Something.

But we didn't. We both proceeded through the school day as if nothing at all was different, with one small exception. During poli-sci, Maya passed me a note. When the folded piece of paper landed on my desk, Leah—who sits next to me—gave me a knowing smirk. Maya and I had become big gossip since Tuesday morning—a first for me, and not something I was relishing.

The note was simple. Maya's phone number, along with the words *Can't wait for tonight! Text me!*

I flushed as crimson as my dice and tucked the paper into my notebook.

For the rest of that period and all through art class, I thought about what I would say when I texted her, running over a thousand different possibilities. I imagined being witty, charming, romantic.

But let's be real. I am none of those things.

In the end, I texted Maya only the most pertinent information about the concert and when I should pick her up.

She responded almost immediately. omg this is going to be amazing! I'm so excited!!

She followed it with her address.

Me too, I responded. See you tonight.

Then I agonized for forty straight minutes about whether I should say more. *Can't wait to see you.* Or *I'm glad you're going with me.* Or *This is literally the best thing that has ever happened to me and I'm sorry in advance if I screw everything up, because I probably will.* 🤪!

But maybe I won't screw everything up, I dare to consider as I stand in front of the bathroom mirror, applying actual product to my hair, something I usually only do for weddings and funerals. As far as first dates go, this one has the potential to be pretty epic, and besides—I've got luck on my side.

I'm not even sure what sort of things I would plan for a first date if it was up to me. I never let myself believe this could happen. Every time I was remotely tempted to ask Maya out—to a movie, or a school dance, or even just to study together—my palms would get clammy and hives would break out along my neck. So that just wasn't going to happen. *Ever.* But if it had? I probably would have taken her to . . . I don't know, a comic book store, maybe? Or out on the boardwalk for a rousing game of Pokémon GO?

But it doesn't matter. Tonight, all the planning has been done for me, and even better, it's all stuff that I know Maya will like. Limousine rides and VIP tickets and meeting Sadashiv—*freaking Sadashiv.* I literally could not have planned a better first date if I'd tried.

"You're not wearing that, are you?"

I freeze, catching Lucy's reflection in the bathroom mirror. She's got a bowl of popcorn in one hand and a sparkling water in the other.

I look down at my clothes, which Pru gave the thumbs-up to not ten minutes ago. Dark jeans, a black T-shirt, my favorite sneakers, because they have awesome dragons on them. (Not to humble brag, but I may have painted the dragons myself.) The soles are starting to fall off, but they're still my favorite clothing item. Not that I have a lot of beloved clothing items.

"What's wrong with it?" I ask.

Lucy sighs dramatically and leans against the door frame. "Oh, big brother. You helpless thing."

My eyebrow twitches.

She knows about the date, of course. *Everyone* knows about the date. We are the sort of family that *shares*, often to everyone's chagrin, and Pru had been delighted to tell the whole story at the dinner table Tuesday night, after we got home from the store. She laid it out in excruciating detail, even embellishing the parts she wasn't actually there for. Fixing Maya's car, being sent to the office on an errand, calling in to a radio station, and all of it culminating in one jaw-dropping moment in front of the whole class: when Jude dared to ask out his forever crush, Maya Livingstone, and she actually said yes!

Honestly, I think Pru is happy that, for once, the focus is on someone else's dating life. Our family likes Quint a lot—Lucy commented once that if he and Pru ever broke up, she would petition to keep him in her place, which seems a little harsh, but I think she meant it as a compliment? Still, it had to get old, especially my parents' endless but well-meaning questions. *What are you and Quint doing this weekend? Are you two going to the dance together? What are you getting him for his birthday?* Et cetera.

But just because Pru was tired of talking about her love life didn't make me excited to spill the details on mine . . . not that I even really have one. *Yet.* What am I supposed to say? Yes, I am taking Maya to the concert. No, we aren't *dating.* Yes, Maya Livingstone. That Maya. *The* Maya.

I couldn't escape the dinner table fast enough.

"The shoes are cool," says Lucy, in what I consider to be a most shocking revelation. Lucy wouldn't say it if she didn't mean it, so . . . *cool.* She takes a sip of her drink. "But the shirt makes you look like a beat poet."

I frown. "Pru said it was fine."

"Pru's boyfriend would wear swim trunks to a Sadashiv concert," she points out. "But I have an idea. Follow me." She pivots, heading to her bedroom. Penny is there, sitting on the upper bunk bed, headphones plugged into her tablet. She pulls them off when she sees me and Lucy.

"Oh, Jude! You look so handsome!"

"No, he doesn't," says Lucy, throwing open her closet door. "But he will."

I make a scared face at Penny, who rolls her eyes behind Lucy's back.

"I still can't believe you won tickets to the Sadashiv concert," Penny says, slumping onto the mattress so that her arm hangs dejectedly over the side of the ladder. "And you're not taking *us*? Life is not fair!"

I bite my tongue. I haven't told them yet that they aren't just any tickets, but VIP tickets. Backstage passes. Maya and I might actually get to meet him.

Lucy and Penny would lose their minds if they knew.

And then probably murder me and steal the tickets for themselves.

"Bring me back some cool merch," says Lucy, pulling a jacket off a hanger and tossing it at me, "and all might be forgiven."

I look at the blazer. It's black with velvet lapels. It takes me a second to recognize it as the tuxedo jacket I wore to our cousin's wedding.

"I thought Mom sold this at a garage sale," I say.

"She tried, but Lucy nabbed it," says Penny. "Said it was too classy to part with. Try it on."

"No, not over *that*." Lucy stops me as I start to slide my arm into the sleeves. "You'll look like you're going to a funeral."

"Well, where else am I going to perform my beat poetry?"

"You need something casual to tone it down. Something *you*, like the shoes, but not as attention-grabbing." She thinks for a second, her gaze sweeping up and down. "Do you still have that gray T-shirt with the weird dice?"

"The D20? Yeah, of course."

She nods. "Perfect."

"Try not to be nervous, Jude," says Penny. "She's going to love you."

I smile, grateful for the words of encouragement. And who knows? Maybe she's right. Maya may not have fallen in love with me before today, despite years of going to school together, but that's because we've hardly spoken to each other outside of class projects. When she gets to know me, really know me . . .

Then what?

I'll sweep her off her feet?

Who am I kidding? I'll be lucky if I can get through this night without vomiting all over my hand-painted Vans.

"Sure she is," says Lucy, without as much enthusiasm. Then she grabs me by the shoulders, staring intensely into my eyes. "But, Jude? *No nerd talk*."

"Lucy!" cries Penny. "He needs to be himself."

"I agree," says Lucy, nodding. "Just less nerdy. You're not going to impress her by recapping all the Avengers movies in chronological order, or explaining the intricate rules of . . ." She waves one hand through the air. "Wizard lairs, or whatever."

I frown. "You literally just told me to wear my Dungeons and Dragons T-shirt."

She holds up a finger. "Your obscure Dungeons and Dragons T-shirt. Subtle nods to your interests are fine, but keep it chill."

I swallow. I have no chill.

As if sensing my anxiety, Lucy sighs. "Just ask questions about her and her interests, and you'll be fine."

"I can do that."

Lucy starts to smile, then thumps me softly on the chest. "For the record, I do agree with Penny. If she gets to know you like we do, she is going to love you."

"Thanks, Luce." I give her a sideways hug, then wait for her to pretend to be annoyed by the affection and brush me off.

I hurry back to my room to change my shirt. Lastly, I snatch my red dice from my desk and shove it into the jacket's inside pocket.

There's no way I'm leaving it behind tonight.

Chapter Eleven

It's a short ride to Maya's neighborhood. I know she lives off Vista del Sol—only because Quint mentioned it once, having been to her birthday party in middle school—not because I stalked her or anything. But I've never been to her house. There are some pretty nice homes in the area, the sorts with lion statues flanking their pillared stoops and working fountains in circular driveways, but as the limousine pulls up to the curb, a part of me is relieved to see that Maya's house isn't some behemoth mansion. It's bigger than my house, with a better manicured yard and flower beds, but not overly fancy. White stucco walls, red-tiled roof, a front door painted bright Mediterranean blue and a lemon tree out front. It's . . . welcoming.

I step out without waiting for the driver, who gives me a disapproving look, because evidently you're supposed to wait for him to open the door? I was never taught proper limousine etiquette.

I square my shoulders and approach the blue door, clutching the bouquet of tiger lilies I picked up at the grocery store that afternoon.

My hand shakes as I ring the doorbell.

I don't even have time to start panicking before it swings open. A broad-shouldered Black man with short hair and a trim goatee stands in the doorway, grinning at me. Maya's dad, I presume.

"You must be Jude. Aw, you brought me flowers? You shouldn't have!"

I swallow the lump in my throat. "Um . . ."

"I'm just kidding. Come in! I'm Myles, and let me tell you, my daughter is so excited for tonight. She was *shaking* when she got home on Tuesday." He extends his hand toward me with an appreciative nod. "Sadashiv concert. Well played."

I smile awkwardly and try to stammer out a few words that don't make me sound like a total goon, but I'm so nervous that honestly, I have no idea what I say to him. I accept the handshake, and even though he's a head taller than me and looks like he would actually know what to do with a bench press machine, he doesn't have one of those overly aggressive man-to-man handshakes.

"Dad, you better not be giving him a hard time," says Maya, appearing at the top of a staircase.

"What? Me?" he asks, affronted. "Don't worry, your mom has given me clear instructions to be on my best behavior. 'Don't grill the poor boy, don't embarrass our daughter, don't make her date *nervous*.'" He squints at Jude. "You're not nervous. Are you?"

"No, sir," I lie, clutching the flower stems so hard it's a small miracle they don't snap in my grip.

"See?" Myles looks pointedly at his daughter. "He's fine. And he even brought me flowers! We're getting along great."

Maya rolls her eyes before turning her focus on me. "Hi, Jude."

"Hi," I respond, a little breathless as I take her in. Her black hair is scooped up into a high ponytail, the ends spilling around her ears like a shimmering waterfall. I think maybe I'm imagining the shimmer, but no— she's dusted her hair with glitter, and has glitter on her eyelashes, too. With a silky white blouse and a pink skirt that swings around her legs as she descends the stairs, she looks like a magical fairy that's just stepped out of the pages of a children's book. A really gorgeous magical fairy. "You look . . ."

I realize then that I should have finished that sentence in my head before I started to speak it out loud. Nothing sounds right. *Amazing. Incredible. Stunning.* They're all true, but the words get hung up, rotating on repeat in my head, and warmth is flooding my cheeks as I struggle to pick one, to say something—anything.

Maya's smile widens. "I'll take that as a compliment."

I swallow and nod.

"You look nice, too." Her gaze lands to the flowers. "Are those . . ."

"Oh, right." I hold up the lilies. "These are for your dad."

Myles barks a laugh as I hold the flowers out to him. Even Maya giggles in surprise, and it's the most magical sound in the universe. I would spend hoards of goblin gold to hear that sound again. To *cause* that sound again.

"No, no, I know you're just being nice now," says Myles, waving his hands.

I give the flowers to Maya as her mom appears in a doorway. I recognize her from various school functions over the years. She wears her curly hair cropped short, but otherwise she and Maya look a lot alike, including the freckles and the sort of smile that puts people immediately at ease. Usually. I'm such a nervous wreck there's no putting me at ease in this moment.

"You must be Jude. I'm Cynthia."

"It's nice to meet you."

"Do you know about what time you'll have Maya home by?"

"The concert starts at seven thirty," I say. "So maybe ten or so?"

She nods. "That's just fine. If it runs much later, Maya, you can text and let us know. Sweetheart, do you want me to take those, put them in water?"

"Thanks, Mom," says Maya, passing the flowers to her. Then Maya takes my arm and lightning jolts through my body.

"All right, we don't want to be late. Bye, Mom! Bye, Dad!"

I wave disjointedly with my free arm. They tell us to have fun as Maya guides me outside, but my senses are flooding with a potent mix of exhilaration and terror. Maya has her arm wrapped around mine. Maya is touching me.

Somehow it hadn't really felt real until just now, this exact moment.

I am going on a date with Maya. An actual, honest-to-god date.

Maya draws up short on the front stoop, staring at the limousine. "Oh, wow. The radio station sent this?"

"Yeah. It's pretty cool inside. There's, like, a refrigerator. And buttons that make it light up like the Starship *Enterprise*."

Maya glances at me, and I cringe inwardly, remembering Lucy's warning. *No nerd talk.*

But Maya's smile only grows. "Are you ready?"

Nope.

"Yeah, let's do this."

She all but drags me toward the waiting car, and I can feel the giddiness in her step, the way her smile is brighter than the setting sun as the chauffeur holds the door open for us.

"I'm so glad you asked me to this, Jude," she says as we settle onto the leather benches. Then, to my absolute shock, she slips her hand into mine, our fingers interlacing. "This is literally a dream come true."

My brain explodes. My hand is on fire. "Yeah," I choke. "Me too."

In the next second, though, her hand is gone.

"Is that a remote?" Maya launches herself to the opposite bench and grabs a remote control off a tray beside the ice bucket, which has been stocked with Pellegrino. "What do you think it does?"

"Engages warp speed," I answer automatically.

Gah. I am bad at this.

Maya doesn't respond, just starts pushing buttons.

Within seconds, the interior of the limo is transformed into a tiny nightclub. Bass-driven music starts to thump from hidden speakers, and a band of lights around the ceiling shifts from purple to blue to pink.

"Wow," says Maya, sitting so that she is facing me, her eyes wandering around the limo. "I bet a lot of unsavory stuff has happened in here."

I snicker. "There's a reason these aren't blacklights."

Maya lets out a peal of laughter and makes a show of setting the remote back where she found it, like she's no longer sure she wants to be touching the thing. She turns back to me, and I notice her heels are bouncing on the floor, making her knees jump up and down, up and down. She's practically vibrating.

"So," she says, leaning forward, "I have to ask. Do you even *like* Sadashiv?"

"Oh. I mean . . ." I scratch the back of my neck, where the blazer's tag is itching against my skin. "I've never *met* him, so . . ."

Maya scrunches her face into the cutest grimace of all time. "That's a no, then."

"That's not a no." I consider the question. "His music isn't my favorite, but I don't hate it or anything."

"Oh, good. You should say that when we meet him. *I don't* hate *your music or anything.*"

I laugh, leaning against the cushioned seat. "My younger sisters are obsessed with him. He's clearly talented. We play him at the store sometimes. He sounds good."

Maya's eyebrows quirk upward. "Keep going. He's more flattered by the second."

I press my hands into the bench seat. "If you want to know the truth, I just . . . sort of feel like the old standards have been done. How many people have covered songs by Sinatra and Nat King Cole? Like, a lot, right? I don't think Sadashiv does anything really interesting to make the songs his own. But that's just me."

Maya nods understandingly. "When we meet him, you should suggest that he record some originals."

"You think so?"

She leans forward, punching me on the leg. "*No,* you absolutely should not say that! He sells millions of records! He does not want career advice from a couple of random high schoolers from Fortuna Beach."

I laugh, feeling some of my anxiety start to ebb away. No one is more surprised than me, but . . . this feels comfortable. Ish.

Maybe I shouldn't be surprised, though. This is why I like Maya, have always liked Maya. She's the sort of person who puts people at ease. Who can make anyone feel worthy of her presence, even if they're not.

"Well," says Maya, crossing one leg over the other. "Even if you're not a fan, I'm really happy that you're taking me to this tonight."

"I'm really happy you said yes."

We fall into silence. Well, except for the pounding music. There's an unspoken truth in the air, filling up the limo like bad perfume. The fact that I have had a crush on Maya for forever. The fact that I have wanted to ask her out for years. And she knows it. We both know it.

Would she have still said yes, if it was to anything other than a Sadashiv concert? What if I'd invited her to go for ice cream? Or go to the arcade? Or don her nicest corset and join me at the annual Renaissance Faire?

It doesn't matter, I try to tell myself. We're here now. She *did* say yes. And we are here. And we are . . .

Not speaking.

Maya's gaze is on the tinted windows, her lips twisted to one side, and I can see her struggling to think of something else to say.

I imagine a tiny Penny on my shoulder, Lucy on the other.

Be yourself.

Be yourself, but less *yourself.*

I suck in a long breath. "So . . . do you know where you want to go to college yet?"

Ugh. Really, Jude? Way to ask a question with all the cool factor of a nosy great-aunt.

But Maya takes it in stride. "My parents met at UCLA, so there's a lot of Livingstone pride there. But I don't know. I sort of think it would be neat to study abroad. Maybe go to Oxford or Melbourne or something." She rolls her eyes toward the ceiling of the limousine. "I don't really have anything figured out yet."

"Who does?" I say, even though I'm actually surprised by her answer. Pru already has a ten-year plan in place for after high school, and for some reason, I'd expected Maya to be the same. Her scores always put her at the top of our class, and she certainly *acts* like she has everything figured out. Maybe she's just being humble?

"How about you?" she asks.

"Oh—um. Not really sure. I figure I'll probably go to community college for the first couple years, get my associate's. After that . . . I don't know. Art school, maybe. If I can get in."

Her expression lights up. "Yes! For illustration?"

"Yeah, maybe? Or, graphic design?"

"That would be amazing. Your drawings are so good."

I squint one eye closed, a half wince. "I'm not really that good."

"Oh, please. We took art together in sixth grade, remember? You were great even then."

"You remember my drawings from sixth grade?" I ask, stunned.

"Of course. You were the best artist in class. I was terrible. To this day I rely on stick figures."

I'm tempted to push back on this description, to say that she's probably better than she gives herself credit for, but . . . I don't remember *her* artwork from sixth grade. I barely remember her being in that class. Which is weird, because that was definitely after the fateful field trip that made me fall in love with her. Wouldn't I have noticed her? Memorized everything she did?

"I'm sure you're a better artist than you think," I say.

"I'm sure I'm *not*," she counters. "But you definitely are." She kicks me with the toe of her shoe, and I realize I'm keeping a mental tally of every time she touches me, even if it's seemingly meaningless. Is this flirting?

No.

Maya wouldn't.

With *me*?

"Impossible," I breathe.

She tilts her head to one side. "What?"

"Oh! Um. Getting into art school, it's . . . borderline impossible. It's really competitive."

"That might be true," she says thoughtfully. "But someone has to get in. So why not you?"

I grin at the argument—logical and simple.

And maybe she's right. Especially now that I have the magic of Lundyn Toune on my side . . .

Why not me?

Chapter Twelve

Traffic gets heavy as we approach the concert hall. Police are positioned around the intersections, guiding cars and pedestrians. But rather than pulling into the parking garage with the rest of the vehicles, the limo turns toward the stadium and pulls up to a security checkpoint. Maya and I can't hear what passes between the driver and the security guard, but a second later we're pulling through.

The limo stops outside a set of nondescript metal doors, unremarkable except for the sandwich board that reads VIP ENTRANCE and the man with the clipboard and headset standing in front of them.

The driver opens the door for us. As we emerge from the limo, Maya takes my arm and I can feel her energy like static electricity. The sun is setting behind the stadium, casting us in shadow, but the sky overhead is glowing pink. Even though the guy with the clipboard looks like he could snap my whole body like a pencil, he smiles when I give him my name.

His pen slashes through a line on the clipboard. "Have a good time," he says, pulling open the door.

We enter a dull corridor lit by retina-burning fluorescents. "I've never been somewhere with an actual bouncer before," I say.

"Right?" says Maya, keeping her voice low even though no one else is around. "This is so cool."

We head down the hallway, following the sound of chatter and music. Not Sadashiv's music, but quiet instrumental jazz. The hall curves to the left, and we come upon a set of open doors, where a crowd of a hundred people or so has gathered. A buffet table against one wall boasts platters of cheese and grapes, and a bartender in the corner is pouring white wine into plastic cups.

We stand in the doorway for a moment. We are by far the youngest people in the room, and I'm hit with a strong sense of . . . *not* belonging.

I swallow hard. "Are you thirsty?"

"I'm okay," says Maya. "I'd be too scared of spilling on myself, right before meeting Sadashiv. Oh my god, Jude, are we really about to meet Sadashiv? I'm so nervous!" She turns to me with a look that is supposed to be anxious, maybe, but is beyond adorable. My heart twinges.

"You know, my little sister Penny plays the violin. Has for years," I say. "And she always gets really nervous before a recital, so a couple years ago, I told her that when she goes onstage, she just needs to pretend that she's a Level 12 wizard walking into a room full of goblins. You know that you're powerful enough to vanquish them all with, like, one spell if you want to. But you don't have to, and it would be a waste of a perfectly good Meteor Swarm spell, so instead you can just . . . charm them. And they'll fall in love with you, because they can't help it."

Maya stares at me, her face unreadable.

"I mean," I add hastily, "not that *you* need help charming anyone."

Maya's lips curl into a shy smile. She looks almost flustered.

The tag in my blazer starts itching again. Or is it just the feeling of mortification when I remember, once again, that I'm supposed to be normal tonight? Confident. *Cool.*

Not talking about wizards.

"That's really sweet," says Maya. "Does it help her?"

Or maybe talking about wizards wasn't *such* a terrible idea.

I consider for a second. "I think so. She hasn't mentioned it in a while, but she said it helped once, a long time ago."

"Excuse me, Jude? You must be Jude! The high schooler, right?"

I swivel to see an Asian woman in a neon-pink jumpsuit, a glass of wine in one hand. She looks vaguely familiar, but I can't place her until she puts a hand to her chest. "I'm Vanessa Hsu, from KSMT!" It clicks then, and I realize that I've seen her on a billboard promoting her morning show before.

"Oh, yeah, hi. I'm Jude."

"I *love* your name. Please tell me you're named for the Beatles song."

"Yeah. My parents are big fans."

"Who isn't?" she says. She has one of those exuberant, over-the-top personalities, the sort of person who talks really fast and excitedly and never lets a moment of uncomfortable silence pass her way without being thoroughly crushed beneath an avalanche of rambling commentary.

Probably what makes her such a good radio personality.

"Oh my goodness, look at the two of you!" says Vanessa, stepping back and scanning Maya and me from head to toe. "You are just the cutest couple I have ever seen! I never looked this good when I was a teenager, let me tell you. I wore Hello Kitty sweatshirts until I was twenty-three, and don't even get me started on my bangs. But you—wow! How are you doing tonight? Are you having a good time? Did you try the appetizers? Are you excited to meet Sadashiv?"

Maya beams at her, even as her hold tightens on my arm. "So excited," she says, not quite meeting Vanessa's energy level. "I'm an enormous fan. When Jude asked me to be his date to this, I almost passed out. I still can't believe I'm really here, and I'm going to meet him face-to-face. It feels too good to be true."

"But you're so young!" says Vanessa. "Definitely younger than Sadashiv's usual demographic. How did you become a fan?"

"Well," says Maya, drawing out the word as her gaze flits to me, then back to the DJ. "This is totally embarrassing, but actually . . . it was kind of because of you."

Vanessa starts. "Me?"

"Before I had my license, my mom would take me to school every morning, and she loves your show, so it was always playing in the car. And you would play Sadashiv's music, and . . . I just fell in love with it. I swear, the first time I heard his voice, it was like having an out-of-body experience. I'd never heard anything so beautiful. Then one day you mentioned how cute he was, so I looked up his picture, and . . ." Maya lets out a dramatic sigh and pretends to fan herself with one hand.

"Yes! He is so dreamy!" says Vanessa.

"*So* dreamy," Maya agrees. They laugh, like sharing an inside joke, and a part of me wonders if I should feel jealous of Sadashiv. I mean, I do feel jealous a little, I guess. Or at least, I used to, when I first heard about Maya's humongous crush on him. But then, he *is* considered one of the world's sexiest men, so . . . it isn't exactly like we're in competition.

And besides, she's not hanging on to *his* arm right now, is she?

"I better keep mingling," says Vanessa, "but it was so great to meet you. Have a nice time tonight, okay?"

As she walks away, Maya turns back to me with an almost impish smile and whispers, "How'd I do?"

"What do you mean?"

She nudges me with her shoulder. "I was using my Charm spell on her. Couldn't you tell?"

A surprised laugh bursts out of me. "Charm Person successfully cast. You've earned fifty experience points."

At the other end of the room, a freckled woman with auburn hair and enormous earrings claps her hands a few times. The crowd falls into a hush. "Hello, and welcome! I'm Erika. I'm a publicist with Hearthfire Records, and we are so thrilled to have you joining us tonight. It's going to be a great show! I know you are most excited to meet our star of the evening, so I'd like to have you all line up right outside in the hallway and we will guide you to the signing table, where you can meet Sadashiv and receive a signed tour poster. Pictures are allowed, but we ask that you remain on this side of the table, please. Now, if you'll follow me, right this way."

A few middle-aged women literally squeal as they hurry to be at the front of the line. Maya and I end up somewhere near the middle as we're all shepherded into the hallway. It feels a bit like elementary school, actually, like we're lining up to head to the playground. The line winds down the hall and curves around a corner, so we can't see the signing table, but it moves pretty quickly, and the entire crowd is buzzing with excitement and nerves.

"I feel like I'm going to be sick," Maya whispers.

I snort, thinking she's making a joke—but then I look at her face and reconsider.

"He's just a guy," I say. "He's human, like the rest of us."

She guffaws. "Yeah. Right. He's so talented, and so attractive, and so . . . *romantic.*"

I smile. "So that's all you're looking for in a guy?"

I want to bite back the words immediately. I'd meant them as a joke, but they come too close to the unspoken truth of my enormous crush.

For a second, Maya looks away, and it is awkward as hell. But then she perks back up. "Tell me about your T-shirt."

I glance down at the gray tee with the white twenty-sided dice. "What about it?"

"It has something to do with Dungeons and Dragons, right?"

"Um." Heat pricks at my neck. "Yeah."

No nerd talk.

"I've never played. How does it work?"

I frown, feeling a little bit like I'm opening a treasure chest without rolling a perception check first. Like this is bound to be trap.

But Maya seems honestly curious. Or at least, like she wants a distraction.

"Well," I start, sorting through the billion possible answers to that seemingly simple question. How *does* it work? "The dice are used to . . . determine things. In the game. Like . . . if you want to see if an object has been cursed, you would cast a Detect Magic spell, and then you'd roll to see whether or not you succeed."

Maya is watching me, listening intently. "Okay," she says slowly. "So if you roll a high number, then the object is cursed?"

"Well . . . no. The roll just determines whether or not you can detect it. The Dungeon Master decides whether or not the object is actually cursed."

"Who's the Dungeon Master?"

"I am."

Her eyebrows raise. "That sounds important."

"I guess. I come up with the campaigns, and help guide the other players. Try to come up with surprises for them, and challenges they have to overcome. I make up the puzzles that need to be solved and decide when they run into a horde of monsters . . . that sort of thing."

It sounds as ridiculous out loud as it does in my head, but for some reason I keep talking, hoping to stumble onto the words that might convey a little bit about how it isn't just a group of friends playing make believe. How it's about teamwork and puzzle-solving, imagination and storytelling. How it gives you a chance to become someone new. To have magic and strength and power. To save the day, sometimes. Or sometimes you just goof off and hunt for treasure and kill orcs and get lost in the woods until you stumble onto something amazing, and how I've started making a comic that will follow our newest campaign but I can't work too far ahead, because things always change when we're playing and—

Maya's eyes widen excitedly. "You're making a comic?"

My gut twists. I shouldn't have mentioned that. "Oh. Yeah. It's not very good, though. It's just a hobby."

"Can I read it?"

I reel back. The thought of Maya reading my comic, the one with the beautiful elven statue that looks like *her*? The very thought makes me want to swan dive into the lava pit of Mount Doom.

I'm epically relieved when a voice interrupts us, keeping me from having to answer.

"Okay, you two. Go on."

Maya turns around, facing the front of the line. And it's us. *We* are the front of the line, and the publicist is beckoning us forward.

We turn the corner into a small room with a potted plant and a couple of posters from artists who performed at this concert hall years ago, and there at a table in the center of the room—sits Sadashiv. As startlingly gorgeous as he looks on the cover of the teen magazines Penny likes, but also looking . . . younger. It's easy to forget when people cast around words like *world's sexiest man* and women twice his age are swooning over him.

But here, right in front of us, he seems almost human.

Maya halts. For a moment, she is as motionless as the statue in my comic, staring speechlessly at the man who is smiling serenely back at us, twiddling a black Sharpie in his fingers.

"Good evening," he says in a posh British accent. "How are you tonight?"

Maya makes a sound that is a bit like a whimper, and if it were possible for eyes to turn into giant hearts like they do in anime, I know that's what hers would be doing right now.

Funny, that. Sadashiv is a famous singer, with millions of fans all over the world. Maya is just a normal girl. But somehow, in that moment, it occurs to me that her crush on him isn't unlike my crush on her. She has him up on a pedestal, not unlike the pedestal I put her on in my comic.

Something about that realization gives me courage. Maybe it's because I'm not a huge fan of Sadashiv—he's just a guy with a nice voice who sings sappy love songs that he didn't even write—but I don't feel nervous at all as I place my hand on Maya's back and nudge her toward the table.

"We're great," I say. "I'm Jude, and this is Maya. She's a huge fan."

"It's a pleasure to meet you both." Sadashiv takes a poster off the stack beside him. He hardly looks at it as he scrawls his signature across the bottom. "I've got to admit, my music tends to draw an older crowd. It's nice to see some younger faces in the audience."

"You're our radio giveaway winners, aren't you?" says the publicist. "The high school students?"

"Yeah. We go to Fortuna Beach High," I say. "I wasn't technically supposed to be on my phone during school, but . . . no regrets."

"I bet not," says the publicist.

"Fortuna Beach?" says Sadashiv, drumming the cap of the Sharpie against the table. "That's close to here, isn't it? I've heard it's quite nice."

"Yeah, it's not bad," I say.

"I love you," Maya suddenly spits out, as if these words are all she can manage. "I mean. I love your music. So much."

He grins. "You like the old standards?"

"I do now. I mean, your last album. I fell asleep to it every night for, like, a month after it came out. It's just . . . so beautiful. Your voice is beautiful."

Sadashiv smiles at her, but I can tell he hears this about a million times a day, and that maybe it's lost some of its novelty. "You're very kind. I'm looking forward to being back in the studio soon. I hope you'll like the next album just as much." He takes another poster and scrawls his name.

"Do you think you'll ever do original songs?" I ask.

Maya shoots me an alarmed look, but Sadashiv doesn't bat an eye.

"I've often thought about it," he says. "I love the old songs, but I know there are a lot of talented songwriters in the world today, too."

"A friend of mine is a songwriter."

"Oh?"

"I mean—she wants to be. She's really great. She doesn't have any songs out in the world yet, but we're recording her first video tomorrow, for a competition hosted by the Condor Music Festival. She might even get to perform."

"How exciting," says Sadashiv, though I can tell he's just being nice now. "What is your friend's name?"

"Ari. I mean—Araceli Escalante."

Sadashiv slides both posters toward us. "That's a great name. I'm wishing her the best of luck."

"Thanks," I say. "I'll tell her you said that."

Maya and I take our posters.

"Let's get a picture!" says the publicist, turning us around. We smile as a camera flashes, then we're being ushered away. Behind me, I can already hear Sadashiv greeting the next group in line.

"I can't believe that just happened!" Maya cries as soon as we're out of earshot. "Look! He drew a heart!" She holds up her poster, and I see that he did indeed draw a neat little flourishing heart at the end of his autograph.

"What?" I say, holding up my own heart-less poster. "Why didn't I get a heart?"

She hums teasingly. "This Charm spell really does work."

Another man with a clipboard gives us a couple of rubber bands to wrap around the posters, then leads us to the concert hall. The seats are filling up fast, the crowd a jostle of excited noise. We're shown to our seats in the second row, so close to the stage I can see the silver knobs on the amplifiers. There's a whole band's worth of instruments, ready to accompany Sadashiv onstage. Drums and a piano, guitars and trumpets, even a saxophone.

"This is incredible," says Maya, shaking her head in wonder. "These seats must cost a fortune!"

"I sold one of my kidneys to pay for them. Not a big deal."

She slides her gaze toward me and studies me for a second, her expression thoughtful. "Thank you, Jude. Really. I can't even . . . I'm just so happy to be here tonight. With *you*."

The way she emphasizes that makes my heart jump into my throat. For a second, I am awestruck at how beautiful she is. How the stage lights catch on the sparkles dusted across her eyelids. How her lips curve in a way that's just a tiny bit teasing, a tiny bit flirtatious.

Then Maya peels her gaze away and spends a moment rolling up her poster and securing it with the rubber band. "So . . . this might be weird," she says, and my brain hurries to finish her thought.

This might be weird, but I sort of have a thing for scrawny, pale guys, and I think you're even more attractive than Sadashiv!

This might be weird, but I've actually been in love with you since that field trip in fifth grade!

This might be weird, but I just realized you're my soul mate!

"And you can totally say no," she goes on, "but do you think maybe I could play Dungeons and Dragons with you sometime?"

My world stutters to a stop. "What?"

"It's sounds really cool, the way you describe it. Like, that could be really fun."

I spend an inordinate amount of time waiting for the punch line. The *got you good! Should have seen the look on your face!*

But it doesn't come.

"What?" I say again.

"If there's room for one more person?"

"Oh. Uh. Sure. Yeah, if you want to. Actually, we kind of need a new player for this campaign. Matt had to drop out, so . . . But we're supposed to start this weekend. We play on Saturdays. And I'm sure you're busy—"

"I'm not busy." She settles back into her seat. "I'd like to come."

I wait, giving her one more chance to drop that *just kidding* on me. She doesn't.

"Okay. Yeah. Of course you can join us."

Her smile is pure brilliance.

We're silent after that, Maya taking in every detail. The lighting, the instruments, the stagehands who make occasional appearances, tending to last-minute adjustments. Meanwhile, my thoughts are reeling, trying to picture what it will be like to play D&D . . . with *Maya*. For Maya, to be in the campaign, a campaign *I* created. She'll see my drawings. Experience the world I designed myself. Get to know some of my closest friends.

And I can't decide if this has the potential to be the best thing that's ever happened to me . . . or a complete disaster.

I'm still waffling between these two very distinct possibilities when the lights dim. The crowd cheers. The band comes out first, picking up their instruments. Then Sadashiv struts onto the stage, looking perfectly at home in front of five thousand screaming fans, his own face projected to the size of a house on the screen behind him.

The music starts—an intro of blaring, upbeat horns, as Sadashiv takes the microphone.

He opens with a Frank Sinatra tune that Dad sometimes plays at the store.

"Luck be a lady tonight . . ."

100

Chapter Thirteen

I have to get up for school in three and a half hours, but I can't fall asleep. Memories of the evening before spin through my thoughts—every smile, every touch, every time I thought maybe, *just maybe*, this could turn into something.

The date was perfect. There's no other word for it. I made Maya laugh. We had a great time.

At least, that's how I'm feeling about it.

But how do I know if Maya feels the same way? How do I take this from one date to . . . many dates? How do I build a bridge between the Sadashiv concert and . . . I don't know. A first kiss? Dating? Happily ever after?

A door squeaks quietly, followed by the soft padding of feet as someone comes down the basement stairs. A small someone in Teenage Mutant Ninja Turtles pajamas. I can't see Ellie, but I'm familiar with the particular way she walks down my steps in the middle of the night. The way she starts out quick, but then gets slower as she nears the bottom of the stairs, uncertain when her feet are going to hit the carpeted floor. I don't have to see her to know she's clinging to the rail with one hand, while her other arm clutches her beloved stuffed squirrel.

Then she's darting across the carpet and crawling under the covers.

"Hi, Ellie," I whisper, scooting closer to the wall to make room for her.

"Hi, Jude," she whispers back, curling against my side.

It's been this way since the fall, when my parents determined Ellie was too big to keep sleeping in the toddler bed they'd set up in the master bedroom, and they needed their own space back. So Ellie's bed was moved into Prudence's room, which I'd expected Pru to argue strongly against, but she actually accepted it without much grumbling. Except, according to Pru, Ellie doesn't spend a whole lot of time in her own bed, preferring to climb up and snuggle with Pru or—on nights when Pru feels stifled and kicks her out—trying her luck with Lucy, Penny, and occasionally even me, despite how she often said that my room in the basement gives her the creeps.

"I didn't know if you were home," she says.

"I didn't get back until late. You were already asleep."

She yawns. "How was your hot date?"

I smirk. "Who said I had a hot date?"

"Everyone." She shifts around, tucking the squirrel under her head like a pillow.

"It went good," I say. "I like this girl a lot. And it seemed like maybe she likes me, too."

"Of course she likes you," Ellie says, without even a hint of doubt.

"Yeah, well . . . I don't know. It seems too good to be true."

The words feel like the truest thing I've said in weeks.

Maya is friendly to me, always, but she isn't *into* me.

I just happen to be the guy who won tickets to the Sadashiv concert, and I'm sure she would have gone with anyone who presented her with such an irresistible invitation.

Well . . . maybe not *anyone*. But I doubt she would have picked me, if given a choice.

Does that matter? I try to tell myself it doesn't. Because she did go with me, and we had a great time, and now maybe she's seeing me differently. For the first time ever, maybe she's seeing me as a guy she could really like.

"This is my chance," I whisper. "I can't ruin it. I have to find a way to show her that I can be right for her. But . . . how am I supposed to do that?"

The sound of Ellie's long, steady breathing proves that she isn't going to be any help at all, not that I expected her to be. What kind of guy takes dating advice from his five-year-old sister? Even *I* know that's a terrible idea.

But then it occurs to me that I have other options, that maybe aren't so terrible at all.

———————

"Lucy, I need your help."

Lucy pauses in the middle of fancy-braiding her hair and looks at me in the bathroom mirror. "With what?"

"I thought maybe you could help me decide what to wear today."

Yeah—it didn't sound quite so desperate when I was coming up with this plan. But the way Lucy's eyes widen makes me want to take it back immediately.

She hastily ties off the braid and spins to face me. "It went well! *Yes.* Are you dating Maya Livingstone now?"

"What? No. We're not . . . The date went well. And I just . . . But no."

"But you want to be."

"I've *always* wanted to be."

"Of course," she says. "And now you need to act the part and impress her. I love this!" She grabs my wrist and drags me down the hall, down two flights of stairs, into my room, where she immediately throws open my closet doors and starts pawing through the clothes messily piled up on the shelves. She yanks out a pair of green corduroy pants that Mom bought me a while back that still have the tags on them.

"Do these fit?"

"Um . . ."

"Put them on." She throws them at me and keeps digging.

I change in the bathroom, and Lucy goes through three different shirt-hoodie-button-down combinations before deciding on a plain white hooded sweatshirt that I always thought was too small, but Lucy insists is supposed to fit that way. "But keep the sleeves pushed up, like this," she says, demonstrating the proper way to wear a sweatshirt, which I've evidently been failing at my entire life. Lastly she grabs a pair of black sneakers.

I make a face. "Those kind of give me blisters."

"Then wear thicker socks."

I frown. "I thought . . ."

"What?"

"I mean. I didn't think you're supposed to wear socks with those? But . . . okay." I open a drawer and pull out a pair of socks. When I turn back around to take the shoes, Lucy yanks them away from me, her expression horrified.

"No-show socks, Jude! You're supposed to wear them with . . ." She lets out a disgruntled noise and casts her eyes skyward. "You are so lucky to have me."

I'm doubting this, but don't say as much.

She digs through my drawer and finds a pair of short white socks. Another gift from Mom that I've never worn, because . . . they were so short. What's the point of socks that short?

Turns out, the point is to wear them with these shoes.

Lucy declares me ready. I grab my dice, and we head back upstairs so I can take a look in her full-length mirror.

And I'm . . . underwhelmed?

I mean, I look different, and not bad. But I'm not sure it's *enough*.

The reflection still looks like me. Indistinct blond hair. Too-big lips. Too-pasty skin. Just in a more hipster packaging now.

"It was slim pickings I was working with," says Lucy, standing back with her arms folded, inspecting me. "But it's an improvement. We'll have to go shopping this weekend."

"Shopping?"

"You asked for a makeover."

"I did not—"

"Don't argue with me." She gives me one more once-over, then nods approvingly. "All right! Let's go to school!"

I'm still skeptical, until we head to the kitchen, where the rest of my family is waiting at the breakfast table.

"Jude, finally!" says Penny. "How was your—" She stops, staring at me. Then she looks at Lucy. Back to me. Then trades a wide-eyed look with Pru, who has stopped spreading jam onto a piece of toast.

"What?" I say, suddenly self-conscious. I look down at my clothes.

"Drip check," Penny says knowingly. "Is this for Maya?"

"*No.* I just . . . I thought . . ." With an uncomfortable glare, I grab a waffle from the freezer and put it in the toaster. "Shut up."

"I think it's sweet you're getting dressed up for a girl," says my mom.

"You're all acting like I'm wearing a suit and tie or something. It's literally just a sweatshirt."

"One that is remarkably lacking in tears, stains, or logos pertaining to any media franchise," says Pru.

"And I like those pants on you," says Mom. "They fit well."

My cheeks are sweltering. Why is this waffle taking so long?

"I'm just trying something new," I say.

"Yeah, for a *girl,*" Penny insists.

"How was the concert?" asks Dad, and I'm not sure if he's grilling me on my date or trying to help me by changing the subject.

"Good," I say.

"What was good about it?" Mom asks.

The waffle pops. I grab it, bouncing it from hand to hand until it cools. "Sorry, can't talk. We're going to be late."

I snatch the keys from the counter and head out. I pause halfway down the steps that lead to our small back alley. Turn around. March into the kitchen.

Pru is smirking, holding my backpack out for me. I take it from her with a grumbled thanks.

"You do look nice," she says quietly as we file out to the car. Then she opens her mouth as if to add something else, but seems to think better of it.

"What?"

She shakes her head, her hand on the passenger side door. "It's not a *big* change, but it's enough that people are going to notice. You've always hated being noticed, but lately . . ."

I swallow hard. I'm still blushing, and that was just from my family noticing me.

But I survived being the center of attention during that stupid coin-flip experiment.

I survived asking Maya out in front of the whole class.

If people notice me just because I'm wearing something other than a Hellfire Club T-shirt? I'll survive that, too.

No—I won't just survive. I will *bathe* in their attention. I will guzzle it down like a pint of ale at Bork's Tavern. And I will like it.

Because the sort of guy who deserves Maya is the sort of guy who isn't afraid of a little attention.

And starting now, I will make myself that guy.

Chapter Fourteen

"Are we still on for recording Ari's video tonight?" Pru asks as we get out of the van.

"Of course. Why wouldn't we be?"

Pru pulls her backpack onto her shoulders. "I'm just saying. We would understand if you made other plans."

With Maya, I realize she's suggesting.

"No," I say, as we step into the school courtyard. "No other plans."

And then: *weirdness*.

I sense it immediately. The way some sophomores fall quiet as we pass by. The way Bristol Eastman looks up from the book she's reading to give me an appreciative once-over.

"Sheeeeesh," someone says appreciatively, and I'm pretty sure they're talking about me.

"What is happening?" I whisper to Pru.

"You took out one of the most popular girls in school, and everyone knows about it," she answers. "And now you show up looking like you actually put some thought into your clothes for the first time ever, and people are noticing." She pauses, before adding, "I told you so."

"Oh god." I keep my eyes on the ground as we head toward our bench, where Quint and Ezra are joking about something. "I just wanted *Maya* to notice, not *everyone*."

"Jude, look at me."

We stop walking, and I turn to meet Pru's serious expression. "I don't care if you're wearing Superman pajamas or a three-piece tuxedo. You are my brother, and you are incredible, and it's okay to be noticed once in a while. It's okay to . . . want things for yourself. Like, for girls to check you out. And for people to get to know you. And for the girl you've liked for *forever* to finally notice you. You deserve all of that."

I stare at her, making sure she's done with her sisterly encouragement, before I say, "I haven't owned Superman pajamas since I was ten."

"Yo! Prudence! Jude!" says Ezra. He's sitting on the back of the bench, waving a handful of cash at us.

"Now what is he up to?" Pru mutters.

"You got five bucks? Ten?" asks Ezra as we make our way over. "What can I put you down for?"

"What are you talking about?" asks Pru.

"Word has it that Principal Jenkins just announced an early retirement, so I'm taking bets on the reason behind it. So far the general consensus is a midlife crisis exacerbated by too many years surrounded by hormonal adolescents. But there's also a strong contingency of people who think she's involved in some sort of scandal—possibly drug and/or sex-tape related."

"Seriously?" mutters Quint.

Ezra smirks. "You think you know people, right? I've also had two guesses that she's quitting so she can run for public office next year, and one guess that she's joining a hippie commune outside of San Francisco. So." He looks at me. "What do you got?"

"How should I know why Mrs. Jenkins is retiring?"

He rolls his eyes. "No one knows. That's the whole point. If you get it right, you get a wad of cold hard cash. If no one gets it right, then you get your money back. Minus my small bookkeeping fee. Obvs."

I shrug, tucking my hands into my pockets. "I don't know." I definitely can't see our principal doing anything scandalous. A midlife crisis? Maybe? "Maybe she's decided to pursue her lifelong dream of writing the next Great American Novel." In my pocket, the dice seems suddenly cold against my fingers. I frown, hesitating. Then I add, "No—scratch that.

108

She's gonna write romances." The dice warms slightly. "About pirates, probably."

There it is again, that weird pulse.

"*Nice*," says Ezra, writing it down. "I'm giving you real low odds, but points for originality. That'll be five bucks to play."

"And you didn't want to take statistics this year," says Quint as I shrug and pull out my wallet.

"Missed opportunity," says Pru. "That class is really just a front to teach us all illegal gambling."

"It's only illegal if you get caught," says Ezra.

"That's not actually true," says Pru.

"How about you, Prudence?" Ezra goes on, taking my money. "What can I put you down for?"

"Character witness," she says. "When you all get in trouble for taking bets on a teacher's private life."

Ezra makes a swoony face and puts a hand to his chest. "You would do that for me?"

"No. But I'd do it for Jude."

"Thanks, Sis," I say distractedly, because Maya just walked into the courtyard. She's with Katie, heading toward their usual table. For just a second, Maya's gaze darts toward me and—I am not making this up—we share a *moment*. Her lips turn upward, just slightly. She tucks a curl of hair behind one ear. She turns back to her conversation.

My heart is drums and cymbals inside my chest.

"*Dude*," says Ezra. "I saw that come-hither look. Go! Get over there, man!" He shoves me so hard in Maya's direction I stumble, barely catching myself before I fall face-first onto the concrete.

I turn back to Ezra with a glower. "I don't need your help, thanks."

He holds up his hands defensively. "I know it. You are a butterfly climbing out of your cocoon. I'm just proud to be here to watch you fly."

My brow creases. Pru and Quint are giving Ezra the same looks—a little baffled, a little annoyed.

Then Quint shakes his head and starts talking about our poli-sci assignment. I'm allowed a chance to exhale. My attention meanders back to Maya, who's sat down now. Janine and Brynn have joined them. They're not looking at me. Maya's probably telling them about the concert, but that doesn't mean she's talking about *me*.

My feet feel heavy—cemented to the ground.

It would be so, so easy to stay right here. Keep my eyes down. Avoid her attention, avoid *her*. Just like I always have. No risk of embarrassment. No risk of rejection.

But that guy? The wallflower who never takes any risks?

He doesn't get the girl. He doesn't *deserve* the girl.

My palms are hot and itchy, but before I know it, my feet are moving, almost of their own accord.

I feel the shift of eyes around me. The intrigued whispers.

I try not to panic, but who am I kidding? I am panic personified. My insides feel like a shaken-up can of soda. Fizzy and churning, and not in the good way.

There's a moment when I think of turning back. I could still change course. Veer right and head to class, pretend that was my plan all along.

But then Maya looks up and spots me. She sits straighter. Her friends notice, and then their eyes are on me, too. Katie puts a hand over her mouth and giggles, and there's a hint of cruelty to the sound, and if I don't survive this, please let my gravestone say something cool, like:

Here lies Jude—a noble pilot who died in service to the Rebel Forces.
His sacrifice ensured freedom for entire galaxies.
He shall not soon be forgotten.

Or, you know. Something like that. Feel free to keep brainstorming in my absence.

My breath catches when I reach Maya and her friends.

Holy hell, what am I thinking? I shouldn't be here. *Why am I here?*

But Maya smiles at me, and says quietly, easily—"Hi."

"Hi," I say back.

Brynn and Janine exchange looks, but Katie just leans forward, cupping her chin in one hand as her eyes travel slowly down to my shoes, then slowly back up again. "Hello, Jude," she says, her voice infused with a thousand meanings that I don't dare to try and interpret.

"Um," I start. I know I'm blushing. "I was just . . ."

What? What was I just doing? Thinking? Saying? What is wrong with me?

This is the worst idea I've ever—

"Yes," says Maya.

My lips part.

Her grin widens. There's a sparkle in her eye, like maybe she's teasing me, or maybe she's amused by me, or maybe she feels sorry for me, and maybe all of the above, and maybe something else entirely.

Crap. Where's Ezra? Where's Lucy? Does anyone around here sell a Maya decoder ring?

"Yes?" I ask her.

"To whatever you're asking," she says.

Brynn makes an *oooh* sound and nudges Maya with her shoulder.

"Uh . . . I actually just wanted to say . . ." My brain is exploding. I need to wrap this up. I need to get out of here. "I had a good time last night." I grimace, my voice growing tight. "That's all."

Katie snickers, but Maya just leans back, still smiling. "I did, too."

"Cool," I say, and did I really just give her a thumbs-up? Who is even in control of my body at this point? "Well. That's all. I'll see you in class." My face is burning as I turn away. I shove my hands into my pockets and clutch the dice like it's my security blanket.

"Jude?"

I groan inwardly. No, please, just let me escape this. I will never again pretend that I could possibly attract the attention of a girl like this. I'm done pretending. I'm done.

Gritting my teeth, I turn slowly back. "Yeah?"

"Do you want to sit with us at lunch later?"

Her friends gasp. Literally *gasp*. And look at her like she's lost her mind. Heck, I'm looking at her like she's lost her mind.

Did Maya Livingstone just invite me to join her for lunch? Like, in the cafeteria? Surrounded by people we go to school with? People with thoughts and opinions and judgments? People who will *talk* about us?

"Your sister, too," she adds, nodding in a direction somewhere behind me. "And Quint. And . . . EZ?" Her expression becomes less enthused, and I remember that she and Ezra were lab partners in biology last year, and yeah, I'd probably be a little traumatized after working with him for a full year, too.

"Oh. Thanks," I say. It comes out a little squeaky, so I clear my throat and go on. "Pru and Quint have second lunch. I guess I can mention it to Ezra."

Whether Maya can sense my feelings on the matter or she herself isn't Ezra's biggest fan, she leans toward me and whispers, "Or not? That would be fine, too. So . . . I'll see you then?" She grimaces. "I mean, I'll see you in first period, obviously. And second period. But then . . . lunch."

The look she has then—like *she's* the awkward one, saying awkward things—makes me fall in love with her even more.

"Yeah," I say. "Lunch."

Chapter Fifteen

"Were *we* invited to eat at her lunch table?" asks César, after I've done my best to explain why I won't be sitting with them today. He, Matt, and I are in line in the cafeteria, pushing our red plastic trays along the bar, but none of us are paying much attention to what the lunch attendants are putting on our plates. Russell said he had a big idea for a new scene in his novel, so he rushed off to the library as soon as the bell rang. Russell cares as much about my girl drama as I care about national sports—which, after all the stares I've gotten today, is sort of refreshing.

"I don't know," I tell César. "She didn't mention you guys. But it would probably be okay?" I glance at them. "Do you *want* to eat at her lunch table?"

They hesitate, looking at each other, unspoken words passing between them.

"Not particularly," Matt finally admits. He looks a little guilty about it, but honestly, I get it. I'm not entirely sure *I* want to eat with her. But I figure I can't be considered as potential boyfriend material if I won't hang out with her during school, right?

And it really isn't about hanging out with Maya. She's intimidating enough. But Maya *and* her friends? What am I supposed to talk to them about?

I find myself intentionally dragging my feet as we make our way through the line. Wasting time as I decide over mashed potatoes or corn bread.

"So?" asks César. "Are you going to?"

"I have to, don't I?"

We reach the end of the line, where a display case of red Jell-O cups jiggles up at us. I make a face. Jell-O is disgusting. I could have sworn I saw people with brownies earlier, but when I ask the lunch lady, she shrugs apologetically. "We ran out a few minutes ago. Want a Jell-O?"

I shake my head. "No thanks." She hands two cups to my friends, and we head toward the cash register. While I'm waiting, I scan the cafeteria and spy Maya's table. *Why* do they have to sit right in the dead center of the cafeteria? It's like they *want* people to look at them.

Katie, Janine, and Brynn are there, along with Raul, Tobey, Serena, and a couple of seniors whose names I don't know.

"You don't *have* to," whispers Matt, perhaps sensing the terror that is clogging my throat as I try to imagine walking over there. Sitting there. Acting like I belong there.

He's right. I don't have to. But do I want Maya to like me? Do I want Maya to see me as someone she could spend time with? Someone who fits into her world? Yeah, more than anything.

But do I *actually* fit into her world, or am I just fooling myself?

"Hey! Hey, you!"

Matt nudges me, and I turn to see the lunch lady beaming at me and holding up a small plate with a perfect chocolate brownie on top. "I found an extra one! Must be your lucky day!"

I smile and take the plate from her. "Thanks," I say. Then I turn to my friends and give them a solemn look. "I'm doing this."

They return the look, all seriousness.

"Go get it, man," says César.

I'm not sure what *it* is, but I push up the sleeves of my sweatshirt like Lucy showed me, pick up my tray, and head into Jabba's Palace.

And no, I'm not picturing Maya in a gold bikini or anything like that. Get your mind out of the gutter. I'm just saying, I'm like a Jedi knight entering a highly protected lair that is fraught with danger and tension and a whole lot of people who would love to watch me get devoured by a rancor.

114

I arrive at the table and stand there for a second, feeling supremely uncomfortable. Janine notices me first. She perks up, slapping Katie on the arm, who in turn gets Maya's attention.

"Oh, hey!" says Maya, nudging Raul beside her. And just like that, people are shifting around. Scooting down the bench. Making room.

For me.

"Sit down," says Maya, gesturing to the bench beside her.

So I do.

"Oh, man!" says Tobey. "You got a brownie? They were out of them when I was up there."

"I think I got the last one," I say. I look from him to my plate, then at Maya, and back to Tobey. "Uh . . . do you want it?"

"Really? Yeah!" He takes the brownie.

And just like that, the group around me returns to whatever conversations they were having before I arrived. Like nothing has changed at all.

I release a held breath.

Brynn asks about the concert, and Maya carries the conversation while I pick at my food. She tells them about the VIP party, and meeting Sadashiv, and the heart he drew on her poster. She takes them through his performance, moment by moment, in such exacting detail that I feel like I'm experiencing it all over again. She remembers a lot more about the concert than I do. Not even twenty-four hours later, and I've already forgotten just about everything about Sadashiv and what songs he sang. All I really remember is the way Maya smiled at me before the show started. The way she glowed in the light of the stage.

"All right, enough about Maya and her magical date," says Janine. "Here's the important question." She arches an eyebrow and meets the gaze of every guy at the table. Raul, Tobey, even *me*. "Which of you losers is taking me to junior prom?"

This sets off a chain reaction. Hoots. Guffaws. More than one suggestive comment. Flirting. And my face turning tomato-red. Not that anyone thinks for a second that I plan on asking Janine out, but there's an underlying question that seems just as obvious.

Am I going to ask Maya to the dance?

Should I? Is it too soon? Would she say yes?

Is *that* what she was referring to this morning, when I was so desperately tongue-tied?

Yes . . . to whatever you're asking.

Hope flutters along every nerve, but I can't bring myself to look at her, while Tobey makes a big show of asking Janine to go with him to the dance, and she . . . rejects him. This inevitably leads to another chain reaction, as the massive burn turns into a massive joke. Tobey doesn't seem upset at all, though. He just laughs it off with the others and starts opening up a ketchup packet for his fries.

How?

I would crawl off into a hole if Maya rejected me in front of everyone like that.

"Yo—Jude the Dude!"

The yell is so loud I literally jump—at the same instant that a stream of ketchup from Tobey's packet laser-beams its way right toward me, missing the sleeve of my sweatshirt by mere millimeters as I turn toward the voice.

Beside me, Maya gasps, then laughs. "That was close."

"Whoa, sorry about that," says Tobey—not sounding very sorry at all—as I grab a napkin and wipe the splotch of ketchup off the bench between me and Maya.

Ezra—the source of my bellowed name—appears a second later at the end of the table, arms spread wide. "How did you know? I must have your sources."

"What are you talking about?" I ask.

"Mrs. Jenkins! The bet! You nailed it!"

I gape at him, waiting for it to click.

"I got the lowdown from Miss Claremont. Mrs. Jenkins just scored a publishing deal. Turns out, *Swooning on the Seven Seas*, book one of a new pirate romance series, will be hitting shelves next year."

116

"You're kidding," I say.

"*Dude*. There's no way you pulled that out of nowhere. You sly dog." He's scowling and smiling at the same time as he pulls a wad of cash from his back pocket. "I'm no math genius or anything, but based on my calculations, this belongs to you."

He flips through the bills, counting out a bunch of money, then holds it out to me. When I'm too stunned to take it, he smacks the pile down on my tray, right next to my cold potatoes.

"No cap," he says, pointing a finger at me. "Next time, I want in on your gossip mill, before you take me for all I'm worth."

With that, he tips an invisible hat to the rest of the table, winks at Serena, then does a fancy spin on his heel and marches back off through the cafeteria.

Serena laughs. "He is so weird."

I'm stunned at the nods of agreement. Ezra is a treasure in the Fortuna Beach High School social circles. He is bold and ridiculous. The ultimate class clown. Teachers hate him—in part because they can't *really* hate him. And students? They adore him, for all his antics, for all the entertainment he's brought us over the years.

He's not weird. *I'm* weird.

What sort of upside-down universe have I stumbled into?

"Holy hell," says Serena, grabbing the pile of cash off my tray and counting it. "I guessed that Mrs. Jenkins was quitting to take care of an ailing parent. How did you know?"

"I didn't. I was just making stuff up."

Raul snorts. "Yeah, right. That's some lucky guess."

I smile uneasily. Yep. *Lucky guess.*

Serena hands the money back to me. "What are you going to do with your winnings?"

"Probably buy the headless Ned Stark Funko Pop," I blurt out.

It takes a second, but then Katie lets out a laugh that borders on a cackle. "Don't tell me you collect those dolls!"

My chest constricts. *Seriously*, Jude? I force a laugh. "Just kidding. I'll probably . . . you know, start saving up for the next time Sadashiv is back in town? I hear those VIP tickets aren't cheap."

"Aw, that's sweet," says Brynn, giving Maya a meaningful look.

I don't think I imagine the way Maya shifts a bit closer to me. But it isn't until the conversation has moved on that she leans closer, her voice low. "Am I really going to have to wait that long for you to ask me out again?"

I inhale sharply and meet her eye.

That smile is back. The one that's a little teasing, and the tiniest bit unsure of herself.

Before I can even begin to think of a response, the bell rings and everyone jumps up from the table.

Maya catches my arm before I can head off to fourth period. "About tomorrow," she says. "Is it still okay if I crash your shindig?"

It takes an embarrassingly long time for my brain to catch up and realize she's asking about D&D night.

"Yeah, of course."

"Your friends don't mind?"

I follow her gaze to where César and Matt are waiting by the exit doors, watching us. César, to my horror, raises his arms in my direction, pumping them in the air like a cheerleader.

Of course, Matt won't be there, but I should probably tell César and Russell and the others that Maya is going to be joining us. I completely forgot. I guess I wasn't sure it was real.

"They don't mind," I say.

"Great," says Maya. "Text me the address."

She heads off in a different direction, her bookbag slung over her shoulder. I wave after her.

It's only then that the feeling of nausea I've had all morning finally starts to fade.

Chapter Sixteen

Quint and Pru are in their element. Quint's been moving chairs and shelves and lamps around for the last thirty minutes, trying to set up the perfect "frame" in the corner of the record store, while Pru has been gleefully checking things off a list she made the day before. She keeps talking about submission guidelines and entry forms and metadata and hashtags—evidently it isn't enough that Ari record her first song and post it online. To Pru, this is Ari's chance to launch her songwriting career. And while Pru may not know much about music or filmography, she definitely knows about promotion and marketing and career management. Or, at least, she does a good job of pretending she knows about these things.

For her part, Ari seems content to pick out riffs on her guitar strings and wait for Pru and Quint to tell her what to do.

As for me, I'm working.

Sort of.

Business has been slow all afternoon.

"So," says Ari, fingers dancing along the guitar neck. "The date went well?"

I haven't told her much. I haven't told anyone much of anything, because what am I supposed to say? There was a limo. Sadashiv signed our posters. Maya grinned at me like I had moved the heavens to bring her to that concert, when really all I did was make a lucky phone call.

"Yeah," I say. "It was great."

Ari smiles, but it's tight-lipped and doesn't reach her eyes.

She's probably nervous. She's still playing around on the guitar, and it amazes me how she can play and talk at the same time. Sometimes I wonder if her brain even recognizes what her fingers are doing, or if it's all muscle memory at this point. I also wonder if she's playing a riff she knows or if she's just making it up, testing out new combinations of notes, writing a song, subconsciously, even now. I don't recognize the melody.

"Don't even bother trying to get more details out of him," says Pru. She has the laptop that she and I share for schoolwork propped up on the far end of the counter. I think she's setting up Ari's brand-new YouTube profile, which I guess I'm supposed to be making a header graphic for at some point? "That's all he'll say about it. 'Great. Yeah. Fine. Limos are neat.'" She scowls at me. "Not like going on a date with Maya isn't a huge flipping deal."

I shrug uncomfortably. "What do you want to know?"

Pru grins like this is exactly the question she wanted me to ask. "Did you kiss her?"

I blanch. "God, Pru."

"What? That's *the* question! Give me *something*."

"That's . . . no. I'm not going to talk about this." I'm blushing again, but my perennially red face hardly fazes Pru anymore.

She sighs, then shoots a knowing look at Ari. "He didn't kiss her."

I half expect Ari to jump in, to make some teasing comment. To nudge or pry or . . . something. It isn't like my crush on Maya hasn't been well-documented and discussed and dissected over the years, between both of them.

But Ari doesn't say anything. In fact, she seems engrossed in her playing again, her shoulders tense.

"But the date must have been good," Pru continues, "because she asked Jude to eat with her at lunch today."

Ari looks up, her gaze curious. "What was it like meeting Sadashiv?"

I could kiss her for changing the subject. "He was nice. You know, for a billionaire."

"Probably not a billionaire," says Pru. "Record labels take a lot of upfront money from the artists."

"I'm sure he's not hurting too bad," I say. "And—oh! Ari, I mentioned you to him."

Her eyes go wide. "Me?"

"I told him I had a friend who's a really talented songwriter. I gave him your name, and he wished you luck on the competition."

"Wow." She stops playing. "Sadashiv has heard of me. That's . . . weird."

"Yeah, meeting him was weird. I thought Maya might faint at one point, like those girls at Beatles concerts back in the sixties."

"Is he as dreamy in real life as he is in the magazines?" This comment comes from Quint. He's set up his phone on a tripod and is making minuscule adjustments to its positioning.

I consider. "I mean . . . yeah. He pretty much looks like he's been photoshopped into reality. Again, he seemed nice, though. Like, he knows he's famous and could probably get away with being a jerk, but he's made the conscious decision to be decent instead."

"Hey, Ari?" says Quint. "Could you sit on the stool so I can check the lighting?"

Ari takes her place as requested, but she looks supremely uncomfortable as Pru and Quint both study her through the phone screen.

"We could use more lighting on this side, to counter the light coming in from the windows," says Quint.

It's still strange to hear Quint using his professional voice. For years, I thought of him as a toned-down version of Ezra. A class clown, a goofball. The guy everyone loves but doesn't take too seriously. He changes when he's behind a camera, though. He's more confident, more focused, discussing things like shadow and depth.

Pru disappears into the office and returns with yet another desk lamp. She sets it up next to Ari, and she and Quint go back and forth for a few minutes, moving the lamp around to different surfaces, trying it with and without the lampshade, while Ari sits in the center of it all repeatedly telling them that it doesn't have to be perfect, and repeatedly being ignored, because not being perfect isn't a thing that Pru believes in.

"Are you doing your new song?" I ask, in part to distract Ari.

She looks at me and takes in a nervous breath. "Yeah. I think so. I mean, I'll play it, and you guys can tell me if it's awful, and then we can do one of my old ones, I guess. But, yeah. I really like this song? I think it's . . . I think I'm happy with it."

I smile. "I'm sure it's great. But if it's not, Pru will tell you."

"You won't?"

I scoff, and point my thumbs back at my chest. "Biggest fan, remember? You can do no wrong in my eyes."

Ari beams and looks away.

Finally Quint declares that the lighting is perfect—so long as we can record the video in the next forty minutes before the sun sets and we lose the daylight coming in through the windows.

"Let's do a quick sound check to see if the mic is working," he says. "Can you play something?"

Ari strums a few chords and starts to sing. The change is immediate. I watch how her shoulders drop, how the tension in her face eases.

She starts with an Adele song, but she makes it her own, trading out Adele's powerful vocals for her own sweet, almost fragile voice. Ari has told me more than once that she doesn't like her singing voice. Despite how great she is in front of an audience, despite how much she loves playing music, she's complained for years that her voice just isn't that great. But it's okay, because she doesn't want to be a performer, she just wants to write songs for someone else to perform. She wants to be behind the scenes, creating music and lyrics that other people will love, that will make them feel something. She doesn't care about being in the spotlight.

Even so, there are times when I hear her sing that I think she must have an absurdly skewed idea of what her voice sounds like, because . . . I kind of love it. You know that cheesy line where they say "she has the voice

122

of an angel"? That's what Ari's voice is to me. It's not powerful, it's not robust, it's not *loud*. But there's something about it that is so soothing, so endearing, so pure. She just doesn't give herself enough credit.

"So, what did you two talk about?"

I start, not realizing that Pru has come to stand beside me. She's keeping her voice low while Ari and Quint fiddle with the recording equipment.

"Just her new song. She's worried it's not any good."

Pru furrows her brow, then understanding hits her. "Not you and Ari, you goon. You and Maya. You were alone with her for more than four hours. What did you talk about that whole time?"

"I mean, we weren't *alone* for four hours," I say. "We were surrounded by five thousand screaming middle-aged women. And not a small sampling of middle-aged men, now that I think about it. And we didn't have to talk because, you know. Sadashiv was there. Singing and stuff. It was kind of a perfect first date? Like going to a movie. Takes all the pressure of conversation off."

"Okay," says Pru, drawing out the word in annoyance, "and the rest of the time, when Sadashiv wasn't singing?"

I pretend to think, as if I haven't gone over every moment of last night a thousand times, replaying it from every angle. "At one point, we talked about D&D."

Pru's face falls. "You didn't."

"It's not like that. It just . . . came up, and she was . . . interested. She kept asking questions. She even asked if she could play. Sometime. With us."

Pru's expression becomes horrified. "Play D&D? With you and your friends?"

"Why are you looking at me like that?"

"Because I've met your friends. Tell me you didn't say yes."

"Of course I said yes. It was her idea. Why would I say no?"

Pru lets out a hoarse laugh, which Quint chastises, reminding us to be quiet. With a quick apology, Pru drags me farther away from our makeshift recording booth. "Jude, I love you, and I think D&D is cool, and it makes you happy, and that's all that matters, and your friends are really nice, and I've got nothing against them, blah blah blah."

"Wow," I deadpan. "This is going to be harsh, isn't it?"

"It's *Maya*. You've been in love with her for years. Literally *years*. And now you have a chance with her, and you're going to woo her with a role-playing game?"

"It can be romantic," I say, more than a little defensive. "People fall in love playing D&D all the time."

Her eyebrows tick up.

"Look, I'm not sure it's a great idea either, but *she* asked. She seemed genuinely interested. And what if . . . what if she actually starts to like me back?" It's almost painful to think it, much less say it. That slim, tenuous, near-impossible hope that this could actually turn into something. "What am I supposed to do, just never talk about this thing that I really love? That I spend literally hours of my free time on? Am I never supposed to introduce her to my friends?"

"No," says Pru, "but maybe you could get to know each other first? Maybe you don't jump right into the part where you get drunk on imaginary mead and storm the imaginary castle?"

"I'm not saying you're wrong, but . . . you weren't there last night. And everyone always says to be yourself. So, this is me. Being myself."

Rather than look encouraging, Pru stares at me with something like pity. "And after your D&D night, are you going to put on your Jedi robes and practice casting spells with your magic wands?"

A muscle twitches in my eye. "Jedis don't use wands."

"My point is—"

"I know what your point is," I interrupt. "I get it. And I know you're trying to be helpful, but . . . again, it was *her* idea. So I'm just going to go with it and see what happens, because what else am I supposed to do?"

Pru tilts her head. "You could ask her out on another date. A real date. With just the two of you. No D&D friends, no screaming Sadashiv fans."

Quint clears his throat, and we both turn to see him and Ari staring at us. "Are you done picking apart Jude's love life?" asks Quint. "Because I think we're ready."

"Right, sorry," says Pru. "What should I do?"

"Nothing. We're good. We just need some quiet." Quint presses record on his phone and nods at Ari. "When you're ready."

Ari's gaze lingers on me a long second before she tears her attention away. To Quint. To the phone. She fidgets, sitting taller and adjusting her position on the stool. She exhales sharply and draws the guitar closer to her body. I look from her to the phone screen, where the limited view shows her lit up in an almost shimmering light. The mural of stars behind her gives a cool, slightly mystical vibe. Professional, but not pretentious.

She looks pretty, too. I don't think about it much, because I'm used to seeing Ari in the vintage dresses she loves, all beautiful and self-assured on that stage, ensorcelling crowds with her music. But she's extra pretty today, with gloss on her lips and her hair done into a braid around the crown of her head. She's wearing a yellow dress dotted with white roses, and in the light from the lamp, she's ethereal. Almost . . . elven.

Araceli the Magnificent.

The thought makes me grin, and that's the stupid look I have on my face when Ari glances up again and our eyes meet. For a second, she goes still, and I shrink back, wishing I could explain to her that I wasn't laughing at her or anything, that I was just . . .

I was just . . .

Thinking that she is absolutely lovely.

Ari licks her lips. I can tell she's nervous, but her voice doesn't waver as she looks into the camera. "Hi! I'm Araceli Escalante, and this is a song I wrote called 'Downpour.'"

Then she starts to play. Her fingers strum a few chords, then pick out a slow melody, before she starts to sing.

Never could say when it started
Crept up like a storm in the night
Not sure when I got so brokenhearted
This love, a crash of thunder
This love, a flash of light

Yeah, my love, it isn't a sunrise
Was never the day shining through
Here comes the rain, and I'm crying again
Caught up in the downpour of me loving you

We used to be sunshine and ice cream,
Kicking sand at the sun going down
Oh, you and me, how easy it seemed
But now I can't be wanting
'Cause this wanting is dragging me down

Ari opens her eyes, growing more comfortable as she loses herself in the music. She's singing to the listeners, to the world, to her future fans, because she's incredible, and the world needs to hear her songs. It's so clear to me in that moment, more clear than it's ever been, that she is special. She's going to create things that move people. She's going to write songs that inspire people all over the world, that make us feel more connected, that help us put our own feelings into words in a way we couldn't do on our own.

Yeah, this love, it isn't a sunrise
Was never the day shining through
Here comes the rain, and I'm crying again
Caught up in the downpour of me loving you

A skip in the record and flickering lights,
Don't mind if the power goes out tonight

Heart beating loud, another sleepless night,
A breath I can't catch and my hope taking flight

I glance at Pru, wondering if she's feeling as proud and happy as I feel. But to my surprise, Pru looks . . . sad. Concerned.

Her eyes dart to mine.

I mouth the word. *What?*

Pru stands straighter and shakes her head. The moment passes, her strange expression smoothing out as Ari finishes the bridge to the song and launches into the final chorus.

'Cause my love, it isn't a sunrise
Was never the day shining through
Here comes the rain, and I'm crying again
Caught up in the downpour of me . . .
The downpour of me loving you

The last chord rings out, and we all hold our breath until the notes have faded into silence. Then Ari flashes a relieved smile at the camera, nervous once again.

Quint stops the recording, and we all break into applause.

"How was it?" Ari asks. "Be honest. If it's terrible—"

"It's not terrible," Pru says emphatically. "It's beautiful, Ari."

"Really," agrees Quint. "We can do a couple more takes if you want to, but . . . I thought that was great."

"Yeah? You really liked it?"

"Loved it," says Pru. "It felt very . . ." She hesitates. "Unguarded. In a good way."

Ari laughs, the sound a tiny bit forced. "The lyrics just came to me when I was lying in bed a few weeks ago. Who knows? Maybe it came from a movie I watched or something."

Pru returns her smile, but I can tell she wants to say something else. To dig further.

I'm beyond confused. The song is amazing, so whatever Pru is worried about, I know that isn't it.

"Whatever inspired it," Pru finally says, "it's really good."

Ari looks down, running the pads of her fingers along the guitar strings. "Let's hope the judges feel the same way."

Chapter Seventeen

True to her word, Lucy takes me to the thrift store Saturday morning, and I am regretting my entire life by the time we're finally finished. But I guess it's successful, because we come back home with bags full of faded jeans and dark jackets and shirts in various colors that have no funny quip, no pop culture reference, no . . . nothing.

Boring.

And *scratchy*.

I change into one of my new tees as soon as we get home, then hurry to get set up for the campaign.

We converted the basement into my bedroom when Pru and I were nine years old. The bunk beds we'd shared up to that point were passed down to Lucy and Penny. The spiders were swept out, and carpet was put in. The room still feels pretty dated, with wood paneling on the wall and ancient light fixtures that may or may not start a fire at any moment. But the resulting space feels equal parts sanctuary and dungeon.

Which is fitting, given that the group and I usually host our campaign nights here.

I set up two card tables and throw a black sheet over them, then bring down the chairs from the dining room. I make popcorn and empty a bag of Fritos into a big mixing bowl. Usually I let the rest of the group grab a drink from the fridge and bring it downstairs with them, but this time I dig a cooler out of our garage and fill it with ice and nestle in some sodas and sparkling waters. I debate ordering pizza. I debate asking Mom to bake us some cookies. I debate a lot of things.

Usually, our D&D nights are relaxed and laid-back and fun.

I am not relaxed right now. I am not laid-back. I am not having fun.

I hadn't really thought it through when Maya asked if she could come play with us. I got hung up on the whole idea of her wanting to spend time with me, and maybe even being interested in this hobby that I really love, and in that excitement I ignored some big-picture things I probably shouldn't have ignored. Namely, the fact that Maya still scares me on a very visceral level, and can I really be an effective Dungeon Master with her sitting at the table?

Maybe this is what Pru was trying to warn me about. Not just that Maya would be hanging out with my admittedly oddball friends. Not just that we would be playing make believe for hours, giving her an unfiltered view into my own imagination, which, let's face it, is a little bit like giving someone a front-row seat to your subconscious, and all the good and bad therein.

But there are also little considerations that, at the moment, don't seem little at all.

Maya is going to be at my house. In my bedroom.

What if she doesn't like the snacks we serve? Should I order pepperoni on the pizza? What if she's vegetarian, or gluten free? I should know these things, but I don't. Why didn't I ask?

And she's going to meet my little sisters, and Ellie hasn't learned enough about social constructs to realize when she shouldn't *ooh* and *aah* over her big brother's possible new girlfriend and ask inappropriate things like, "Are you going to get married?" and "Are you going to have children?" and "Do you love my brother?" and is it too late to encourage them to all go out for ice cream or something? It would make me really happy if no one else is here when Maya arrives.

"Whoa," says Pru, standing at the bottom of the basement steps with a laundry basket balanced on one hip. "This is the cleanest I've ever seen this room."

130

I look around, at the made bed, the shelves I've spent the last three hours dusting, the carpet I actually vacuumed. "Is it too obvious that I'm trying to impress her? Should I, like . . . mess things up a bit?"

"No, no, I like it. It's cozy." She glances at the card table. "The pumpkin spice candle is a bit much."

"Yeah, you're right." I blow out the candle.

"I folded your laundry," says Pru, setting the basket on my bed. "You seemed stressed, so . . . you're welcome."

"Thanks." I start shoving the clothes into my closet. "Have you talked to Mom and Dad? Asked them to, you know, not make a big deal of this?"

"Jude, you're making a way bigger deal out of this than anybody else."

"After that encouraging speech you gave me yesterday about what a colossal mistake it is for me to include her in the game, I might be feeling a little on edge."

"Sorry," says Pru, and I almost think she means it. Like, she is sorry that I'm so nervous, but she also hasn't changed her opinion. Pru is not, generally speaking, an opinion-changer.

With the exception of Quint, I guess. She *really* changed her opinion about Quint, after spending our entire marine biology class last semester complaining about how lazy and inconsiderate he was. Turns out she was wrong . . . and she was even willing to admit it (eventually). So maybe there's hope for her yet.

"Okay," I say, slamming shut the last drawer and taking in a deep breath. I look around, debating if I should hide the Funko figures on my shelf, but decide against it.

Be yourself, be yourself, be yourself.

How can such common advice feel so uncommonly useless?

My attention lands on the table. The black sheet, the bowls of snacks, the Dungeon Master's privacy screen, the grid boards, the tiny pewter figurines of goblins and dragons and orcs, half of which I painted years ago before I started getting bad hand cramps.

"Is it too late to cancel?" I say, a hint of a whine in my voice that I'm not proud of.

Pru looks at me. Opens her mouth. And . . .

The doorbell rings, its distant cheerful melody echoing down the staircase.

Pru's look turns empathetic. "You've got this."

"Do I?" I say. "Because earlier you made some very convincing arguments that suggested I do not have this."

"Yeah," she says, cringing. "I have some concerns. But I love you, so . . . I hope this goes well."

"I appreciate that."

I take the stairs two at a time, Pru following after me. I hear the front door open and Penny's overly excited voice—"Hi! You're Maya, I'm Penny, Jude is so—"

"Maya!" I say, a little breathless. I skid to a stop in the foyer. "You made it. Awesome. This is Penny. She's one of my sisters. Come in."

Maya is smiling, a little nervously, as she steps through the door. She's holding a bag of tortilla chips and a jar of salsa. "Hi, Penny. You were with Jude when he came to my rescue after my car broke down, weren't you?"

"Yes! That was me!"

I chuckle uncomfortably. "And you know Pru." I gesture behind me.

Pru waves. "Hi, Maya."

"Hey," says Maya. "Are you going to play with us tonight?"

Pru makes a face. "Um, no. I'm meeting up with Quint in a while. But you'll have fun."

The way she says it is almost convincing.

A gasp echoes down from the upstairs. "Is that her?" says Ellie, peeking through the banister rails. "She is so pretty!"

I cringe. "And that's Ellie." I glance up and see Lucy also leaning over the railing. "And Lucy. These are . . . wow. They're all here. These are all my sisters. Everyone, Maya. Maya—my sisters."

Maya laughs. "Hi, everyone. It's nice to meet you." She turns to me and holds up the chips and salsa. "I brought snacks. I figured that's probably the quickest way to get your friends to like me."

And there it is again—that adorable hint of uncertainty. Something akin to shyness.

I've never in my life thought of Maya as shy. She's always been friendly and popular and gorgeous and out of my league, yes. But shy?

"You really don't have to worry about that," I say, even though in saying it, I realize that I don't know if it's true. Girls and crushes and real-life stuff don't really come up with the D&D group. We're not those kinds of friends, I guess, and since the concert I've had way more anxiety wondering what Maya would think of *them*, not the other way around.

"Okay, so you can follow me," I say, and head downstairs. I hear a few teasing, singsong goodbyes from my sisters as we descend into the basement. I hold my breath, trying not to overthink every little thing as Maya surveys my bedroom, but it's impossible not to wonder what she's thinking. Is she judging the Batman poster? The old sketches of monsters I long ago tacked up on the wall? Is she inspecting the books on the shelf, a shocking number of which depict medieval swords and dragon wings on the spines?

Is she regretting this yet?

"So . . . Pru and Quint," says Maya, setting the chips and salsa on the table. "I will admit, I did not see that coming."

I laugh, but it's a little strained. "You and everyone else who has ever met them." I rock back on my heels. "Last summer Pru volunteered at the animal rescue center that's run by Quint's mom, and next thing you know, they're dating. Honestly, I think Pru might have been more surprised about it than anyone. But I think they're happy."

"They seem like a good fit," says Maya. "In an opposites-attract sort of way."

The ensuing silence is short but stifling. My thoughts are racing, because on one hand I do not want to be talking about my sister and her boyfriend, but on the other hand, I can't help trying to read between the lines. Is Maya suggesting that she and I, too, could be a good fit? In an opposites-attract sort of way?

Maya glances at the table. "You said I should get here early? To create a character?"

"Right! Yeah. Have a seat."

I take my usual place at the end of the table, but set down the privacy board so it isn't like I'm hiding from her, and hand her the character template I printed out earlier. "Did you give it any thought yet?"

"Yes," says Maya, her eyes lighting up as she scoots in her chair. "I want to be a tiefling fighter."

I gape at her. The way she says it. The way she is literally *speaking my language* makes me want to jump across this card table and . . . do things.

But my speechlessness is also a result of the fact that . . . this is not at all what I expected her to say. A tiefling fighter? I struggle to picture it. Tieflings are humanoid creatures whose blood has been infused with magic from the infernal realms, giving them an almost demonic appearance—tails, fangs, and badass horns that project from their skulls. And fighters are, as you might expect, masters of weaponry, trained in all forms of combat. They're fearless in the face of danger, and can mete out death in a ruthless, almost clinical way.

I compare that mental picture to the character in my comic—the eladrin cleric who had been cursed by dark magic, trapped in the form of a statue for years, waiting to be saved. In the comic, the character inspired by Maya is beautiful, imposing, and elegant, just like she is in real life.

But she was also a statue, and I guess . . . pretty devoid of personality, now that I think about it.

At my silence, Maya's expression starts to fall. "Did I get something wrong?"

"No! No. I'm just . . . surprised. A tiefling fighter. That's . . . cool. Really cool. Have you thought about names yet? Because tieflings tend to

134

follow particular naming conventions. Not always, but they usually have names taken from the Infernal language, or—"

"Or virtue names," says Maya. "I looked it up. Do you think Grit works as a virtue name? Because I was thinking of calling her Grit Stone-splitter."

I blink. "That is an awesome name."

She beams. "Thank you."

"And you do know that tieflings have horns? And tails?"

"Yep," she says. "I had this idea that maybe Grit's tail was scarred in a gruesome battle years ago, and she's kind of self-conscious about it, so she keeps it hidden most of the time."

I nod slowly. "Sure. Yeah. Um. Here, you can write that down." I tap the top of the page, and Maya starts to write her character's information in her looping, half-cursive script. "We don't have any tieflings in the group yet. Or fighters, actually. She'll be good to have in the group."

"I've been thinking about her all day. I've got a whole backstory worked out and everything. I want to be . . . I think it's chaotic neutral?"

"Your alignment. Yeah. Chaotic neutral would be like . . . like a free spirit. You're not really concerned with being good or evil, but you value your freedom and following your heart."

"Yes, exactly," says Maya, her eyes shining. "I have this idea that Grit grew up in a really dismal orphanage, with a lot of rules and restrictions, and now that she's away from all that, she's sworn to always let her instincts guide her. She wants to live a full life, full of new experiences and meeting new people and not be stuck in these tiny boxes that people try to put her in, where she always has to try to be what everyone expects her to be all the time. Instead, she can go out in the world and be adventurous and spontaneous and fall in love and have fun—" Maya cuts herself off and the moment of enthusiasm vanishes into discomfort. "Sorry. I'm probably way overthinking this."

"Not at all," I say. "Actually, it's really good to think about backstory and how it made your character who they are. It makes it a lot easier to play them authentically, and figure out what sort of decisions they would make in different situations."

Maya frowns at me. "Then why do you look so skeptical?"

I grimace. "I'm not. I'm just . . . surprised. It's not the character I'd envisioned for you, I guess."

"Oh? What had you envisioned?"

"An eladrin," I say immediately. "Which is a type of elf. With summer magic. An affinity for nature. Lawful good, or maybe chaotic good."

Maya's eyebrows raise. "Given this some thought, have you?"

I laugh. "Not really. I just . . . I guess that's how I see you. In a way."

"As an elf?"

My heart thumps, and I hesitate. Half of my brain screams not to respond, to change the subject before I say something I'll regret. The other half knows this is not the sort of opportunity one should pass up, no matter how great the risk.

"As someone who brings beauty and warmth and goodness with her wherever she goes."

I hold her gaze just long enough to see the compliment register, then I look down and pretend to be sorting my notes for tonight's campaign. "So, uh, I have some extra dice that you can use. The next step is to roll for Grit's stats."

I hand her my set of dice. The old resin ones, not the mystical twenty-sided dice that almost never leaves my pocket now. I talk her through the rest of the character creation process and Maya tackles every step with enthusiasm, brilliantly concocting more of Grit's backstory as she fills in her character sheet with ability scores and equipment. Maya is already talking about Grit like she's a real person—a connection that some players don't develop until they've been playing the game for weeks, or even months.

I'm more than a little impressed. I'm in *awe*.

By the time the doorbell rings again, most of my fears have evaporated. I never should have doubted the magic of Lundyn Toune.

Clearly, Maya is going to fit in just fine.

136

Chapter Eighteen

"How dare Matt abandon us!"

These are the first words out of Noah's mouth as they burst into my house. They start unlacing their knee-high boots to leave by the door, even though literally no one else takes off their shoes when they come to our house. "And for something as cliché as making money? What kind of priority is that? I am so embarrassed to be related to him. I'm seriously considering disowning him for this. I also have half a mind to boycott that fish and chips place and—" Noah looks up for the first time and notices that we are not alone in the foyer. That it isn't César or Russell or Kyle at my side. Noah draws up short. "Hello, new person."

"Noah, this is Maya. Maya, Noah."

Noah peels off the boots and sets them by the front door before shaking Maya's hand.

"You don't go to Fortuna Beach, do you?" Maya asks.

"No. Orange Bay Science Academy."

"Noah is Matt's cousin," I offer, by way of explanation. "Matt Kolden?"

To which Noah adds, "Except I'm disowning him, because he ditched us." They tilt their head, studying Maya. "Are you Matt's replacement?"

Maya glances at me, uncertain, and I'm saved from answering by another ring of the doorbell.

The rest of the group is on the front porch. I usher them inside, and we all crowd into the foyer that blends into our family's living room. I try to introduce everyone to Maya, but my nerves are getting to me, and I can tell that Maya is doing her best to not be overwhelmed by new names and new faces and—

Yeah, let's take a breather. Check in. How are *you* doing? Feeling overwhelmed by all the new additions to this story?

Okay, let's get through this. For the fanartists.

We've got César. Mexican American, with a wave of brown hair that tends to have a mind of its own. He's skinny, like me, but he's the first to point out that he could whoop me in an arm-wrestling contest any day of the week. Not that we've actually done that. In the game, he plays Goren the Gruesome, an impulsive human sorcerer with a taste for bloodshed and violence. (But in real life, he's a nice guy, I promise.)

Russell and Kyle are both sophomores at our school, and have been friends since Kyle moved to Fortuna Beach in middle school. Despite being a year younger than me, Russell looks like a full-on adult. He's pale and hairy, built like a football player with an honest-to-god *beard*, just like his author idol, George R. R. Martin. His character is Celryn the Grave, a shadow elf monk who is easily the most logical member of the group, and tries his best to keep the others focused on whatever they're supposed to be doing.

Kyle, his best friend, is Korean American, and if you ask my younger sisters, they'll tell you he's the cutest of all my friends, with shaggy black hair and an ear piercing. He is also emphatically cheerful, not unlike his forest gnome druid, Querth Nulga.

Lastly, we've got Noah, who is the most recent addition, having joined the group last fall at Matt's insistence. Noah is pale like me, with short, spiky hair that is currently dyed violet, though they are always changing it. Noah is a senior, and thus the oldest of our group, but they're also the shortest, which could be why they chose to play a badass halfling rogue named Starling Morve.

And then there's Maya. You know her already. Beautiful. Confident. Girl of my dreams. Also, evidently, playing a tiefling fighter named Grit Stonesplitter, and yes, my fingers are totally itching to sketch out her character as soon as possible.

And oh . . . hey! I'm Jude. Should we have done this sooner? Sorry about that. I am pale and scrawny and self-conscious about my lips, which Pru says make me look like a pouty male model, which I just cannot accept is a compliment. I am tall, though. It's fun being tall. Cute old ladies at the grocery store look at you like you're Superman when you grab the pickles off the top shelf for them and you don't even have to stand on your tiptoes. That's pretty great.

Cool. Got it? Moving on.

Everyone already sort of knows Maya, at least in passing—except for Noah. But Noah is outgoing and talkative and all the things I wish I could be, so by the time we're all settled in at the card tables downstairs, most hints of strange newness have evaporated. Noah is explaining why Starling abandoned their previous group of bandits to join our little family of misfits, and Kyle is talking excitedly about the last campaign, when Querth saved the whole gang by translating a Druidic riddle and figuring out how to stop a deadly nest of sentient vines that had captured the group, and César is insisting that he helped, too (he didn't), and Russell is giving me an impatient look like he's regretting not bringing a book to read while we get through all the social niceties.

And Maya looks . . . nervous, I guess. But not in a *what am I doing here?* way. More like in a *this is new, but I'm here for it* way.

I know there was a time, like a hundred pages ago, when you were thinking, *Dude, why do you like this girl so much?*

But you get it now, right?

"Okay," I say, opening up my notebook to the pages and pages of notes I've made for our new campaign. "We left off with Starling, Goren, Celryn, Querth, and Brawndo at Bork's Tavern and Inn in the small village of Talusia. As you all make your way down for supper one afternoon, the bartender calls Querth over and hands him a letter."

"Oh, yes, I love getting mail!" Kyle says, in his chipper Querth voice. "I take the letter back to the group and read it."

I nod. "Querth reads the letter aloud," I say, then drop my voice in an attempt to mimic how Matt would always speak for his character,

139

Brawndo. I feel silly at first, with Maya listening in, but I figure—if we're doing this, we're doing this.

> *My good friends,*
>
> *Though our adventures have been a source of pride, camaraderie, and occasional riches, it is time for me to fulfill my destiny. I have gone to join the king's army in order to fight in the southern war. I will find you again once the war is through. Until then, farewell, and do not follow Goren into any unfamiliar dungeons. As history has shown us, it is always a terrible idea.*
>
> *Yours,*
> *Brawndo*

"He joined the king's army?" shouts Noah. "That traitor!"

"Traitor or not, let us wish him well on his journey," says Russell. "I raise my drink to our fallen comrade." He mimes holding up a tankard of ale.

"He isn't fallen yet," says Kyle. "He literally just left."

"Yeah, but it's Brawndo," says Noah with a smirk. "He won't last two hours on a battlefield."

"True," Kyle says thoughtfully. "In that case, I buy a round of ale for everyone in the tavern, and lift my cup in honor of Brawndo."

"To Brawndo!" César, Russell, and Noah cheer, while Maya looks on, her gaze bouncing between each of them.

"All right," I say. "Querth, deduct two silver coins from your purse to pay for the drinks." As Kyle makes a note, I go on, "As you complete your toast, the door to the tavern swings open and in strides a tiefling dressed in traveling gear, a broadsword at her hip."

Maya sits taller in her chair. "That's me! Wait. Is that me?"

I chuckle. "That's you. So—what do you do?"

140

Maya hesitates, her momentary enthusiasm fading into uncertainty. The others wait. I know they could jump in with any number of prompts to help her get started. A greeting, an observation—even picking a fight, which is César's answer to just about everything. But we all wait to see what Maya will do first, to let her decide how she wants to introduce her own character.

Her eyebrows bunch briefly, but then the moment passes. Her expression clears, set with determination and a spark of glee. "The tiefling shouts, 'Give me ale, or give me blood!'" Maya punctuates the demand by slamming her fist on the table, nearly knocking over my privacy screen.

My eyes widen in surprise.

Grins split across the faces of the group. Even subdued Russell nods appreciatively.

"Well said," whispers Noah, before settling a hand on Maya's wrist and leaning closer. "But you don't have to say 'the tiefling.' You can just talk as your character."

"Oh, okay." Maya wiggles her shoulders. Her smile is huge, like she's been waiting all her life to yell those words and not be judged for it. "Um. Now what?"

I grin at her. "The bartender looks up . . ."

I have no coin to offer for your service, but I assure you there will be treasures to be found in the temple.

And I can also reward you by...

...writing an epic ballad in your honor upon your victorious return!

COUNT US IN!

Chapter Nineteen

It is the strangest night of Dungeons & Dragons I have ever experienced.

Not just because Maya is there—though that's definitely part of it.

Not just because Maya is playing a fighter and . . . weirdly enough, she is playing her character *really well* as the players set out on their quest through the forest and encounter their first obstacle—a pack of giant weasels. Maya is so into the mindset of Grit Stonesplitter that once the battle is over and the remaining weasels are trying to run away, she throws a handful of popcorn at the board, shouting, "Get back here so I can rip your spines out with my bare, bloodied hands!"

We all gape at her, speechless, until Maya sheepishly sinks back into her seat. "Sorry."

But Noah just beams, delighted, and looks at me. "Screw Matt. We're keeping *her*."

And then Russell informs us all (with a completely straight face) that a group of weasels is called a *boogle*, and how a person knows that, I have no idea, but the whole night dissolves into hysteria pretty fast after that.

But possibly the strangest part of the night is . . . me. And my dice. And my bizarre streak of impossibly lucky rolls.

Since I'm letting Maya borrow my dice, I've been using my magic D20. And I'm not, like, *great* at math or anything, but even I know that on a twenty-sided dice, the odds of rolling a twenty on any singular roll are . . . well, one in twenty.

And yet, for every time I roll to determine initiative or the strength of one of the NPCs or see how well-concealed various traps and treasures are as the characters do their perception checks, the number comes up the same.

Twenty.

Twenty.

Twenty.

The others start giving me strange looks. We've played together enough, excepting Maya, that I'm pretty sure no one thinks I'm cheating, because what reason do I have to cheat? Things are more interesting when some treasures got discovered. And it is definitely more fun when the players stand a fighting chance against any opponents I throw at them.

I become grateful for my privacy screen, which prevents the players from seeing my rolls. I start to lie—rolling the dice, seeing that same twenty glinting up at me, and just pretending that I rolled some other random number instead. Seven. Sixteen. Two. It doesn't really matter. The game continues. My lucky streak continues. But tonight, it doesn't feel lucky. It just feels . . . annoying.

It's almost ten o'clock by the time we call it a night.

"I can't wait to hear this epic ballad," Kyle says as he packs up his books and character pages.

"Ballad?" I ask.

"The bard promised us a song," he says. "When we break the curse. So when this campaign is over, you're going to owe us a song, Dungeon Master."

I chuckle. "Right. Luckily, I might know of a real-life bard who can help with that."

They all stow away their handbooks and dice and figurines, smiling and laughing as they replay some highlights from the night. I'm somewhat astounded to see that Maya is acting every bit a part of the group.

Like she's been playing with us for years. Somehow, she and Noah get on a friendly rant about favorite K-dramas, which leads to them exchanging phone numbers and making plans to get together and rewatch some favorites.

Maya lingers behind after the others have gone, insisting that she wants to help clean up, especially since she—no, since *Grit* had gone a little overboard with that popcorn. There isn't much to do, though, and we mostly work in silence. She carries up the empty bowls to the kitchen sink, while I disassemble the card tables and take them out to the garage.

"This was really fun," says Maya, folding the tablecloth.

"Yeah, it was," I agree. "You fit in really well." Which is true. Tonight was *great*, actually. There were times when I forgot that the prettiest girl in school was sitting at the table. For a while, I stopped being nervous. I stopped being self-conscious. I stopped being anything but the Dungeon Master, and it felt just like hanging out with my closest friends. Just like normal.

It had been great.

But it hadn't been *romantic*.

I scratch the back of my neck. "Do you want to . . . stay awhile? We could watch a movie or something?"

Her look turns apologetic. "Thanks, but I should get home."

"Right. It's late. Um . . . I'll walk you out."

We head upstairs and out to the driveway.

"I'll see you at school on Monday," Maya says, pressing the unlock button on her key fob. The headlights blink.

"Yeah. Definitely."

As Maya is reaching for the car handle, I gather my nerve. "Maya?"

The next few moments are a comedy of errors. Maya swings open the door as I lean forward, and the corner of the door smacks into my chest so hard it actually knocks the wind from me. I stumble back, stunned.

"Oh!" Maya cries out. "I'm so sorry! Are you okay?"

"Y-yeah," I say, rubbing my chest and trying to bury the pain. It doesn't hurt *so* bad, I tell myself. It's more a pride thing, really.

And also, confusion.

What the heck, Luck?

Maya looks horrified at first, and then . . . suspicious. "Were you going to . . ."

She doesn't say it, but the words are there, clear as the moon in the starless sky.

Was I going to kiss her?

Yes. Yes, that had definitely been the idea.

"Just thought I'd . . . hold the door open for you," I say, coughing. "Gentleman . . . type . . . stuff. It was a misguided attempt."

"Oh." She chuckles weakly. "That was an accident."

"I know. I'm fine. Uh . . . drive safe, okay?"

She nods. "Good night, Jude."

"Night."

I stand in the driveway and watch until her brake lights vanish around the corner, then I head back into the house. In the bathroom, I tear off my T-shirt to inspect the damage, but despite a small red mark, it doesn't look nearly as bad as it felt. The embarrassment is lingering longer than the wound.

What was I thinking, leaning in to kiss her like that?

I go down to my bedroom and pull out my sketch pad, but I don't draw anything. I just flip mindlessly through the pages, while my brain replays the most memorable moments of the campaign. All of my friends joking around, reminiscing about all the dumb things Brawndo had done during former campaigns. And Kyle insisting that they pause the entire quest so he could stop and help a family of snails safely across the road, which drove César absolutely mad—especially when the snails turned out to be magical and gifted Kyle with a tiny bottle of healing elixir. Then there was the time when Noah and Maya went off on a tangent about spineless mercenaries, until they were both laughing so hard that Maya was wiping away literal tears. Eventually Russell cleared his throat and reminded them that they were going to be devoured by a dire wolf if they didn't do something.

The whole night surpassed every expectation.

So why do I feel like something went catastrophically wrong?

It doesn't make any sense.

I need to ask her out again, I decide. Just like Pru said. A real second date.

Which would be . . . what, exactly? We could rent scooters on the boardwalk, or . . . I don't know. A picnic on the beach?

Nothing I think of seems right. I try to picture me and Maya on these excursions. I try to picture myself being charismatic and charming. I try to picture her laughing at my jokes. But no matter how hard I try, even in those fantasies, I can't get her to laugh as hard as she did with Noah tonight.

I'm imagining things. I'm overreacting. I'm just being my normal self, full of self-doubt. Nothing new to see here.

Things are going great. They couldn't be better. This magic that's come inexplicably into my life is infallible.

I can win Maya's heart. It will just take a little luck.

And I have all the luck in the world.

Chapter Twenty

"*Jude.* Stop goofing off," says Pru. "We're here to work!"

"Sorry, I know," I say hurriedly, not taking my eyes from the screen or my hands from the controls. "But I've never gotten this far before. I can't stop now!"

Ari's house has a lot of cool things, things that definitely make it the preferred hangout spot when we can't spend any more money on nachos at Encanto or ice cream cones at the Salty Cow. For starters, Ari is an only child, so the very fact that she doesn't have three younger sisters vying for control over the TV, phone chargers, snacks, and general living space is a bonus. She also has an in-ground pool in her backyard that is far superior to the blow-up pools my parents still buy—and replace—every year. And her den is top-notch, with a wall-to-wall record collection (many purchased at Ventures, of course), a big-screen TV, two vintage arcade games, and a pinball machine.

I could spend hours killing time at Ari's house. I *have* spent hours killing time at Ari's house. Full afternoons reading a book on her patio while she and Pru laze around on floaties in the pool. Entire days locked in a head-to-head pinball competition. (Ari always wins. But then, she does *own* the machine, so I figure she probably gets more practice than we do.) Entire evenings studying and writing papers, while Ari picks out different records neither of us have heard before, and Abuela keeps us energized with a seemingly never-ending supply of fresh fruit dusted with Tajín, lime, and chamoy sauce. (Which is too spicy for me because I'm a wimp, but I've learned to search for the slices of mango and watermelon with the least amount of sauce on them, whereas Ari likes to drink the juice left at the bottom of the bowl like it's a rare delicacy, no matter how many times we've had it.)

Sometimes I almost feel more comfortable at Ari's house than mine. I love my family, but there's just something about the quiet comfort here that I rarely get at home.

Right now, though, I'm less concerned with quiet and comfort, and more focused on maintaining my streak in this Pac-Man game.

"Oh wow," says Quint, looking over my shoulder. "I think you've beat EZ's highest score."

My chest warms with a tinge of pride. It's not often I feel like I've beaten Ezra at anything.

On the screen, the little round monster munches and runs, munches and turns, munches and flees, dodging colorful floating ghost guys. I'm in a zone, my hands nimbly pushing the joystick. Up, left, right, down, up up up—

It's almost like I can't *lose*.

Which is when I realize. This isn't *me*. This is the magic!

My hands pause on the controls. The purple ghost that should have attacked my round-faced dude inexplicably heads the other direction.

My heart sinks.

What's the point of winning if it's already decided?

"That's weird," says Quint.

"Maybe there's a glitch on this level," I mutter, before I intentionally run Pac-Man into another ghost.

Game Over.

"Finally," says Pru, as the game flashes the new high score and asks me to input my initials. "Can we do this now?"

"Sorry." I turn toward the couches. Pru is sitting with the computer on top of a throw pillow on her lap. On the other side of the couch, Ari is nervously braiding a strand of her hair while she stares at the screen. Her attention jumps up to me, and for just a second, I catch her gaze swooping down over the new jeans and plaid button-up that Lucy talked me into. She said I could wear it over just about any T-shirt—yes, even my nerdy ones—and with the lower buttons done up and the sleeves cuffed to my forearms, it would still look good.

And even though I feel a little awkward, when I catch glimpses of myself in the mirror, I kind of like it.

And when Ari bites her lower lip and looks quickly away, I kind of like that, too.

I scratch behind my ear and sit down in the space between them, while Quint takes the recliner.

"There are eight million files here," says Pru. "Which one are we supposed to be looking at?"

"Okay. So . . ." I take the laptop from her. "Here's the original video. And here's the one that Quint adjusted the sound on. And here . . ." I take a deep breath and click an MP4 file. "Is the final video. But!" I pause the video before it can start playing and look at Ari. "Before we watch it, just know that nothing is set in stone. If you hate it, we don't have to keep it."

"Hate what?" says Pru, her voice suspicious. She is generally suspicious of anything that wasn't her idea first, but I'm used to winning her over. "What did you do to her video?"

"Nothing," I say. "I just added a few graphics. But if that's against the contest rules, or Ari doesn't like them, they're easy to take off."

"We didn't talk about graphics," says Pru. "You were just supposed to add the credits and the subtitles, so the robot translators online don't mess up Ari's lyrics."

"Yeah, I know, and I did. I also . . . embellished some things. I had some extra time this morning, and I was inspired, so . . ."

"Let's just watch it," says Quint.

Ari nods. "I'm sure I'll like it."

"Don't say that," I tell her. "Because you might not, and there's no pressure. This is your video, not mine. I just thought maybe it would help it stand out in the competition. Not that you need that. The song is great as it is."

I mean that. I've had her song "Downpour" stuck in my head all day, and I memorized the lyrics while I was working on the video. I barely finished it an hour ago, before we left to come to Ari's house, which means I haven't had time to dwell on what I've done. To analyze the additions I made from every angle. To question and doubt and worry about it, which means that all the anxiety that would normally have been spread out over days or weeks is all bunching up inside me right now.

I exhale and click play on the video. The musical intro begins, with the credits in the bottom corner, just like a real music video. "I think there's a way we can adjust the settings so people will be able to watch it with or without subtitles—" I start to say, but then the first graphic appears, and Pru and Ari gasp. I clamp my mouth shut, nerves tingling throughout my whole body.

Quint jumps up from his chair and comes around to the back of the couch so he can watch over our shoulders.

The graphics are simple line drawings, like chalk doodles that float in and out of the frame in time with the song. A shining sun in the corner as Ari begins to sing, quickly replaced with storm clouds and a flash of lightning. Rolling waves in the frame beneath her guitar. A little sailboat rocking by. Ice cream cones and beach umbrellas and spinning records spewing tiny music notes around Ari's head.

I'm critical of each and every one of them. I mean—for one morning's worth of work, it's not *awful*, and I'm grateful for that one summer I spent an undue amount of time learning Adobe After Effects, thinking that someday I'd like to turn our D&D campaigns into mini cartoons, until I realized how much I absolutely despise the tedious nature of animating and I was definitely better suited for comics.

Still. It could be better. Those waves could be slower, to better match the rhythm of the song. That lightning bolt was too big, almost distracting. During this chorus, the breaking hearts are a little too cheesy.

I don't realize I'm chewing on my knuckle until Pru reaches over and pulls my hand away.

The video finishes with a pale green screen, the credits scrawling in my own sloppy handwriting. Ari for singing and songwriting, Quint for videography, Pru for production team, me for editing, plus a special thank-you to Ventures Vinyl. At the very end, a cloud sweeps across the screen, clearing out the text and leaving a single small heart behind.

The video ends.

"It's okay if you hate it," I start. "I made another version, without the—"

Suddenly, arms are around me, hugging me from the side. "I *love* it," says Ari. She grabs my head and pulls me closer to her, kissing me on the cheek.

My face flames.

"It's perfect!" she continues. "It looks like a real music video. Except, you know, without a bunch of fancy costume changes and a million-dollar budget."

"Are you sure?" I say, even more nervous now with Ari's arms around me. "I wasn't sure if maybe special effects are against the contest rules or something?"

Pru takes back the computer. "I'll check the small print to be sure, but I think I would have remembered something like that. And I've gone through the hashtags to watch other entries, and lots of people are try-ing to make their videos stand out by doing different camera angles and strobe lighting and . . . Actually, there were some with costume changes, now that I think of it. We should be fine. And I agree with Ari—I loved it, Jude. It fit the song perfectly."

Ari gives an excited squeal and releases me.

I sink into the couch cushions.

"All right, enough chitchat." Pru opens up Ari's brand-new YouTube channel. With a few clicks, she uploads the file, chooses a thumbnail image, and pastes in the description with all the necessary details about the festival competition.

When she's done, she passes the computer to Ari. "You do the honors."

Ari sits up taller and reaches for the touch pad. On screen, the arrow hovers over the publish button.

"Wait." I settle my hand over hers.

Ari's whole arm tenses.

"I know this is weird," I say, my fingers tingling where they lie flush against her skin. "But I've been feeling really lucky lately, so . . . maybe some of it will rub off on you."

Quint snorts. "If EZ were here, he would have a field day with that comment."

Pru turns and glowers at him.

Ari gives me a hesitant smile. "I'll take all the luck I can get."

Together, we publish the video.

I pull my hand away, and we all sit there staring at the screen, where an image of Ari and her guitar, with a little white heart over her shoulder, sits at the top of her otherwise empty channel.

"It looks lonely," says Quint. "You're going to have to record more songs."

Ari hums thoughtfully. "You know, I've been thinking about that. It was kind of fun making this. Maybe we could make more?"

"Absolutely," says Pru, hopping to her feet. "Now that we've made one, the next will be faster, easier, cheaper to produce. Basic economy of scale."

Quint chuckles. "Not to mention that Ari has a whole bunch of great songs that people might want to hear."

"Well, yes," says Pru. "Obviously, that, too."

"What about entering the contest?" asks Quint. "Does that part happen automatically now?"

Ari shakes her head. "I need to submit the entry form, but I've got it filled out except for the link to the video, so it will only take a second."

Pru side-eyes me. "Do you need to help her with that, too, Jude? Let more of your luck rub off? Or are we going to trust in her hard work and talent for this part?"

"I've never said anything against hard work and talent," I say, my hand still tingling. "But even you can't deny it. Things have been going my way lately."

Pru opens her mouth—presumably to deny it—but she hesitates. Her gaze darts to Ari, and her jaw clenches briefly, before she turns back to me with a smile that seems almost . . . resigned? "You're right. It certainly seems that the odds are ever in your favor."

Chapter Twenty-One

The magic of Lundyn Toune does not let me down. A homework assignment that I thought was lost miraculously reappears in my binder when the teacher asks for it. I stop to tie my shoelace and find a ten-dollar bill on the sidewalk. And even though I forget to put my favorite cereal on the grocery list, my mom remembers to pick some up anyway, and that *never* happens.

The luckiest thing of all, though, is that sitting with Maya and her friends at lunch becomes progressively less uncomfortable as the week goes on. I even dare to talk once in a while, and maybe I'm imagining it, but I think I'm sort of charming them? It's mentally draining, I'll admit, to listen to their conversations and constantly be searching for things I can respond with that are either interesting or clever or both, but when I do and everyone laughs, I feel like I'm totally nailing this. One time I even catch Serena giving Maya a *who would have thought?* look that I interpret as a really good sign.

Despite all that, it still takes me until Friday to work up the nerve to ask Maya out on a second date. She says yes and we agree to meet up after school, but do I just imagine the way her smile is more reserved this time? And why is it that her response doesn't fill me with the same heart-jolting ecstasy it did the first time? I chastise myself, knowing that this is not something I can take for granted. The potential to be dating *Maya*. The novelty of impossible good luck might wear off, but that never could.

And besides, no amount of coin flipping or dice rolling can make me worthy of calling Maya Livingstone my girlfriend. If this magic disappeared tomorrow, would she still see me as a guy she could like? A guy she might fall for?

I can't become complacent until I'm sure that the answer to that question is yes.

———————

"Oh, that's just beginner's luck!" shouts Maya as my golf ball sails through the mouth of the shark, down the tube, out onto the lower level of the putting green, and straight into the little plastic cup.

Hole in one.

And that is the precise moment when I begin to question if mini-golf was a good idea. I smile nervously as we head down to pick up our neon-colored balls. Maya had gone first, and it took her six shots to get it in the hole, but she insists that she's just getting warmed up.

I wish I could think of some witty remark, but I'm busy trying to figure out how I'm going to make it through the rest of the course without Maya thinking that I'm some sort of putt-putt prodigy.

Or that I'm cheating.

I'm not sure which would be worse.

"It's not *completely* beginner's luck," I say as we make our way to the next hole, the one where the ball is supposed to go up and over a small pirate ship. "I have played mini-golf before."

She doesn't need to know that the last time I played was with my family, and I don't think Ellie was even born yet.

"Are you a golf savant?" says Maya, setting her orange ball down on the starting mat and lining up her club. "Because despite my lackluster showing on that first hole, I am actually pretty good at this game, and I will not let you intimidate me, Jude Barnett."

For some reason, I like it when she uses my full name, and I can feel myself relaxing. "I'm sure I just got lucky that time."

Maya takes her swing, and the ball goes straight up the ramp, past the wooden masts, and down the other side. It comes to a stop about a foot away from the hole. "There is no luck in putt-putt golf," she says, casting me a solemn look. "This is a serious game of skill and strategy."

She gets the ball into the hole with one more swing and records her score while I line up my club. This time, I try to send it off-course and . . .

The ball strikes the side of the ship and bounces back, returning to almost the same spot I hit it from.

Maya makes a pleased sound in her throat, and I exhale with relief. After the D20 fiasco last weekend, I half expected the magic of Lundyn Toune to defy the very laws of physics to ensure I got another hole in one. Whoever would have thought that there could be times when a person just doesn't want to be all that lucky? Turns out, sometimes it is better to be average.

By intentionally skewing my shots, it takes me four tries to get over the pirate ship, and I use the same strategy for the next few holes, hitting my ball into the water once, and landing in the same sand trap twice.

We fall into an easy rhythm. To my surprise, Maya fills most of our conversation with talk of our D&D campaign. She's even started writing out her character's backstory, thinking it would be fun to turn it into a short story or something. Not that she would ever share it with anyone. Her friends wouldn't get it, she says, and she's never posted anything online, and probably it isn't that good, anyway—her words, not mine—but she's having fun all the same. She talks about how she used to come up with stories when she was a kid, where she would put herself in as a character and pretend she was a ninja or a paleontologist, and sometimes she would write her stories down, but it has been so long and she'd kind of forgotten about it. She talks with a lot of nostalgia, like she's connected with a beloved part of herself that has been neglected for too long.

If you're wondering whether or not I get many words into this revealing monologue of hers, the answer is . . . not really, no. But I don't mind. If Maya wants to talk my ear off about her long-buried dreams of fantasy adventure, who am I to stop her?

Maya has lots of ideas about where the campaign might be heading. Actually . . . some of them are pretty good. Maybe even better than what I've got planned.

"You know," I say, "you'd make a good DM."

Her eyes widen. "No way. I wouldn't even know where to begin."

"After you've played for a while, you'll get a feel for how it works. Coming up with a campaign is sort of like writing a story without any characters. Part of the DM's job is to keep the game on track, but it's more about improvising so everyone has a good time. Honestly, I think you'd be great at it."

She preens, even as she's shrugging modestly. "It seems like a lot of work."

"It is. But it's fun, too."

She hums thoughtfully while I take my next shot. "Maybe," she says, as my ball ricochets off the walls inside the miniature windmill, then pops out the other side and straight into the hole.

She scowls. "Now, that one was definitely a lucky shot."

"Sorry?"

"Why? I'm still beating you," she says, writing down the score.

She does beat me in the end. It's not that I intentionally let her win, I'm just way more focused on not getting a hole in one on every shot, so I stop paying attention to how she's doing, and it turns out, she *is* good. As we return our clubs, the attendant gives Maya a WINNER sticker, which she proudly sticks to her shirt like a badge of honor.

"Does the loser buy dinner in this game?" I ask, tucking my hands into my pockets. Squeezing the dice.

The smile Maya gives me is borderline flirtatious. But rather than my confidence skyrocketing at that look, I immediately question if that was too cheesy, too fake, too . . . *not me.*

"I could eat," she says.

I nod, suddenly unable to hold her gaze. "I know a place."

Chapter Twenty-Two

We walk to Encanto, my favorite restaurant. Pru, Ari, and I have spent enough hours studying here after school that the owner, Carlos, doesn't even bother to ask our orders anymore, just brings us the usual.

"I've never been here before," says Maya. "But I've walked by it a million times."

"I come here a lot," I tell her. "The food's delicious, and the owner's really nice."

There's a SEAT YOURSELF sign inside the door, so I lead her to our favorite booth. We slide in, and Maya grabs the menu out of the little holder stand on the table. "What do you usually get?"

"I really like the tostones and Ari usually gets the nachos. Plus appetizers are half-off right now," I say, pointing to the happy hour menu. But then I worry that maybe that makes me sound more cheap than practical, so I add, "They've got great fish tacos, too."

"That all sounds good," says Maya, putting the menu back and glancing around. "Oh, look. It says they have karaoke every Tuesday." She waggles her eyebrows at me. "Should we come back and sing sometime?"

I grimace. "*No*, thank you."

Her expression turns surprised, and I immediately regret my reaction.

"I mean—I'll come back with you anytime you want," I amend. "But I'm not one for singing in public. I don't even like to sing in the shower when I know people are home."

"I'm not much of a singer, either."

"Ari likes to come and sing on Tuesdays once in a while," I say. "Sometimes she even talks Pru into it. You should join us sometime."

"I'd like that."

"Jude, is that you?" Carlos says, appearing at our table with two glasses of ice water. "I hardly recognized you without the usual gang. Who's this?"

"Hey, Carlos. This is Maya. We go to school together."

"You go to *school* together," repeats Carlos, in a way that makes it sound like this simple fact holds twelve layers of unspoken meaning. "Well, I hope you're being good to this guy," he says to Maya. "He's one of the good ones. The usual, Jude?"

Cheeks flaming, I look at Maya, and she shrugs. "When in Rome."

"Yeah," I say. "The usual."

Carlos nods. "And to drink?"

We both order Sprites, and as Carlos walks away, Maya gives me an intrigued look. "You really *are* a regular."

"Yeah, this was one of Ari's favorite places when we met her, and it's close enough to home that Pru and I could ride our bikes before we had our licenses. It was just the three of us for a while, but now of course Quint comes a lot, too. And Ezra. And Morgan—you probably haven't met her. She used to volunteer with Pru and Quint. She's going to college up in San Francisco now, so we haven't seen her in a while, and . . . I am rambling. I'm sorry."

Maya barks a laugh. "Please, after I talked your ear off about my tiefling backstory earlier? Honestly, it's refreshing when you start to open up. You're always so quiet."

Naturally, this comment only serves to make me clam back up. I busy my hands by undoing the strip of paper around the napkin and silverware. "I don't usually have much to say."

"You don't have much to say? Or you don't think people want to hear it?"

"Both?" I crumple the paper strip into a tight ball and flick it across the table. It bounces off the salt shaker. "Mostly I think a lot about comic books and D&D campaigns . . . and most people aren't super interested in that."

"I'm interested."

She says it so genuinely that I can't doubt her, especially after how much fun we had last weekend, and how much thought she's been putting into her character.

"I'm still trying to wrap my head around that," I tell her. "Never in a million years would I have imagined . . ." I trail off, worried that I'm on the verge of saying something embarrassing.

"What?" urges Maya. "That I have an imagination? That I like stories with magic and adventure, too?"

"Not that," I say, then pause as Carlos brings our drinks. I use the interruption to try to form a coherent thought. "It's like, this obviously isn't some cliché teen movie where I'm the nerd kid who gets stuffed into lockers by the popular jock, and you're the cheerleader who enjoys . . . I don't know. Shopping, or whatever."

Maya makes a face, suggesting that I might want to get on with a point, and I grimace. "But there are still . . . you know. Social circles. And you've always been in one circle. The one that joins school clubs and runs for student government and gets voted for prom court, and . . . stuff."

"You do know that we don't actually have a prom court at our school, right?"

"Oh. Yeah, of course."

I definitely did not know that.

Seeing the truth on my face, Maya laughs and shakes her head. "Have you even been to one of the dances?"

"No," I say. "Because I am in one of the other circles. The social circle that . . ."

"Plays fantasy games," she says.

"And watches anime and reads novels about dragons and goes to sci-fi conventions and Renaissance Faires and, like, actually wears costumes to them."

Maya's eyes widen with . . . glee? "Do you really?"

Oh god.

I look away.

She gasps, leaning forward. "Do you have pictures? Can I see? What kind of costume? Did you wear a kilt? Armor?" She narrows her eyes. "Were you an elf?"

"*No*," I say sheepishly. "I was a human. A human . . . wizard."

Her eyes twinkle. "If you don't show me a picture, I bet your sisters will."

"Not Pru. She's loyal to me." I sigh heavily. "But the rest of them would definitely sell me out in a heartbeat."

She laughs. "I wouldn't take advantage like that. Though I would like to see it." She hesitates, before adding, "I'd actually love to go sometime." She takes a long sip of her drink, nose wrinkling from the carbonation. A waiter stops by a minute later with our food.

We eat in silence for a while, before Maya says, a little *too* airily, "Do you ever feel like you've missed out on something and now you're not sure if you can go back and try again?"

I tilt my head at her, suspicious at her tone. Like she's pretending it doesn't mean much, which makes me wonder. "What sort of something?"

"I don't know. Just . . . something."

We fall silent again. The restaurant is growing more crowded for dinner service. Carlos shakes a cocktail behind the bar.

When she finally speaks, it isn't at all what I expect her to say. "They aren't circles, Jude. They're boxes."

I pause, a piping hot tostone halfway to my mouth.

Maya clears her throat and meets my gaze again. "It may not be a cliché teen movie, but it does still feel sometimes like we've had these roles assigned to us. For me, I think it's because I've spent my whole life wanting people to like me. I want to have friends. And I want to get good grades and for our teachers to think, wow, she does really good work. And I want my parents to be proud. And—I mean, not that you don't want those things, too, but for me it's like . . . like I don't remember choosing who my friends were and what activities I was going to be interested in, it all just sort of happened. You start hanging out with people in elementary school, and they like certain things, so you start to like those things, too. The same movies, the same sports, the same . . . *everything*. But then . . ." Her brow pinches. She glances at me, then looks away. "There was this one time in . . . eighth grade, maybe? I saw this poster at school. One of the clubs was hosting an anime movie night, with movies by . . . what's his name? The guy who did *Howl's Moving Castle*?"

"Hayao Miyazaki," I say.

"Right. Well, I'd actually seen *Howl's Moving Castle*. My dad took me to a special showing at the Offshore Theater, and I really liked it. So I told my friends that we should go to this movie night, and I remember Katie acting like it was the weirdest thing I could have suggested. Like, who wants to go watch cartoons with a bunch of kids we don't even hang out with, and the cartoons aren't even in English? And I . . . I laughed with her, and I agreed. What a dumb idea. But secretly, I always sort of regretted not going."

She exhales slowly and finally takes a bite of her food.

"I went," I tell her.

She pauses in her chewing, then swallows and nods, her lips twitching at the corners. "Of course you did. Was it amazing? Did I miss out on what could have been the best night of my life?"

I think back. "It was in the auditorium, and they projected the movies onto a big screen. There were only maybe . . . twenty of us? Twenty-five? And someone ordered pizza. And . . . of course, Miyazaki's films are incredible."

Maya looks wistful. "See? That sounds great. Whereas I was probably at another sleepover where we painted our nails and played truth or dare, just like every other sleepover." She cringes. "Don't get me wrong. I like my friends, it's just . . . Honestly? I had more fun playing D&D last weekend than I've had in a long time."

These words should probably fill me with satisfaction, except Maya looks so sad when she says them.

She winces. "Don't tell them I said that. Obviously."

"I won't," I say. Then, hesitantly, "So just to be clear . . . you're planning to break up with your friends because you're a closeted nerd?"

Maya laughs. "*No.* They're still my friends. I just sometimes feel like we're different people now than when we met. And the things that I think sound really cool and fun . . . I don't even think I could bring them up without being laughed at, or looked at like I've betrayed them somehow."

"Things like . . . watching anime," I clarify. "And going to Ren Faires. And playing Dungeons and Dragons."

She gives me a warning look. "I know that wasn't sarcasm I just heard, when I am spilling my heart out to you right now."

I scoop some mild salsa criolla onto my plate. "Sorry. It's just . . . you make it sound like you're joining a cult or laundering drug money or something. You just want to plunder an imaginary dungeon once in a while. Literally millions of people all over the world like this game. I mean, what did everyone say when you told them? Did they threaten to send you to nerd rehab?"

I'm trying to be funny, but Maya doesn't laugh. If anything, she looks guilty as she takes a drink of her soda.

"Oh," I say. "You haven't told them."

"I'm not embarrassed, I swear. I just haven't . . . It hasn't come up. But obviously they know that you and I are hanging out together."

Hanging out, I think. *Not dating.*

"It's okay," I say. "You can tell them whatever you want. Or don't want. But really, what are you afraid would happen? Do you really think they're going to abandon you, just because you found a new hobby?"

"Maybe not," says Maya, sounding completely unconvinced. "But I'm not sure I want to find out."

I frown. "They welcomed *me* easily enough."

"Because *I* welcomed you."

I open my mouth. But then shut it again.

Maya picks at the tostones.

Finally, I gather my thoughts enough to say, "The things we like are

168

only a part of who we are. This doesn't change you. Just like hanging out with me doesn't change who you are, either."

Her smile is faint. "Thanks, Jude. And thanks for inviting me out tonight. I do like hanging out with you."

My heart leaps. I return her smile, and for a second, I feel it. This gravitational pull between us. We're close enough in the booth that I could lean toward her, tilt my head down, close the space between us, and—

Panic tightens my chest and I break eye contact first. Clearing my throat, I reach for my drink and take a few long gulps.

When I dare to look back at Maya, she's digging through her small purse for something, and I sense that maybe she feels as awkward and uncertain as I do. Did she *want* me to kiss her? I wish there was an easy way to tell. All the movies make it look so easy, like you'll just know when the time is right.

But all I know is that this booth, with just the two of us in it, feels suddenly crowded.

And Maya still isn't meeting my eye.

"You know," she says suddenly, "I bet there's some alternate universe where I did go to that movie night. And in that universe, I think you and I are probably really good friends."

The words expand between us. Taking up all the air. Pushing against my chest.

Really.

Good.

Friends.

"Yeah," I say, my voice strained. "I bet you're right."

Chapter Twenty-Three

The house is inordinately quiet when I get home, and it takes me a minute to remember that Mom and Dad were taking Penny and Ellie to see the newest Marvel movie. (Without *me*? I know.)

I'm not really hungry, but I go into the kitchen anyway and take the Nutella jar from the cabinet. Nothing like a little bit of post-date stress-eating when you have absolutely no idea if you just royally botched another chance to kiss the girl of your dreams.

I unscrew the Nutella lid, then lean against the counter and scoop out one huge spoonful. I eat it slowly, because a mouthful of Nutella is far less enjoyable than one might think.

I barely taste it.

What is *wrong* with me?

With a groan, I put the Nutella away and reach for my phone.

I briefly consider texting her, but I don't know what I could say that wouldn't make me sound desperate. Instead, I open my emails.

My heart jumps into my throat.

Jude,

Your art submission will be published in the July issue of the *Dungeon*. You will receive payment in the form of a check within the next seven to ten days.

I really admire your unique style and

perspective, and would love to see more work from you for future consideration. Please feel free to submit additional work to this email directly.

Best regards,
Ralph Tigmont
Art Director, the *Dungeon*

"Holy crap," I mutter, reading the email for a second and then a third time. This is happening, for real. I'm going to get paid for my drawing. And the art director—an actual art director—wants to see more of my work. He gave me his direct email. That seems . . . important.

My mind floods with visions of artistic acclaim. Next, my work will be selected for the magazine's cover. Then other magazines will come calling—*Nerd Today* and *Dragon Script* and then, I don't know, like, the *New Yorker* or something. People will commission stuff. Hollywood will want me illustrating movie posters, and publishers will put my comics into print, and my original pieces will sell out every time they're displayed in Artist Alley at Comic-Con.

This is an opportunity. I have to seize it, right?

Nerves humming, I grab my backpack and sit down at the table, pulling out my sketchbook. I flip back through the most recent comic sketches—just a few goofy pages about Araceli the Magnificent coaxing a ragtag group of treasure hunters to go on a quest to save her wizard, and the first phase of their adventure.

I can't share these with anyone. They're too cheesy, and packed full of inside jokes that no one but my friends would appreciate. Now that I know the *Dungeon* wants to see more of my work, I feel like I've been wasting my time on this comic. I should have been pushing myself to create something more original. I need to focus on getting published and building a respectable portfolio, now that I have my foot in the door.

And yeah—I know what you're thinking. I'm clearly just using this as a distraction to take my thoughts off of the painful end to tonight's date with Maya.

But why do you say that like it's a bad thing?

The fact is, I haven't been drawing much lately, ever since my drawing was first accepted. I guess I've been plagued with . . . something. Artist's block? The overriding terror that they picked my art by mistake and any day now I'll get the apology email, along with a kindly worded postscript urging me to look into other hobbies?

I page through my older drawings. Warlocks. Druids. Trolls. Treasure chests and sword fights, and everything is boring, boring, boring.

What did Ralph Tigmont see in the piece I submitted? What did he like about it? He mentioned my unique style and perspective, but as far as I can tell, nothing I've done is unique at all. It's all been done a thousand times. The drawings aren't *bad*, per se. I mean, I still struggle with arm length sometimes, and the way this rogue elf is gripping his daggers is all wrong, and what was I thinking, putting this fighter in such stereotypical battle armor? It's like I haven't had a single original thought in my entire life.

Shaking my head, I dig out a pencil.

Okay. No big deal. I'll just draw something new. I'm motivated now. I know what they're looking for.

Just kidding.

I have no idea what they're looking for.

But if I did it once, maybe I can do it again.

I start to sketch.

After a few minutes, the lines coalesce into a warrior wearing a flowing cape, surrounded by a pile of skulls.

Ugh. Predictable.

I turn the page. Start again.

A girl. A fighter. With a sword and armor that is . . . curiously skimpy?

Objectification and impracticality, all in one go. *So* original. I'm a freaking pioneer of the cultural arts.

A new page.

I draw a dragon perched at the top of crumbling castle ruins, and it's garbage. Absolute garbage.

I don't have a unique perspective. There's nothing unique about me at all.

And that's when it hits me.

I am an impostor. This is what creators mean when they talk about impostor syndrome, except it isn't just a syndrome—it's real. That piece I submitted before was a fluke. A once-in-a-lifetime miracle. A one-hit wonder. The only good thing I will ever produce, and it's over. I won't even cash the check they're sending. I'll just frame it, so that fifty years from now I can look at that check on my wall and reminisce about that one time I had a drawing published in my favorite magazine. That one time I made something worthwhile. The one time I didn't completely suck.

No—that's not even true. I had the dice then. That's how my drawing got chosen. It wasn't me. It wasn't the art. It was the *dice*.

Which means it wasn't really earned at all.

The kitchen light flickers on. I start and look up to see, not one of my sisters, but *Ari*.

She's standing in the doorway wearing a black tank top and flannel pajama pants that are covered in small pink hearts.

"Sorry, didn't mean to startle you," she says, seeing my expression. "I was just getting a glass of water." She cocks her head at me, taking in my notebook. "Did I interrupt a stroke of midnight inspiration?"

"I wish," I mutter, slamming the notebook shut and rubbing my eyes. "What are you doing here?"

"Slumber party," she says, filling a glass from the water pitcher we keep in the fridge. "Pru wanted to keep an eye on the competition, so to speak, so we've been watching videos of other contest entries."

"Have there been any good ones?"

"Oh my gosh, *so* good." Ari slips into the nook across from me. Rather than saying this with a fearful or nervous tone, she seems invigorated. "Even if I'm not a finalist, it would be worth it to go to the festival just to hear some of them perform. I've subscribed to so many new channels tonight." Her lips twist mischievously as she leans closer, voice dropping to a whisper. "But between you and me, I think I had the best video. The graphics you made were super cute."

"I'm glad you liked them. But if you're a finalist, it will be because your song is great. It has nothing to do with me."

"We'll see. A lot of the entries are really great, but . . . I think I have a chance."

"Of course you do."

She wiggles her shoulders, a cute habit she has when she's proud of herself but trying to be humble. Then she inhales sharply and fixes a curious look on me. "Pru said you were out with Maya tonight?"

I swallow and reach for my pencil again, liking the comfort of its familiar feel in my fingers. "Yeah. We went to the boardwalk. Nothing special."

"Not every night can be a Sadashiv concert."

I dig the lead of the pencil into the crease between the notebook's cover and spine.

"Things are going well?" Ari asks.

"Yeah," I say. "Great."

Ari tilts her head to one side.

"What?"

"Nothing . . . ," she says in that annoying way that makes it clear there's *something*. "It's just really easy to tell when you're hiding something."

The lead on my pencil snaps, and I curse under my breath. "I'm not hiding anything. It's just weird to talk about this. I mean, Pru doesn't give us updates on every single date she and Quint go on."

"No," says Ari thoughtfully, "but . . . you can always tell that she's happy afterward. Really happy."

Her words strike a tender spot in my chest, bringing back every doubt I've felt since leaving Encanto. Since . . . well, before that. Since forever, I guess.

Something nags at me, whispering and unsure.

I've been on two dates with Maya now. I've gotten to know her, the real her, far more in these past weeks than I ever have in all the years we've gone to school together, and she's even more awesome than I thought. Funny and creative and surprisingly easy to talk to. A part of me likes her more than ever.

But it's a different sort of like. This sort of like isn't an all-consuming fantasy, bordering on obsession. It isn't the agonizing knowledge that I could never be worthy of her. It isn't the bittersweetness of a crush doomed to be unrequited for all eternity.

I like Maya in a way that's real and tangible and . . . different than it used to be.

I just can't figure out what's different about it.

"Jude?" says Ari. "What is it?"

I shake my head. "Nothing. I don't know. Maya's great. Really."

Ari sips at her water, watching me over the rim of the glass.

I scratch the pencil eraser against my scalp. "You know what I think the problem is? Our first date, when we went to the concert . . . it was perfect. Beyond perfect. And now there's just a lot of pressure to make *everything* perfect. But also . . . where do you go from there? VIP tickets, the limo, meeting Sadashiv. It's not like I can top that. So we're just . . . figuring out what's normal, I guess. Getting to know each other."

Ari takes another sip of her water, then looks away. "It takes time."

"Right? That's what I keep saying."

A smile flutters across her lips. "So you are dating, then? Officially?"

My stomach flips, thinking of Maya's words.

I do like hanging out with you . . .

Really good friends . . .

"I don't think anything is official," I say, wondering if I should tell Ari about how I had a chance to kiss Maya and I didn't take it. Maybe that's the problem, though. Maybe if we were officially dating, I wouldn't have panicked like I did.

"It's pretty incredible, isn't it?" says Ari.

I glance at her. "What is?"

"You and Maya. You liked her for *so long*. And now, it's like . . ." She shrugs. "You're just . . . dating. Just like that."

I laugh—a throaty, incredulous laugh.

Ari frowns at me.

"Not *just like that*," I say. "It's terrifying. And exhausting. It's like I'm in competition with myself. My past self. Always trying to one-up yesterday's Jude. This date needs to be more fun. More special. More romantic. How does anyone keep up?"

Ari frowns. "Maya makes you feel that way?"

"Maya? No. I don't know. She's never said anything, it's just . . ." I trail off. I don't know what I'm trying to say. My feelings have been such a jumble, I'm not even sure how I'm feeling anymore—about Maya, about anything. "It's got to start feeling normal at some point, right? Like Pru and Quint. They're so at ease around each other. But with Maya . . . it's not even like it used to be, where I would get around her and just clam up and feel like I had nothing to say and just try not to make an idiot of myself. Now it's more like . . . things are starting to feel normal. Comfortable, even. But not in the way I thought they would."

Ari is watching me, listening intently. "I'm no expert," she says, trailing a finger around the rim of her glass, "but isn't the whole point to just have fun and enjoy each other's company? If you hold yourself up to these impossible standards, then it will never feel good enough, and you'll always be worried that you're disappointing her, and . . ." She frowns, looking almost pained as she continues, "I know this is a big deal and you've had a crush on her for ages, and I am happy for you, but . . . don't think for a second that you aren't a catch, too, okay? Any girl would be lucky to be with you. That includes Maya."

I smile, but my heart isn't in it, because I don't really believe her.

"Thanks, Ari, but—"

"No," she says, so forcefully it steals the next words from my mouth. "I'm serious, Jude. You're . . ." Her shoulders jerk upward in an awkward shrug. "You're a really great guy. You need to know that."

The air crystallizes around us, and I hold her gaze for a second. Five seconds. An eternity.

She looks away first, and my heart skips.

There are words she isn't saying. I can practically see them, like a blaring neon sign over Ari's head. I can hear them, sung to a tune that's been playing in my head all week.

Caught up in the downpour of me loving . . .

"There you are."

We both start. I didn't hear Pru coming down the stairs, but she's standing in the doorway looking at us with suspicion etched into her face. "What's going on?"

"Nothing," I say—too loud, too fast. Even though it's the truth. *Nothing* is going on. Maybe I imagined, for a second, that Ari was trying to say something . . . suggesting that she . . .

But that's absurd.

She was just being nice, and I'm tired and confused.

"I was asking Jude about his date," says Ari, standing and opening the dishwasher to put her glass in, because even though she's a guest, she also sort of lives here.

"And?" says Pru. "How was it?"

"Fine," I say. "Why does everyone keep asking me that?"

Pru's eyebrows shoot up. "Oh no. What happened?"

"Nothing." I look between them, suddenly annoyed. "We played mini-golf. We had dinner at Encanto. It was great. And no, I'm not hiding anything." I shoot a scowl at Ari, but she just turns and looks at Pru, and they share some sort of silent, psychic communication that is clearly about me hiding something.

"Never mind," I mutter. "I'm going to bed."

I grab my notebook and brush past them, but the second I'm standing on the landing, looking down into the shadows of my basement bedroom, I'm overcome with a feeling I can't quite place.

Solitude, maybe? The knowledge that another sleepless night awaits me, full of thoughts of Maya and luck and comics and campaigns and songs with lyrics that send shivers down my spine.

I heave a sigh and turn back around. "Actually, Ari said you guys were watching the other entries for the competition?"

Pru folds her arms, a *what of it?* expression on her face.

"Mind if I join you?"

Chapter Twenty-Four

The sound of pen scratching across paper wakes me up. I squint an eye open. I'm not in my bed. I have a crick in my neck. My right hand is throbbing with the painful jabs of pins and needles.

I sit up. I'm lying on a comforter on the floor of my bedroom. My bleary eyes land on Ari sitting cross-legged not far away, her back to the bed. She has a sketchbook in her lap and is bent over it, her dark hair falling like a curtain in front of her face, her pen flying across the paper.

"Ari?"

She looks up. "Sorry," she whispers. "Did I wake you?"

"No." I pause. "Well, maybe. But it's okay." I try to shake some feeling back into my hand. I glance over at the bed, where Pru is sleeping, curled up on her side against the wall. Disheveled blankets suggest that Ari must have slept beside her. I don't remember falling asleep on the floor, but we were up really late watching dozens, maybe hundreds of videos that had been submitted with the competition's hashtag—some really good, others laughably bad. "Is that my sketchbook?"

"I hope you don't mind. I woke up with these lyrics in my head and needed to write them down. This was the first paper I saw."

I rub my palm into my eye and yawn. "No biggie."

"Okay. Then stop talking until I'm done with this."

I smile sleepily and nod as Ari turns her attention back to the notebook. For a second she stares at the paper, her pen poised above it. Then she hums a short melody to herself, falls quiet, and starts to write. After a few seconds she pauses, her head bobbing to some song only she can hear before she starts to write again.

Once I can feel my fingers, I get up and stumble toward my dresser. I'm still wearing the clothes I wore on my date with Maya, so I pull out some sweats and one of my favorite T-shirts and head to the bathroom.

After I change and brush my teeth, I find myself staring at my reflection, wondering if I should brush my hair, too. It's pretty rough, sort of matted on one side and all tangled on the other. I run a hand over my chin, where there's the slightest hint of stubble. Should I shave? Would it look better, or does the stubble make me look more mature?

I'm reaching for the shaving cream when I pause.

What does it matter? It isn't like I have someone to impress.

My hand hovers over the can. Five seconds. Ten.

I end up shaving anyway.

It's just basic hygiene.

When I get back to the basement, Ari has set the pen down on the carpet beside her and is flipping through the sketchbook pages.

"Get your song written?" I ask.

"It's a start." She turns another page. "I'll keep working on it, but I think it has potential." She holds up the sketchbook, showing me the page she's looking at. "Is this me?"

I go still, seeing the most recent comic book pages. I rack my brain, trying to remember what was in it. Ari coming to the tavern and meeting the adventurers and sending them off on their quest.

Nothing worrisome.

I don't think.

"Sort of," I say. "Araceli the Magnificent, remember?"

She smiles and runs a thumb along the sketch. "It's a fun story so far. I like how you illustrate everyone and their characters. They're all so easy to love. Makes me want to know what will happen next." She turns back the pages until she finds her song and rips it out. "I hope I get to read it when it's done."

180

"When what's done?" mumbles Pru. She sits up, squinting at us from the bed.

"Just a comic I started."

"You're writing a comic?" she says, as Ari's phone dings.

"It's just for fun. A comic, graphic novel . . . thing. It's nothing. I'm just messing around."

"Can I read it?"

"You're not in it," I say.

Pru squints one eye at me. "But Ari's in it?"

Perhaps more defensively that necessary, I say, "The story needed a bard."

The story did not *need* a bard, but Pru doesn't have to know that.

Ari gasps loudly, halting Pru's questions. "You guys! No way. *No. Way.*"

I trade a look with Pru, who throws back the covers and scurries out of bed. We gather around Ari, staring down at the email on her phone.

> **Subject: Condor Music Festival Songwriting Contest Entry**
>
> **Congratulations! We are pleased to inform you that your song, "Downpour," has been selected as one of our top ten finalists . . .**

That's as much as we read before Ari and Pru are squealing so loud they could wake the rest of the family two floors above us, and then Ari's arms are flung around us both and we're all jumping around—even me, because it would be weirder not to.

"Let me see it again," says Pru as soon as we've calmed down. She grabs the phone out of Ari's trembling hands. I still have one arm slung over Ari's shoulder, and she doesn't move away, but she's so giddy she probably doesn't even notice. Her hands are cupped around her face, eyes shimmering as Pru reads the email out loud.

"All finalists are invited to perform on the festival's Albatross Stage at five p.m. next Sunday. The grand prize winner will be announced following the performances. If you are unable to attend the festival, we also welcome you to join the celebration virtually. Please respond to this email by this Wednesday, latest, so that we can prepare for any special arrangements. Being present and performing is not necessary to win the grand prize."

"I can't believe this is happening!" says Ari, falling back on the bed and hiding her face in her hands.

"Hold on, there's more," says Pru. "Attached to this email are two complimentary tickets for you and a guest. Additional tickets can be purchased through our website at a discounted price using the code 'song-finalist.' Thank you for entering our competition. We wish you the best of luck."

Pru lowers the phone and gawps at Ari. "You're going, obviously."

Ari moves her palms to her cheeks. Her eyes are shining as she stares at Pru, even as her lips purse with uncertainty. "It's a long drive. What, close to three hundred miles? I mean, I could go down Sunday morning, but depending on how late it goes, I might not get back until after midnight."

"So?" says Pru.

"It's a school night."

Pru fixes her with a *look*. "You can miss school the day after performing the song *you wrote* at a music festival! What are your teachers going to say? No, we don't want you to follow your dreams?"

I clear my throat. "You know, if Pru of all people is advocating for playing hooky, you should probably play hooky."

Ari bunches her lips to one side, considering. "Obviously, I want to go. But also . . . I don't know if I really want to drive the wagon all that way by myself. What if it breaks down?"

"You won't be by yourself," says Pru. "I'll go with you, obvious . . ." She trails off, her shoulders dropping. "Wait. That's when they're transferring Luna and Lennon to their new zoo. Quint and I were going to go together."

"Which you *have* to do," says Ari emphatically, sitting up again.

Pru frowns at her, and I know how much she hates that she might not be there for Ari on such a momentous night. "What about your parents?" she says. "They would take you, wouldn't they?"

"My mom is taking some client out to look at a bunch of houses that day. I guess they made an offer on some mansion that overlooked the water, but got way outbid, and it was, like, a whole thing. But Dad could take me. Maybe. Or what if . . ." She tugs on a strand of her hair, something she always does when she's thinking hard about something. "I mean, this might be a really terrible idea . . . but what if I asked EZ to go with me?"

My chest tightens like it's just been struck with a phaser set to stun. "Ezra? Are you kidding?"

"He knows cars, right? And every time he sees the wagon, he makes some comment about wanting to look under its hood, and I'm starting to think he means it literally, not suggestively."

"Almost certainly both," says Pru.

"Could you stand to be in the same car with him for that long?" I ask.

Ari laughs, like I'm joking. "He can be a bit much, but I don't mind."

I bristle some more. "But he's so . . . irresponsible."

They both look at me.

"He's been working at the same mechanic shop since he was, like, twelve," says Pru. "That seems pretty responsible."

"Yeah, but he's so . . ." I struggle, searching for the right word, but nothing is right. *Obnoxious? Ridiculous? Flirty?* Finally I give up. "I just think that one of us should be there, too. Me or Pru. We're your best friends."

"I would love that," says Ari, "but I know this zoo transfer is a really big deal for the center, and you usually work on Sundays, and—"

"Dad will cover for me. You know he'll be ecstatic when he hears about this. It's fine."

Ari goes still. "Do you *want* to come?"

"Of course I do!"

She looks briefly surprised, but then flashes a grateful smile.

"I do, too," moans Pru. "I'm so bummed to miss this!"

"I'll record the whole thing," I tell her. "I promise."

"What about Maya?" starts Ari, picking at lint on her pajama pants. "Do you want to invite her to come with us? You, me, Ezra, and Maya?" She inhales sharply. "Could be fun. Right?"

The question hangs between us. When she says it that way, it seems obvious. The four of us. Ezra, because he's good to have on hand if a car breaks down. Maya, because I want to spend more time with her. And I can be there to support Ari.

It'll be a win-win.

But it also sounds an awful lot like a double date.

And that's the part that has my stomach roiling as I smile and say, "Yeah. That sounds perfect. I'll ask her at D&D tonight."

Chapter Twenty-Five

The week passes quickly. I sleep in Sunday morning, exhausted from a night of questing that ran way longer than they usually do, but only because we were having so much fun that every time I suggested we wrap it up, the group insisted that we keep going—Maya the loudest of all.

"We're so close to finding this temple!" she shouted, as the clock ticked past eleven. "We can't stop now!"

"We might have to stop now," I said. "If we finish the adventure tonight, what are we going to do next Saturday?"

To which she shot me an unimpressed look. "You're the Dungeon Master. You'll figure something out."

But when I reminded her about the festival, even she had to concede that we'd better call it a night.

"There you are," says Dad as I make my way to the kitchen, already dressed. "I was about to send search and rescue out for you."

I smile faintly and dig around in the cupboards, before pulling out a box of cereal. Mom is reading a book at the table, a half-eaten bagel beside her. The TV is on in the living room, playing one of Ellie's favorite cartoons.

"Isn't Ari supposed to be here soon?" Dad asks, pouring himself a cup of coffee from a nearly empty pot.

"Ten," I say through a yawn. Bowl. Spoon. Milk. My cereal routine is pretty automated at this point.

"Ten o'clock," says Dad, tsking to himself. "Your sister was out of here before six."

I frown. "Six? That's early even for—" I pause, remembering. "Right. Luna and Lennon are going to the zoo today."

"You're going to have so much fun at the festival," says Mom, bookmarking her pages with an old tattered drawing that Ellie made of a unicorn. "You know, your dad and I went on a date to Condor once, years ago. How are things going with Maya?"

"Good," I say quickly. "Really good."

Which is true. I no longer feel that panicky, nauseous feeling every time I see her, which definitely seems like a step in the right direction.

On the other hand, over the last week it's sort of felt like we've hit some sort of stagnation in our . . . whatever we are. Maya and I don't hold hands, or even really talk to each other much at school. I still sit at her table during lunch, but I don't say a whole lot, just let the conversation carry on around me, feeling as much like an outsider as ever.

There have been times when I've looked over at Matt and César and Russell and wondered what they were laughing about, feeling a sharp pang of envy.

All that aside, though, Maya was thrilled when I invited her to the music festival. And yeah, maybe that was more because she wanted to get out of helping her parents with a garage sale they were planning, and also because she likes music festivals and is excited to see Ari perform, and maybe it had virtually nothing to do with . . . you know. Going with *me*.

But still. She was *thrilled*.

Mom smiles. "Maybe one of these days you can invite her over for a family dinner, rather than just squirreling her away in the basement and keeping her all to yourself."

"You make me sound like a serial killer."

Dad barks a laugh. "I had that same thought!"

Mom sighs. "I didn't mean it that way. But we would like to get to know her."

"Sure," I say. I'm debating whether or not I should tell them that Maya and I aren't really *serious* yet, when Mom glances out the window. "Ari's here."

186

I follow her gaze out the kitchen window as Ari's turquoise Ford Falcon pulls up to the curb, Ezra already in the passenger seat.

I finish my cereal and put the bowl in the dishwasher just as Ari is coming into the house, not bothering to knock. Ezra is right behind her, his grin like a ray of freaking sunshine.

"Morning, Barnett family!" he bellows.

"Are you ready?" says Ari, sounding a little breathless. "Are we still picking up Maya?"

"Yeah," I say. "Let me grab my stuff."

"You're not planning on doing homework, are you?" says Ezra, eyeing my backpack. "This is a road trip, dude. There is no homework on road trips."

"Just bringing my sketchbook in case we have time to kill."

"You overachievers are so cute." Ezra shakes his head. "When you get bored, you want to, like, create something. Do something productive. Work on your art." He clicks his tongue. "The only adequate response to boredom is well-intentioned, poorly executed mischief that may or may not land you in jail."

I've been around Ezra enough to know that this is *probably* just a joke, but I still ask, "Have you ever been in jail?"

"Not yet," he preens. "But I'm young and ambitious."

"Well, that's promising," says Mom, giving Ari a hug. "Good luck at the festival, sweetheart. We're rooting for you."

"Thanks," says Ari with an anxious smile. "I'm trying not to think too much about it."

"Just try to have a good time today. And be careful driving," says Mom, giving me a hug, too.

"*I* won't be driving," I say. I'm intimidated as hell by manual transmissions. Ari has offered to teach both me and Pru since we got our licenses, even though she herself isn't, like, the greatest at it. She still kills the engine on a regular basis and is terrified of going up hills.

"I'm telling *all* of you to be careful," Mom says. "Call us if you need anything."

She pulls away, then Ezra surprises her by going in for a hug, too. Mom complies, even though I think she's only met Ezra one other time, and I can tell she hasn't made up her mind about him yet. Makes two of us, I guess.

We head out to the car, and I toss my bag onto the back seat. I glance into the back of the wagon and see Ari's guitar case and a small metal toolbox, which I assume is Ezra's.

We wave to my parents on the porch. Ari turns the engine and pops the clutch. The second we pull away from the curb, Ezra raises his arms over his head and whoops. "*Road trip!*"

We pick up Maya and hear a lot of the same admonishments from her parents as we heard from mine. But within ten minutes of pulling out of her driveway, we're on the freeway, music blasting from Ari's Bluetooth speaker as Ezra scrolls through the music on her phone. "These are some bizarre playlists," he says, feet kicked up on the dashboard. "Taylor Swift, Aretha Franklin, Blondie, and . . . Larkin Poe?"

"They're a sister singer/songwriter duo," says Ari. "They're amazing. You must be looking at my girl power sing-along playlist."

"Yeah, because I didn't recognize any of the artists on your *Dreary Days* playlist." He scrolls to a different screen. "Julieta Venegas, Eurielle, Taska Black, Metaxas, Ximena Sari . . . er . . ."

"Sariñana," says Ari.

"Ximena Sariñana," says Ezra, looking mildly impressed. "Her name is almost as great as yours. Also, here's a song by . . . *elbow*? That can't be real a real band."

"It is. Just pick something and play it," says Ari.

Ezra turns to her. "Do you just, like, scour Spotify for the most obscure tunes, or what?"

"Just because a musician isn't well-known in the States doesn't make them obscure," says Ari. "And some of the singers on that playlist have been my biggest inspirations. Besides, we work in a record store. We're always being introduced to new music."

It's thoughtful of her to include me in that statement, given that when I'm working I pretty much just rotate between the same three Led Zeppelin albums. (Robert Plant was a big Tolkien fan, and there are a bunch of *Lord of the Rings* references in his lyrics. I like what I like.) Although once someone sold us the soundtrack to the original Super Mario Bros. game, and I played it for six hours straight until my dad put it out on the sale rack for twenty-five cents and I never saw it again.

"Oh yeah, this is the one," says Ezra.

Ari meets my eye in the rearview mirror, and I can tell she's wondering if she should be scared—the answer is yes. Whenever Ezra is excited about something, we should all be scared.

She grins, as if she's read my mind.

A horn section blares over the speaker, followed by Sadashiv singing "One for My Baby (And One More for the Road)."

Maya laughs. "EZ! Are you a Sadashiv fan?"

"Um, who *isn't*?" he says, turning to face us from the front. "I was devastated when Jude took you to that concert instead of me. *Devastated*."

"Hold on," I say. "Is this song on one of Ari's playlists?"

"Of course," says Ari. "There's a reason he sings the old standards, you know. Something about them is universal—themes that relate to us even eighty years after they were written. I figure I can learn something from that."

Ezra scoffs. "Songwriting genius, blah blah blah. You know you just like his velvety-smooth voice. That's some sexy shit, right there." He makes a purring noise in his throat.

"He isn't wrong," says Maya.

Ari shrugs, then puts on her blinker to switch lanes. "He *does* have a nice voice."

"And hair," Maya adds. "You should have seen him up close and personal. It's hard to believe he's even real."

"Now you're just rubbing it in," says Ezra.

"Just imagine," I say, staring out the window at the Pacific Ocean, blue and shimmering. "Someday a group of teens could be heading off to a music festival, scrolling through their playlists, and they'll put on 'Downpour' by Araceli Escalante."

Ari meets my gaze in the mirror again. "I only imagine it about ten thousand times a day."

"Me too," says Ezra. "My song coming up on the radio, T. Swift singing it like she's basically serenading me."

"T. Swift?" I ask.

"I mean, Ariana Grande would work, too. I'm not picky."

"Wait, wait, wait," says Maya, leaning forward so far that the aftermarket seat belt locks up on her, "what do you mean *your* song?"

"Didn't you know?" Ezra gestures at himself with both hands. "I am the inspiration behind the tune."

A coldness trickles down my spine, even as Ari turns to him, mouth agape. "What? No you're not!"

She says it . . . but she's blushing.

I look back out the window.

This is just Ezra, being his ridiculous, charmingly self-centered self. Ari doesn't . . . It isn't like they . . .

I can't manage to finish the thought. The idea of it is too weird. Ari and Ezra? I mean, he flirts with her all the time, sure, but he would also flirt with a palm tree if it gave him the time of day.

"It's just a song," says Ari. "It's not inspired by anyone."

Ezra slaps a hand to his chest like he's been struck with an arrow. "You destroy me, Escalante. Don't ruin this fantasy for me."

"Not every song has to be about something . . . or someone," she says.

"Your protestations speak volumes," counters Ezra.

Ari scowls. I can tell she wants to argue more, but what's the point? She just refocuses on the road, her expression shuttered, a blush on her cheeks. And I can't help thinking that Ezra is right.

Her protestations do speak volumes.

But what exactly is she protesting?

Chapter Twenty-Six

The drive to the festival consists of:

A drive-through espresso stand for blended, caffeine-laden milkshakes.

Twisty, scenic roads that alternate between breathtaking views of the ocean followed by towering pine trees.

One stop at a gas station to fill up the tank and purchase enough snacks to feed a small band of barbarians.

One Sasquatch sighting.

A whole lot of inane comments from Ezra.

Some theories from Maya on what the Temple of Lundyn Toune will hold for her and the gang, and the observation—twice—that the way Noah plays their halfling rogue is absolutely hilarious.

Reviewing the musician lineup for the festival we're headed to, since no one other than Ari has bothered to check it yet. I recognize two performers: Araceli Escalante, and . . . the Beach Boys! Until it turns out to actually be a Beach Boys tribute band, not, like, the actual Beach Boys. But Maya and Ari are excited to catch a number of the shows, while Ezra moans that he missed some grunge band that played on Friday.

(Okay, I made up the Sasquatch thing.)

Ari grows increasingly tense the closer we get to our destination. I can tell because when Ezra offers to drive for the millionth time, Ari finally relents, pulling over to the side of the road and releasing her white-knuckled grip on the steering wheel. It's early afternoon once we arrive at the festival and pay twenty dollars to park in the biggest field I've ever seen. Even from the far reaches of the parking lot we can hear the distant sounds of music. Ari grabs her guitar, and we head toward the entry gates.

The festival is an explosion of stimuli as we scan our tickets and receive a festival map and schedule. Crowds of people mill about. The wafting aromas of fried foods come at us from every direction. And we are inundated with music—music booming from distant stages where the headliners are playing, a guy playing a guitar and harmonica right at the entrance, and hip-hop thumping from a huge speaker not far off, where a small crowd is watching a group of break-dancers.

"I'm going to find the information booth," says Ari, scanning the map, "and make sure I know where I need to be and when."

"We'll come with you," I say.

Ari smiles gratefully but shakes her head. "Go enjoy the festival. Maybe we can meet back up for that Latinx pop band? That's . . ." She scans the schedule. "On the Albatross Stage in an hour."

"Perfect," says Maya, grabbing my arm. "Let's go walk around. Check out these booths."

"I'll stick with Escalante," says Ezra. "In case the talent needs some muscle." He flexes his bicep.

Ari rolls her eyes but doesn't argue, and together they wander off, getting quickly lost in the throng.

"Come on," says Maya, pulling me in the opposite direction before I've had a second to digest the twist of disappointment in my stomach.

"Shouldn't we stick together?"

Maya gives me an indecipherable look. "They'll be fine. What do you want to do?"

Stick together, I think. But instead I shrug. "Whatever."

We wander through a lane of canvas-sided tents hawking everything from jewelry to wind chimes to paintings of famous bands and musicians. We pass booths offering airbrushed tattoos and face painting and actual piercings. (Maya jokes that I'd look pretty hot with my ear pierced. At least, I think she's joking?) We pass an eating area where people are scattered around a bunch of tables, listening to a three-piece band on a small stage. Then an art exhibit of acoustic guitars decorated to look like famous paintings—*Starry Night*, *The Scream*, Andy Warhol's soup cans. We pass a dance troupe defying the laws of gravity, while onlookers enjoy candied nuts and tiny doughnuts from a nearby vendor.

I'm surprised when we stumble onto an entire area designated for kids, with toy instruments to bang on, tables to make arts and crafts, and even a stage for performing karaoke, on which a girl not much older than Ellie is belting out Katy Perry's "Firework."

"I should have brought my sisters," I say.

"Maybe next year?" says Maya, nudging me with her shoulder.

"Maybe." I consider, before adding, "Ari will probably be on the main stage by then."

"I wouldn't doubt it." We turn and start heading back into the main thoroughfare. "Do you like having lots of siblings?"

I think for a moment. "I don't dislike it. It can be weird, being the only guy. I mean, there's my dad, but he spends a lot of time at the store. And it's like, Pru's technically the oldest by seventeen minutes, but she doesn't seem as concerned with the whole 'older sibling' thing as I am. I want to be a good role model, and be there for them when they need me. I don't think Pru feels it the same way I do."

Maya smiles. "I bet you're a really good big brother."

I'm not great with compliments, so I don't say anything.

"I'm an only child, so I always wondered what it would be like. I really wanted a sister when I was little."

I think about what my parents said, about how I should invite Maya over sometime, for something other than D&D. She could hang out, get to know my sisters, play Go Fish with Ellie and make collages with Penny until her fingers stick together from all the glue.

But before I can think of how to word such an invitation, Maya gasps delightedly at a display of jewelry in the next booth. She heads to check it out, oohing over spiraling silver earrings and pendants cut from a variety of stones.

While I wait for her, I scan the nearby booths. There are handmade percussion instruments and racks of bohemian clothing and a super creepy cat that's staring right at me and light-up wands and bubble guns and—

I do a double take.

Yep. There's a cat sitting on a round table covered with a silky purple cloth. The cat has green eyes and is as black as a displacer beast, and it is definitely staring right at me.

Creepy.

I'm so unsettled by the cat's unblinking stare that it takes me a second to notice the middle-aged woman sitting at the table, too, beckoning to me with waving fingers.

I tense and look around. But no, it's clearly me she's looking at.

Swallowing, I make my way across the path. The woman doesn't *look* like a fortune teller. At least she doesn't look like the fortune teller at the Renaissance Faire, who was decked out in more scarves and costume jewelry than my grandma's vanity. *This* woman is wearing jeans and a flowy blue shirt, her straw-colored hair trying to escape from a messy bun on top of her head.

"Young man, your aura is very divided," she says, by way of greeting. It's the sort of statement one of my NPCs would say when the adventurers stumble onto a surprise caravan on the road, and normally I would laugh to hear it spoken with such gravity. Except the woman looks legitimately concerned, and I bite my tongue.

"Thanks?" I say. "But I don't really want a . . ." I glance at the sandwich board beside her, listing palm readings, tarot readings, chakra balancing, and an assortment of crystals for sale. "Anything," I finish.

She smiles, apparently unbothered. "We don't always want what we need," she says, "which is why I'm going to give you some advice."

"Um . . ." My eyes go to the sandwich board again, and the prices that seem a little astronomical.

"Free of charge," she says, as if . . . you know, she can read my mind. *Weird.* She reaches out and scratches the cat's neck. It immediately starts purring, leaning into her pets. "Cosmo likes you, and he's worried."

I don't want to be disrespectful, but I can't help my eyebrow twitching up with skepticism. The *cat* is worried about me? "That's . . . nice," I say, starting to think about how I can extricate myself from this conversation as quickly as possible. "But Cosmo doesn't need to worry. I'm good. Great, actually. I'm probably the luckiest guy you'll meet all day."

I don't mean for it to sound sarcastic, but it comes out that way, and I wince.

The woman gives me another soft, close-lipped smile. "Are you familiar with the Taoist parable of the Farmer and his Horse?"

Oh boy.

"No?" I say, giving a quick glance around. *Maya? Come rescue me?*

"Don't worry," the woman says, a teasing glint in her eye. "I promise to make this quick." She straightens in her chair, and I curse the upbringing that taught me how unforgivably rude it is to walk away when someone is talking to you. "There was once a farmer who owned a beautiful horse," she begins. Yikes. Should I sit down for this? "Whenever his neighbors passed, they would say, 'You are so lucky to have such a fine horse!' To which the farmer would shrug and reply merely, *Perhaps*. Then one day, the farmer forgot to latch his gate, and the horse ran off. 'What terrible luck,' said his neighbors, to which the farmer replied, *Perhaps*. A few days later, the horse returned, along with a half dozen wild horses it had befriended. Again the neighbors cried, 'Now you are rich! You are so lucky!' But the farmer said only, *Perhaps*."

I frown, sensing a pattern. But more than that, wondering why she's telling me this.

"A week passed, and while the farmer's son was breaking in one of the wild horses, he fell off and broke his leg. 'Ah! What horrible luck,' exclaimed the neighbors, but yet again the farmer only shrugged and said, *Perhaps*. The very next day, soldiers passed through their small village, demanding that all able-bodied young men come to fight in the war, but the farmer's son, with his broken leg, was spared. 'You are so lucky!' the neighbors said, but once again, the farmer merely replied, *Perhaps*."

The woman finishes and starts to pet her cat again.

"Wow. That was great," I say, once it seems clear that she's finished.

"You understand?"

I stare at her. "Yeah. Totally."

She stares back at me.

"Not really," I admit.

Her smile warms. The cat purrs louder and flops onto its side. "You will."

The truth is, I *do* get the concept behind the parable—that not everything is as it seems, and how we respond to a situation is more important than the situation itself, or . . . something like that. But I'm not sure why she's telling *me*. I wonder if she can really see something in my aura. If she can tell that I've been touched by uncanny good fortune. If she can see that I'm in possession of magic.

No lost horses or broken legs here.

"There you are!" Maya grabs my arm. "Look, I found this." She holds up her hand to show a sterling silver ring that depicts a small dragon wrapped around a green egg-shaped stone.

"Cool," I say. "I like it."

Maya glances at the woman, then around at the booth. "Oh, I love tarot readings! But . . . we have to meet Ari and EZ."

The woman inclines her head to us, her smile never fading. "Enjoy the festival."

I wave awkwardly as Maya and I turn away. Even though a part of me is relieved to escape the woman's knowing gaze and eerie cat, there are questions burbling up in my thoughts that I wouldn't mind asking her. Why was this good luck given to me? What does it all mean? Is Ari going to win the contest? Is my good luck going to last for the rest of my life? Is Maya "the One," or am I just fooling myself, about everything?

Something tells me she wouldn't have given me any straight answers, even if I did have the guts to ask. But maybe I don't need psychic guidance. Maybe all the answers are right in front of me, and have been right in front of me all along, and I just need to stop doubting myself and doubting the magic and just trust, for once, that everything really is going to work out how it's meant to.

"Jude? What's wrong?"

I pause and look at Maya. She's holding my hand, and I hadn't even noticed. Now, noticing, I feel the warmth of her palm. The softness of her skin.

Her brow furrows. "What did that fortune teller say to you?"

"Something about . . . luck," I stammer.

She laughs, like she should have guessed. "Well, that makes sense. You are *abnormally* lucky."

"You've noticed?

"Uh, *yeah*. The concert tickets? The coin flips? That random bet on Mrs. Jenkins? It's hard not to notice. What do you have, a four-leaf clover stashed away somewhere?" She jokingly pats the pocket on the chest of my shirt, and my heart leaps at the touch.

No . . . It *should* leap at the touch.

Which, I guess, is not exactly the same thing.

"Maya," I say, and something in my tone stops her. Her expression goes serious. She's still so close. "I've liked you for a really long time."

Even as I say it, cold sweat prickles at the back of my neck.

Maya's lips form a small, surprised circle, even though I don't think this is a big revelation to her. I've always known that I wasn't any good at hiding my crush—from her or anyone else. I'd just never planned to *act* on it, until that day when I won the radio contest, and the power of the dice gave me the courage to finally do something about my feelings.

"I have been lucky lately. But not because of any of those things you've mentioned. I've been lucky because I'm finally getting to know *you*. And you're even more amazing than I always thought."

Music swirls around us, but I hardly hear any of it. All I see is Maya. All I feel is the erratic pounding of my heart.

Maya's look of surprise turns into a small smile, and in that moment she looks almost bashful. She peers at me through her eyelashes, then seems to reach a decision. She tilts her face up toward mine.

I glance at her lips.

I take in a breath.

And I kiss her.

Chapter Twenty-Seven

Fireworks.

Trumpets.

Shooting stars.

A symphonic crescendo.

The rest of the world fading away until there's only us, alone at its center.

Okay—clearly, Hollywood has given us some pretty hefty expectations of what kisses are supposed to be like. And it's not that I had *high* expectations. It's not like I thought the world would stop turning on its axis. It's not like I thought my lips would touch Maya's and a Level 8 Sunburst spell would explode around us or anything like that.

But if my expectations were low . . .

No, not low.

If my expectations were *realistic* . . .

Why do I feel so disappointed?

I break the kiss and pull away, already trying to mask the uncertainty roiling inside me.

Maya's eyelids flicker open. We hold each other's gaze for a second, but I can't read her.

Then a tiny wrinkle forms between Maya's eyebrows. She opens her mouth, looking like she has bad news. Terrible news. Looking like she is about to break my heart.

"We should probably hurry," I say. "They'll wonder where we are."

Maya hesitates. Regret and uncertainty.

Then she starts to smile. A knowing, polite smile.

"Yeah. Let's go."

We start to make our way back through the festival and . . . crap, crap, crap. Can we rewind? Pretend that never happened? Can I get a do-over? But what good would that do me when I have absolutely no idea what just went wrong? We had music. We had the aroma of cinnamon and sugar. We had *me* and *her* and six years of yearning . . .

Maybe I'm overreacting.

I'm definitely overreacting.

It's not like it was *bad*.

It wasn't bad. I don't think.

Was it bad? Am I a bad kisser? These things take practice, right? There are bound to be some road bumps. Not knowing which way to tilt your head, or what to do when your noses smash together, and yeah, in my nervousness, I maybe moved a little too fast, and I should take my time and go slower, and next time I will go slower, and . . .

Is there going to be a next time?

Yep, I'm definitely overthinking this. For all I know, Maya thinks it was a perfectly sufficient first kiss.

But maybe—whispers a small and very annoying voice—*maybe it isn't just about what Maya thinks.* Maybe the bigger problem is that I didn't feel what I thought I would feel. What I think I should have felt.

What is wrong with me?

The fortune teller's words come back to me, an unhelpful whisper. *Your aura is very divided.* What does that even mean?

"There," says Maya, pointing. I hadn't realized we'd made it to the Albatross Stage until I spy Ezra standing near a curtained-off section to the side of the crowd, holding Ari's guitar case. The stage is crowded with the Latinx group, which boasts a full horn section and a bunch of percussion instruments I don't even know the name of. The crowd all around us is dancing to the high-energy music.

"Ezra, hey," I say, glancing around. "Where's Ari?"

200

"Getting changed." He juts a thumb toward the curtains, and as if on cue, the fabric shifts and Ari emerges. She's changed out of the denim shorts and Ventures Vinyl tee she was wearing on the drive and into a long white dress that is lacy and flowy and makes her look like a bohemian druid gifted with some celestial power.

"Holy smokes, Escalante," says Ezra. "Bringing the heat!"

"You look beautiful," adds Maya, every bit as genuine, if not quite as loud.

"Thanks," says Ari, cheeks tinged pink. "Our performances are being filmed today, so . . ." Her gaze alights briefly on me, and I know I should say something. A compliment. Something simple, but honest. *You look nice.* That'd be easy enough.

She does look nice.

Superlatively nice.

But for some reason, my tongue is glued to the roof of my mouth, and she looks away before I can unstick it.

"This band is so good," says Maya, having to yell a little when the music launches into a particularly loud horn solo.

We find a place to sit on the grass. Ezra takes off his shirt and lays it down so Ari can sit without getting grass stains on her white dress, which is simultaneously chivalrous and a very obvious excuse for him to go shirtless for a while, and it takes all my willpower not to roll my eyes at the gesture.

It isn't long before Maya hops back to her feet. "I have to dance to this," she says, reaching a hand toward me. "Jude?"

I recoil. Which is a perfectly acceptable reaction to someone asking you to dance in public.

She gives me a look. "Oh, come on. Please?"

"I'll dance," says Ezra.

Maya hesitates, giving me another chance. But then she shrugs. "Okay!"

They head off, making their way toward the stage where hundreds of people have gathered into a turbulent, jostling mess of bodies and limbs and sweat. A lot of sweat.

"Are you having fun?" Ari asks.

I turn to her. "Yeah. This has been great," I say. Which isn't a *lie*.

I consider telling her about the weird interaction with the fortune teller and Cosmo the Cat, but for some reason, I hold my tongue.

Your aura is very divided.

Instead I ask, "Have you caught any other bands?"

"We sat in on a rock group on one of the smaller stages," she says, "but just caught the end of their show. They were good, but this is next level. You can feel the influence of nueva canción in their music, with the defiant lyrics, and those woodwinds!" The lyrics are all in Spanish, so after a second, Ari scoots closer to me and goes on. "This song is all about empowerment and love and embracing the beauty of Latin culture. Oh, and look!" She points at the stage, her eyes shining. "That girl on the right, playing what looks like a lute? It's actually a charango! I've never seen one in person before."

I grin at her. "You're nervous."

Ari's face crumples. Then she laughs. "*Terrified.*"

I chuckle and scoot closer still so we don't have to yell quite so loud. "Yeah. You get extra music theory-ish when you're nervous about performing. Of course, I would rather go swimming with sharks than get up and perform on a stage like that. It's really impressive that you're here, Ari. And I know you're going to do great."

She pulls her knees into her chest. "Thanks, Jude." She smiles at me, though there's something a little sad lingering behind her eyes. "I'm glad you're here."

"I wouldn't miss it. I know Pru is really sorry she couldn't come."

She nods. "I know."

"So . . . ," I say, tilting my head to one side, "would Araceli the Magnificent be proficient in charango playing?"

Ari dreamily clasps her hands under her chin. "She would be a charango master!"

The band finishes their set, and we cheer with the rest of the crowd as they take their bows. A lot of the audience disperses, heading off for food or to check out what's happening on the other stages around the festival. But a lot of people remain, too. Lounging on their blankets and beach towels, pulling drinks out of coolers. Maya and Ezra return, grinning and breathless. Maya sinks down onto the grass beside me, which is when I notice how close Ari and I have gotten in their absence. Ezra sits cross-legged on Ari's other side and starts listing all the food vendors he saw earlier and trying to decide what he's going to eat later.

It takes a while for the stagehands to clear off the slew of instruments, drum kits, microphones, and amps, getting ready for the contest finalists.

"Hey, Escalante, check it." Ezra holds up a piece of grass. No—not grass. A shamrock. A four-leaf clover. "Found it for you." He winks.

I gawk at the clover as it passes from Ezra's fingers to Ari's, feeling strangely . . . betrayed. Obviously, if any of us were going to find a four-leaf clover and give it to Ari as a special gift, it should have been *me*.

"Wow," says Ari, twirling the clover between her fingers. "I haven't found one of these since I was a kid."

"We have a big patch of clover in our backyard," says Maya. "You can find a ton of four-leafers. I think it must be a genetic mutation or something."

"So they're not really that rare," I say, and it comes off sounding more bitter than I'd intended.

Ezra gives me a look, like I've offered a challenge, then whips out his phone. After a second, he holds up the screen. "Maya's mystical clover patch aside, this says they are about one out of every five thousand clovers. Seems pretty rare to me."

I frown. Again . . . why didn't *I* find it?

"Thank you, EZ." Ari opens up the case of her guitar and tucks the clover inside. "I'll take all the luck I can get today."

"As a proud Irishman, I am pretty much the world's leading expert on all things luck." He hesitates before adding, "And also a ridiculous amount of superstition."

Ari laughs. "You might have four-leaf clovers, but I bet we Mexicans have more superstition than you do. We are steeped in it."

"That sounds like a challenge." Ezra clears his throat before proclaiming earnestly, "Did you know it is considered unlucky to"—he ticks off on his fingers—"dream about nuns, kill a spider, kill a hedgehog, wear gray to a wedding, or cross the path of a feisty redhead?" He lowers his voice, adding, "A woman, that is. Us ginger men are fine. Gotta love a little sexism in your superstitions. *Oh!* And also, you can't give anything away on Mary Day."

Maya frowns. "What's Mary Day?"

"No idea. Something to do with Mother Mary? I think it's in August? But I get around that one by just never giving anything away."

"You literally just gave away a four-leaf clover," I point out.

"Crap. Didn't think of that. Anyway . . . it's not Mary Day. I'm pretty sure." He looks at Ari. "So what do you got?"

She considers. "Let's see. It's unlucky to sweep dirt out of your front door. Or decorate with seashells. Or travel on a Tuesday. And you should never step on a grave . . ."

Ezra rolls his eyes. "That's unlucky everywhere."

"Oh! You're also not supposed to watch a dog . . . um . . . do its business." Her cheeks go scarlet. "It will give you pimples."

We all stare at her, and when it's clear she's serious, we burst into laughter.

"Classic," says Ezra. "That explains some things."

"How about black cats?" I ask, thinking of the creepy feline in the fortune teller's tent. "That's definitely unlucky, right?"

Ari nods her head. "Very."

"Wrong," says EZ. "They're lucky to us."

I draw back, surprised. "Really?"

"Oh yeah. Be good to the cats, man. They've got sorcerer's powers for sure, and they can use them for good or evil. But if you're good to them, they'll be good to you."

I can't tell if he's joking. I also can't tell if EZ is trying to flirt with Ari, or if she's trying to flirt with him back, and I'm weirdly relieved when a short, curvy woman thumps the microphone, pulling our attention back to the stage.

"Hello, everyone! Are we having a great time at the Condor Music Festival?"

The crowd cheers. Though there's significantly fewer people than there were for the last group, it's still a good-size audience. And the setting couldn't be more beautiful. The rolling grassy hill, the horizon of towering pine trees, the approaching dusk giving an orange tinge to the festival at our backs.

Suddenly, my fingers twitch in a way that hasn't happened in a week or more.

I should draw this.

I've felt pretty uninspired since my lame attempts to sketch something new that would be worth submitting to the *Dungeon*. It might be nice to sketch out a scene that has nothing to do with fantasy or fandom for once. Something low-pressure.

Onstage, the woman is explaining the songwriting competition and how entrants from all over the country submitted music in nine different musical genres. I pull the sketchbook and pencil from my backpack while she goes on about their esteemed panel of judges, all professionals in the industry, and the harrowing task they were given to narrow the entries down to just ten finalists.

I draw the stage first. The scaffolding on either side, the backdrop, the lights, slowly working my way out to include the trees in the background, the audience out front with their coolers and blankets.

"And what a treat we have for you today," says the host. "Of our ten finalists, *seven* were able to join us here at the festival, and they are going to be performing their songs for us live! What an amazing opportunity to hear some up-and-coming talent!"

The crowd applauds.

"Before we get to the live performances, we're going to play the videos from the three finalists who could not join us in person tonight."

A screen behind her lights up with a projected video.

A boy around our age sits at a grand piano. He introduces himself and his song, then begins to play.

The song is good. *Really* good, actually. The lyrics all about chasing a dream that seems just out of reach.

Next is a college-aged woman with a soulful voice. Her song is poetic and profound and has something to do with sailors and gold and taking a chance and . . . Honestly, I don't really get it, but it sounds cool.

Lastly, an older man with a ukulele sings an achingly sad love-lost song about someone named Georgine.

And then it's time for the live performances.

I feel Ari inhale sharply beside me as the woman returns to the microphone. I lean toward her and whisper, "Do you know what order you'll be performing in?"

"I'm fifth," she whispers back.

Fifth. It seems like forever to wait, but the performances go quickly. A husband and wife performing a song they co-wrote. Then a boy who can't be much older than Penny, singing and playing the piano. Then two women—cousins, I think—one on guitar, one singing. They're all really good, and even though I'm enormously biased in favor of Ari, I can admit that she has some real competition today.

It's only the fourth performer who leaves me scratching my head a little. She's in her early twenties and takes the stage with exuberant energy, before proceeding to sing about . . . seltzer water? Am I mishearing this? I frown skeptically as the song goes into the first chorus—*oh so sparkly, with no calories* . . .

I can't help making a face. Out of how many hundreds of entries, *this* was a finalist? Am I missing a deeper meaning here? I sneak a glance around at the rest of the audience, surreptitiously as I can, and feel justified to see that lots of people look befuddled.

She'll be an easy act to follow, at least.

As she's finishing the song, Ari reaches for my hand. I jolt and turn to her, but she's watching the stage with wide eyes, chewing on her lower lip.

I turn my palm up and lace our fingers together, giving her hand a squeeze. "You've got this," I say. "You're here for a reason."

"What reason is that?" she says, her voice barely above a squeak.

"Because the world needs the music of Araceli Escalante."

She swallows and looks at me, and—my heart lurches so quickly I almost choke on it.

I understand why she doesn't want to get her hopes up, but this isn't some ludicrous fantasy. She could really do this. Sell her songs so the world can love and enjoy them. Ari has more than earned the opportunity to stand on that stage. She's talented, obviously. But she also works tirelessly to become better, every day. She writes a song and then agonizes over every word and every note, always pushing herself to be better, to keep improving. And she puts so much emotion into her writing. So much passion. So much of *herself*.

"I didn't want to hurt EZ's feelings earlier," Ari says, leaning closer so only I can hear her, and even that is difficult over the music coming from the giant speakers, "but you're my actual good luck charm."

I stare at her. "What?"

She smiles shyly and releases my hand. Onstage, the girl takes her bow as the audience applauds politely. Ari stands and grabs her guitar.

"Break a leg!" calls Maya, and I jump at the sound of her voice. For a second, I'd forgotten she was there.

Ari heads toward the stage, just as the emcee calls, "Next up, please welcome—Araceli Escalante!"

Maya and Ezra both scream so loud they'll probably be hoarse later, but all I can do is clap. My head is spinning like I've just downed a whole jug of Bork's signature mead.

I grab my pencil again and twirl it aimlessly between my fingers, because my palms are feeling sweaty, and there's always been something comforting about holding a pencil in my fingers. I don't draw, though. I keep my focus on Ari as she ascends the steps and makes her way to the center of the stage.

"Thank you," she says, sitting down on the stool they offered her and settling the guitar across her lap. "It's an enormous honor to be here today. This song is called 'Downpour.'"

She plays the intro that's as familiar to me now as any song we play at the store, and when she starts to sing, I'm struck by the same mixture of emotions that flurried through me the first time I heard it. *Every* time I've heard it.

There's pining in her voice, honesty in her words. And there's Ari, glowing beneath the setting sun, looking so beautiful.

Something stirs inside me. Something so strong I can't deny it, even though I know I've felt it before and managed to deny it just fine. This time, it's inescapable. Ari, who I so badly want to see win this contest. Whose song is incredible. Who, herself, is *incredible*.

Who is . . . my friend.

And definitely not the girl I kissed not even an hour ago.

Mother of Mordor, what is wrong with me?

When Ari's song is over, I feel somehow both jittery and numb as I clap along with the rest of the audience. I distantly hear hollers from the crowd, whistles of appreciation.

Ari returns to our spot on the grass, trembling with adrenaline. Maya gives her a hug. Ezra gives her a double high five—and then also pulls her in for a hug. It would be weird, wouldn't it, for me to just sit here and not make eye contact and not say anything? Even though that feels safer in the moment. I have the sensation of teetering on a precipice that could fall out from under me at any second, but I also stand. I also hold out my arms and smile and try not to breathe as Ari wraps her arms around my waist and accepts the embrace like it's a perfectly normal friend thing to do.

"You were great," I whisper into her hair.

My insides are a thundercloud as I release her and drop back down to the blanket, pulling my sketchbook closer like a shield.

I barely hear the last two performers.

Finally the emcee returns, clutching a large envelope like she's giving an award at the Grammys. The screen at the back of the stage changes to show a projected computer screen with three livestreamed videos—the three songwriters who couldn't come in person. They're all grinning. They all look anxious and scared and hopeful, just like Ari.

"It is truly my honor to announce this year's winners for the Condor Music Festival songwriting competition," says the host. "As a reminder, our grand prize winner today will receive five thousand dollars plus three days at a recording studio with a top producer to record their album!"

My hand twitches toward Ari, when from the corner of my eye I see Ezra moving closer to her. Putting his arm around her shoulders.

My hand twitches back to my own lap.

The woman opens the flap of the envelope and pulls out a card. "Our third place winner is . . . Trevor and Sierra Greenfield!"

The husband-and-wife duo. They take the stage, beaming. The woman hands them a tiny guitar statue, and they take a step back, hugging each other.

"In second place . . . Araceli Escalante!"

My heart lifts. Second place!

Then plummets. Second place?

Ari scrambles to her feet, beaming as she makes her way to the stage. Her hands are clasped over her mouth, and if she harbors even the tiniest bit of disappointment that it isn't first place, it's impossible to tell.

She accepts her guitar statue and steps back alongside the third-place winners. Then she finds us in the crowd and bounces excitedly on her toes, holding up the award statue. "Second place!" she mouths.

The three of us all give her thumbs-up, but then Maya says, "I liked hers the best. I really thought she was going to win."

The part of me that dislikes any sort of conflict rises automatically to the defense of the judges. Music is subjective, after all. Different people, different tastes. There was a lot of talent up on that stage.

And yet . . . I really thought she would win, too.

209

On the stage, the emcee asks for a drumroll, and all around us, people thump their hands against their thighs. "And our grand prize winner is . . . Ginger Sweet!"

A girl screams and jumps to her feet right in front of the stage.

My brow tightens.

The seltzer water girl?

"Hold on," whispers Ezra, "wasn't she the one that sang that god-awful love song to LaCroix? That song was the worst."

Maya and I don't respond, but a quick glance tells me that Maya is equally bewildered. Of the ten finalists, this girl was the last that I would have picked to win. And I might just be imagining it, but it seems like some of the cheers subside into confusion as the girl runs onto the stage to accept her award.

The emcee beams widely as she hands over the third little guitar. The girl takes it, still squealing, her free hand pressed to her cheek as she bounces on her toes.

"I can't believe this!" she says into the mic. "This is amazing! Thank you!"

"Ginger, tell me," says the host, "what inspired this song?"

"Oh my gosh, it's so funny! I was at this restaurant having pizza with my friends, and we all ordered soda waters, and I was just, like, blown away by how bubbly it was—just like me, because everyone is always saying how bubbly I am, and then I just had to write about it, you know?" She breaks out into giggles and waves at the camera that's been livestreaming the show.

It's subjective, I think. *Different people, different tastes.*

But . . . Ari's song was *so good*.

In fact, all the other finalists were good. And a lot of the videos we watched when Ari stayed over were great, too.

But . . . *this* is the grand prize winner? Really?

I can't make sense of it.

As the emcee wraps up their time on the Albatross Stage, it all feels a little anticlimactic. People pack up their blankets and head back into the festival before the booths close, or to catch one last performance on another stage, or to head home after a long day of music and festivities.

Ari leaves the stage. She's stopped by dozens of people as she makes her way across the lawn. Congratulations and handshakes. As she gets closer, I catch some of their comments. How much they loved her song. And at least one person telling her they thought she should have won.

Ari smiles graciously and accepts their compliments, all the while clutching her second place award to her chest.

I know it isn't logical, but a part of me can't help but feel like I let her down.

So much for being her good luck charm.

Chapter Twenty-Eight

"I'm not disappointed," Ari insists as we make our way back to the car. The sun is setting, and a rush of people are pouring out of the festival around us. "Second place, out of *all* the entries that were submitted? This is the best thing that could have happened to help me kickstart a real songwriting career."

"Second best thing," Ezra amends. "Winning, obviously, would have been the best thing."

She rolls her eyes. "Fine. Second best thing. My point is that it feels really good to be recognized. People like my song! I'm thrilled."

"As you should be," says Maya.

"But also—you should have won," adds Ezra. "And we all know it. You were robbed."

"Or at least, *she* shouldn't have," Maya mutters. The thought we've all been thinking.

"It was rigged," says Ezra, like it is an inarguable fact.

Maya shoots him a warning look. "Just because we didn't like it—"

"No, nuh-uh. This is not an issue of subjectivity or whatever. Everyone in that audience heard all ten finalists, and I'm telling you, every one of them thought hers was the worst. Because it was! It shouldn't have even been a finalist to begin with." He clicks his tongue. "Someone was pulling strings, and Ari got robbed."

I frown, considering. I'm not usually one for conspiracy theories, but in this case, it almost seems more plausible than believing *that* song was chosen as the winner.

"Who were the judges?" EZ asks.

Ari shakes her head. "I don't know. The contest page just said it would be voted on by industry professionals."

EZ hums knowingly. "I bet you anything she's got some rich uncle on the judges' panel or something."

"You don't know that," says Ari, but her expression . . . pursed lips, shadowed eyes. She feels the same way we do, even if she's morally opposed to openly criticizing another musical artist.

"It doesn't matter," I say. "You were great, Ari. The crowd loved you."

She smiles. "It was nerve-racking. But thanks." She sighs heavily. "I understand why songwriters have to perform our own music to get noticed, but . . . I can't wait until I can just hand the songs over to a professional and let them do the scary part."

We pile into the car—Maya and I in the back again, and Ari driving, even though Ezra offers to take the wheel. Then we sit in the parking lot for half an hour waiting for the line of cars to move. Darkness creeps quickly across the sky, and by the time we're pulling onto the road, Ari has her headlights on.

We're mostly quiet for the long drive. Just freeways and semitrucks and the moon appearing through the darkness.

Quiet, that is, except for EZ, who must have an allergic reaction to silence, since he fills the void of conversation and playlists by voicing every inane thought that pops into his head.

"Anyone else want to move to Michigan and apply for a license to hunt unicorns? That's a real thing. Not that I want to kill a unicorn. I'm not a *monster*. But I would like the paperwork that says I'm allowed to, if I so choose.

"Who do you think was the first person to eat lobster? I mean, seriously? Who looks at that freaky monster from the sea, with its shell and its claws and its creepy antennae things, and thinks . . . I bet that is *delicious*?

213

"Did you know that humans grow two meters of nose hair in the course of a lifetime? How awesome would it be if they never fell out and we all had nose hair hanging down to our toes? Jude, you should put *that* in one of your comics."

It would annoy me, except sometimes he manages to elicit a laugh from Ari, and the sound warms me to my core, which then spurs on an unexpected sourness in my mouth that might be jealousy, and that freaks the hell out of me.

I can't be jealous of Ezra and the way he flirts shamelessly with Ari and the way she sometimes acts like she might like it.

I can't *like* Ari. She's Pru's *best friend*. And one of mine, too, for that matter. We've grown so comfortable with each other that she can tease me about my mindless doodles and I can show her my comic and not want to crawl into a cave, and she can sleep on my bed and it isn't weird. Liking her would definitely make that weird.

Oh.

And also Maya.

The girl who has consumed my thoughts since childhood, filling me with a steady spring of pathetic, romantic hope. The girl I finally have my chance with. The girl who—I realize, suddenly, I haven't been dreaming about lately, not like I used to.

When did those daydreams stop?

I still like Maya. Knowing her better, I actually think I might like her even more now.

But what if I never actually *liked* her, like I thought I did? I was sure it was love. Pure, indisputable, all-encompassing love.

But what if I'd been in love with the idea of her? What if some part of me had actually liked that she was unattainable? Because unattainable is safe. Unattainable means I never have to do anything. I never have to try. I never have to put my heart on the line.

While falling for someone else . . . falling for a best friend . . . falling for *Ari* . . . would be anything but safe.

I need to smother these rebellious emotions and bury them where they lie.

"Um . . . guys?" says Maya suddenly. "Does anyone else smell smoke?"

We all tense, sniffing the air. And . . . yeah. That's definitely smoke.

"Oh no," says Ari, instantly panicked. "What do I do?"

"Panic," says Ezra.

Ari looks at him, eyes round.

"Naw, just joking. There's a gas station right up there. Just pull off, and I'll check it out."

The smell has intensified by the time we pull off the freeway and under the overhang of the fluorescent-lit gas station. As we all step out of the station wagon, I can see a waft of smoke escaping from the hood.

"It's probably just overheated," says EZ. "This has been a lot of driving for this old beast."

He opens the hood. Ari, Maya, and I crowd in around him, but I'm not sure why. It's not like we're going to be useful here. I'm met with a sense of déjà vu, this engine every bit as foreign to me as Maya's was, though this one boasts a lot more rust and a lot less plastic.

"Between the two of you," says Maya, "I'm sure you can fix it. Right?"

Ezra gives her a look. "Two of us?"

"You and Jude." She nods at me with an encouraging smile. "My car was having issues a while back, and Jude took one look at the engine and figured out the problem like that." She snaps. "It was kind of magical."

"Really?" Ezra drawls, giving me a skeptical look.

"I just got lucky," I say uncomfortably, clearing my throat. "While we're here, anyone want anything? Coffee? Snacks?"

After taking EZ's and Ari's requests, Maya and I head into the convenience store. I fill up four Styrofoam cups with coffee, while Maya browses the snack aisles in search of chips, gummy candies, and trail mix. I'm opening my seventh little packet of hazelnut creamer when I spy the brightly lit vending machine in the back corner. Not a vending machine for food or drinks, but one for scratch tickets.

I know you're supposed to be eighteen to buy scratch tickets, but . . .

I glance toward the cash register. The clerk is staring at her phone, not paying me any attention.

I may not be able to hand Ari the grand prize from tonight's competition. I may not be able to fix her car.

But there is one thing I can do.

I make my way over to the machine and scan the options. My attention latches on to a scratch ticket near the bottom with a green shamrock on it and a heading at the top: *With a Little Luck*. They're five dollars apiece.

I glance at the cashier one more time before feeding in a twenty-dollar bill and selecting four of the shamrock tickets. They pop out of a slot in the bottom. I snatch them up and tuck them into my back pocket before heading back for our coffees.

The car's hood is still up when we make our way outside, Ari holding a flashlight while Ezra does who knows what. We hand Ari her coffee and set Ezra's by the front tire where it won't get accidentally kicked over.

Maya and I sit down on the curb to wait, and a part of me is grateful when she pulls out her phone so there isn't any pressure to make small talk, which sounds exhausting right now after the turmoil of today's super inconvenient feelings.

I pull out my phone too and start scrolling through social media. Some people from school doing the newest dance craze. A gamer I follow showing off exclusive swag from Emerald City Comic Con. Some of our school's drama kids posting photos of the backdrops for their upcoming production of *The Wizard of Oz*.

A post from Pru makes me pause. It's a clip from a local news outlet, where a reporter is interviewing her and Quint. In the background, Quint's mom, Rosa—the founder of the Fortuna Beach Sea Animal Rescue Center—stands beside employees from the zoo, while two sea lions play in a pool in a brand-new enclosure.

I play the video. Pru and Quint tell the reporter about how Luna and Lennon were rescued. My sister is in her element as she recounts how

Lennon was found, sick and malnourished, on the beach during the Freedom Festival.

"Once we got Lennon to the rescue center and he met Luna, they became best friends immediately," Quint says. "We knew neither of them would be able to survive in the wild, so we wanted to start socializing them right away, in hopes that we could transfer them to a permanent home together. As you can see, now they're inseparable."

The camera pans to the sea lions. As if they'd rehearsed it, the sea lions both flop up onto the deck beside the pool, practically snuggling. The reporter makes a heartfelt *aww* sound.

"Speaking of becoming inseparable," says Quint, drawing the camera back to him. His countenance has changed slightly, his expression newly hesitant. "I may have asked Lennon and Luna to help me out with a little surprise."

Beside him, Pru frowns. Deeply. "What surprise?"

Quint flashes a mischievous smile. Then he turns and gives a thumbs-up to his mom. Rosa grabs two small wooden boards that had been lying at her feet and whistles. Both sea lions perk up as Rosa tosses the wood into the pool.

The sea lions dive in, their bodies skimming through the water. They catch the two boards in their mouths and, in one elegant movement, cross the pool to where Pru and Quint are standing with the reporter. Luna and Lennon pop their heads up, showing off the boards. The camera zooms in on the words that have been painted across the slick wooden surfaces.

Dear Prudence . . .

Will you go to prom with me?

The reporter gasps. The camera pans back to show Pru, her mouth open in surprise. She lets out a bewildered laugh.

Then she smacks Quint on the arm. "On TV? Seriously?"

He chuckles. "Is that a yes?"

"Of course that's a yes!"

Grinning, Quint goes to kiss her, and the reporter steps away, drawing the focus of the camera with her. "If that isn't a memorable day at the zoo, I don't know what is!"

The video cuts out. The little replay icon appears.

I shut my phone off. Happy for Pru, happy for Quint, happy for Rosa and the zoo and my sister's favorite sea lions. But mostly, distracted by a plaguing thought.

Prom.

Well—junior prom. Despite the posters all over school, I've given it hardly any thought, but I know it's coming up soon.

I've never once gone to a school dance, and I hadn't planned to start now.

But . . . Maya might want to go. Probably.

I should ask her.

Probably?

I *want* to ask her. Because I want to be Maya's boyfriend. It's what I've always wanted, and one day of conflicted emotions isn't going to change that. If I don't get my head on straight, I'm going to risk losing the best thing that's ever happened to me.

I am in love with Maya. Period. End of story.

And I will prove it.

I take in a breath and turn to her, ready to make my (albeit lackluster) promposal right there and then—when the slamming of the car hood makes me jump.

"All right," says EZ, wiping his hands down the front of his pants. "Our chariot awaits."

I jump to my feet, heart skittering. Yeah, you're right. I can do better than asking a girl to prom while sitting on the curb outside a gas station in the middle of nowhere.

"Jude, did you drop these?"

I turn around to see Maya holding up the scratch tickets.

"Oh! Yeah." I check my pocket, but sure enough, it's empty. "I got these for us. I thought, who knows? Maybe one of us will get lucky."

It's difficult to keep a straight face as I say it, because, *hello*. I'm the guy who flipped heads fifty-seven times in a row. Of *course* I'm going to get lucky. It wouldn't surprise me if all four of them are winners.

This time, Ari accepts Ezra's offer to drive and we pile back into the car. Ari finds some coins in what used to be the ashtray and passes them around. EZ asks if he has to share a cut with me when he wins millions.

"Just invite me on your yacht sometime," I tell him. For a minute, the car is filled with the quiet noise of scritch-scratching. I uncover my lucky numbers, then wait for the magic to take over. Not just to match the lucky numbers, but also to uncover a coveted shamrock that will triple the prize money.

I scratch. And I scratch—

"This one's a dud," says Ezra, tossing his ticket to the floor of the car.

"Mine, too," says Maya. "Oh well."

I swallow.

Scratch, scratch, scratch . . .

Ari sighs. "Nothing here."

They all turn to watch as I scratch off my final number.

My . . . *losing* . . . number.

I blink.

"Well?" says Ari.

"It's . . . a loser."

I squeeze my eyes shut. Then open them and blink again, rapidly this time. Waiting for the numbers to change. To rearrange themselves. To reveal how I won, because of course I won, I *always* win. I have the magic of Lundyn Toune on my side. I have my lucky dice.

"Dude," says Ezra with a chuckle in his voice. He reaches into the back seat and grabs the ticket away from me. "There's no need to take it personally."

Feeling betrayed, I press my hand to the outside of my jeans pocket, feeling for the familiar, comforting lump of my mystical D20.

I freeze.

The world tilts and goes dark.

The air leaves me in one horrified breath.

No. No, no, *no*.

I feel the other side, then reach my hands into both pockets.

But they're empty.

The dice. It's gone.

And so is the magic.

Chapter Twenty-Nine

The whole drive home, I'm tempted to ask Ezra to stop and turn around. We have to go back to the festival. I have to search for it.

But I know how that will sound to everyone, so I don't say anything. Even as my stomach roils. Even as my heart withers. How could I have lost it? When? *Where?*

The next day, I look up the festival and call the phone number listed on their website. I ask if anyone turned in a red twenty-sided dice. I stay on the line, fingers tightly crossed, as the woman on the other end checks with their lost and found. But no luck. I give her my phone number, and she promises to call if it turns up.

I hang up, overcome with dread.

How could I have been so careless? I don't even remember the last time I saw it or felt it in my grip. I'd gotten used to it always being there. I'd gotten complacent and now . . .

Now the magic is gone.

No—not *gone*, as I soon discover.

The magic, as it soon becomes apparent, has *turned on me*.

Those scratch tickets were just the beginning.

Over the next week, I lose every coin flip, giving Ellie her choice of everything from the game we play on Monday night (Frozen Memory Match) to the movie we watch on Tuesday (*Frozen*) to the dinner I cook for us on Wednesday when Mom and Dad are out for their monthly date night (mac and cheese). I know I should probably give up on the coin-flip thing, but I can't help holding tight to my hope that my safety net hasn't been pulled out from under me.

That hope slowly wanes.

The minivan gets a flat tire one morning on our way to school.

The soles of my favorite dragon shoes finally give up and split from the rest of the shoe—in first period, so I'm stuck walking around with floppy soles the rest of the day.

At lunch, the toppings mysteriously slip right off the crust of my pizza and right onto my brand-new sweatshirt, leaving a triangular-shaped splotch of tomato sauce that doesn't wash out.

The laptop I share with Pru gets a virus, and it takes hours for me to recover a bunch of my artwork files, and I'm still not even sure I got them all.

The printer jams when I'm trying to print a last-minute report.

My locker door jams when I'm already late for fifth period.

My pointer finger gets jammed into the basketball during gym . . . and of course it's my drawing hand.

My other classes don't go any better. I guess I've gotten into the bad habit of not studying—what's the point when I ace every exam effortlessly?—so when I bomb tests in both astronomy and Spanish, can't answer any of the questions in English class, and forget all about our statistics and poli-sci homework, I feel the full, shameful weight of the disapproving frowns from my teachers. I blabber a number of inane excuses that I know they aren't buying, and vow to try harder, my cheeks burning.

Even the one class I've always loved, visual arts, turns into a drag as we move from drawing into a unit on watercolor. I break a paintbrush and spill water all over my work—*twice*—before Mr. Cross asks me to spend the rest of the period tidying up the supply cabinet instead.

But wait—*there's more*.

I discover a cockroach in my bedroom, and we have to call in an exterminator, forcing me to sleep on the lumpy living room sofa for two nights while noxious gases permeate the basement.

The cactus that Lucy gave me for Christmas dies. (I didn't even know you could kill a cactus.)

My debit card goes missing, and I have to cancel it and order another one and spend a week without any access to spending money.

For the first time in months, I get a pimple on my forehead and hives on my chest *at the same time*.

The hot water runs out when I'm in the middle of shampooing my hair. Someone drinks all the milk so there's none left for my morning cereal. And when I'm helping Mom carry in the groceries, I stub my big toe on the porch steps, trip, and send the bag of groceries spilling into the front garden bed. The carton of milk we just bought explodes all over my legs, before seeping down into the dirt. Add to all that the fact that I still haven't managed to ask Maya to prom. With the dance less than two weeks away, I know I'm running out of time. And I can't explain it, but I also feel like I'm running out of chances to prove that we are meant for each other.

To prove to everyone—to Maya, to myself, to the world—that I didn't royally screw up by using the magic of Lundyn Toune, a magic that has utterly deserted me . . . to ask out the wrong girl.

———————————

"Mom, did you get more popcorn at the store?" I call, digging through the cupboard.

"No," Mom yells back from upstairs. "Put it on the list!"

I groan. The grocery list isn't going to help me much tonight. I add it to the notepad on the fridge anyway, then go back to digging. I manage to find a bag of tortilla chips that aren't *too* stale, some fancy salted nuts, and a half-eaten package of Oreos.

It will have to do, I decide, pouring the chips into a large bowl. Bonus—we have a jar of salsa in the fridge, and some queso dip in the pantry.

Mom comes in while I'm scooping the dip into a microwave-safe dish.

"Hey," she says, sounding a little breathless. "What are you—*oh*. Saturday. Right." She massages her brow.

"Is everything okay?" I ask.

"Oh, yeah. There's just been a lot to try and keep track of lately." She sighs and pours herself a glass of wine from an open bottle in the fridge. "Between tax season and getting everything in order for Record Store Day . . . honestly, every day that goes by when all five of you kids end up at school and no one misses music lessons or sports practice or play-dates, and dinner is on the table and the house didn't burn down—I'm calling it a win." She takes in a deep breath and leans against the counter.

"You set a high bar for parenting," I tell her, putting the cheese dip in the microwave and setting it for a minute.

Mom smirks. "We can't all be perfect all the time. Is there anything you need for tonight?"

I shake my head.

"All right, then. I told Penny I'd take her to the music store to pick up some rosin tonight, so if we're not here, that's probably where we've gone. I'll take Ellie, too, so she doesn't bother you."

"She's no bother," I say. And it's true. Ellie almost never comes down to the basement during D&D nights, but when she does, it's pretty easy to set her up on the carpet with a few tiny pewter figurines and let her play make believe on her own.

"I really do appreciate you, Jude. Your dad and I lucked out, in more ways than one." She puts a hand on my shoulder, and I bend down so she can kiss my head, just like she did when I was little.

The doorbell rings and Mom raises her glass to me. "Have fun storming the castle."

Maya and Noah are on the front step, and Maya is laughing so hard she's leaning against the porch rail and holding her stomach like it hurts.

Noah grins innocently. "I may have broken our fighter."

I gape at them. "What did you say to her?"

"Nothing."

"Goren—Gruesome—" Maya stammers between breaths.

224

"Aah," I say, nodding. "Yeah, Noah is very good at impersonations."

"I don't know what you're talking about," says Noah. "I have nothing but the utmost respect for our bloodthirsty friend. I would never impersonate him in a mocking manner."

"That was—so—spot-on," gasps Maya, wiping away literal tears.

I usher them inside, and Maya manages to gather herself by the time we carry all the food downstairs.

The doorbell rings again while we're setting up, and I take the steps two at a time. Russell and Kyle are on the porch. As I let them in, César pulls up to the curb.

"Tonight is the night!" says Kyle. "You should know that I'm not leaving here until we have conquered this temple, killed some monsters, and broken this curse."

I smile, but even I can tell that it's weak. "We'll see where the night takes us, I guess."

We raid the kitchen for sodas before making our way downstairs again. Maya and Noah are deep in conversation, facing each other across the card table.

I clear my throat, and they both look up, seemingly startled.

And . . . guilty?

"Everyone ready? César, you have your dice?"

"Oh, crap!" he says, springing to his feet. He forgets them in his car pretty much every other week.

As he heads back up the stairs, I shuffle my papers absently. My stomach is in knots, but no one seems to notice how nervous I am. It strikes me how it's taken hardly any time for Maya to become an integral part of our group. They're all talking about what happened last in the campaign, and Kyle is complimenting Maya on her quick thinking when they all came across those mean little sprites, and Maya looks genuinely flattered by the praise.

I realize it then. Of all the unexpected twists of the universe—Maya Livingstone is one of us now. And that is *bizarre*.

"All good there, DM?" asks César.

"Huh?" I hadn't realized he'd come back already.

Everyone is staring at me.

"What's up?" says César, taking his seat and setting his dice on the table. "You look freaked out about something."

"I'm just seeing what we've got coming up," I say, swallowing. "I, uh . . . got some last-minute inspiration and made a few small changes to the campaign. Nothing you all need to worry about. I just . . . you know. Want to make sure I didn't miss anything."

"What are we waiting for?" says Russell, who has a low tolerance for small talk.

"I'm almost ready." I take in a breath and look around at the group, my gaze alighting on Maya last. She's fidgeting with a tiny tiefling figurine, the one Noah lent to her to represent her character way back on day one.

I absently grab my twenty-sided dice.

My completely normal, nothing special, entirely unmagical dice.

Anything more than a ten, and I do this.

My thumb caresses the soft planes and angles of the dice.

No—anything more than a five.

I roll the dice, hidden safely behind the screen. It tumbles across my notes.

Comes to a standstill.

And it's . . .

A one.

Critical fail.

I stare at it. That single digit laughing at me.

I close my eyes, discouraged.

But . . . am I really going to let a dice make my choices for me? One that doesn't even have mystical powers?

No. No, I am not.

I am the Dungeon Master, and I am in charge here. Not luck. Not magic. Not the Temple of Lundyn Toune.

"All right," I say, snatching the dice back into my palm. "The quest had been long and treacherous . . . ."

The moment the question is out, I know this was a bad idea. I feel it in every bone of my body. I sense it in the way everyone is staring at me. Mostly in the way Maya is staring at me.

Not like she's flattered. Or happy. Or excited.

More like she's . . . queasy?

My promposal hangs in the air between us, along with a stifling amount of uncomfortable silence.

I swallow. "For the record, this is me, now. Jude. Not the statue." I lower my privacy screen so there's nothing between me and Maya. "Maya—will you go to junior prom with me?"

Maya's mouth opens, but no sound comes out. For whatever reason, she looks at Noah, then back at me.

"Jude," she says quietly. "Can I talk to you . . . somewhere else?"

"Oh, damn," mutters César. "That's not good."

Kyle punches him in the arm.

Russell grumpily takes a handful of trail mix and starts picking out the M&M's. "Does this mean we didn't actually break the curse?"

"All of you, zip it," says Maya, pushing back her chair.

I follow her up the stairs, even though I don't really understand what the point is. I already know everything I need to know.

Lucy and my dad are watching a true crime documentary in the living room, and Pru is doing homework in the kitchen, so we end up outside. Maya sits down on the front step. Part of me would rather stay standing, because I can run away faster, I guess, but I sit down anyway.

"Jude—" she starts.

"No need to drag this out," I say quickly. I realize that I'm still holding the resin D20. I pass it idly from palm to palm. "You can just say no."

Maya bites her lower lip. Her expression looks genuinely pained. "I can't *just say no*. This last month . . . I have had so much fun with you. Really. I mean, it's been weird at times, right? Because I always sort of knew you liked me? And I . . ." She makes a face. "Don't take this the wrong way, but I wasn't really interested in you before. But it turns out I actually really like hanging out with you. And being here, playing

D&D . . . I love this, and . . . I do like you, Jude. A lot." She hesitates. "I just . . . don't know if I . . ."

"Maya. I get it."

She grimaces.

"It's okay," I add.

"I don't want to hurt you," she whispers. "I'm hoping we can be friends. But I also understand if . . ." She looks down at her hands, fingers making knots in her lap. "If that isn't going to happen."

It's probably the nicest rejection a guy could hope to get. And even though it *is* a rejection and there's a stab of disappointment in my gut, I also feel a wave of relief at her words, and a sense that I've known all along that we weren't meant to be together, despite years of pining. Because that's all it was. Pining. Not a relationship. Not reality. Just an impossible fantasy.

The reality is that being *friends* with Maya might actually be better.

I fold my fist around the dice and rub my brow, chuckling to myself.

"I'm really sorry, Jude."

"Don't be," I say. "Honestly . . . if all this hadn't happened, there's a good chance I would have been in love with you for the rest of my life."

I meet her gaze again. She looks so sad. So very, very sorry.

But I don't want her to feel sorry. Or guilty. Or any of that.

I settle my elbows on my knees, fingers mindlessly fidgeting with the dice. "I'm glad you said no."

"Jude . . ."

"No, I mean it. I had to try one last time. Because you're right. I have liked you for years. And I wanted it to work out, because that would prove that this crush wasn't so hopeless after all. But . . . I already knew, I think. I've known for weeks. We don't have what Pru and Quint have. Or . . ." I pause, realizing that she's still holding the little pewter figurine. And in that moment, something else clicks. Something I should have noticed sooner. "Or . . . what Grit and Starling have, for that matter."

A short, startled laugh bursts from Maya, before she turns away, hiding her face from me. "Starling is a flirt."

"Maybe," I say. "But Noah is a really good person. And I know I've never heard you laugh like you do when you're around them."

Maya tugs at one of her curls.

"Maya, you're incredible. You know that already, but in case you haven't heard it in a while. And I am so lucky that I got to go on a couple of really great dates with you. Ten-year-old me has been having the time of his life this past month, going out with the girl of his dreams and realizing that the real you is even, like, a thousand times more amazing. And I am always going to be the guy who was one hundred percent devoted to you for almost our entire school career."

Maya looks at me again. "This is a pretty good speech," she says. "You're sort of making me regret my answer."

I grin. "Don't. It was the right answer."

She nods. "I know."

I sigh and stuff the dice into my pocket. It doesn't warm against my skin. It doesn't pulse lifelike in my palm. It's the wrong dice, and it's no help at all.

"Friends?" I ask, holding my hand toward Maya.

Her lips turn upward. But instead of shaking my hand, she leans closer and pulls me into a sideways hug. "Friends."

Chapter Thirty

"No Ari today?" asks Dad.

I look up from the chapter of *The Great Gatsby* that I've been struggling to get through all morning. Dad stands on the other side of the counter, going through yesterday's mail. "Uh, no. Her mom's got some big open house today and asked Ari to help out with it. I think she's on champagne-and-fresh-baked-cookies duty."

Dad barks a laugh. "Elena gives out champagne at her open houses? Just for coming to take a look?" He shakes his head and tosses a catalog into the recycling bin. "Maybe we should try that here."

He suddenly goes still, holding a large flat package, the sort that we usually get specialty edition records sent in. "Jude, this is it," he says. "Hand me the box cutter."

He opens the package carefully, making sure not to damage what's inside as he peels back the cardboard flaps.

I lean closer. On top is a letter, which Dad scans quickly, then sets aside.

Next is a certificate with a blue fancy scrollwork border. Though I'm reading upside down, I easily make out the most important text, bolded in a large font:

Certificate of Authenticity.
Paul McCartney signed *London Town* poster.
Authentic.

The album poster and album lie underneath, barely visible beneath a layer of protective plastic.

Dad beams at me. "There you have it."

"Amazing. Now what?"

He hands me the certificate and starts taking off the packaging. "We'll get it framed, I guess. Hang it up somewhere."

"Did they say how much it's worth?"

"No, that would be a question for an appraiser, although until something is put up for sale, you never really know how much someone will pay for it. Not that it matters. I am never parting with this album." He gets the wrapping off and grins down at the poster with Sir Paul's signature. "Hiding in plain sight all this time. Who would have thought?" He carefully slides the poster back into the album jacket, then gathers up the plastic and cardboard packaging. "Oh, hey, before I forget. Do you think you could place our order for Record Store Day special releases today? I've been putting it off, but your mom and I went over the budget, and we should be good to get those ordered up."

"That's cutting it close, isn't it?" I glance at the calendar. Record Store Day is in two weeks, the same weekend as junior prom.

"It isn't ideal," he agrees. "Hopefully we won't need to pay for expedited shipping, but if that's what it takes . . ." He shrugs. "Those special releases are a huge draw this time of year. Gotta give the people what they want."

"Sure. I'm on it."

I swivel to the computer as Dad takes the recycling out to the dumpster in the alley behind the store.

I've only begun to fill out our order when a woman wearing an expensive-looking shawl comes up to the counter with a stack of records.

"Did you find everything you were looking for?" I ask.

"Yes, yes, you have a very nice selection," she says in a thick Indian accent, tapping her fingers on the top album. Sadashiv's newest record. "I especially love all this British Invasion music."

I laugh, though I'm not sure if she's trying to make a joke. I guess he could be considered British Invasion for Gen Z?

"I saw Sadashiv in concert recently," I say, ringing up her purchases (which I see also include the Yardbirds and the Hollies, so some classic Brits, too).

"Oh?" says the woman, opening her purse and counting out some cash from her wallet. "Did you enjoy it?"

I hesitate, not entirely sure how to answer. I *did* enjoy that night . . . even if things with Maya ultimately didn't work out how I'd hoped.

At my hesitation, the woman laughs. "Maybe you are not his target demographic. To each his own."

"I actually liked it more than I thought I would," I say, neatly stacking up her purchases before sliding them into a paper bag, then counting out her change. "I hope you enjoy these," I say, passing her the bag.

"That looked like a good sale," says Dad, as soon as the woman is gone. "How many records did she buy?"

"Nine or ten," I say.

"Not bad." He pulls out a box of our most recent intake of used records and starts evaluating the condition so they can be priced. "You know, your mom and I watched some of the videos on Ari's page last night. They turned out really great. Pru says you had a hand in that."

Feeling self-conscious, I go back to filling out our order for Record Store Day. "I didn't do much."

"Regardless. We're really proud of Ari. And of you." He sighs. "You know, someday we're going to be selling records with her songs on them. And I'll get to tell all her adoring fans—that girl is like another daughter to me. I've known her since she was yea big . . ." He holds his hand at waist-high.

"We met Ari when she was twelve," I say. "Not four."

"Twelve? Really? *No*. It feels like she's been part of the family for way longer than that."

I shake my head. "It was right after we started seventh grade. Mom took Lucy and Penny back-to-school shopping, and Pru and I were doing homework up at the counter, and you had Ellie strapped into one of those baby carrier things?"

"Oh, yeah, I loved those days," Dad says nostalgically, pressing a hand to his heart. "I miss having a baby around."

Commenting on this seems like a surefire way to get another sister, so I don't.

"And Ari came in with her dad, and the two of you were gushing about what it's like to watch little girls grow up, or something like that. I remember you let him hold Ellie for a while. And the whole time, Ari was buzzing around the store like she'd found paradise. Oh, with that binder she always carried with her! Remember the binder?"

Dad's eyes widen. "I forgot about that. Haven't seen it in a while."

"I think she's gone digital now," I say, surprised at how nostalgic *I'm* suddenly feeling, remembering that purple binder covered in retro stickers of peace signs, daisies, a VW Bug, A guitar that looked a lot like the one she inherited from her grandfather. On the inside—sheet protectors and pages and pages of albums that twelve-year-old Ari had kept religiously organized. By genre and alphabetical by artist, it had been her master list of all the albums she already had in her collection (most of which were actually her dad's collection), along with an ever-growing wish list of albums she still wanted to find.

"You and David were so busy talking that she kept coming up to me and Pru and asking where to find things," I say. "And we were pretty clueless, but I tried so hard to help her. To pretend like I knew what I was talking about. Like I was a total expert on Ventures Vinyl, 'cause . . ." I trail off, my cheeks going pink.

Because I wanted to impress her. I wanted to impress that exuberant, quirky, music-loving girl, who had shown up in my parents' store like a ray of unexpected sunshine.

Dad's voice is soft. "That's right. You hit it off right away, didn't you? I'd forgotten all about that."

238

I smile wanly. "Why is it so quiet in here? I don't remember the record stopping."

I busy myself changing out the record on the turntable, but my thoughts are still on that first meeting with Ari. How eager I'd been to find any excuse to keep talking to her. How disappointed I was when she left, more than an hour later, a stack of albums clutched in her arms.

It wasn't until later that night, lying in bed thinking of the girl with the electric smile, that the guilt had set in. By then, I'd long sworn my eternal devotion to Maya Livingstone. The girl I was sure was my soul mate. How could I be so fickle, to feel my heart so easily stirred by a pretty stranger?

That's when I decided to double down. To prove my allegiance, my unerring love, for Maya. I would not be swayed. I would not give in to the way my heart fluttered a little whenever Ari came to the store. I would squash those rebellious feelings into submission, and I would never give in to them again.

So that's what I did, to the point where I'd forgotten all about that giddy rush that swept over me every time I saw her. As her visits to the record store became more frequent, it became easier and easier to pretend I'd never felt anything at all. As the three of us became inevitable friends and started spending time together outside of the store, I started to believe that friendship was all I'd ever wanted. All I'd ever felt.

I was loyal to Maya, the girl I never expected to want me back, and it was easier to immerse myself in love unrequited than to let myself imagine something else might be possible. Something that involved risks and uncertainty and heartbreak and rejection. Something that was real.

My hands finish going through the motions of setting a new record on the player. Flipping the switch to start it spinning. Lowering the needle.

I barely hear it, though. I don't even know what record I just grabbed off the top of the stack. I'm too lost in my own thoughts. Too struck with the most uncanny of realizations.

Okay, class. What have we learned today?

That apparently, I am the most oblivious, lovestruck dumbass in all of Fortuna Beach.

"Where'd I put that *London Town* record?"

I start and turn to look at my dad. He's got his hands on his hips, a deep frown as he surveys the area around the counter. The computer and keyboard, the clutter of assorted merchandise, the remaining mail that needs to go back to the office, the box of records to be priced and put out for purchase. It takes a long moment for his words to register.

"Oh, it's right—"

I freeze, my hand reaching halfway to the spot on the counter where Dad set the album with the certificate of authentication.

There's nothing there.

"I swear it was right—" I inhale sharply. "Oh no. Oh, crap."

Dad gives me a worried look.

"I think . . . I think it might have gotten mixed up with that stack of records that I just . . . that that woman just . . ."

Painful understanding flickers in my dad's eyes. "Her credit card. We can find her name . . ."

I shake my head. "She paid with cash."

Dad flinches.

We look at each other in dreadful silence for a long while, guilt clawing at my insides. It's gone. Just like my magic dice, the *London Town* album with the signed poster is gone.

The Curse of Lundyn Toune strikes again.

Chapter Thirty-One

My dad breaks the news about the lost Paul McCartney autograph while flipping grilled ham and cheese sandwiches in a skillet. My family is dismayed, but my dad tries to be gracious about it, skipping over the part where it's entirely my fault.

His generosity only makes me feel worse.

"Mistakes happen," he says, carrying the platter of sandwiches to the table, along with a roll of paper towels. "It's not a big deal."

After some uncertain glances, my family takes their cue from him. Agreeing, wholeheartedly. Totally not a big deal.

Except it is. It's an even bigger deal than they realize. Further proof that my luck is backfiring on me. Further proof that I've been cursed.

What if it's going to be like this forever now? Just one misfortune after another, for the rest of my pitiful life?

No—I can't start thinking that way. There has to be a way out of this. A way to break this spell.

If only I hadn't lost that dice.

"This came for you in the mail, Jude," says Mom. She wipes her buttery fingers on her paper towel before grabbing an envelope and passing it to me over Ellie's growing pile of discarded crusts.

At first I'm sure it will be more bad news, so I don't even care if I leave grease spots on the paper as I tear it open and pull out . . . a check. Fifty dollars, with my name typed neatly onto the recipient line. The *Dungeon*'s logo—a stylized *D* with medieval iron bars across it—is in the corner.

"Nice," says Pru, punching me lightly in the shoulder. "I guess you're officially an *artiste* now."

I smile half-heartedly.

The envelope also contains a notecard from the art director who emailed me before.

I look forward to seeing more of your work.
—Ralph Tigmont

I stuff the note back into the envelope. "Can I be excused? I've got some homework to get to."

I don't wait for their response, just abandon my sandwich as I slide out from the table.

I'm halfway down the stairs when Pru stops me. "Jude, wait. Is everything okay?"

I turn back to her. "What do you mean?"

"You've been really quiet lately." She rolls her eyes. "I mean, quieter than usual. Actually . . . you've been acting kind of strange all week."

I tap my fingers against the stair rail. "I kind of fell behind on some classes. Been trying to get caught back up. And things are ramping up at the store, trying to get ready for Record Store Day."

She's silent for a while. There are times when I swear Pru and I can read each other's thoughts, so I force myself to think about anything other than Ari. My brain circulates through homework. (Jay Gatsby is as much a hopeless sap as I am.) Then to the store. (Ari sitting on the counter, tuning her guitar.) Then to the campaign. (I might need Ari's help to write that epic ballad, now that the adventurers broke the curse.) Then to my comic. (Wizard Jude couldn't see what was right in front of him, either.)

Why is not thinking of Ari so hard all of a sudden?

"Did you finish your campaign last weekend?" says Pru.

See? Mind reading. It's a twin thing, and possibly the closest thing to a superpower I'll ever have.

"Yeah, it went well. Everyone had a good time."

242

"And Maya is . . . a permanent part of the group now, or what?"

"I guess so. I still hope Matt will come back for the next campaign, but it was fun having Maya there. She actually fits in pretty well."

Pru nods slowly. "That's nice."

I sigh. I can see where this is going, so might as well save us some time. "*And* we've decided to just be friends."

Pru squeezes her fist in an excited I-knew-it gesture. "I could tell you were hiding something. When did that happen?"

"I wasn't *hiding* it," I mutter. "We talked last weekend. We both felt this makes more sense."

"And you're . . . okay?"

"Yeah, actually. I like Maya, but I'm not in love with her. Not anymore." *If I ever really was*, I think, but don't add.

I can see Pru mulling this over, maybe trying to decide if she believes me or not. But I must be convincing, because she slowly nods. "Who would have thought? Maya turns out to be a natural for role-playing games, and you fall *out* of love with her?"

"Yeah," I say, dragging a hand through my hair. "I didn't see it coming, either."

Pru bids me good night and I retreat to my bedroom as soon as possible, feeling awful in more ways than one. My colossal mistake with the album is bad enough, but for it to have happened right on the cusp of my incredibly inconvenient realization that I might have feelings for Ari?

Real feelings?

My head has been spinning all day.

I don't know what to do. I don't know if I should do anything. I mean, there's no rule that says I have to act on these emotions now that I know about them. I can just go on as normal. Pretend nothing has changed.

Can't I?

Why are you looking at me like that?

Seriously though. For a while there, I was the luckiest guy in Fortuna Beach. I could have had anything I wanted. I could have asked out Ari, and the universe would have bent itself to my will. I could have entered some sweepstakes and won a trip for two to a tropical location and whisked Ari off on a romantic getaway where of course she would have fallen in love with me.

But I didn't. And I can't possibly ask her out now.

Obviously.

I mean . . . can I ask her out?

No. Of course not. If she says no, if she doesn't feel the same way . . . we are screwed. Our friendship, ruined. It will never not be weird. And then Pru would be mad because I made things all awkward and she would be stuck in the middle, and I don't want to do that to her, either.

Unless . . . unless it's possible that Ari might feel something for me, too?

I'm almost afraid to hope, but there could be a precedent here. I mean, we've always been close. The sorts of friends who tease each other and touch each other . . . almost like flirting. Like, four years of flirting that I somehow completely missed.

But without knowing for sure, I feel trapped by indecision. If I go on like nothing's changed, then I'll never know if I stood a chance.

If I risk telling her the truth, then I not only risk rejection . . . I risk our friendship, too.

Ugh.

I could really use a distraction.

I pull the art director's note back out of the envelope.

I've been putting this off for too long, trapped by indecision and the certainty that my first acceptance was a complete fluke, boosted by a lucky power I no longer have.

So if it's pointless, and anything I try is going to fail now . . . I might as well get this over with.

I turn through the pages of my notebook, looking for anything I might deem remotely submission-worthy.

I pause when I get to the first chapter of the comic. I read through the pages. Araceli the Bard singing about the adventures she and the wizard have been on as they arrive at the lost temple. Fighting off a horde of goblins. Teasing each other. Trusting each other.

It's like my subconscious has been sending signals for months, trying to get me to see the very obvious truth. This comic isn't about a wizard who tries to rescue a maiden-turned-statue, a girl literally stuck up on a pedestal. It isn't some epic tale of star-crossed love and broken curses and defying impossible odds.

This is about two friends who share inside jokes and have witnessed each other at their best, and at their worst. This is about the sort of love where two people can sit in silence for hours at a time and never feel weird about it, perfectly content just to be together.

Still a love story, but a different one than I'd imagined.

I massage my brow and skip through the rest of the sketch book, until I stumble onto the page I was working on at the festival. The stage and the trees and the audience with their lawn chairs and paper boats of carnival vendor snacks. I never finished it. I never added the star performer.

This is it, I realize. My next art submission.

I don't even care if it's any good. I don't care if it's what the *Dungeon* wants or not.

I pull up a picture of Ari on my phone, one of us at Encanto—me and Ari and Pru and Quint and Ezra all squeezed into our favorite booth on karaoke night. Trish Roxby, host of karaoke night, took the photo. In it, I have my arm around Ari, like it's nothing.

I set the phone up against a stack of textbooks and start to draw Araceli the Magnificent on the Albatross Stage, strumming her lute while literal magic swirls and sparkles in eddies around her.

When it's done, I add a caption: *The Minstrel and the Music Festival.*

Then I email it to the art director before I can question myself. Again. There. Done.

One terrifying task complete. Proof that I can put myself out there. I can risk rejection and move on with my life . . . with or without magic.

So now that I've got that out of the way . . . what am I going to do about Ari?

Ask her out.

Or don't ask her out.

Tell her how I feel.

Or ignore how I feel until the end of time.

Try to figure out how Ari feels about me.

Or avoid ever seeing her again.

Back and forth. Back and forth. Thoughts spinning, spinning, spinning.

Okay. Pause.

How about this?

I just . . . don't decide anything. I don't decide to tell Ari how I feel. I don't decide to *not* tell Ari how I feel.

I let luck decide for me.

I know, I know. But hear me out. Yeah, maybe luck and I haven't been seeing eye to eye lately, but that doesn't matter. If Mr. Robles has taught me anything, it's that luck is a numbers game. Throw the dice enough times, and eventually you'll hit it big. (Just hope that the house hasn't emptied your pockets already.) Flip the coin enough times, and it has to land in your favor. And it only takes one lucky break to end a losing streak.

That's just basic math.

And I have an idea.

Chapter Thirty-Two

To be fair, my brilliant idea is . . . objectively not so brilliant. That doesn't deter me from putting it into action over the next few days, though.

I spend hours after school scouring the internet for things I might be able to win for Ari, as proof of my affection. But not just that. If I can win something—*anything*—it will prove that I *can* get lucky again, even without that stupid dice. Even without the magic.

It will prove that I'm not cursed.

And—wow. I never realized how much free stuff is just given away, all in the name of promotion.

Free guitars. Free speakers. Free amps. Free in-ear monitors. Free recording software. Free music lessons. Free trips to Nashville and Austin. Free studio time. Free song critiques. Free earrings shaped like music notes and necklace pendants made out of guitar picks and bracelets crafted from recycled guitar strings.

I enter every online sweepstakes I can find. Everything that seems like it might be even remotely appealing to Ari. Anything that I might win and present to her with a flourish. *Here, Ari. I won you these sweet vinyl decals! You can put them on your guitar case, and every time you look at them, you can think of me. Also, what do you say about forgetting this whole "friends" thing and giving Happily Ever After a try?*

Too much?

Yeah, maybe a bit much. Full disclosure: I have no idea what I'm doing, in case that wasn't obvious. I've barely caught my breath from the realization that I find Ari painfully attractive. I'm still reeling from the knowledge that my desire to kiss her outweighs every other desire I've ever had—that includes Maya, art school, and every Funko in existence. I'm still reeling when I think about how I've always felt happier in Ari's presence than with anyone else, no matter where we were or what we were doing, and yet somehow I *didn't realize it until now*.

Anyway—my point is that all of this is just a numbers game, and the numbers are going to tell me what to do next. Enter enough sweepstakes, and I'm bound to win something, and that something will be my ticket to a more-than-friends conversation with Ari.

Hey, it worked with Maya.

And if I *don't* win anything? Well then . . . I guess it wasn't meant to be.

———————

I check my emails first thing every morning, just to see if any of my hard work has paid off yet. (Don't think it was hard work? You try proving you're not a robot by picking the crosswalks out of eighty-seven square grids, and then come talk to me.)

My heart leaps when I open my inbox on Friday. *So many emails!* But after a quick scan, I realize that none of them are proclaiming me as the winner of anything. They're just proclaiming that every one of those sweepstakes I entered also put my email address onto a mailing list. I've never seen so much spam.

> *New gear on sale! Lowest prices of the year!*
> *Refer your bandmates for bonus points!*
> *Is your outdated recording software holding you back?*
> *We can make your song go viral!*
> *Sign up for our new songwriting course!*

Get your album produced FAST! Overnight shipping available!

Live music is trending in your area! See this week's hottest shows!

Can't read sheet music? We can help!

Bargain prices on our hottest selling accessories! Don't miss out!!!

I bend over my desk, rubbing both hands into my hair. Maybe the whole sweepstakes idea was a long shot. Maybe I'm not going to be able to rely on luck this time around. Maybe I need a new tactic.

Just because I can't win something, doesn't mean I can't *buy* her something. Maybe one of those sales mentioned in my abundance of spam emails will give me an idea for a good Ari gift? A new tuner? A case? A guitar humidifier? *What is a guitar humidifier?*

You know what? Let's hold off on the gift idea until I've done more reconnaissance. I could also keep things simple. With . . . like, flowers.

Ari, I know for a fact, loves daisies.

But what would I say if I sent her flowers?

> *Saw these and thought of you! That's all. Nothing to see here. As you were.*

> *That friends-to-lovers trope really worked out in that Yesterday movie that you and Pru love so much. Let's discuss.*

> *Roses are red, violets are blue, these are not roses or violets, but I know you like daisies, and I like you!*

Lucy might have been right about my beat poet potential . . .

As it turns out, it doesn't matter what I would say in the card, because when I go to look up the prices for a bouquet of daisies, no daisies are available. Because there's a *national shortage of daisies*.

The Curse of Lundyn Toune has officially gone nationwide.

Groaning, I tilt back in my chair and cover my face with both hands. Think, Jude. *Think.*

I do think. For a solid ten minutes, I *think*. But I'm not getting anywhere.

I need to clear my head. I'm definitely not in the mood to draw anything, as I haven't heard back from the *Dungeon*. I'm tempted to play video games or zone out in front of the TV for a while, but I'm still behind in most of my classes.

I try reading *Gatsby*, but that just makes me wonder which of us is more clueless—Gatsby or me? I put it down after only a couple of pages.

The statistics homework is full of words like *bivariate* and *regression* and *coefficients* and—crap, I'm going to need Pru's help with this, but she's out with Quint tonight.

At least I can get started on the next visual arts assignment. Mr. Cross sent us each home with a lump of air-dry clay and we're supposed to use it to practice sculpting.

I knead the clay until my knuckles ache, but it feels good, actually, pouring my emotions into something like this. My palms are already rusty red by the time I form the lump into something resembling a flower.

A daisy.

It looks like something Ellie would make.

I crumple it all in my fist and try again.

This time, the clay turns into something resembling a guitar.

Then an old station wagon.

What exactly am I trying to prove here? That whenever I have a crush, I become devoid of all other thoughts?

I start over again. I'll make a figure—a larger version of the small figurines we use to represent our characters in D&D. That should impress

Mr. Cross, right? I try to take my time, and even watch a YouTube video on sculpting for beginners. A torso and legs, a traveling cloak, long wavy hair, a lute . . .

A bitter laugh escapes me as I sit back to look at the figure. It's not amazing work, and I haven't added many details yet, but it isn't half bad for my first attempt.

Maybe *this* could be my gift to Ari?

Is that creepy?

It seems like it might be creepy.

Heaving an exhausted sigh, I pick up the figure, secured to a paper plate to keep it from toppling over, and set it in the corner of my room to dry. Not sure why I bother. With the way things have been going, I'll probably fail this assignment, too. I was probably supposed to sculpt something specific. Like a cat. It doesn't matter how good of a sculpture I make, there will be something wrong with it. The curse will make sure of that.

I slump back into my desk chair. My hands are dry and crusty from the clay, and I try to pick the chunks out from beneath my fingernails.

Thinking of cats makes me think of the fortune teller at the festival.

Divided, she said. My aura was *divided*.

Could she have been talking about my feelings, divided between Maya and Ari?

Well, if that was the case, I certainly don't feel divided anymore. And as far as her story? The farmer and the horse and the moralizing?

Not helpful. I thought fortune tellers were supposed to offer some guidance, some wisdom, some *clarity*, not just tell cryptic fairy tales that don't—

I gasp.

Wait.

That's it.

The idea hits so hard that I lose my balance, tilting too far back. The chair crashes onto the carpet.

"Should have seen that coming," I mutter, scrambling to my feet. The good news is that I avoided squashing my sculpture by a mere six inches, so . . . maybe my luck is taking a turn for the better?

I leave the chair where it is and dash upstairs. I poke my head into the living room and see Mom watering plants and Lucy reading a graphic novel on the couch. Not who I'm looking for. I head up to the second floor. The door to Pru and Ellie's room is open, and I can hear Ellie talking to herself.

I peek inside to see Ellie kneeling in front of the dollhouse she got for her birthday a couple of years ago. She's holding Disney's Jasmine in one hand, Rapunzel in the other, and it sounds like Jasmine is trying to convince Rapunzel that she really does have to go to the dentist, otherwise all her teeth are going to fall out. Funny, I'm pretty sure my parents had that exact talk with Ellie a few days ago.

I knock on the door. "Hey," I say, stepping into the room. "Do you still have that Magic 8 Ball?"

Ellie tilts her head at me. "Yeah. It's in there." She points to the small wooden toy box that lives next to Pru's bookshelf. "Why are your hands all red?"

"Had to make something out of clay for art class."

She gasps excitedly. "Can I make something?"

"Uh—not right now." I dig through the assortment of dolls, accessories, ponies, and random craft supplies, and find the Magic 8 Ball buried at the bottom. "Can I borrow this?"

She's pouting about the clay, but nods anyway. I thank her and head out of the room, back down two flights of stairs, back to my bedroom. I walk past the fallen chair and sit on the edge of my bed, clutching the plastic ball in both hands.

If I can't rely on luck to give me the answers I'm looking for, I'll try a different tactic.

A different kind of magic.

I'll ask the universe.

I squeeze my eyes shut.

"Does Ari like me?" I ask out loud, cringing even as I say it, because, *yeah*, I get how pathetic that sounds. But if we're doing this, we're doing this.

I give the ball a shake and hold my breath as I flip it over. My hands are leaving rust-colored fingerprints on the shiny plastic as the little triangle bobs up against the glass.

Reply hazy, try again.

"Okaaay," I say. "I guess there are worse answers. To be more specific—does Ari like me? Like, like-like me."

Shake, shake. Stare.

Outlook not so good.

My chest tightens.

"Are you sure?"

You may rely on it.

I scowl. Is this ball being sassy to me right now?

After a second, I ask, "Is there any hope of her liking me in the future?"

Without a doubt.

I sit up straighter. "Really?"

As I say it, the little triangle tips against the glass, to a new answer.

Very doubtful.

I deflate, pressing my brow to the cool plastic. "Jerk." I sigh and give it another shake. "Should I ask Ari out?"

As I see it, yes.

"Oh, is that how you see it? But why—since evidently, I don't have a chance."

Shake.

Wait.

Better not tell you now.

"Uh-huh. Would she say yes?"

Most likely.

I press my fingers into its sides until my knuckles turn white. "Should I ignore everything you're telling me?"

Yes definitely.

I snort.

"Is the universe playing a practical joke on me right now?"

It is decidedly so.

"It certainly feels that way." I lower the Magic 8 Ball into my lap, lips pursed together. It really does feel like some unseen power is toying with me. But . . . "Why me?"

I look down.

Sigh.

Give it one last shake.

It seems to take it a long time, as if the Magic 8 Ball is thinking. Then, finally, the little triangle appears out of the blue.

Ask again later.

I let out a guttural groan and flop back on the covers. "The dice never talked back to me," I mutter, feebly tossing the Magic 8 Ball onto the floor.

It lands with a sickening, squishy *thud*. My whole body flinches. Then I let out a pathetic noise, somewhere between a laugh and a sob, as I cover my face with my hands. I don't need to look to know that I just flattened Araceli the Magnificent. So much for my luck taking a turn for the better.

Chapter Thirty-Three

"You sounded great tonight," I say, in a tone that is totally friendly and casual and in no way gives away the fact that I spent most of this open mic night wondering what would happen if I pulled Ari into the back room, and—

"Thank you," Ari says, beaming at me as we stack the chairs against the wall. "We had some fun performers tonight. I thought that guy who was playing his own acoustic blues songs was fantastic."

"Yeah. He was great," I say, even though I barely heard any other performances all night.

"You're *kidding* me," comes my dad's voice from the back room—more than a little irritated, which is unusual for him, and therefore extra disconcerting.

Ari and I exchange a look. The store closed ten minutes ago, and only the three of us are left.

"Dad?" I call. "Everything okay?"

He emerges a second later, pulling a frustrated hand through his hair. "I just got a notice that our shipment for Record Store Day has been delayed. Hundreds of records—the ones you ordered? The special promotions that are the entire point of Record Store Day?" He raises his hands in exasperation. "Stuck in a warehouse. They haven't even been sent out yet. They're saying they won't deliver for another two weeks!"

My heart drops. The records that *I* ordered.

Of course they would be delayed.

"Crap. I'm sorry, Dad."

He stands massaging his brow with one hand, the other planted on his hip, stress wafting off his body in waves. "Not your fault, obviously."

I swallow hard.

"You'd think they'd have their act together. It's only the biggest sales day of the year!" He looks around at the store, shaking his head. "What are we going to do? If we don't have any special promos going on, what's the point of participating this year?"

"It's still a great day to show people how important we are to the community," says Ari. "A locally owned business that supports the artist community . . . that's not nothing."

I smirk at Ari. "You've been spending too much time with Pru."

Dad sighs. "I know you're right. It's not . . . *pointless*. We can still hope for a good turnout, and increased sales. But it's so frustrating. I'd drive to the warehouse and pick up the shipment myself if they'd let me!"

"We still have a week," I say. "Maybe something will change. Or we can come up with something else to make the day special. Get customers excited."

"I'll talk to Pru about it tomorrow," says Ari. "You know she lives for this sort of challenge."

Dad nods, though he looks unconvinced. "That she does."

"You should go home, Dad," I say. "You've worked every day this week. Ari and I can finish closing up."

He looks between us, and I expect him to argue, but then he rubs his brow some more and nods. "I think I'll take you up on that. Thanks. Both of you. I'm sure I'll have a clearer head about this in the morning."

After Dad leaves, Ari and I finish putting the chairs away.

I walk to the end of one of the display shelves and wait for Ari to grab the other side so we can roll it back to its normal place, but Ari stands with her head crooked to the side, studying the store.

"Ari?"

She twirls toward me. "I'm going to mop," she says, with a determined nod.

"What? Now?"

She heads to the back room. After a second, I hear the water running in the large utility sink, and I walk back to see her filling our mop bucket with sudsy water.

"It's after nine o'clock," I say. "Why are you mopping?"

"Because it's filthy," she says. "When was the last time these floors were cleaned?"

I consider this, and don't have an answer. Not since I've worked here, I don't think.

"Exactly," says Ari, thrusting the broom into my hands before grabbing the mop for herself. "And now is the best time to do it, when all the furniture is pushed off to the side. We'll have to do it in two stages. We'll do the part that's clear now, then move all the shelves into the front part of the store and do the back. You sweep up the big chunks first, and I'll follow after you with the mop."

"Okay, but . . . why?"

She rolls her eyes. "Your dad is clearly very stressed out about Record Store Day. We can't make those records magically appear, but don't you think it would be a nice surprise for him to show up tomorrow and have the store looking a little bit nicer?"

To be honest, I'm not sure that clean floors are the sort of thing my dad will notice, but I can tell Ari's heart is in the right place. So I take the broom and get busy.

For a long time, we work in silence. And no, it isn't weird.

There are no awkward vibes between us. Why would there be? It isn't like I'm analyzing every look she gives me, or every time we bump into each other, or wondering what it means that she's humming to herself while she works, practically waltzing around with the mop.

Eventually Ari breaks the silence by telling me about some new song she's been working on that she's really excited about, and I tell her some of my early ideas for our next D&D campaign, and it feels like old times. Like nothing has changed at all.

Except for when Ari's feet give a tiny skip that I'm not sure she's even aware of, and my heart exactly mimics the movement.

That part is new.

I give my head a quick shake, trying to erase the vision of the long threads from her frayed jean shorts swaying against her thighs.

Once we're done with the front half of the store, we move over the furniture and repeat the process with the back. Once we're done, we both stand back to admire our work.

"It's beautiful," says Ari.

"I would eat off this floor," I tell her.

She taps her fingers contemplatively against her mouth. "I would *dance* on this floor."

I peer at her from the corner of my eye, but she's already prancing over to the record player and digging through the bin of records beside it. "What album should we christen the space with?" she asks.

I don't bother making a suggestion, because she's the one with the encyclopedic musical knowledge. I watch her pull a record from its jacket and set it on the turntable. She lowers the needle, and the store fills with familiar crackles, more noticeable in the silence than they are during the day.

Then an almost eerie voice coupled with a hypnotic drumbeat.

"The Beatles?" I say, as John Lennon starts singing about *grooving up slowly* . . .

"*Abbey Road*," says Ari. "One of the best albums of all time. It seemed fitting."

Then she's grabbing my hands and pulling me into the center of the room.

"Whoa, whoa, whoa," I say, jerking away. "What are you doing?"

"What?" she says, apparently unbothered as she starts to dance circles around me, her arms reaching gracefully toward the ceiling. "No one else is here."

258

"There are people outside," I say, gesturing to the bare windows. "They could see everything."

"It's late! There are no *people*," she says. But she doesn't push, just keeps vibing to the music. *Come together, right now* . . .

I swallow hard, heat flaming across my cheeks as I watch her. I try to mold my expression into something skeptical, something aloof, but it's not easy. Not when her long hair is swinging against her arched back. Her feet tapping, spinning, tiptoeing across the new floor. Her hips swaying in perfect time with the music.

She looks back at me once, and there must be something truly mortifying about my expression, because she barks out a laugh and punches me in the shoulder. "Are you really just going to stand there?"

"Yep," I croak.

"Come on, we are celebrating! Another successful open mic night, a soon-to-be-successful Record Store Day, no matter those stupid shipping delays! What else can we celebrate?"

"I thought we were celebrating clean floors."

"That too!" She keeps dancing, attempting to get me to move with her. I staunchly refuse, which only makes her try harder, until it becomes a game. Her shoulders rubbing against mine. Her hands molding my body into poses that are almost dancelike. Ari is singing along now, too. *Got to be good-looking, 'cause he's so hard to see!*

My heart pounds along with the drums in the background, and I am so grateful when the song finally comes to an end.

"Welp, that was fun," I say, heading toward the record player.

"No, wait!" Ari says, laughing as she latches on to my arm. The next song begins. Slow and sweet and hypnotic. One of the Beatles' most well-known love songs.

Something in the way . . .

"I know you'll dance with me to this one," she says. "You have to."

Panic rushes through me. "Why do I have to dance to this?" I ask, trying to keep my voice from feeling strained.

"Because if you're taking Maya to prom, you're going to have to slow dance."

My lips part in surprise. Doesn't she know?

But no—how could she? I haven't said anything about it.

"Come on, wimp," she says, taking my hand and placing it on her waist. The movement is so fast, so no-nonsense, I hardly register what's happening until it's done. The feel of her soft shirt under my palm, and the smallest sliver of bare skin where her shirt rides up. My breath catches in my throat. She settles one hand on my shoulder, takes the other into hers. Old-fashioned slow dancing. "Just one song?"

My heart is thumping madly, like it's trying to escape. Does she feel the way my arm is shaking? Is my hand sweating too much?

Every instinct is telling me I need to escape from this, and fast, before things get dramatically out of control.

Before Ari realizes—

"Jude," she stays sternly. "Don't make this weird."

"It's already weird," I respond immediately.

She sighs, and I can tell I've disappointed her. "You're hopeless."

"I'm sorry."

"Literally all you have to do is sway a little."

"Yep. Sway. Got it."

But I don't. I do not sway, and since she's apparently waiting for me, neither does Ari. We stay perfectly still, her gaze on my shirt and mine on a single strand of dark hair that has curled rebelliously away from the others.

Five seconds pass.

Ten.

We meet each other's eyes.

Then, in unison, we both start to laugh.

Big, rolling, breathless laughs. The kind of laughter that has Ari buckling forward until her forehead smacks me on the chest. Then her hand is over her mouth like she might be able to hold in the uncontrollable giggles, and that just makes me laugh even harder.

I pull her closer and wrap my arms around her shoulders. Just a hug. Just two friends, sharing a moment of temporary madness spurred on by temporary awkwardness.

By the time we're catching our breath, Ari is tucked into my arms, her head beneath my chin, rubbing tears from her eyes.

"You *are* hopeless," she says again.

To which I blurt out, "I'm not taking Maya to prom."

Ari goes still for a heartbeat.

She pulls away, and I reluctantly allow it, though one hand lingers uncertainly at her waist. "What?"

"Junior prom. Any prom," I amend. "We've decided to just be friends."

"Oh, Jude. I'm sorry. Are you okay?" She lays a hand on my arm, and for some reason, this prompts me to edge closer again. Just a tiny bit. Just enough to keep her close to me.

I shouldn't want to keep her close to me.

I do, though.

It's a problem, but I *do*.

"I'm fine, actually." I swallow. "It turns out I don't like Maya as much as I thought I did. At least . . . not in that way. I've thought about it a lot this week, and . . ." I don't know how to finish that sentence.

Soft music swirls around us but we aren't dancing. And since it seems way weirder to just stand there, motionless, in something halfway to an embrace, I take a breath and reach for Ari's hand. She starts at the unexpected movement, but as soon as I start dancing, swaying gently back and forth, Ari follows. She lets me lead her in slow, steady turns around the store. Our feet sliding inch by inch, shuffling slowly to the beat of the music.

"This might sound strange," I say, once I've had a moment to gather my thoughts, "but I think maybe my crush on Maya was like . . . a defense mechanism."

She keeps her eyes on me, but something has changed. When she was urging me to dance with her before, she was carefree and eager. But now there's something guarded in her expression. "What do you mean?"

261

"I never planned on asking her out. Taking her to the concert was kind of a fluke, and if I hadn't won those tickets, I never would have done it. So it's like, having this huge crush on her was *safe*. I never had to act on it. Because when the feelings are real, then the risks are bigger, and . . . that's a lot scarier."

Ari looks like she's trying to puzzle through my words, like maybe I've been speaking in code. And I guess, in a way, I have been.

Because speaking in code is safer, too.

"But once I did ask her out," I continue, "and got to know her, she wasn't just this impossible dream anymore. She's real, and she's great, but . . . we're not right together. And I'm okay with that."

Ari doesn't respond. The tips of her hair brush against the hand I have spread against her lower back, and it's nothing but sheer willpower that keeps me from taking a strand of that hair and wrapping it around my fingers. Feeling its softness. Running my hand down its length.

I would give up my Lego *Millennium Falcon* to know what Ari is thinking in that moment, but she doesn't say anything about my genius revelation. She doesn't say anything at all.

"You were right," I say, once the silence has stretched out for too long. "This floor is made for dancing."

She makes a sound that's almost a chuckle, but it's quiet and distracted.

We stop dancing and Ari tilts her face up toward mine.

We are close. Really close. She is breathtaking, and I don't know how I managed to pretend otherwise for so long. How have I never paid any attention to the way my heart aches when she touches me? And this tingling in my lips—is it new, or am I just now recognizing it for what it is?

"Ari," I murmur, even though I don't know what I want to say. I just want to say her name. Just want to hear it, and know she's here, and this is real, this is actually happening, and . . .

My fingers curl into the fabric of her T-shirt.

Ari inhales, a quick, wavering breath. But she doesn't pull away, and she's looking at my lips, and I—

I slip.

I'm not even *moving* and yet, somehow, my heel catches on a slick spot from the mop water and next thing I know, I'm falling backward, pulling Ari down with me. We both yelp and land in a heap, Ari halfway on top of me, her elbow in my stomach. Pain ricochets from my butt all the way up my spine from landing on the hard floor.

I groan.

"What just happened?" says Ari. "Are you okay?"

"Yeah. I slipped. You okay?"

"Yeah. Mostly surprised."

I meet her gaze, still cringing from the pain. Ari is on her side, propped up on one palm, her hand on my chest, legs tangled with mine, and despite my bruised backside and my bruised ego . . . this isn't a terrible place to be, either.

Until the door to the record store swings open, the string of bells rattling as loud as a fire alarm.

We might be on fire for as fast as we pull away from each other.

"Ari!" shrieks Pru, hurrying toward us and waving her phone in the air. "You are never going to believe this!"

Chapter Thirty-Four

Pru freezes then, frowning at us on the floor. "What's going on?"

"Nothing," we both shout, scrambling to our feet. I don't notice the song coming to an end until the next song on the album starts to play—the jaunty and disturbing "Maxwell's Silver Hammer," which is not romantic in the least, thank you, music gods.

"I slipped," I stammer. "Why are you here?" I look at the clock—it's after ten.

Pru looks at the mop and the damp spots on the floor, and her effusive smile returns. "Dad said you stayed late at the store, and I wanted to show Ari this in person. Ari's gone viral!"

"Viral?" says Ari, sounding only a tiny bit breathless. "What do you mean?"

She's collected herself a hell of a lot quicker than I have. She seems almost unaffected by that . . . thing . . . that almost happened, whereas I am doing my best to will the heat from my face. I busy myself by going over and stopping the record player. Then I put my hands in my pockets to keep them from shaking and wish, for the thousandth time this week, that my dice was there when I reached for it.

So either Ari is a way better actor than I am, or—that thing that almost happened was more in my head than hers. Because I'm pretty sure that I almost kissed Ari, that I definitely *would* have kissed her if Pru hadn't come barging in. Was I just imagining the way Ari was leaning in closer? The way her eyes were beginning to close? Was I trying to interpret signals that weren't actually there?

Ari has always been affectionate. The sort of friend who isn't embarrassed to hug you goodbye or snuggle into your side during the scary parts of a movie or do a thousand other little things that I would have thought were flirting if it was anyone else.

Just because she asked me to dance on this perfect, wide-open dance floor doesn't mean she wanted me to kiss her. It was just . . . Ari. Being Ari.

Wasn't it?

I'm so caught up in my thoughts that it takes me a hot second to get caught up on whatever Pru is so excited about, though she's been rambling nonstop since she interrupted us. Which I'm glad she did.

Obviously.

Really, really glad.

So glad I sort of want to take her phone and chuck it through the window.

Pru's cheeks are flushed as she talks, a combination of her excitement and the fact that she probably just rode her bike here all the way from home—I see it leaning against the wall outside.

"Someone filmed your performance and the awards," says Pru. Ari takes the phone from her, and they both focus on the screen. "I looked up footage from the past few years they've hosted this contest, and they typically get a few thousand views. But this one already has more than fifty thousand, and the comments are *not* nice."

"Not nice?" I say, my hackles rising instinctively. "To Ari?"

"Oh no, everyone loves Ari," says Pru. "Most people think she should have won, or really, any of the other finalists. That girl who did win is a joke."

Ari winces. "That's terrible. They don't even know her!"

Pru sighs and gives Ari an impatient look. "And when has that ever stopped people from criticizing someone on the internet?"

"I'm just saying, she is a person," says Ari. "With feelings. Even if people don't like her song—"

Pru waves her comment away. "Yes, yes, people are jerks. That's not the point. Ari, this is the best thing that could have happened to you."

Ari's brow creases. "How?"

"Because a regular old songwriting competition hardly gets any interest, unless maybe that song goes on to be in the Top 40 or something. For the most part, contests like this are ignored by the general public. But controversy!" Pru beams like she's just been offered a shopping spree at the Container Store. "People like controversy. They're even hypothesizing that there could be foul play involved, and trying to look into the judges to see if anyone could have pulled some strings to get this girl picked as the winner. Now, I obviously don't know if that's true or not, but it has created speculation and it has people talking, and look!" She grabs the phone back and opens a new window with Ari's video.

My eyes widen as I see how many hits it has—ten times more than the last time I watched it, and her subscriber count has increased exponentially, too.

"There are even reels of people lip-syncing to the song!" Pru scrolls to a couple other social media channels to prove it. We watch, stunned, as two girls about Penny's age belt out a heartfelt rendition of "Downpour."

Ari presses her hands to her cheeks. "I can't believe this."

"As your manager, I advise you to put out more content," says Pru.

Ari is speechless, still staring at the phone screen.

"Promptly," Pru adds.

Her tone startles Ari into looking up. "Oh. Um. I do have a few new songs . . . or we could record some of my older ones . . ."

"Whatever you're comfortable with," says Pru. "I don't want you to post anything that isn't ready yet, but this has the potential to get you and your songs a lot of attention. Strike while the iron is hot!"

Ari smiles, looking a little dazed.

"Also, I have a proposition for you," Pru continues, her whole face lit up. "What would you say about performing at this year's Record Store Day?" She says it like it's a bigger deal than it really is, even selling the

266

idea with a big sweep of both of her hands in the air, like she's framing an invisible banner overhead.

Ari frowns, and I get her confusion. She's performed here during every open mic night for months. "Sure?"

"You're not seeing the vision," says Pru, grabbing Ari by both shoulders. "You're it, Ari. The big draw! A local, award-winning singer/songwriter whose song went viral before she even got her first publication deal. This is huge, and if you agree, I am going to promote the heck out of this. We'll announce it on your channel, of course, but I bet I can get local media attention on this, too. The *Chronicle* loves stories like this."

Ari's eyes widen, a little nervous, but she says, "You're my manager, so I guess . . . promote away!"

Pru does a wiggly happy dance. "Music to my ears."

Chapter Thirty-Five

Hey, Ari. I was wondering if you'd be up for getting dinner tonight?

Too casual.
Delete. Delete. Delete.

Hey! Just out of curiosity, have you seen the new Marvel movie yet?

Not casual enough.
Delete. Delete. Delete.

Surprise! I have major romantic-y feelings for you. Text Y if you feel the same way. Text N to stop receiving these texts.

Delete. Delete. So much delete.

Was thinking of going to karaoke tomorrow. Wanna go?

Unnnnnnggggghh.

I must have typed a hundred different texts into my phone these past few days, but nothing sounds right. Everything sounds either too cheesy or too serious or not serious enough. It's either too chill or it's too intense, like I will be positively devastated if she rejects me.

I keep reminding myself that this isn't a declaration of love. This is just a friend . . . asking out another friend . . . to see if maybe we could become something more than friends.

No big deal.

But every time I'm about to hit send, my insides squeeze and a cold sweat breaks out on the back of my neck and I delete the text as fast as I can.

And this is *Ari*. I've texted Ari so many times. Hell, I've probably sent a thousand texts *just like this*—inviting her to movies and dinner and—well, not karaoke. Ari's the one who always drags me and Pru along to karaoke night. Like it's *no big deal*. Because it's not!

And yet I see Ari now whenever I close my eyes. The way her gaze darted to my mouth when I was sure I wanted to kiss her. When I was sure, however briefly, that she wanted me to.

My pulse stutters, just like it did then. My skin flushes. My mouth goes dry.

And I hate this. I hate that these inconvenient emotions have made me nervous to talk to Ari. *Ari*, of all people. It's unnatural. Ari, Pru, and I have been attached to each other since seventh grade. We've ridden our bikes countless times up and down the boardwalk. Shopped for matching Halloween costumes (my personal fav: Mario, Luigi, and Princess Peach, and yeah, Pru really rocked that mustache). We've fought over the armrests in the movie theater—and rubbed elbows on my own couch at home, and on *her* couch, for that matter. Hell, this is the girl who has *literally slept in my bed.*

I mean, I wasn't in it with her, but still. That's a thing that has happened, more than once.

I'm just about to gather my courage and hit send (no seriously, I'm going to do it this time), when a new email notification pops up. I'm only too happy for the distraction, so I click over right away, and—

Oh.

Hello Jude, thank you for your recent submission.
I'm afraid it is not right for us at this time, but please
do keep us in mind for future submissions.

Best,
Ralph Tigmont
Art Director, the *Dungeon*

I read through it once and instantly hit delete.

I'm disappointed, but not surprised. I hadn't really expected them to take the drawing of Araceli the Magnificent onstage at the Condor Music Festival. If anything, the rejection has me feeling numb. Almost . . . resigned.

Shoulders slumping, I set my phone aside and try to return to my work, which I was actually making great progress on until I got waylaid by a rush of inspiration to text Ari and ask her on a not-a-date that has the potential to turn into a date, but that clearly isn't working out for me, so—back to the task at hand.

The website DIYVinyl.com popped up along with the influx of newsletters and promotions that have been pouring into my inbox since my flurry of sweepstakes entering. It's a service for printing your own vinyl records, promising quality sound and quick delivery. I've never given much thought to what goes into producing an actual vinyl album, but they've made the process pretty easy so far.

So this is my newest brilliant idea.

I will make Ari an album. I will have it printed and shipped in time for Record Store Day. I will surprise my dad with an exclusive record to sell at Ventures, I will surprise the world with the very first Araceli Escalante song collection, and I will surprise Ari with this thing that she may not even know she wants, but I really, really think she is going to like.

This is my big gesture. My silent declaration.

Not bad, right?

I was worried I wouldn't be able to find enough audio files to fill both an A and B side, but luckily, Pru and Ari have been hard at work uploading new songs to Ari's YouTube channel. Though none of them have gotten as much attention as "Downpour," her views and subscribers are shooting up daily. The hardest decision has been figuring out which songs to pick, as I consider things I've never considered before, like the musical flow between songs and whether or not this album should "tell a story."

But that's a dangerous path, because if there is a story, I want to be a part of it, and I'm not sure if I am. Ari sings about love a lot. She sings about heartache and feelings unrequited. She sings about hiding and pretending and trying to move on. Could anything here be inspired by me, or is it the height of arrogance to even ask that?

Finally, I make my selections and upload them to the site.

Next comes the hardest part: artwork. I've been thinking about it all day, but haven't figured out the Just Right Thing yet. A photo of Ari and her guitar? Something from her video, or one of our open mic nights? I've gone through her socials and Pru's, looked back through countless photos of us together, and . . . yeah, okay, maybe wasted a lot of time staring dreamily at pictures I never thought to stop and admire before. The way her nose scrunches up when she's mid-laugh. The way her lips quirk to one side when she's about to tease me about something. The way she mindlessly chews on one knuckle when she's trying to think up the perfect song lyrics.

There are a lot of great photos of Ari, pictures that make my heart squeeze so tight I almost can't breathe. But for the cover of her first album? Nothing seems *right*.

And then . . . an idea.

I pick up my phone again and open my folder of scanned art. Right at the top is the sketch I did of Araceli the Magnificent onstage at the music festival, the audience listening rapt in front of her.

It may not have been what the *Dungeon* was looking for, but for this . . . it might work. Actually, it might not be bad at all.

Except, something's missing.

It takes me a second to find the original artwork. I make a few copies, then spend an hour adding sparing strokes of watercolor until I'm happy with it. (I guess I did learn something that day in visual arts, despite all my fumbling around.)

The back of the album, I decide, will be black with white line art like the doodles in her first video. A cloud with a lightning bolt, swirls of waves down below, a sailboat, and a few tiny hearts beside the song list.

The hardest part is figuring out how many copies to order. How many will actually sell at the store? But in the end, I just order as many as I can afford.

My finger hovers over the "complete order" button for a long moment, remembering when I put my hand over Ari's to post her first video. Back when I was luckier than King Midas.

Of course . . . in the end, I guess he wasn't all that lucky, either.

I brace myself and place the order.

Exhaling, I sit back.

I hope they arrive in time.

I hope she likes it.

Also . . . I should probably do some homework.

A merciful knock interrupts me just as I'm pulling *The Great Gatsby* from my bag. "Yeah?"

Penny pokes her head down the stairs. "Are you busy?"

"Uh . . . nope," I say, tossing the book onto my desk and shutting the laptop. "Not really."

She hops down the stairs, her violin clutched in one hand. "I was wondering if you would listen to my solo."

"Oh. Yeah, sure. When's your next recital?"

"A week from Wednesday."

"Let's hear it."

She beams at me and raises the violin, nestling it under her chin. It takes me a second to realize she doesn't have her sheet music with her. I know she's been working hard to memorize more of her parts lately, and I'm impressed before she even starts to play.

Penny draws the bow across the strings. The sound warbles at first. There's an aura of uncertainty, of doubt.

But then the tempo picks up, and the nerves seem to fade away.

I grin, watching her play. I've heard this before. A bunch of times, in fact, as she's been practicing for weeks now. But I haven't really *listened*. I notice the precision of the bow, the way she sways in time with the music, the way her brow is furrowed in concentration, even as the movements appear second nature.

I'm no violin aficionado, but I'm pretty sure she nails it.

I am ridiculously proud of my little sister as she finishes and lowers the violin to her side.

"Brava," I say, clapping. "Penny, that was fantastic."

She bounces happily on her toes. She doesn't ask if I mean it. She doesn't have to. "Thanks. I think that was the best I've done so far."

"I know you've been practicing a lot, and it really shows," I say. "Hey—you should think about playing at the store on Record Store Day. I know you said you don't like playing solo in front of a crowd, but you're really good. People would love it. Mom and Dad would love it."

I expect her to resist the idea, like she always does at open mic night, but she doesn't. Spots of pink appear on her cheeks as she taps the bow idly against the side of her leg.

"Actually, I sort of had an idea, but . . . I don't know."

"What is it?"

"You know Ari's song? 'Downpour'? The one everyone's been talking about?"

"Yeah, of course." No need to tell her that I easily make up a couple thousand of those plays on YouTube.

"I haven't talked to Ari about this or anything, but . . . I was listening to it last week, and I sort of . . . came up with a solo? Like, for the bridge."

"A violin solo?"

She nods shyly.

"Penny! That's awesome. Ari would love that."

"You think so?"

"Definitely. You should talk to her about it. The two of you could perform together."

She digs a toe into the carpet. She looks unsure, but also excited.

"Want me to ask her?"

Relief wells in her eyes. "Would you?"

"Yeah, sure. But I know she's going to love the idea."

She bounces in place. "Thanks, Jude!" She surprises me with a sideways hug, careful to keep the tip of her bow from poking out my eye, then turns and bolts back up the stairs.

I'm still smiling after her when my phone dings. I glance down.

Ari: Sure!

My heart stutters.

Sure? Sure *what*?

Oh no. That last text . . . it didn't . . . !

I grab my phone and sit on the edge of my bed, unlocking the screen. My texts glare up at me, and there it is, the most recent one I sent.

Was thinking of going to karaoke tomorrow. Wanna go?

And Ari's reply.

Sure!

My breaths are suddenly stilted as I sort through the rush of panic and the subsequent rush of elation.

I did it! I texted her! I asked her out! By accident, but still. And she said *yes*.

Not "don't count on it." Not "ask again later." But *yes*.

I start to laugh, a bit giddily. Dinner. Karaoke. With Ari. Tomorrow!

Three dots appear—Ari typing something else.

I tense, holding my breath, anticipating her next words.

I thought you'd never ask.

I've been thinking about you all day.

I'm really looking forward—

I'll see if EZ wants to come too.

Fizzle, fizzle, die.

Eyes rolling back into my head, I collapse onto my pillow.

Eons later, I sigh and type out a response.

Cool. I'll check with Pru and Quint. See you there.

Chapter Thirty-Six

Things girls like, according to Hollywood:
 Flowers
 Chocolates
 Expensive jewelry

Things Ari likes, according to observation:
 Thrift store bargains
 Popcorn drenched with Tapatío
 Discovering obscure indie bands that no one
  else has ever heard of

"What are you working on so studiously over here?"

I slap my hand over my notebook and turn innocent eyes up to Carlos. "Nothing," I say quickly. "Just notes for a school project."

Carlos gives me a look, then peers down at my hidden notebook. One eyebrow ticks upward. "Uh-huh," he says. "Meeting someone special again today?"

"Special? No. Not at all. What makes you think that?"

His frown deepens. Meanwhile, incriminating heat is rushing into my cheeks.

"Just Pru and Quint," I say. "And . . . Ari. They should all be here soon. I think. Might be a few minutes."

A group in the next booth starts cheering loudly. I gesture lamely at the big-screen TV behind the bar, where a basketball game is playing. "Big game tonight?"

Carlos's expression becomes even more suspicious. "First game of the playoffs."

"Oh." I nod. "So . . . that's a yes?"

Shaking his head, Carlos says, "Do you want to order now, or are you going to wait for everyone?"

"Uh—no, I'll go ahead and order."

"Tostones, nachos, Shirley Temples?"

"You know us well," I say. "Oh, but um . . . extra cherries in Ari's drink. And—you know what, put some extra ones in mine, too?"

Carlos rocks back on his heels. "You got it."

"Oh, and jalapeños. On the nachos. Please."

He hesitates. We usually request to have the jalapeños removed, because Pru and I don't care for them, though sometimes Ari will ask for them on the side.

"If you insist," he says. "Anything else?"

"That's it for now. Thanks, Carlos."

As he walks away, I glance down at my notes, which are, upon further examination, completely useless. What am I going to do? Woo Ari with spicy snacks and a gift card to Annette's Consignment?

With a groan, I tear out the page and crumple it up.

"That better not have been a new drawing."

My spine stiffens as Ari slides into the half-circle booth. She's wearing her plaid shirt, the one that looks like it's been laundered to within an inch of its life, like it's held together by clouds and unicorn fur.

Which is to say—soft. It looks really soft.

She scoots in all the way until she's right next to me, and I know—logically I know—that she is leaving space for Pru and Quint and Ezra. But also, illogically—*she is right next to me. Practically touching me. I can smell her hair.*

"You're early," I stammer, clenching the crumpled page tighter in my fist and panicking momentarily that I might drop it and she might pick it up, and through some weird twist like in the movies, all would be comically revealed . . .

For better or worse.

With these muddled thoughts in my head, I miss her response.

"So?" she says.

I blink. "So what?"

She gestures at the paper. "You know how I feel about the needless destruction of fine art."

I scoff. "Naw. This is just . . . notes. For something I'm working on. I ordered for us already. Hope that's okay. Nachos."

"Yum." She smiles, but I can't hold her gaze. My heart is a staccato drumbeat. From the corner of my eye, I watch Ari unravel her silverware from its paper napkin, and I have a nearly irresistible urge to take her hand. Maybe I don't need to wait for the albums to arrive to show her how I feel about her.

What would happen if I just . . . *told her*?

I sit straighter. Take in a breath and don't let it back out again.

I start to reach for her hand, at the same time that she moves the fork to her other side and—

"Ow," I say, jerking back.

Ari gapes. "Oh! I'm sorry! Are you okay?"

"Yeah, fine," I say, looking at the four little indents at the base of my thumb where the fork got me. I clear my throat and drop my hands into my lap, squeezing them tight.

Carlos appears with a tray of Shirley Temples balanced on his palm. "Here we are," he says, setting down the four pink, sparkling drinks. "And extra cherries for the two of you." He slides our drinks to me and Ari, and we thank him.

Normally when we get Shirley Temples, Ari takes the cherries from my drink without even asking, because we both know I'm going to give them to her anyway. But this time it seems imperative that she knows I *want* her to have them, not that I'm just letting her get away with something for the sake of tradition. "Here," I say, plucking out the little toothpick speared through three red cherries. I go to drop them into Ari's drink, but one of them slides off the tip of the toothpick and drops, bouncing off the rim of the glass and into Ari's lap.

"Ack, sorry." I reach for the cherry as Ari bends over to see where it went.

Our foreheads collide.

"Oh!" Ari backs up, rubbing her brow.

I'm cringing. "Sorry. I'm sorry."

Letting the cherry go, wherever it landed on the floor, Ari sits up, laughing. "We're clumsy today."

"Evidently," I mutter.

Ari's grin starts to fade. "Is something going on?"

"No. Why? What do you mean?"

"You just seem . . ." She hesitates. "I don't know. Nervous, or something."

"Do I?" I say, intending to lie and insist I'm not nervous at all. Nothing to see here, folks. But then I think, *If ever there was a perfect opening, this is it.* "I mean. I guess I am. Maybe. A little."

She turns toward me, giving her full attention, her expression open and patient and completely oblivious to the fact that she is *not* making this easier. "What is it?"

"Um. So." My saliva turns thick and sticky in my mouth, and I can't look at her for more than a second at a time. Despite how many times this week I've thought about what I might say to her when this moment came, my thoughts are barren now, like I've never strung a full sentence together in my life. "Weird story. Well—I mean, not so weird. But maybe a little weird?"

Ari frowns, waiting.

All right, Jude. It's like peeling off a Band-Aid, right? Just—get it over with. Put it out there. The more you prolong it, the more painful it will be.

I force myself to look at her.

"It's just that . . . Ari, I really like—"

The bar explodes around us.

Not, like, a literal explosion. Just—excited, over-the-top hollering from every direction.

Ari and I both jump and look around. People are standing up, yelling at the television, where men in basketball jerseys are storming onto the court, surrounding one of the players, screaming and jumping up and down.

"Guess they won," says Ari.

"Guess so." I pause, before adding, "It's the first game of the play-offs."

"Oh." She turns back to me. "What were you saying?"

I scratch the back of my neck and consider beating a hasty retreat. But no. I'm here. I've come all this way. "Right. So . . . I was saying. We've been friends for a long time, right? Which is . . . great. You're great. And . . . and I . . ."

I might hyperventilate.

Ari leans closer, looking concerned. "Jude, you're kind of scaring me. What is it?"

"I was just wondering if you . . . would you ever . . . consider . . . maybe going on a—"

"Date night!" yells a voice, making me jump. *Quint.* "Been a while," he says, as he and Pru slide into the booth on my other side. "This brings back memories."

I force a smile and shift over to make room for them. Closer to Ari. She stays where she is, and now our thighs are pressed together. My pulse ratchets up even higher. I realize that I'm still clutching the torn-out notebook page in one hand, and I surreptitiously slide it into my jeans pocket.

"I thought EZ was coming," says Pru, counting the four beverages.

"He is," says Ari. "He had to stop by the garage, but he'll be here soon."

"I wasn't sure," I say. "So I didn't get him a drink."

"He can order his own when he gets here," says Pru, pulling her beloved binder from her backpack. "We've got business to take care of."

"We do?" asks Ari, wrapping her hands around the condensation-slick glass, the remaining cherries bobbing at the top of the ice. "I thought we were here for karaoke night."

"That too," says Pru. "But first—if it's okay with you—I was hoping we could record a new video for your social channels promoting Record Store Day this weekend."

"I already did that," says Ari. "I posted twice last week about—"

"I know, I know," Pru says hastily. "And your posts were great. But I thought we could do one more video about how this Record Store Day, we're having a special guest . . ." Pru raises her eyebrows.

"Me?" asks Ari.

"You!" Pru says. Then pauses. "You are still going to perform, aren't you?"

"Yeah, of course," she says. "I'm not sure how big of a draw that really is, though. Does anyone really care?"

"Um, how many views does 'Downpour' have on it again?" asks Pru. "And how many subscribers have you gotten the past couple of weeks?"

"Subscribers don't necessarily turn into sales. Or even people showing up."

"But it can't hurt," says Pru.

"Yeah, you're right. I don't mind doing it," says Ari. "I just don't want anyone to be disappointed. But—um, hold on." She looks at me. "I'm sorry, you were trying to say something before, and we got totally distracted."

"Nope," I say, raising both hands. "Not a big deal. I was just going to ask, um . . . if you talked to Penny? She . . . uh . . . had an idea. For your performance this weekend."

"Yes!" says Ari, pressing a hand to my forearm and killing me slowly. "We talked after school today, and she played the violin solo she's been working on. I think it's perfect! I'm so excited to do it with her."

"Cool. Excellent." I clear my throat. "Cool."

"Okay, then," says Pru, whipping out her phone and opening up the camera, but Quint immediately takes it away from her and starts adjusting the settings. "You know what to say?"

Ari tears her gaze from me. "I guess so. Something like . . . *Join me at Ventures Vinyl in Fortuna Beach this Saturday, in celebration of the annual Record Store Day! I will be performing throughout the day, and I can't wait to see you!*"

"You're a natural," says Quint.

Pru agrees. "Perfect. Just like that, but with more energy."

Ari pastes on an incandescent smile and gives two thumbs up, practically shouting this time. "I can't wait to see you!"

"Even better. This time I'll actually record it."

"Wait, one more thing," I say. "You should also tell people that there's going to be a special surprise at Ventures this weekend. One especially for your fans."

Pru gives me a look. "We were just talking about her performance, Jude. Keep up."

"Not the performance. Something else."

Ari tilts her head at me. "What surprise?" she and Pru ask in unison.

"Uh . . ." I look from Ari to my sister and back. Then, sheepishly, "It's a surprise?"

"Jude," Pru says warningly.

"Trust me. People will love it."

Though Pru looks skeptical, this seems good enough for Ari. She smiles at the camera, and Quint counts her down before starting to record.

They shoot the video six times before Pru is satisfied that Ari hit all the necessary talking points with the right energy level. Pru takes back her phone and immediately starts editing the video . . . or drafting up a caption . . . or whatever she does . . . right as our food arrives.

"Here we go, my hungry friends," says Carlos, setting a platter of nachos and a basket of tostones in front of us.

We all thank him while Ari passes out small plates for everyone.

Pru is reaching for a chip smothered in cheese and Encanto's signature guacamole, when she pauses. "You forgot to order it without the jalapeños."

"Uh—no," I say. "I know Ari likes them. And . . . Quint, too, right?"

Quint nods, a tostone already in his mouth.

"So I figured we could just pick around them. You know, like grown-ups."

Ari giggles. Pru looks displeased but puts some nachos on her plate anyway.

We dig in, and Quint starts telling us about some new marketing initiative that he and Pru are spearheading for the rescue center. Pru wants to do another fundraising gala at the end of the summer and make it an annual thing. She brings up the possibility of Ari performing her viral song there, too.

"Speaking of viral songs," says Quint, nodding toward Trish Roxby, the karaoke host, who has just entered the restaurant with a bunch of equipment on a dolly. Carlos springs around the bar to help her. Trish immediately starts talking a mile a minute, and as she and Carlos walk past, we catch bits of their conversation—some drama about a terrible first date with some guy she met on a dating app. Carlos is laughing at her extravagant portrayal . . . but there's something strained about it.

At first I think I'm imagining things, until I realize that all four of us are staring after them.

Slowly, Pru turns to look at the rest of us, her eyes narrowed. "Carlos is still single, right?"

Ari gasps delightedly, pressing her hands to her cheeks. "He has a crush!" she whisper-squeals. "On *Trish*!"

I look at her out of the corner of my eye. "Didn't *you* have a crush on *him*?" Honestly, it's been so long since she brought up what even she used to refer to as her "schoolgirl crush," I'd all but forgotten about it.

Ari rolls her eyes. "He is a very kind, very good-looking man who owns his own business and knows how to cook. Of course I had a crush on him. Half the people who come here probably have crushes on him."

"Maybe so," says Pru, a singsong lilt to her tone, "but he does not look at half the people who come in here like he's looking at *her*."

We all stare at Carlos and Trish in an unapologetically creepy manner. But neither of them seem to notice, too caught up in Trish's narrative and setting up the karaoke equipment and Carlos practically falling over himself to get her something to drink.

"Why doesn't he just ask her out?" says Pru.

To which Quint, Ari, and I all respond, "It's not that easy."

We all tense and look at each other like people do when they suspect they may have been assimilated into the Borg.

Pru looks duly freaked.

"Resistance is futile," I whisper.

She glares at me, the way she does whenever she doesn't get one of my nerd references. "He is a grown man. And a catch, as Ari has pointed out. If he likes her—"

"Hey, y'all, long time, no see!"

We all jump and turn to greet Trish standing beside our booth. Since I'm terrible at pretending that we weren't just talking about someone, I grab a nacho and pop it in my mouth to keep myself from saying something stupid.

Trish immediately starts cajoling Pru and Ari into singing tonight, and Ari says she has a couple of songs in mind, and—holy jalapeños, Batman, *why is my mouth on fire?*

My eyes bug, and I grab for my drink, accidentally knocking it over. Sprite and grenadine and ice slosh over the table, straight onto my lap. I yelp, but stuck between Pru and Ari, there's nowhere for me to go. "Sorry!" I cry. Without thinking, I grab Ari's glass and take a big drink through the straw. It tames the burning in my mouth, at least a little. "I'm okay," I choke, grasping for my last shreds of dignity as I pass Ari's drink back to her. It's mostly just ice now, and one cherry at the bottom, still impaled on a toothpick.

Pru is pulling napkins from the dispenser and tossing them at me. I take them, trying to appear more grateful than embarrassed.

"Jalapeño?" Ari asks.

"Yeah," I say. "But I'm pretty sure Carlos swapped that one with a ghost pepper."

Ari nods, feigning sympathy. "That was a very mean trick." Then she grabs a chip with *two* jalapeños and pops it into her mouth and chews and swallows like it's nothing.

I gape at her. "Do you even have taste buds, or have they all been incinerated by now?" I take the pile of napkins and dab at my wet pants. Yeah, *that's* a great look. Real suave, Jude.

"Get excited, for the party hath arrived!"

I freeze and cringe, and it is a full-body cringe that I immediately feel bad about, hoping no one else noticed.

Ezra slides into the booth next to Ari, putting me in the middle of our group. "This feels celebratory. What's the occasion? Did you know that National Lumpy Rug Day is coming up? Now, that's a holiday I can get behind. Ooh, can I have your cherry?" He winks suggestively at Ari, then, without waiting for her response, takes a spoon and scoops out the last remaining cherry in her glass and scrapes it off the toothpick with his teeth.

And yeah, maybe I just took a gulp of her drink without asking, but this is different, and the next thing I know, a burning rage is rising up in my chest.

Or maybe that's still the jalapeño.

"The occasion," says Ari, "is karaoke night." She pushes the song binder that Trish gave us toward him.

"Yes! Perfect!" cries EZ, raising both hands over his head. "This is the night you and I make history. EZ and Escalante, our first duet, baby."

Ari's eyes widen. "What?"

"Let's see what they got. Don't worry, I'll find us a good one."

Ari shoots a terrified expression at me and Pru, and given that every time Ezra has come with us to karaoke night, he's either sung "I'm Too Sexy" or "Barbie Girl," I do not blame her for being a little concerned.

Promptly at six, Trish takes the microphone and welcomes everyone. Karaoke night has been going on long enough now that a lot of people are regulars who come back week after week, so there's already a list of people waiting to perform.

We hear songs by Sheryl Crow, Bon Jovi, and the Weeknd before Trish picks up a card and reads "Next up—EZ and Escalante!"

"What?" says Ari, gesturing at him. "I don't even know what song you picked. What if it's one that I don't know?"

Ezra scoffs and gives her a *yeah, right* look as he slides out of the booth.

Ari makes an annoyed sound in her throat, but she follows him anyway, smoothing that soft plaid fabric around her hips as she heads up to the stage. That small movement makes my mouth go dry. I reach for my glass and try to take a sip before remembering it's empty.

The song starts up, a short percussion intro, a hint of a steel drum, then background vocals—*Aruba, Jamaica, ooh, I wanna take ya . . .*

"Kokomo" by the Beach Boys, one of my dad's favorite bands.

Ari gives Ezra a disbelieving look as he launches into the first verse. Ezra sings with gusto, but it's clear by the third line that he doesn't actually know the song all that well. With a roll of her eyes, Ari steps in to save him. She does know the words, and she sings on key, even if she isn't nearly as animated as he is. Ezra has no shame as he dances around Ari, shimmying his back to hers while they go on about jetting off to some tropical island, rolling around in the sand, falling in love . . .

I might actually be sick.

It's impossible to tell if Ari is uncomfortable or enjoying this or just merely tolerating Ezra's antics. And then, as they launch into the final chorus, it happens.

Ezra takes Ari's hand and drops to one knee in front of her. In front of *everyone*.

My world seizes. Tilts. Stutters.

"Ooh I wanna take ya—to prom! Oh prom! Please, let's go to prom! Araceli! Escalante! Go-o to prom! With me! EZ! La da da da da!"

He's obviously winging it at this point, hardly singing along to the music at all as the background vocals fade away. It doesn't matter that he sounds ridiculous. The restaurant is a cacophony of cheers, hoots, wolf whistles, as Ezra Kent promposes to Ari.

286

Ari . . . who looks shocked.

Ari . . . who looks bewildered.

Ari . . . who is starting to smile.

"Jude?"

I barely hear my name over the blood rushing through my ears and the chaos of a whole bunch of strangers rooting for the guy who is asking out the girl that I realized too late that I am in love with.

I look at my sister, who is frowning at me. "You okay?"

"Yeah. Awesome," I say, my voice tense. "Why?"

Rather than answering, she looks down at the napkin on the table. Or what used to be a napkin before I mindlessly tore it to shreds.

I swallow hard and sweep the pieces into a pile, dumping them onto my plate.

Ari and Ezra return to our table. Ezra's got his arm draped loosely over Ari's shoulders. He's beaming like he just won the lottery, because . . . yeah. *He just won the freaking lottery.*

Ari is smiling, too, but it's more nervous, more dazed. Her eyes meet mine and widen in a look of total dismay. A *can you believe that just happened?* look.

I force myself to smile back around clenched teeth.

I'd better get started on that epic ballad right away!

I do hope there aren't any hard feelings between us.

What? Oh! None at all.

Honestly, I think I was caught up in a moment of delusion.

Everything is much clearer to me now.

Including how much the two of you obviously belong together.

He's right. Before I met you, my dreams were filled with thieving and looting and viciously popping the heads off of every stirge I come across.

Bloodsucking little bastards.

But now, my dreams are of you and me. Thieving and looting and killing small obnoxious creatures...

together.

That's the most romantic thing anyone has ever said to me.

I'm just gonna...

Yep.

Okay. Bye then.

Chapter Thirty-Seven

Fine, Curse of Lundyn Toune. You win. I'm not going to fight it anymore. What does any of it matter? If Ari can be into Ezra Kent, of all people, then clearly, I never stood a chance. He and I couldn't be more different. He thrives when he's the center of attention. Lives for the spotlight. Loves getting a reaction from people—laughter, usually, but I think he'll pretty much take any reaction over being ignored. He is confident and outgoing and doesn't care what anyone thinks of him.

Whereas I was perfectly content to fly under the radar before all this happened. To just survive high school unscathed and go on my merry way.

So there. I don't need uncanny good luck. I don't need real-life magic. I certainly don't need love.

In fact, from what I can tell, all I really need . . . is to study.

"Jude, Jude, Jude," says Mrs. Andrews, clicking her tongue. I'm standing beside her desk, ignoring the fact that Maya, Matt, César, and Pru are all loitering in the hallway, waiting for me, even though class ended two minutes ago.

Mortification prickles my skin. A teacher has never asked to speak with me after class before, and I can't recall a teacher ever looking quite so disappointed in me, either.

"I don't know what's happened to you this semester," she says, handing me my test. A D is written at the top. "Is something going on that you want to talk about?"

It's a trap.

"No?"

She sighs, like she hadn't expected anything different, and I wonder how often she has some version of this conversation with her students, and how often they just want to dodge her questions and get out.

"Are you sure?" she asks. "Because you held a solid B plus last semester, and were doing great on all the tests at the start of this unit, but these past few weeks . . ." She hesitates, her gaze darting toward the hallway. I follow the look, and Maya gives me an encouraging wave. Mrs. Andrews clears her throat. "It seems you might be lacking some focus."

This is true. But I know better than to say so. "Can I do some extra credit or something?"

She sighs, disappointed that I'm not willing to dissect my problems with her.

"Fine," she says, waving a hand through the air. "Four pages, due next Monday."

I gulp. Record Store Day is this weekend.

But I guess that's what I get for slacking off all semester, relying on magic to maintain my grades.

"Sure," I say. "I can do that."

Things don't get better in statistics, when the worksheets that I *swear* I completed are nowhere to be found, and Mr. Robles has to mark me down for my fourth late assignment in two weeks. Add to that the fact that I bombed yesterday's test, and all I want is to drown my sorrows in Doritos by the time lunch rolls around. Except Mr. Robles also keeps me after class to talk about my slipping grades, and by the time I make it to the cafeteria, the line has run out of everything but wilty-looking Caesar salad and Jell-O cups, and to add insult to injury, the stupid vending machine eats two dollars and gives up zero chips.

"Dude, it's broken," Jackson yells, unapologetically and unhelpfully, as he strolls past.

I take my tray and sad, sad salad and head toward the table where Maya and the others are already half-finished with their meals, casting a forlorn look at Matt, César, and Russell as I walk past.

"Nice T-shirt," says Katie, in that way she has of making a compliment sound like an insult.

I glance down at the shirt that Penny got me for my birthday—the Hellfire Club logo from *Stranger Things*, season four. I know the shirt was 60 percent off at Hot Topic when she bought it, but still, given that Penny is too young for my parents to let her watch the show and has no idea what Hellfire Club even is, I thought it was a pretty darn thoughtful gift.

But I'm not a complete idiot. I can tell Katie isn't giving me a compliment. This is the first time in weeks I've shown up at school in what used to be my usual uniform—jeans, a T-shirt, my hand-painted dragon shoes, the soles of which have been shoddily repaired with my mom's hot glue gun. I didn't really think anyone would notice.

Obviously, I was wrong.

"Thanks?" I mutter, sliding into my spot next to Maya.

"*Stranger Things* must be, like," continues Katie, "a biopic for you, right?"

I blink slowly. Then—"Yeah. My friends and I have killed many demons in the Upside Down to prevent them from feeding on the clueless humans of our otherwise idyllic town." I pause, before adding, "You're welcome."

"*Snap*," says Raul. "I think Jude just dissed you, Katie."

She cuts a glare to him, and I immediately look down and start stabbing the romaine on my plate and pretending that my cheeks aren't burning. *Again.*

"Dissed by the wand-wielding weirdo?" says Katie. "Hard to be too offended." Her tone is joking, but the way she says it, I can tell she's had that insult at the ready for a while now, even if she's acting like it wasn't intended to be offensive.

"Lay off," says Maya, her tone darkening.

Katie sits back on the bench. "What? It was a joke."

I gaze at my barely touched lunch. I would give anything to be sitting at that other table right now . . .

"What I don't understand is why Jude is even still here," says Katie, heaving a drawn-out sigh.

I whip my head back up, wishing that this question didn't parrot my own thoughts. Countless times this week, I've wondered what I'm still doing at this table. Maya and I are not dating. Were never really dating, and won't ever be dating. But going back to my old table would require . . . I don't know. An explanation? An apology? It would attract attention, not just from the people at this table but from most of the junior class, and I know people would think that I was like a sad puppy slinking away with my tail between my legs after the gorgeous, popular girl rejected me . . . and you know what? This metaphor was broken from the beginning.

My point is—it's easier to just keep on keeping on.

Or . . . it was.

And I thought . . . I guess I stupidly thought that I was welcome here.

"What is that supposed to mean?" asks Maya, her voice taking on an edge.

"The two of you aren't together," says Katie, gesturing between us with her fork. "He started sitting here because he got you tickets to that concert, but now? You're not even going to prom together. You're going with that . . . hobbit, or whatever."

"Their name is Noah," Maya says through her teeth, "and they play a halfling in our game."

Katie snorts. "Right. Your *game*. My point is, it's over, Jude." Her expression turns dramatically pitying. "Maya's not into you. She's willing to go out with one of your nerd friends, but *you* still weren't good enough. It is time to move on before we all feel even more sorry for you than we already do."

"Seriously, Katie?" says Maya. "Jude is my friend! Why do you have to be this way?"

"He is not your friend," says Katie, fixing an intense look on Maya, like *she's* the one being ridiculous here. "He's more like your stalker. He's been obsessed for years, and everyone knows it, and honestly, I think it's cruel the way you're leading him on."

"She isn't—" I start, but Katie keeps going.

"Have you even seen the drawings he makes of you?"

My chest tightens. "What?"

Katie gives me a smug look. "I sit behind you in Spanish class. I've seen that comic. The wizard drooling over the statue that looks so much like our girl here." She laughs harshly. "It is *so* creepy."

"You mean . . . this comic?" says a voice behind me. Maya and I spin around on the bench. I hadn't even known Tobey was behind me, hadn't felt him unzipping my backpack—and now he has my notebook in hand as he dances out of reach.

"Hey!" I shout, launching to my feet, knocking my tray of salad onto the floor in my hurry to get up. Lettuce and croutons go everywhere, but I'm focused only on Tobey as he sprints to the other side of the table. He's flipping through pages. My pages. My drawings.

People are starting to stare.

But what am I supposed to do? Plead with him to give it back? Jump over this table and tackle him?

"Hand it back, Tobey," says Maya, standing now, too. "What are you, four years old?"

He ignores her, eyes bugging wide. "Whoa, you drew this? You're really good. It looks just like her!" He turns the pages so everyone can see the pictures of the statue. Of Maya, graceful and elegant and . . . Maybe Katie is right. Maybe it is creepy.

My stomach twists, and for some reason, I'm tempted to tell them to keep reading. To get to the part with Grit Stonesplitter, the tiefling fighter. That's the real Maya, the one no one here knows except me.

But he flips right past it, while Janine stands up to look over his shoulder. "Oh my gosh!" she squeals. "Is that Kyle, from the track team? He's *adorable*."

I grimace, shaking my head, unable to speak. Please don't pull my friends into this . . .

And then—

"No way!" shouts Janine. "That's EZ! Ah, that is hysterical! And who's that?"

"Ooh la la. Hello, hottie with a guitar," says Tobey.

Shit, shit, shit—

"Hey, let me see," says Raul, standing and reaching for the notebook.

"Yeah, check it out," says Tobey, handing it to him. "We've got some first-class drama in these pages. Jude, who knew?"

But Raul doesn't look at the comic. As soon as it's in his hand, he slams it shut.

"Hey!" says Tobey, but Raul holds the notebook out of reach.

"Stop being a dick." Raul leans over the table, holding the notebook toward me, but my heart is in my throat, and I know my face is the color of a shirt of someone who's about to die on *Star Trek*, and I can't move, not even to take it.

Maya grabs the notebook instead, then all but shoves it into my hands. "Thanks, Raul," she says.

I give a terse nod, not trusting myself to speak. Then, without looking at anyone, I turn, sling my backpack over one shoulder, and walk away.

"Jude?" Maya calls, but I don't look back.

What I want to do is to run, literally *run* out of this cafeteria. Find some maintenance closet and hide until the last bell. I briefly consider faking illness so I can seek shelter in the nurse's office. Is it still faking if I really do puke? Because I'm pretty sure I could manage some puking right about now.

Instead, my social survival instincts kick in, and I seek shelter in the first place I see. My old table, where Matt, César, and Russell are watching me.

"What the hell?" says César, shifting over to make room for me. "What was that all about?"

"Nothing," I say robotically. My jaw is so tight I might actually crack a tooth. *That* would get me into the nurse's office for sure.

To my relief, my friends don't push for an explanation. After a short, uncomfortable silence, they just go back to eating and talking about whether or not anyone can afford to go to Comic-Con this year.

Until, twenty seconds later, they go quiet again.

"Can I sit with you?"

I turn my head, but don't meet Maya's gaze. "Uh—yeah. Sure. Of course."

She slides onto the bench. "I'm so sorry about that, Jude. That was so uncalled-for."

"Not your fault," I say quietly. My hands have stopped shaking enough now that I stuff my sketchbook into my bag.

"I know it isn't my fault, but I never thought they'd be assholes like that. I know Katie can be a . . ." She lets the word hang unsaid. "But she used to be nice, I swear. I don't know why she acts this way sometimes. And Tobey . . . I mean, he's always been kind of a jerk, but Katie likes him, so we tolerate him, and . . ." She trails off.

"It's cool."

"No, it's not." Maya sighs, and her voice grows quiet. "Are *we* okay?"

It takes me a minute to realize she's not just talking about the fact that her friends just ganged up on me, tried to humiliate me. She's talking about the drawings. The statue, the pedestal. The accusations—that I'm obsessed with her, and that she's being cruel by leading me on.

I force a small smile. Finally meet her eyes. "Yeah. We're good."

"Are these seats taken?"

We look up. Raul, Serena, and Brynn stand at the end of the table, trays in hand.

I stare at them for a long moment, then at my friends, with their confused expressions. Then at Maya. But she's watching me—letting me decide.

What is there to decide? Yeah, some of the people at that table have always rubbed me the wrong way, but these three pass the vibe check, as EZ would say. They're definitely cooler than Katie and Tobey, anyway.

"Yeah. Sure," I say.

"But be warned," says Matt, as they start to sit. "We talk about nerdy things at this table. Like, a lot."

"All good," says Raul. "I used to play Magic: The Gathering on the weekends, and she"—he points his thumb at Brynn—"is obsessed with *One Piece*."

This statement hangs over us all, unexpected and weighty.

"*No way*," breaths César. He looks at me. "Did you know that?"

I shake my head. They never talked about it before. Not with the rest of the group, at least.

"Weird," César says. "I feel like we've entered the Twilight Zone, high school edition."

"What about you?" says Russell, skeptically eyeing Serena.

Serena shrugs. "I have no idea what any of you are talking about. But I love Maya, and I kind of can't stand Tobey, but I never felt like I could say anything. And also . . ." She glances at Matt in a way that seems borderline . . . flirtatious? "It's always nice to make new friends."

Matt coughs and accidentally knocks over his soda.

We laugh, but not in a mean way. Just in a . . . well, this-is-new way.

Brynn tosses over a pile of napkins, while Russell tries to explain to Serena what *One Piece* is, and the rest of the table inevitably start talking about the topic that seems to have permeated the entire school: prom. I listen distantly while those who are going make last-minute plans for dinners and rides and after-parties, which is actually just hitting up a late-night taco truck, then playing Cards Against Humanity at Serena's house until they all crash. Never thought I'd be into high school parties, but that doesn't sound too bad. Serena even invites those of us who aren't going to the dance to come over, too, which might be tempting if I didn't have an evening of wallowing planned already.

Brynn asks Maya more about her date, this "hilarious rogue" they've all been hearing so much about, and I'm pretty sure Maya starts blushing. I smile at her, genuinely happy for Maya and Noah, and genuinely hoping they have a great time on their first real date.

"Oh, Jude, that reminds me," says Maya. "I keep forgetting to bring you your dice. It's been sitting on my dresser for weeks. I'll try to remember to put it in my backpack when I get home so I can get it to you before our next session."

I frown. "No, you already gave me my dice back." After our first D&D session, Maya went out and bought her own set, so she didn't have to borrow mine anymore.

"Not the resin set you play with," she says. "The fancy one. The D20. That looks like a ruby?"

I inhale sharply. All sound turns to white noise, a muffled disbelief thundering between my ears.

"What?" I say. "You have my . . . my dice? My red dice?"

"You dropped it at the festival. I picked it up, but they were giving out the awards and I didn't want to interrupt, so I put it in my pocket and completely forgot about it." She smiles—utterly clueless about how this revelation has shaken me to my core.

My dice.

My *lucky* dice.

"Yeah. Yes. Please," I stammer. "I'd love to have it back."

Chapter Thirty-Eight

"There are people outside!" cries Penny, bouncing excitedly. "Actual people! Waiting! In line!"

"Penny, breathe," says Pru. "Before you hyperventilate."

Penny gestures toward the front door. "But isn't that a good sign?"

It is. It's a great sign, actually.

We've been up since dawn, making sure everything's in place for the big day. Pru has been keeping a running countdown on our social media channels ticking down to Record Store Day—*featuring local award-winning songwriter, Araceli Escalante! (And a special surprise!)* She's also been trying to get me to tell her what the big surprise is every chance she gets, but I refuse to say anything.

Pru finishes going over our day-of promotions, along with detailed instructions on how we should handle preorders for the merchandise that never showed up and how we should all be encouraging email list subscribers throughout the day.

"Quint will get off from the center around noon," Pru is saying, checking things off a massive to-do list, "so Lucy, I'm putting you in charge of photography and videography for social media until he gets here."

"On it," says Lucy.

"Mom will mostly be in charge of switching out the records, so long as she isn't having to wrangle Ellie too much."

"I can help wrangle Ellie," I say. "I'm mostly just going to be at the cash register."

"Which, if we're lucky, will keep you *very* busy," says Pru.

I cringe at the L-word, but nod anyway. "If we're lucky."

Pru looks up from her notes. "Shouldn't you all be writing this down?"

"And deny you the pleasure of bossing us around for the rest of the day?" Lucy says. "Never."

Pru starts to glare, but then pauses. "Fair enough. How are we on time?"

"Doors open in five," says Dad.

The one person who's still missing, even more than Quint, is Ari herself. She's bringing her parents and Abuela down so they can watch her perform. But with her arthritis, Abuela doesn't always move super fast, especially in the mornings, so Ari warned us she might be running a little late.

I haven't seen Ari since Tuesday night, haven't even texted with her. Pru said something about her being busy with schoolwork this week, but I can't help but wonder if she's avoiding me. Could she read the truth on my face after Ezra's promposal? Could she see my devastation? Does she know?

And if she knows and she's not talking to me . . . well, then. I guess that answers one question.

Outside, we hear scattered cheers, and Ari appears outside the glass door, Abuela on her arm and her parents behind them. Ari looks startled at the attention, which—yes, evidently, is for *her*. She smiles weakly and waves to the people in line as Pru hurries to let her in.

"Perfect timing," says Pru. "We were just about to open. Dad, will you do the honors?"

Dad steps outside to make a quick speech to the waiting masses and welcome them to Record Store Day at Ventures Vinyl.

"How are you, Abuela?" I ask, carrying a chair over for her to sit in.

"Very good, Jude." She grins as I bend down to give her a hug, but waves the chair away as she takes in the store. "I want to look around first. Araceli has told me about this beautiful mural you painted, and she was right!" She nods admiringly at the stage. "Muy sofisticado."

"It turned out really nice," Ari's mom agrees, beaming at me. "Next

304

time I have a client who wants a personalized mural in their home, I know who to call."

"Thank you, Mrs. Escalante," I say, blushing. Ari's parents have been telling me for years that I can call them David and Elena, but I've never been able to get past *Mr. and Mrs. Escalante*. I envy Pru a little. She didn't even hesitate to call them Mom and Dad way back in middle school, given that they had so quickly become like a second set of parents to her.

As they're browsing the store, I glance over to catch Ari's eye. She's wearing a long crocheted cardigan over a pink sundress, her thick hair braided down her back. She looks beautiful.

But as soon as the thought crosses my mind, Ari quickly looks away.

And that's when I know. She really *is* avoiding me.

My heart sinks down into the pit of my stomach.

So that's that. I gave myself away on karaoke night, and she doesn't feel the same way, and I can't believe I let myself hope, even for a second, and I . . . definitely don't have time for this upswell of emotions because my dad has welcomed everyone and flung open the door and customers are pouring inside.

I take up my spot behind the cash register, but I haven't even been there for a minute before Pru approaches me, looking anxious.

"Okay, Jude, you're up."

I frown at her. "Huh?"

"Your big surprise?" she says, drumming her fingers on the counter. "The thing Ari promised to reveal today, even though she has no idea what it is? People are asking about it."

"Oh. You mean . . . we're doing that now? Right now?"

She doesn't bother with a response, just gives me a *look*.

I gulp. Yep, guess we're doing that now.

By yesterday afternoon I'd convinced myself that my bad luck would keep Ari's records from showing up, but the delivery truck arrived right before closing, along with four heavy boxes.

I go to retrieve one of the boxes from the back room and bring it up to the counter.

"I hope this is good," says Pru, a warning in her tone. "I'd say half the people here came for Ari."

"That's incredible."

"It is. But also . . ." She gives the box a skeptical look. "They have expectations."

"Don't worry, Sis," I say, opening the box. "People are going to love this." I sound more confident than I feel.

"I hope so," says Pru. "Are you going to make the announcement?"

"Announcement?" I pause, the flaps of cardboard half open.

"Yeah. Tell people what the big surprise is? Given that this is sort of your deal."

"Do I have to?" At no point did I consider that I might have to make an *announcement*. The whole point was kind of for the records to speak *for* me.

Yes, this was my way of helping out the store when our merchandise didn't arrive on time, but more than that, this was supposed to be my big moment. My chance to reveal something special to Ari. *For* Ari.

My heart, wrapped up in a vinyl LP.

My big gesture does feel bittersweet now, given my failure to tell Ari how I felt. Given that she's going to prom with a guy who's my exact opposite.

But I still want her to have this. To love this. Even if my attempt at a big romantic gesture is too late. I glance around the store. People are flipping through bins and holding Ventures Vinyl T-shirts against their chests to check the sizes. Mom and Dad are being social butterflies, thanking everyone for coming and asking if they need help finding anything. Lucy seems to be taking a gazillion photos and videos, Penny has disappeared into the back room to get in one last practice on her violin, and Ellie is walking around offering cookies to our customers from a platter. Ari is surrounded by people who seem to be gushing about her viral video. I even see her signing something—are people asking for *autographs*?

"Okay," I mutter to myself, working up my courage. I grab the box off the counter and carry it up to the little stage, apologizing to the people who have to squeeze to the sides of the narrow aisles to let me pass. When I reach the platform, I set the box by my feet and turn on the microphone.

"Uh . . . hello," I say, my heart pounding. I feel Ari's presence just off the stage, the way you feel the sun on your skin on a summer afternoon, but now it's my turn to avoid looking at *her*. "I'm Jude. I work here, and also my parents own the place."

"*Yeah*, Jude! You got this!" shouts Lucy from the back.

I cringe. Wave jerkily.

"So, I know a lot of you are here for today's live performance by our very own award-winning singer/songwriter . . . Araceli Escalante."

I dare to meet her gaze. Ari rolls her eyes at me, but then flashes a cute smile at the crowd, framing her face with jazz hands. A few people chuckle.

"If you've been following Ari on social media, you may also have heard that today we have a very special surprise for her fans."

"I don't have *fans*," Ari stage-whispers.

"Yes, you *do*," Pru says, appearing beside her. "Get used to it."

My hands are sweating. I release the microphone and instinctively stick one hand in my pocket, hoping for courage. A charisma check would be really helpful right about now.

But of course, there's nothing there. Why, oh why, didn't I drop everything to run to Maya's house after school yesterday and get my dice back?

"Pru is right," I say, looking at Ari. "I think we've established that I am actually your biggest fan." I pause, my voice quieting. "Always have been. Always will be."

Ari bites her lower lip.

"Which is why," I say, glancing around at the rest of the audience, "I wanted to do something special. For Ari and for all of you, who are coming to love this girl . . ." My lungs hiccup. "Love *her music*, as much as I do."

Anxiety is beginning to set in, and I realize I need to wrap this up and get off this stage as quickly as possible. "So today, while supplies last, we are releasing an exclusive album that you won't find anywhere else." I pull an album out of the box. It isn't shrink-wrapped (that cost extra), and the card stock used for the jacket is a little thin, but . . . it's real. A real vinyl record, with my artwork on the front and Ari's name printed across the top.

I hold it up so everyone can see, and Ari gasps, covering her mouth with her hands.

"I present to you: *Downpour*, the debut album by Araceli Escalante, featuring eight songs written and recorded by this incredible artist." I pause before adding, quietly, "And also, artwork by me." I squint one eye shut and hold the album toward Ari. "I hope you like it."

"Jude," she breathes, taking the record and cradling it in her hands. She studies the drawing—the elven bard performing onstage at a modern-day music festival. A quiet laugh escapes her as she runs her thumb over the drawing. She flips it over, taking in the doodles, the song list, the credits printed along the bottom. "This is incredible."

She looks up, and there are actual tears shimmering in her eyes, which makes me squeeze my arms into my body and feel like I should apologize, even though I can tell these are happy tears.

"Thank you," she whispers.

Pru strides onto the stage. "Jude, this is brilliant," she says. "Why didn't I think of it?"

Then she's nudging me off the stage and taking the mic. "Ari's exclusive debut album will be available at the counter for anyone who wants to take one home today. And . . . maybe Ari will even sign them after her performance?"

She looks at Ari, who shrugs back. "I guess so?"

"But first . . . ," says Pru, "let's get this party started with our live performance of Ari's viral song, 'Downpour,' with special guest on the violin, my little sister . . . Penny Barnett!"

Chapter Thirty-Nine

I barely hear Ari's introduction as she takes the stage. I feel dizzy and nauseous as I weave through the crowd, eager to get back behind the counter. It feels safer there, where I don't have to give any speeches and no one stares at me and my heart isn't held right there in my palm.

I drop the box of records on the counter, and my dad surprises me by immediately pulling me in for a hug.

"What a fantastic idea!" he says, quiet enough to not interrupt Ari on the stage. "You put these together all by yourself?" He takes one of the records out of the box, looking it over.

"Do you think she likes it?" I blurt.

Dad shoots me a knowing look. "How could she not?"

I inhale deeply, and then there's someone on the other side of the counter, asking if they can buy two copies, and just like that—Ari has made her first sale, while up onstage, she strums the chords of her first big hit.

I complete two more sales in quick succession, but most of our customers are watching Ari as she performs. Penny waits just off the stage, her violin in hand. She doesn't look nervous at all, which surprises me. But then she never looks nervous at her recitals, either, even though she told me once that she sweats so much before a show that she always worries the violin will slip right out of her hands.

Maybe that Charm spell I told Maya about really works.

I wish it would work for *me*.

It isn't until Ari is launching into the second chorus that I feel the tight knot in my chest start to unwind, and I'm able to watch her and listen to her and feel what I feel for her without an endless barrage of worries clouding my thoughts.

Then her eyes meet mine, and for just a second, the world stops, and I think, *I can't be imagining this.*

But she looks away again, down at her guitar. My heart aches. The room feels stifling now. Too crowded. Too warm. Too small for everything I'm wanting and hoping for, and maybe I'm too scared to find out what will happen if I try again.

Penny steps onto the stage during the bridge, playing the violin solo that she wrote herself, while Ari strums along in the background. It's beautiful and perfect, and the crowd cheers when she finishes. Penny bows and steps off the stage while Ari sings the final chorus.

The song ends, the last notes fading away. The crowd breaks into enthusiastic applause. Ari gestures to Penny, and they bow together. "Thank you to Ventures Vinyl for letting me be a part of their annual Record Store Day, and thank you to Penny for joining me onstage, and thank you especially to Jude." Ari smiles at me—a beatific, unbelievable smile. "For making one of my greatest dreams come true. As Pru mentioned before, we have albums for sale, which is . . . *wow.* So . . . I hope you enjoy them. And I'll be back to perform more songs throughout the day. Thank you!"

She steps off the stage and gives her waiting parents a hug, and the room becomes chaos. Some people start browsing the bins and shelves and merchandise again, but a whole lot also make a beeline for the back counter. We sell out of the first box in minutes.

"Jude?"

I spin around, nearly knocking over the Jimi Hendrix bobblehead that someone is waiting to purchase.

"Ari," I say, suddenly breathless. "You sounded—"

I don't get a chance to finish before her arms are around me. Her ear

310

pressed to my chest. The citrus-floral scent of her shampoo short-circuiting my brain.

"Thank you," she says. "The records. They're incredible. I can't believe you did this for me. I mean—and for the store, too. Of course."

She pulls back, holding my arms, which are hanging limply at my sides. Her smile. Her eyes. The way she's looking at me.

"That's all," she says, laughing a little, as if nervous now. "I just wanted to say thank you. You don't know what this means to me."

"Y-yeah. No problem."

She steps back, and I resist the urge to grab her. Pull her close. Bury a hand in her hair. Tell her—

"Jude! Wow, this place is happening!"

My body tenses. Ari and I look over to see that Quint and Ezra have arrived. Quint gladly takes over photographer duties from Lucy, and she wastes no time in snatching the last cookie off the tray, now that her professional duties are fulfilled.

"All right," says Ari, bouncing on her toes. "I guess Pru wants me to sign the records that people are buying? Which is *weird*."

"Tough being famous," I say, and she laughs as she heads for the small signing table that Pru wasted no time in setting up. My attention darts between her and Ezra, my insides twisting as I wait to see how they greet each other. A hug or . . . *please* not a kiss. But Ezra just winks and does a flirty finger-point thing before the crowd swells around Ari, separating her from the rest of us.

The second box of records empties out, too, and Pru has the idea to set a handful aside for Ari and her family and, of course, us. Then my dad has the idea to actually put the album on the turntable so we can all listen to it together.

"Its inaugural play," he says, lowering the needle. "I think we can officially call this my *new* lucky album."

I know he means well, but the reminder of the lost *London Town* record makes me cringe with renewed guilt.

I can't manage to look at Ari, who is signing the records as fast as people can buy them. Her voice starts to play through the speakers, the first verse of "Sea Glass," one of her earlier songs that was always one of my favorites.

"This is so surreal," Ari says loudly, amazement and joy mingling in her voice.

And it's great, for that moment. People are loving Ari and they're loving Ventures Vinyl and my dad's smile is as big as I've ever seen it and complete strangers are going up to Ari's family and saying how proud they must be and Ari is glowing from all the attention and it's good, this thing I did. It's really good. I don't know if it said what I hoped it would say, but it doesn't matter. I helped the store and I made one of Ari's dreams come true and for now, that's enough.

And then . . .

And then.

"Uh-oh," says the woman who is opening her wallet to pay for Ari's record and a handful of others.

It takes a moment for me to hear it, too.

My whole body freezes.

No.

There's a skip in the record. Ari's angelic voice stuck on a jagged loop, repeating the same line over and over and over and over and over—

But . . . but it's *brand-new*.

Dad stops the record. "That's a shame," he says, inspecting the dark grooves. He uses a special brush to make sure there isn't any dust trapped on the vinyl, then starts to play it again.

The skip is still there.

This can't be happening.

"A fluke, I'm sure," says Dad, taking the record off the turntable and replacing it with another one of Ari's. Another record, straight from the sleeve. "It happens sometimes in the pressing process."

He starts to play it again, but I know, *I know* it wasn't a fluke. I can feel it in my soul.

It skips again, in the exact same spot, and that confirms it.

Bile rises in my mouth as I look at the box of unsold records. People in line are frowning, uncertain. Some who have already made their purchases are clutching their receipts and exchanging looks like they aren't sure what to do.

I thought I'd made Ari's dream come true, but I was wrong. There's a skip. The records are damaged. Ruined. Every single one of them.

I shut my eyes and feel my chest collapsing. Why did I even bother?

Lousy.

Terrible.

No good luck.

"Jude?"

I shiver and look up. Ari is watching me, one hand on a half-empty box of records.

"I'm sorry," I say. "It must have been some error in the production process. I can . . ." I swallow hard. "I can contact the company. See about having it reprinted, or . . . I don't know. But these . . ." My voice turns heavy and damp, and *dammit*, I'm not about to cry over this. And it isn't about the record, not really. It's about Ari's dreams and my last-ditch effort to show this curse that it won't rule my life. But I can't say that. No one would understand. "They're ruined. I'm sorry, Ari."

"It isn't your fault. Jude . . . this is still the nicest gift anyone has ever given me."

I smile at her, but it's fleeting and weak, and I would give anything to cast a spell of Invisibility right now.

"Well . . . this is a disappointing situation," says my dad, speaking to the crowd. "Unfortunately, it seems that the records we received are damaged." He looks momentarily stupefied, not sure what to do. He looks at me. Not disappointed, exactly. But concerned. He sighs and forces a smile. "We'll of course refund anyone's money who would like to return their record."

There are disappointed grumbles. People who were in line are turning away.

Dad claps me on the back and says quietly, "It was a really nice thought, Jude."

Then he returns to the turntable and removes Ari's record.

My jaw clenches so tight it aches, and I swear, somewhere, the Curse of Lundyn Toune is laughing.

Chapter Forty

Suffice to say, Record Store Day is a disappointment.

I mean—it isn't all bad. Ari performs throughout the day, and she sounds amazing. Her duet with Penny was a highlight, for sure. And sales-wise, it's probably still our biggest day of the year. But it's not what we were hoping it would be.

My parents don't say as much, but I can see it in their faces. The deepening wrinkles around my dad's eyes. The tightness of my mom's lips. The looks they exchange with each other when they think we aren't paying attention.

Why oh why didn't I think to buy scratch tickets *before* the luck turned on me? That's what any normal person would have done, right? Or given my parents a random string of numbers and told them to go buy a lotto ticket? What sort of loser is gifted infallible good fortune and decides to waste it on magazine art submissions and concert tickets to a singer he doesn't even like?

Those are the questions plaguing me when I get home. Pru is upstairs getting ready for prom, and I know I should go talk to her, tell her to have a good time and all that, but I've been in a bad mood ever since the skip was discovered in Ari's records, and my mood has not improved with time. So I head to my room and slump into my desk chair and proceed to stare dejectedly at my unopened sketch book.

At least I didn't screw things up with Ari, despite all my chances. Because if I had succeeded in telling her how I feel, I guarantee it would have been disastrous, just like everything else. It's pretty clear that I can-not be in love with a girl without turning into an awkward buffoon. At least this way I haven't ruined our friendship.

That's good.

Great, actually.

And if I could just convince myself of that, maybe I would stop feel-ing this overwhelming sense of hopelessness. Maybe I would stop feeling like I screwed everything up.

I'm quite enjoying my wallowing—thinking I might just hang out in this swamp of self-pity until it gives me gangrene—when there's a knock on my bedroom door.

"Come in," I mutter half-heartedly.

"Jude!"

I look up, startled to see Pru jogging down the steps in a knee-length turquoise dress. Tucked under one arm is her beloved day planner, and part of me wonders if she intends to take it with her to the dance.

"We need to think about damage control," she says, sitting on the edge of my bed and opening the planner.

"You look good, Sis. Aren't you leaving soon?"

"Quint's on his way. Don't get distracted. Record Store Day was a bust, profit-wise, but on the plus side, we did get some great media atten-tion. If we can hit our upcoming promotions really hard as we move into tourist season, we might stand a chance."

I try to smile at her, but it's flimsy at best. I don't have the heart to tell her that I'm the last person she wants help from. I'll just ruin everything I touch.

"Pru, can we talk about this tomorrow? I'm tired, and you have a dance to go to."

She glares at me. "*No.* We need to get something put up on Ari's channels immediately. The record was such a great idea, and I know people are disappointed about the skip, but I think we can still spin this in our favor."

My mouth quirks, just a little. "Spin. Good one."

316

She gives me a look, and I realize she wasn't trying to make a pun. Then she shakes her head, annoyed. "We'll explain that there was a mistake in the production process and we're getting it fixed. We can start taking orders for the next batch. I figure Ari can still be teamed up with Ventures—selling through the store's website, so we can share—"

"*Pru.*"

She looks up from her notes.

"Tomorrow. Please."

She opens her mouth. Hesitates. She studies me for a long, uncomfortable moment. One of those twin-telepathy moments that make me feel like a bug under a microscope.

"Tell me what's going on with you."

"What? Nothing's going on with me."

"Is it Maya?"

I hesitate. "Yeah. I guess."

Pru clips the pen back to the papers and shuts the binder. She settles it in her lap and stares at me full-on. "Liar."

I snort. "You're not a mind reader, Pru."

"*Please.* You believe in the twin psychic connection as much as I do."

I wish I could argue with that statement, but I can't. I'll never forget the time I twisted my ankle on the playground in elementary school and Pru, who had been helping a teacher clean whiteboards, actually beat me to the nurse's office. The nurse asked if she'd seen it happen through the windows, but Pru shook her head and said she just . . . *knew*.

Sometimes having a twin is bizarre.

"So?" Pru presses.

"So what?"

Sighing, Pru crosses her arms over her chest. "I know you are as concerned about the store as I am. I know you want to help. So why are you looking at me like you have better things to be thinking about right now, when all you have to be thinking about is that extra-credit paper on *The Great Gatsby*?"

I glower at her. "I do have other things to think about. And for your information, I tried to help the store, and it didn't work, so you know what? I'm giving up. It's all on you now. Good luck."

She looks positively disgusted as she sets the binder beside her. "I get it. That the records were damaged is a huge disappointment. But you can't just give up."

"I like it when you tell me I can't do something. It makes me want to try harder."

Pru scowls, unamused. "The skip in those records wasn't your fault."

I rest my elbow on the desk, massaging my brow. "Pru. Seriously. Go to prom. Have fun. We'll talk about it later."

I hear her drumming her fingers against the top of the binder. I imagine I can hear the gears in her brain, spinning, spinning.

Then—"You could come with us, you know."

I shoot her a disgruntled look. "Yeah. Right."

"I'm serious. You, me, Quint, Ezra . . . Ari. It will be fun."

I shake my head. "I'm good."

"Uh-huh." She chews the pen cap. "It must have been a lot of work, putting those records together. Not just the song list, but the artwork, too. And you spent all that time editing the music video. I bet you really wanted it to be . . . special."

Alarms blare in my head. "What is your point?"

She doesn't respond. Just waits.

I clench my jaw and look away.

"Jude," says Pru. So gently it makes me wince.

"What do you want me to say?"

Another silence.

Then . . .

"Holy ravioli," she breathes. "*Really?*"

"Really what?" I snap.

"Jude!" She's louder now, almost yelling. "*Ari?* Are you kidding me right now?"

I look at her, irritated, and I consider denying it. But . . . what's the point?

So instead I jut my finger at her. "If you say anything to her, I will put the curse of the Spider-Man Broadway show on you, I swear it."

"Hold on," she says, raising her hands. "Are you and Ari . . . ?" She wiggles her eyebrows suggestively.

"No. *No.* There is no 'me and Ari.' She's going to prom with Ezra."

Pru's face crumples. "Oh. Right."

"Yeah. *That* little detail. I'm just the loser who realized he might be in love with his best friend a little too late."

Pru gasps, clamping a hand over her mouth.

I recoil. I hadn't meant to say *those* words. "That wasn't . . . I didn't mean—"

"No stinking way! Since when?"

I groan and heave myself up from the desk chair. "I don't know," I say, starting to pace. "I think maybe for a long time? But I was so into Maya, right?"

She nods, leaning forward. "Indisputable. Go on."

"I think I'd convinced myself that Maya was the only girl I could ever have these feelings for, so I didn't pay any attention to it, and then as soon as I realized that Maya wasn't right for me . . ." I stop pacing, my hands spread wide. "It's like . . . it was so obvious. It was Ari, all along, and I just didn't . . . I couldn't . . ."

"Wow," Pru breathes. "I'd always wondered, but . . . with your crush on Maya, I thought maybe I was imagining things."

"You could tell?"

"Sort of. You and Ari always seemed to have something special." She considers a moment, before going on. "You're different around her. More relaxed than when you're around anyone else. And Ari's never come out and said anything to me, maybe because you're my brother, but I swear, sometimes the way she looks at you—"

My heart jolts. "What do you mean, the way she looks at me?"

"Like you're . . . I don't know. This is cheesy, but like you're her knight in shining armor or something. Like the first time she sang 'Downpour' at open mic night? Or when you pulled out those records today? I could practically see the hearts in her eyes. Plus, there's . . . you know. All those songs she's written."

My pulse skips. "What about her songs?"

"Well, I don't *know* this, but sometimes I've wondered. All those lyrics about unrequited love, and how the guy always seems to be into someone else." She shrugs. "Maybe she was thinking about you."

My head spins. I mean, I've thought it before. Wondered before. But to hear someone else say it's a possibility . . . to hear *Pru* say it's a possibility. Practical, no-nonsense Pru, who knows Ari better than anyone.

It makes me wonder. It makes me *hope*.

She tilts her head. "So . . . are you going to tell her?"

"I've tried," I say, collapsing onto the bed beside her. "But I can't do it. I'm not like you, Pru."

She pulls one knee up onto the blankets so she can face me. "What do you mean, you're not like *me*?"

I gesture at her. Fancy dress, look-at-me lipstick, a binder full of great ideas that she doesn't just share with people—she *forces* them to take notice.

"Not afraid to take risks. Not afraid to put yourself out there, to go after something when you want it. But me? I'm happy being in the background. Where no one scrutinizes you or criticizes you and sure as hell no one ever rejects you." I take in a shuddering breath, then close my mouth and swallow hard. "Maya was never going to reject me, because I was never going to give her that chance. And with Ari, it's a thousand times worse . . . because I want it a thousand times more."

Pru watches me for a long moment, taking it in. Finally, she says, "But you said you've tried? To tell her how you feel?"

"Yeah. I mean. Sort of. But whatever I do, things get messed up, and eventually I'm going to ruin everything. If it was a month ago, then maybe . . . but now everything I touch turns into goblin crap, and I can't risk that. Not with Ari."

"What do you mean? How were things different a month ago?"

"I was *lucky* then." At Pru's skeptical expression, I wave my hand through the air. "I know how this is going to sound, but . . . I think I'm cursed, Pru. The Curse of Lundyn Toune."

She watches me so intently I think she's trying to use her twin psychic powers again. But finally she says, simply, "The Wings album?"

I sigh. "No. Not exactly. There's this temple in our campaign. The Temple of Lundyn Toune. It's cursed, and if someone tries to break the spell but they're not worthy, then they become cursed themselves. And . . ." I roll my eyes toward the ceiling. "I think I'm cursed. At first all this good stuff was happening to me. Like the concert tickets, and the coin flips in class. Remember? I was untouchable. But then I lost my lucky dice, and after that . . . everything just turned on me. And now it feels like I'll never be lucky at anything ever again."

"So . . . hold on," says Pru. "What lucky dice?"

"You know, the one I found at the store. On open mic night. The same night we discovered the Paul McCartney autograph."

"Right," says Pru. "So the dice is from an imaginary temple that's named after a Wings album, and it's cursed you."

"Look, I know how it sounds," I say, giving her a warning look. "But you have to admit, there have been a lot of bizarre coincidences lately and—"

"No, no, I get it," says Pru, staring at me earnestly. "McCartney album. Bizarre interventions by the universe. Random good luck turns into random bad luck. I'm with you."

I scoff. "I'm not even sure I'm with me."

She smiles softly. "Well, I am."

My bedroom door creaks open at the top of the stairs, and Ellie cries, "Pru! Quint is here!"

"Be right there," she calls back.

I sit up and roll out my shoulders. "Go. I'm fine. Really."

She shakes her head. "Tell me more about this temple."

"Pru. Your date is waiting."

"He's fine. Curse. Temple. Go."

I throw up my hands. "I don't know. It's this . . . temple. These ruins.

In the middle of nowhere. And there's a statue, and if the statue decides you're worthy of her blessing, then you're given plus five on all skill throws until the end of the campaign."

Pru frowns, and I wave my hand at her.

"Luck," I clarify. "She gives you really good luck. But if you're found unworthy, then you're cursed."

"How does she decide that someone is worthy?"

I chuckle wryly. "That's the ironic thing. It's not really *her* decision."

I had been so proud of this when I first came up with it, months ago when I was figuring out the rules of this campaign. The mechanics of it all had gotten a little lost in the midst of my promposal and Maya's subsequent rejection, so I never had a chance to explain it to the group, despite how clever I'd felt.

"So there's this stone, right? The Scarlet Diamond. And everyone thinks it's the key to unlocking the temple's magic. But actually—the way to get the temple's blessing is to destroy the stone, because that shows the maiden of the temple that you don't *need* the magic. You're good enough just the way you are. So . . . by destroying the stone, you prove that you're worthy. And therefore . . ."

Pru finishes for me. "Therefore, you win the magic."

"Essentially." I glance at the stairs. "Will Quint be—"

"He's fine," she says again. "He's probably already playing Mario Kart with Penny. But just listen to yourself for a second, Jude. Or . . . listen to me, repeating you." She lifts up both pointer fingers, like this will help me focus on the very important thing she's about to say. "You don't need the magic," she says, enunciating each word. "You are good enough, just the way you are."

"Oh god," I mutter. "I wasn't trying to turn this into a therapy session."

"Well, it *is* a therapy session, and you're welcome," she says firmly. "I mean it, Jude. You're the one trying to convince me that you've been cursed by some fictitious temple. While at the same time you literally just explained how a person breaks the curse." She reaches for my shoulder and gives me a shake. "By believing that you. Are. Worthy. Without the magic. Screw the blessing and screw the curse. Jude, if you really think all these weird coincidences are because of this thing, then it sounds like you have something to prove. Not to any curse or temple, but to yourself."

I wait until I'm sure she's done talking. "Great pep talk," I say flatly. "I am so inspired. Thank you, Prudence. You have solved all my problems. Now please go and enjoy your evening, knowing that you have fixed my life."

The look she gives me then. *Oh*, that look. Sometimes I think my twin sister could be the boss in one of my dungeons.

I slowly scoot away.

"That's it," she says, getting to her feet. "You're coming tonight."

I gape at her. "What?"

"You're coming. Put on a different shirt. Something with a collar."

I look down at my Ventures Vinyl T-shirt. Back up at my sister. "What?"

She juts a finger toward my closet. "Get changed. We are leaving."

"I'm not going to prom."

"Yes. You are."

"*Why?*"

"Because you are in love with Ari, and you have to tell her!"

I gape at her.

Pru puts her hands on her hips, determined.

The silence is thick. As thick as mutagen ooze.

There's a knock on my door, and a second later, Quint comes strolling down, wearing a tuxedo.

"Yo," he says, stopping at the bottom of the steps and taking note of the thick-as-ooze tension between me and Pru. "What's going on?"

Pru pulls herself to her full height and crosses her arms over her chest. "Jude is—"

"Don't you dare," I say.

She hesitates, scowling.

Quint looks between us, and I sense that he's wishing he'd stayed upstairs.

Pru exhales sharply through her nostrils, then a light comes on in her eyes, and she turns to Quint. "Picture this. You are madly in love with a girl who has no idea how you feel about her."

I bite back a groan, but Quint just nods and says, "Yeah, I remember those days."

Pru pauses, momentarily flustered. She even starts to blush, and unlike *me*, Pru is not a blusher.

"Get a room," I mutter.

Pru bats the comment away. "And you have to prove, *somehow*, that you are worthy of her."

"No," I interrupt. "Not worthy of *her*. Worthy of . . ." I flap my hands around through the air. "Anything. Everything."

"The magic," Pru clarifies, snapping her fingers and pointing at me. "Right?"

"There is no magic," I state firmly, contrary to everything I've felt for eons now.

"Disagree. There is definitely magic," says Pru, which is just about the most un-Pru-like thing I've ever heard her say. She turns back to Quint. "So? How do you do it?"

"How do I prove that I'm worthy of . . . magic?" he says, struggling to follow the conversation. "Or love?"

Honestly, I think we're all struggling to follow the conversation at this point. I know I am. How are *you* doing? Holding up okay? Wondering about all those things I promised way back on page one, like the grand adventures and the epic quests and a love that inspired the music of bards?

Stick with me. We're getting there.

"Yeah, sure," says Pru. "Either. Both."

To his credit, Quint seems to give the question honest consideration. "Well," he says slowly. "I . . . guess I take a risk. I tell her how I feel. Or show her somehow."

324

I open my mouth to tell them both that, yeah, obviously, I've *tried* that, but something holds my tongue.

I never had the magic on my side after I realized how I felt about Ari. I'd already lost the dice by then.

"So who is Jude in love with?" says Quint. "We're not talking about Maya, are we?"

Pru ignores the question. I can feel her watching me, but it takes me a long time to dare to lift my eyes.

"Jude?" she says. A question in her gaze. "In the wise words of Sir Paul McCartney . . . you have found her. Now *go and get her*."

I grimace, then grab my pillow and throw it at her as hard as I can, but Pru catches it easily, laughing.

"You did not just quote 'Hey Jude' at me."

"Come on," says Pru. "I have been waiting *years* to use that line." She tosses the pillow back on the bed and snatches up her planner. "So? Are you coming or what?"

I want to insist that it's too late. I've already tried. I've already failed. I am destined for a life of solitude and misery.

But I know, deep down, that these are only excuses. My heart, desperately trying to protect itself.

My modus operandi. Self-preservation at all cost.

But much as I hate to admit it . . . Pru might have a point.

And also Sir Paul. I guess.

"Yeah," I say. "I'm coming."

Chapter Forty-One

"What do you think?" I say, stepping into the living room.

They're all there. My parents. All four sisters. Quint.

And their expressions are . . . mixed.

Pru raises an intrigued eyebrow. Lucy looks horrified. Ellie claps and squeals, "You're a pirate!"

I look down at my outfit. Black slacks and the loose linen shirt that I wore to the Renaissance Faire two summers ago. I decided to forgo the cloak. And the wide leather belt with velvet pouches. And also the sword. So really, I think I've shown a lot of restraint.

"I said to put on a shirt with a collar," says Pru.

"This has a collar." I pull on the wide collar to prove it.

"I like it," says Penny. "You look like Prince Eric."

I give Pru a look. *See?*

"Hey, it's your curse," she says, standing. "Let's do this."

"Also," I say, "I need to make a quick stop."

I feel sick and nervous as Quint pulls up outside Maya's house and I climb out from the back seat. "You can wait here," I say. "This shouldn't take long."

As I walk away, I hear Quint whispering, "So . . . he is or is not in love with Maya?"

My palms are sweating as I approach the front steps. My fingers are shaking as I ring the doorbell.

From inside, I hear hurried footsteps and Maya's voice—"Coming!"

She's radiant when she swings the door open. But her smile stiffens and falls when she sees me. "*Jude?*"

"Hi," I say, taking her in. She's prom-ready in a violet dress, a band of white flowers holding a halo of thick black curls back from her face. Glitter on her lips and eyelids, sparkles dusting her shoulders.

"Wow. You look great."

She does look great. Stunning, actually.

And also . . . increasingly horrified. "What are you doing here?" she asks, a pitch of uncertainty in her voice.

I frown, confused. But then it occurs to me—she thinks I'm here to make a scene. To . . . I don't know, declare some love obsession and beg her not to go to prom with Noah, or . . . something.

My eyes widen, even as heat tinges the tips of my ears. "I'm not here for you," I say. "I'm not . . . This isn't . . . I'm just here for my dice."

Her lips part in surprise. "Your . . . dice?"

"Yeah. You said you found it at the festival?"

"Yeah," she says slowly, "and that I would bring it to you at school next week."

"I know. But I kind of need it sooner. Now. If possible." I hesitate, before adding, with a weak smile, "Please?"

Another car pulls into the driveway. I glance over my shoulder and see Noah getting out of the driver's seat. Their gaze meets mine, confused. "Jude?"

"Noah! Hi. You look . . . dapper." I've never seen Noah dressed up before, but they've gone all out in pinstripe pants and suspenders over a white dress shirt, with a couple of rhinestone barrettes attempting to tame their spiky hair. Hair that is, I realize now, the exact color of Maya's dress.

Awww. Matching. And I think, *Ari would love that.*

"And you look like you're about to break out into a sea shanty," says

Noah, looking briefly amused. Until, all at once, a shadow eclipses their face. "Wait. Are you here for . . . oh. Oh—god." They clutch the stair rail. "You're not over Maya."

"What?"

"I'm a horrible friend. Crap." Noah presses a hand over their eyes. "I should have talked to you. I shouldn't have assumed. I just thought—"

"No! No, no, no. Seriously. This isn't what it looks like," I say, hands outstretched. "I am so happy for you two. I didn't mean to intrude on your night."

"He's here for a dice," says Maya. "Evidently, it couldn't wait?"

I cringe. "I know it doesn't sound like a big deal, but . . . it kind of is. To me."

Maya is clearly annoyed, but she says, "All right. I'll go get it."

"Thank you."

She disappears back into the house.

Noah notices Pru and Quint in the car and waves, before turning back to me, uncertain. "Are you sure you're okay with this? Because I like Maya a lot, but I also value your friendship, and if you're not—"

"Noah, please." I smile, trying to look reassuring. "I am more than okay with this. I swear. I'm really just here for the dice."

Noah rocks back on their heels, not looking entirely convinced. "The fancy red one?"

"Yeah. I thought I'd lost it a while back, but Maya found it." I scratch the back of my neck. "Actually . . . if you want to know . . . that dice sort of gave me the courage to ask Maya out in the first place, and now I'm kind of hoping that it might help me ask out another girl. Someone who's really special to me. Someone I should have asked out a long time ago."

"Wait, *what*?" Maya appears in the doorway again and there—*there*—clutched in her hand. The most breathtaking sight I have ever seen.

Hope wells up inside me as Maya sets the dice into my open palm. It feels exactly the same. The surprising weight. The sharp angles. The strange warmth of it.

"My parents want to get photos of us," Maya says to Noah, before turning back to me. "But first, who are you asking out? And what does the dice have to do with it?"

I wince. I hadn't meant for her to hear that.

"It's a long story."

Maya folds her arms and leans against the door frame.

"Um. Okay." I inhale. "I know this sounds unbelievable, but I sort of think the dice might be . . . magic."

They stare at me.

"I mean, in all reality, maybe it's more like a . . . a magic placebo?" I say, because that doesn't sound quite so far-fetched.

Their confusion doesn't fade.

"The thing is, after I found this dice, I kept getting really lucky. Everything I tried worked out for me. But as soon as I lost it . . . everything went to hell. But now I have the dice again, I can use it to . . . to ask out Ari." I pause. "I guess that wasn't such a long story after all."

Maya straightens, her expression brightening. "I knew it! I knew you had a thing for her! It was so obvious, and I couldn't understand why you thought you were into *me*!"

"I also feel that I could have picked up on this sooner."

"This is great," says Maya. "Are you going to her house?"

"No. Prom, actually. Ari went with Ezra tonight."

"*Oh*," says Noah. "That's why you're dressed like that. This is a quest. You're going to duel for her hand!" They tug on their suspenders. "Sort of sexist, but I also kind of dig it."

"I'm not dueling for her hand," I say. "I just want to tell her how I feel and see if maybe she feels the same way."

Maya beams. "But Noah's right. It is like a quest. You have a magic spell, and you need to find the maiden . . . Jude!" She punches me in the arm. "This is romantic!"

"Thank you?"

"So," she adds, "what do you need from us, Dungeon Master?"

I laugh, but her expression is earnest, and Noah looks equally grave as they take Maya's elbow. "Whatever you need, we're here for you."

"After we let my parents take their photos," says Maya.

Noah juts a thumb toward her. "After that."

Chapter Forty-Two

Writ upon these hallowed pages is the epic tale of the great wizard Jude. It is a story of one hero who faced impossible odds and conquered dark magic (and darker insecurities) as he set off on his brave quest to win the love of the fairest bard in the land . . .

While senior prom is being held at a golf club this year, junior prom, with its much smaller budget, is taking place in our school gym. Quint finds a parking spot, and we step out into a warm spring evening, the air smelling of sea salt and jasmine flowers. I stand in front of the gymnasium, and look at it, really look at it. And in its dark facade I see, for the first time, not a nondescript torture chamber touted as a gateway to physical education.

I see . . . temple ruins, buried deep in a forgotten jungle. Lost to any map. The final resting place of too many explorers to count.

My final frontier. My hero's journey. My epic quest.

She's in there. My destiny is in there. Am I worthy? Of love? Of adventure? Of a happy ending?

Am I worthy of the magic of Lundyn Toune?

"Jude? What are you doing?"

I start. Pru and Quint are already at the doors, looking back at me.

"Sorry," I say, hurrying to join them.

We buy an extra ticket from the table in the hall and step into the gymnasium.

I would like to say that it's been transformed into a wondrous and enchanting palace, but . . . it's still just the gym, albeit with crepe-paper decorations, cloth-covered tables, and a disco ball.

A DJ is set up beneath one of the basketball hoops, and there are a lot of people here jumping around on the court—er, dance floor.

Maya and Noah find us at the entrance, and almost immediately we spy Serena and Raul standing at a table with César and Matt, which surprises me. I hadn't realized the two of them were coming. I find myself searching for Russell and Kyle, too, until I remember they're both sophomores.

I square my shoulders and approach the table littered with plastic cups and confetti.

César spots me first, and his eyes widen as he takes in my pirate-y shirt. He grins and spreads his arms wide. "Dungeon Master! You grace us with your presence!"

Everyone turns to me, and I can feel a slew of friendly greetings on the tips of their tongues, but I raise a palm to stop them. "Adventurers," I say in my most commanding voice, "I need your help."

They all freeze. And there's a long moment in which we're surrounded by the thumping of bass music and the swirl of red and purple lights when I think, *What the heck am I doing?*

But then Maya steps up beside me, arms crossed over her chest. "We're here on a quest to find and woo Jude's true love."

I shoot her a nervous look. "I mean, I didn't use those *exact* words . . ."

She shrugs back at me. "I inferred."

"There's seriously some epic *Princess Bride* stuff happening here," says Noah, already vibing in place to the music.

César throws back his drink. "I'm just here for the ale, but . . . if you need to kill some goblins, I'm your guy."

"I have missed this," says Matt. Then he lifts his arms and flexes his biceps. "Brawndo accepts your mission. Let's plunder!"

Serena looks at Raul. "What is happening?"

"Okay, what now?" asks Pru, as she and Quint crowd in beside us.

I look around, scanning the crowd. It's dim in here, and the gym is big and crowded. "Where's Ari?"

"Who's Ari?" asks Serena.

"That your singer friend?" asks César, reminding me that most of these people have only met Ari in passing, if at all.

"What about EZ?" I press.

At this, everyone glances around. "He was over by the drinks . . . ," says Serena. "But that was a while ago."

"EZ Kent?" asks Raul. "Could be dancing?"

We all look toward the dance floor, but there are so many people. A thriving, gyrating mass of my peers. I cringe to think of Ari among them. Ari with Ezra. Ari with anyone but me.

I swallow hard and say, loudly, "I need to talk to Ari."

Serena asks again, "Who is Ari?"

"Ezra's date," says Pru.

Serena frowns, like the idea of Ezra Kent having a date is baffling to her.

My gaze falls on the stage where the DJ is set up. My heart shudders, but I stuff my hand into my pocket and seize the D20 in my fist. I gather my courage and point. "I need to get on that stage."

They all follow my look.

Maya turns back to me first. Uncertain, but also . . . impressed. "You go get it, Jude," she says. "Come on."

And just like that, I'm being pulled through the jostling crowd. I am surrounded by my adventurers. Fighters and rogues and sorcerers crowding in on every side. Protecting me. Shielding me from the writhing pit of human flesh.

Shielding me from . . .

Goblins.

"Maya! Jude! Wait, are you here together?" shouts Katie.

Maya and I freeze, which brings the entire group to a standstill. Katie leers at us. Janine is nearby, Tobey's arms around her waist as he grinds against her.

Why are there always goblins?

"Is that a *pirate* shirt?" says Janine, with much more snark than Ellie had. "Ahoy, matey."

Katie laughs. "You two are the cutest. Shoo-ins for cutest couple award, for sure."

Maya smiles thinly and grabs Noah's arm, pulling them toward her. "Actually, this is my date. Noah. Noah—these are my . . ." She hesitates.

She hesitates for a long time.

She hesitates for so long that it becomes extremely awkward.

Finally, Maya finishes, "Classmates."

I cough. "*Goblins.*"

Maya breaks into a peal of laughter. Katie looks annoyed and Janine looks confused and Tobey looks like he can't understand why they've stopped dancing.

"If you'll excuse us," Maya says, shouting to be heard over the music, "we are on an epic quest." Then she takes my arm and drags me up to the stage.

"We'll stand guard," she says, giving me an encouraging nod. "We're here for you."

"Thanks," I say, even as my heart swells up, nearly choking me. The DJ is behind a fancy soundboard. She has her eyes closed and giant headphones over her ears, and she's rocking out to the music, lost in her own world, and it takes me a long moment to realize . . .

"Trish?"

She doesn't respond. Just waves her arms into the air.

"Trish Roxby?" I yell, louder this time.

Still—no reaction.

I climb up on the stage and tap her on the arm.

Trish startles and pulls off her headphones. Her eyes widen. "Jude! What are you doing here?" she cries, her southern accent even more stark when she yells. "No—wait, dumb question. You go here! Are you having a great time? It's so good to see you! Oh, look, your sister's here, too!" She waves at Pru behind me.

"Trish, have you seen Ari?"

She fixes her eyes on me and shakes her head. "No, sweetheart. I thought she went to a private school?"

"She's here somewhere. I need to find her."

"Okay?" she says, looking at me, a question in her eyes.

I swallow hard. Gesture at her microphone. "Can I . . ."

Oh god.

"Do you think I could . . ."

Am I really doing this?

"Maybe . . . ?"

Trish looks from me to the mic. "Oh!" she says. "Yeah, it's all yours!"

Dammit. It would have been awesome if she'd said no.

Trish hands me the microphone, then turns down the music and gives me a go-ahead nod.

My stomach lurches as I grip the mic in one hand and face the crowd. The dancing comes to a stop. I haven't even said anything yet, and people are turning to look with curious, somewhat annoyed, expressions. Their eyes sweep over my unconventional attire.

I clear my throat. I'm searching the crowd. For Ari. Or Ezra. But I don't see either of them.

"Hey," I say. My mouth is dry, and my voice falters. I'm strangling the microphone, all the while searching. Where is she? "Uh . . ." My gaze falls on Pru, who gestures at me with her hands, telling me to get on with it. Beside her, Quint is grimacing like he's watching the *Death Star* take out Alderaan and there's nothing he can do about it.

And then there's Maya, who has her elbow linked with Noah's. And Matt, who's giving me two thumbs up. And César, who puts his fingers in his mouth and whistles.

My adventurers. Who would storm any castle, invade any dungeon, take on any goblin horde. For once, they aren't here for their story. They're here for *mine*.

I pull the dice out of my pocket and rub my finger over its familiar triangular planes.

I am a Level 12 wizard, and I hold magic in my hand.

Please let this work.

I drop the dice, hearing it clatter on the stage by my feet.

Bolstered, I press on. "I'm sorry to interrupt the music, but I'm looking for Ari. Ari, are you here? I know this is awkward, but I really need to talk to you."

People look around. First at their friends and dancing partners, then the crowd at large. Ari doesn't go to our school. She came with me and Pru to last year's bonfire party, but I don't expect too many people to remember her from that.

"Ari?" I say again.

Someone in the back yells—"Ari's not interested!"

I flinch.

Mortification is creeping over me. My face is burning. My stomach is writhing.

But I came here on a quest, and I will not fail.

I am a Level 12 wizard facing a room full of goblins . . . but I don't need to charm them, or even defeat them. All I care about is finding Ari.

Roll for perception. Roll for persuasion. Come on, dice, help me out here.

"There is a girl who came here tonight with another guy," I say, my voice gaining strength. "And I know it's kind of a dickish thing to try and make a move on someone else's date, but this girl . . . she really means something to me. And I have to tell her that. I just need her to know that I would do anything for her. Even humiliate myself in front of literally my entire class, just to let her know that she is extraordinary in every way, and I—"

Did I just hear my name?

"I . . . um . . ."

Yes. There it is again.

"Jude!"

I pause, squinting into the crowd, shimmering beneath the disco ball. I think that was—

336

"Jude the Dude!"

I spot him then. Ezra Kent, pushing his way toward the stage, arms waving wildly.

"EZ," I say, gulping. "Look, I know this isn't cool on a lot of levels, but I am in love with—"

"She's not here," EZ shouts, stopping just off the stage.

I blink at him. "What?"

"Ari's not here. She changed her mind. Told me yesterday she just wants to be friends. It was, like, the sweetest rejection of all time." He laughs and gestures at the girl beside him. "I came with Claudia tonight."

Claudia, who already looked bewildered, now turns to him aghast. "Hold on. You told me you'd been trying to work up the nerve to ask me for a month. But you asked another girl first?"

"A month, an hour. Potato, potahto," he says. His grin brightens. "But you're the girl who actually came tonight, which makes you my favorite."

Claudia lets out a disgusted noise and storms away to a chorus of *ooooh*s from our classmates. EZ shrugs apologetically at me, yells up— "Rootin' for ya, dude!"—then chases after her.

I stand there, slack-jawed, not sure what to do next.

Ari isn't even here.

And I am . . . dressed up like a pirate.

Making an epic love confession.

On a stage.

Under a disco ball.

In front of almost the entire junior class of Fortuna Beach High.

Some people are smiling at me, like this thing I've done is sweet and admirable. Others are laughing. But most, I'd say, are cringing—glad it isn't them.

And I . . .

I don't really care.

I don't care if I'm a laughingstock when I show up to school next week.

I don't care if Tobey and Katie and Janine and all the other jerks spend the rest of the school year tormenting me over my shoddy attempt at a big romantic gesture.

I don't care if I'm the butt of every joke from now until graduation.

All I care about is that I am here. On the stage, in the spotlight, microphone in hand, proclaiming to the world that *I am worthy* . . .

Of love. Of attention. Of glory. Of romance. Of adventure. Of magic.

And yet . . . I have been found wanting.

"Nice try, simp," someone shouts. Then another voice—"Play some music!"

"Jude?" says Trish. "You all right, sweetheart?"

I nod and give her a sheepish smile. "Sorry about that," I say. "I guess that didn't go according to plan."

She takes the microphone from me. "It was a valiant effort. If I were Ari, I'd feel pretty damn lucky."

I smile, but my heart isn't in it.

Trish starts the music again as I stumble off the stage. I remember my dice at the last moment. Looking back, I see it there, twinkling innocently by the sound equipment. On top? A sad, golden number one.

Critical fail.

Betrayal hits me in my gut as I grab the dice and stuff it back into my pocket. I don't look at Maya or Pru or any of my friends. The crowd parts for me as I stagger toward the exit.

"Jude?" says Pru, chasing after me. "Are you okay? We can drive you to Ari's house. We can—"

I spin toward her. "No, Pru. I'm just going to walk home."

She frowns. It will take an hour on foot. "We can take you . . ."

I shake my head. "Thanks, for everything. But I just need some time. Enjoy the dance."

I nod at Quint, wave at Maya and the others.

And I go.

Chapter Forty-Three

I don't go home. Not right away. At first I just wander. But it must be easier to wander downhill, and in Fortuna Beach, going downhill usually leads you to the ocean, which is how I end up at the boardwalk. And then—Ventures Vinyl.

I let myself in through the back door using the keypad that Mom had installed because Dad has a bad habit of forgetting his keys at home. I make my way to the front of the store. For a second I just stand in the doorway, looking out into the shadows. There's enough light coming through the front windows that I can make out the peaks and valleys of the bins and shelves, the merch tables, the framed posters with glass that glints when a car passes by outside.

I have never been here when it was so quiet. There's always music playing, and the constant drone of work and laughter and family and, on the best days, Ari. Humming to herself, always.

I turn on the lamp on the counter, leaving off the overhead lights. It's still dim, but in a way that's cozy and serene.

And right next to the lamp, haloed in its golden sheen, is Ari's record. Araceli the Magnificent.

I don't even want to touch the record, for fear it will burst into flames in my hand.

I make my way around the counter. Past the hanging T-shirts with the logos I designed. The concert posters and Beatles memorabilia on the walls. The vintage Ventures clock with the hands made to look like surfboards.

I run my fingers over the records in their bins. Jazz. Blues. Alternative.

I stop when I get to the end of the aisle and look at the stage in the corner. The microphone. The amps and speakers. The acoustic guitar is set on a stand in the corner—what was once my guitar, during that brief stint when I took lessons years ago. Dad held on to it, and has had it available in the store for years now, in case a customer ever wants to just pick it up and strum some music—which is an idea that absolutely terrifies me, but you'd be surprised how many people do it. At least once a day, some stranger picks up that guitar, sits on that stool, and plays a song. Like it's nothing. Like they aren't terrified of being judged, ridiculed, mortified.

I could never do it. Not when the store was open and people were actually here.

Although . . . I guess what I just did at the dance was a hundred times worse.

I step onto the stage and pick up the guitar. Sitting down on the stool, I strum the open strings once, then grasp the neck. My fingers curve into an A major chord, one of the few I can remember. I strum again, trying to remember the words I wrote in my comic.

"And there ends our tale of the great wizard Jude," I sing to myself. "Something, something . . . turned to stone. He may have got the glory, but he never got the girl, and forever he will stand there . . . alone."

A last strum rings out to the empty store and fades away.

Not bad.

I mean, it's better than a song about seltzer water.

I pick mindlessly at a few more strings . . . until I hear a clatter, familiar and loud in the otherwise silent store. I look down as the dice rolls across the stage and hits the guitar stand before coming to a stop. It must have fallen out of my pocket. Or *leaped* out of my pocket. The thing certainly seems to have a mind of its own.

I stare down at its shimmering golden numbers, the sparkles of red that dance across the stage beneath it.

Another *one* glints up at me.

I guess it wasn't impressed with my performance.

Well, you know what?

I wasn't super impressed with its performance, either.

I slide off the stool and return the guitar to the stand before scooping up the dice. My lucky dice. My Scarlet Diamond.

This was supposed to fix everything. Bring back the luck. Reinstate the magic.

And it failed.

Not just failed . . . This stupid dice betrayed me.

Wrath boils inside me. I hate this stupid thing. I hate the luck and I hate the curse and I would have been better off if I'd never found it to begin with.

I could throw it in the ocean!

Or . . .

Or I could melt it!

You know. If I had a kiln. Or a pet dragon.

Gah.

"How do I get rid of you?" I shout. Setting the dice down in the center of the stage, I look around, searching for something big and heavy and powerful.

Where is a freaking battle-axe when you need one?

I don't have a battle-axe, obviously.

I grab the stool instead and raise it over my head. I let out a furious, guttural scream and swing the stool—

Nope. *Nope*. Resist the Dark Side, Jude.

I manage to stop myself just before the stool makes contact—probably saving our stage in the process. I growl. Set the stool down. Look around again. I still don't know what the dice is made out of, but something tells me it would win the fight against a wooden stool.

This time, I grab the dice and the microphone stand and take them both out onto the front sidewalk. I look around, but the street is empty, all the shops long closed for the night. I see a set of headlights a few blocks away, but I don't care.

I'm determined now. Determined to see this through.

"I don't need you!" I say, setting the dice on sidewalk. "I don't want you!" I grip the microphone stand. "Or your magic!" Raise it over my head. "Or your stupid luck!" I let out a howl of anger and swing the stand down, aiming its heavy base right at the red, glinting stone—

The force from the blow reverberates up my arms, sending me stumbling back against the wall of the store. I'm stunned, feeling like my arms are about to disconnect at my shoulders. My teeth vibrate in my skull. My eyes blink and squint, clearing away the red from my vision.

Exhaling a shaky breath, I hold up the microphone stand. The base now sits crooked, bent where it connects to the rod.

And there on the sidewalk—the dice. Destroyed. Bits of jagged stone or glass or whatever it is are scattered across the pavement, hints of gold now seeming dull in the streetlight.

My shoulders sag. My anger leaves me all at once.

I feel . . . ridiculous. Standing there panting while the wind tugs at my hair and my billowy pirate shirt.

And then . . .

And.

Then.

The car I noticed before pulls over to the curb, pinning me in its headlights. I recognize the loud thrum of its engine moments before it shuts off. The headlights dim. The door opens.

"Jude?" says Ari, climbing out of the driver's seat. "What are you doing?"

I'm rendered speechless as she shuts her car door and walks toward me, pulling a sweater tight around her shoulders to ward off the chill coming in from the ocean.

I can only imagine what I look like right now, with my partial costume and crazed expression and broken mic stand, hovering over a shattered twenty-sided dice.

I don't know how to answer her question, so I ask her, instead, "What are *you* doing here?"

She looks from me to the microphone stand to the bits of broken red stone. Her expression is curious and bemused, but she just tucks a strand of hair behind her ear as she walks past me into the store.

I follow behind her, feeling like I'm walking through a virtual reality dreamscape. It looks real, it *feels* real, but something keeps nudging at my brain, telling me it can't possibly *be* real.

"I wanted to get some of my records," says Ari, opening up one of the cardboard boxes left behind the counter. "I know you're planning on sending them back and having them redone, or getting your money back, but Abuela asked if she could send some to our family in Mexico. Even with the skip, she thinks they'll be collectible someday." She makes a face, like she thinks this is highly questionable. "So I thought I'd stop by and grab some before they get sent off."

"You couldn't come in the morning?" I ask. "Don't you work tomorrow?"

She opens her mouth, then closes it, frowning. "It just . . . seemed important that I come tonight." She laughs at herself. "Anyway, what are you doing here? And why are you dressed like a pirate? And what do you have against that poor microphone stand?"

Swallowing, I set the stand back on the stage. It tilts precariously to one side, but doesn't fall. Then I open my arms and look down. "It was supposed to be heroic. Penny said I looked like a prince."

Ari grins, more than a little teasing as I make my way down the main aisle between the record bins.

"That Penny's got good taste," she says. "Is this for a D&D thing?"

"No. I went to the dance."

Her eyes widen. "Really? With who?"

"Nobody. I mean, Pru and Quint. And some people from the D&D group."

Is that relief in her eyes? Am I imagining it?

"Was it fun?"

"No," I say hastily. "It was terrible."

But I'm laughing when I say it, so Ari smiles, too. "I'm sorry to hear that. So, then . . ." She looks around the store, because of course, I didn't answer her question. *Why am I here?*

"I went because I was looking for you," I say, reaching the end of the aisle. "At the dance."

"Oh." Ari straightens. "I wasn't . . . I didn't go."

"Yeah. I got that."

She looks down, mindlessly pulling on a strand of hair. "EZ really caught me off guard at karaoke night. I said yes at first, because there were so many people watching, and I didn't want him to feel bad. But after I had some time to think about it . . ." She makes a guilty face. "I like EZ. But just as a friend." She tilts her head and meets my eye again. "You could have just texted me, you know."

I cross my arms nervously over my chest. "I wanted to see you. In person."

"Okay," she says. "Here I am. Is something wrong?" She starts to look suspicious. "And why did you want to look 'heroic' tonight?"

I already feel awkward with my arms crossed, so I uncross them, but that feels weird, too. I settle one hand on the nearest bin, wishing my heart would stop flipping over in my chest. I glance down, trying to remember all those smart, romantic things I said at the dance, when I thought Ari was there.

My gaze lands on the album next to my hand, and all language evaporates from my brain.

An Elvis album. The title? *I Got Lucky.*

I swallow and look across the aisle to the other side. Another album catches my eye, right in the front of the bin.

Bruce Springsteen's *Lucky Town.*

And on the counter behind Ari—Ronnie Wood, *Mr. Luck.*

Heart pounding, my gaze darts up to some of the album art displayed on the wall. Dawes's *Good Luck with Whatever.* And on the other side of the store . . . Britta Phillips, *Luck or Magic.*

I slam my eyes shut, rubbing the bridge of my nose. *No.* No more luck, good or bad. No more magic. I don't need it, and I don't want it. I am worthy without it.

"Jude?" asks Ari. "Are you feeling okay?"

I look up. She's taken a step toward me.

"Here's the thing," I say tightly. "Life is an adventure, right?"

She hesitates. "I . . . guess?"

"Yours will be, at least. You're going to make amazing music. You're going to have people falling over themselves to work with you and record your songs. This is just the beginning."

She looks startled, even as a hint of a pleased smile turns up her lips. "Thank you?"

"And I'm going to apply to art school. I don't know if I'll get in, but I'm going to try. And maybe someday I'll make comics or illustrate album covers or . . . I don't know. Make concert posters or design fantasy novels or something. And that will all be pretty cool, too."

She nods slowly. "Okay . . ."

"And lately, I've realized that I . . . that I . . ." I squeeze the edge of the bin tighter, but I can't move past that statement. No matter how I try, no words seem right.

I think about a million moments over the years. A million smiles. A million little touches. I think about slow dancing to the Beatles, and Ari calling me her good luck charm, and I think about how I'm *caught up in the downpour of me loving you.*

And I might be a fool, but I hope.

I hope.

I breathe Ari's name. A whisper and a laugh and a magical incantation.

Then I take a deep breath and close the distance between us. I take her in my arms and I bend down and I kiss her.

Chapter Forty-Four

Fireworks.

Trumpets.

Shooting stars.

A symphonic crescendo.

And when she kisses me back . . . it is a freaking Level 8 Sunburst spell.

Chapter Forty-Five

She's in my arms, the ends of her hair brushing against my knuckles, and both of her hands in my hair and, great mother of Gandalf, I am disintegrating by the time I manage to pull away.

Struggling for breath, I lean against her and watch as her eyelashes flutter open.

We stare at each other a long, speechless moment.

Slowly, Ari slides her hands down my neck. Her thumbs brush against my ears. Fingers spread across my shoulders then stop at my chest, where my heart is thundering beneath the surface.

Finally, the words come.

"I want to be with you," I say. "On whatever quest or adventure we go on. I want to be with you. Always. All the time. And I hate that it took me so long to figure that out."

She makes a sound that's a bit of a laugh and a bit of an exhale.

"Jude . . . I—"

A knock raps against the front door.

We both yelp—but rather than jumping apart, we draw closer together, her body tucking instinctively against mine.

"What *now*?" I mutter.

A man is standing outside the front door, fully visible through the glass. Even in the dim lighting, I can see that he's smartly dressed in a khaki sport coat and long plaid scarf.

"Who is that?" says Ari.

"I don't know," I say.

But then the man smiles at us and gives us a casual wave, almost more of a salute, and—

Holy crap.

I *do* know who it is.

"Wait a minute . . . ," says Ari. "He kind of looks like . . ."

"Sadashiv," I whisper.

And it is.

Freaking *Sadashiv* is standing outside Ventures Vinyl at half past ten on a Saturday night.

Beside me, Ari whispers to herself, "This dream just got weirder."

I almost laugh when I glance at her. Except—I think she might be serious. "Do we let him in?"

"A world-famous singer with multiple platinum albums? Yeah, Jude. We let him in."

We make our way to the front, and I open the door. "Uh . . . hello?"

"Good evening," he says in that suave British accent. "I'm so sorry to intrude. Strangest thing—my car just got a flat tire. Hit this . . . *thing* in the road." He lifts up a piece of jagged red stone. On one edge I can see a glinting gold twenty.

"But then I saw your store and that there were people inside, and I hope I'm not interrupting. May I come in?"

"Uh . . . yeah. Sure." I step back, and he strides into the record store. Behind him, across the street, I see a sleek black sports car, the sort of car that celebrities drive. The sort of car that's worth more than the mortgage on this building. Now with one flattened tire.

Sadashiv turns in a circle in the center of the store, his gaze sweeping over the walls. "So this is the famed Ventures Vinyl. It looks larger in the photos, but it's really quite quaint, isn't it?" He pauses to inhale deeply. "Ah, I do love that smell. Every record store has it."

Ari and I exchange mystified looks.

He pivots on his heel to face us again, the movement a bit like a dance step. Then he spots a garbage can beside the counter. Without a second's hesitation, he tosses the broken bit of dice into it. Like that's all it is. Garbage. A sharp piece of rock that flattened his tire, and nothing more. He turns back to us, grinning the grin that has broken a million hearts. "I can't believe you're here. What are the odds that my car would get a flat right outside this store, and even in the middle of the night—here you are! What terribly good luck." He holds a hand toward Ari. "Araceli Escalante. It is beyond a pleasure."

My eyes widen. Ari looks like she's about to faint. Or swoon. Or both.

She manages to shake his hand. "You know who I am?"

He chuckles. "I've been following you on social media. Ever since the music festival and that horrifically botched award ceremony."

Ari opens her mouth, but nothing comes out, so she shuts it again. She shoots me a bewildered look.

"*You* have been following Ari," I say incredulously. "And you know about the music festival."

"I do. My producer was one of the judges. After the awards were announced, he told me that he was quite certain there was some under-handedness in the judging process. It turns out the grand prize winner was related to one of the other judges, which should have been cause for disqualification."

"Huh," I say. "So EZ was right."

"Shady business, that," says Sadashiv, "and it's led to quite the controversy. But that is all irrelevant now. What struck me most when I first heard about the competition was the name of the second place winner. *Araceli Escalante.* Very memorable, isn't it?" He chuckles, smiling at me. "I remembered the name from when you and I met backstage. It is nice to see you again, though forgive me for not recalling *your* name."

"It's Jude."

"Jude! Ah, yes, like the Beatles song." He slides one hand into his pocket, somehow managing to look both effortless and like he's posing for a fashion spread. "As it is, I recalled the name of your songwriter friend, and when I heard about the controversy, I searched up her song and . . . well, I rather like it." He beams at Ari, who leans against the nearest shelf. Definitely swooning. "I've been following your social media ever since. You've accomplished quite a lot in a short period of time."

"Th-thanks," says Ari.

"The story gets stranger still," says Sadashiv. "Do you mind if we sit?" He looks around and spots the stack of chairs against the wall that we used for Ari's audience earlier. Without waiting for a response, he pulls down three chairs and sets them up in an intimate little circle. "That's better," he says, taking the seat closest to the stage and crossing one leg over the other knee. He could be royalty, the way he carries himself.

Ari and I sink into our own seats with significantly less grace.

"What story?" I say, not sure how anything in this night could get *stranger*.

"The story of how I knew about this store," says Sadashiv. "And how it is so serendipitous that I happened to end up here tonight. Where to begin." He leans back in the chair, staring up at the ceiling. "I recently purchased a second home off Bayview, about a mile from here. I'd been wanting a second home in Southern California for some time, as I find myself so frequently in the area for recordings and awards shows and the like."

"As one does," I mutter.

"Bayview?" interrupts Ari. "Not the Greenborough estate?"

He looks at her, astonished. "Why, yes, I think that might be the name of the previous owner. You're familiar with it?"

"My mom's a real estate agent," Ari says. "She had a client looking at that house. She was pretty upset when some anonymous buyer swooped in and paid over asking price for it."

"*Ah*," says Sadashiv, daring to look chagrined. "Well . . ."

"It's okay," says Ari. "I'm pretty sure her client found another multimillion-dollar house to buy. They're kind of a dime a dozen around here."

She's joking, but I don't think Sadashiv can tell as he just nods and says, "I'm glad to hear it."

"Anyway, sorry," says Ari. "Go on."

"Yes. Well . . . after I'd moved in, my mother came to visit from London. And my mother . . ." He laughs affectionately. "She has quite a fondness for music stores. She likes to make sure they have . . . well . . . *my* albums in stock. It's quite embarrassing, really. But she's also become a bit of a collector. So, while she was out one day, she stopped in here and bought some records, but when she was showing me her purchases, she noticed that one record was put into her bag by mistake."

"*London Town*," I whisper. "That was *your mom?*"

Sadashiv grins. "It was. She felt bad about the mistake, especially given the certificate of authentication. A *signed* Paul McCartney poster. Wow." He spreads his hands out, eyes toward the ceiling. "I am an enormous fan, as you might imagine. Met him at the Grammys last year. I was positively starstruck."

"I know the feeling," whispers Ari.

"Anyway, my mother had to return to London the next day, but I promised I would bring the record back to this Ventures Vinyl at the first opportunity. I meant to do it sooner, or have my assistant drop it off, but between moving into the new house and media interviews and trying to get into the studio for my next album, things have been hectic. And *then* . . . ," he goes on, like there's more. Could there be *more*? "I saw your video, Araceli, promoting Record Store Day at . . . well, here. Ventures Vinyl. And while I don't like to admit this to many people, I've always been a bit superstitious. Signs from the universe and all of that. I thought maybe the universe was just reminding me that I still need to return that record, but now, with the car situation, I have to wonder if there's more to it than that."

He beams, his story evidently finished.

A silence settles over us. My brain is on overdrive, piecing together everything he's told us and everything I know to be true. So many random coincidences, leading to here. Sadashiv in our record store and . . .

And *what*, exactly?

"You weren't kidding," says Ari. "That is a strange story."

"I thought so as well," says Sadashiv. "And now, as we're here, this might be a perfect opportunity to discuss a business proposition."

Ari's gaze slides to me, then back to him. "With . . . me?"

"I mentioned trying to record my new album. As it happens, my record label and I have decided it's time to do something different. Go beyond the old standards. We're looking to do an album of original songs, and are hoping to work with some up-and-coming songwriters. I thought we could discuss the possibility of my recording some of *your* songs."

Ari doesn't respond.

"If you're interested in licensing the rights, that is."

She still doesn't respond.

I extend my leg and kick her.

Ari starts. "Y-yes," she stammers. Her hands have started to tremble. "I'm interested. Definitely interested."

"Fantastic," says Sadashiv, clapping his hands together. "I'll have my people be in touch. This has been quite a fateful meeting, hasn't it? But it is late, and I won't keep you any longer." He stands up, and Ari and I both jump to our feet. He shakes both of our hands, then starts to head toward the door.

He pauses, though, his attention landing on one of Ari's records propped up on a shelf by the stage. He picks it up, then glances back at us. "Do you mind if I take one of these? It might very well be collectible one day."

Ari lets out a strangled, delirious giggle.

But I still have a few of my wits about me (not many, but a few), so I say, "What about *London Town*?"

"Yes, of course," he says. "I'll make sure to have my assistant drop it off this week."

He gives us a one-fingered salute, then heads back out into the night, popping up his jacket collar and adjusting his scarf. Only then do I notice another car has pulled up outside, and I wonder if it's his assistant or a chauffeur or if he just called an Uber before he came inside.

The door swings shut, and Ari and I stare at each other for a very long time.

"I'm dreaming," Ari finally says. "No one can possibly be this lucky all in one night." Then her face crumples with disappointment. "It's been such a good dream, too."

Warmth floods my cheeks, thinking of the kiss that I can still taste on my mouth, the hands I can still feel in my hair.

"I don't think we're dreaming," I say, stepping closer.

"No? Sadashiv showing up? In the middle of the night? Wanting to record my songs?"

"It is . . . improbable," I concede. "We'll call it an anomaly."

She laughs, but there's a sad, mournful sound to it. "And *you*? Are you an anomaly, too?" She reaches for the wide linen collar of my shirt, her fingers traipsing across the fabric and sending goose bumps down my arms. "I've been waiting for you to kiss me since we were twelve years old," she says quietly. "And here you are. And . . . you're dressed like a pirate. Why a *pirate*?"

My heart swells. "Since you were *twelve*?"

"Since the very beginning," she says emphatically. Then, confused, "I didn't even know I had a thing for pirates."

I lean closer, pressing my brow against hers. "I'm sorry for making you wait so long. It won't happen again."

"You say that now, but when I wake up . . ."

I grin. "I'm not going to be able to convince you that this is real, am I?"

"This isn't real," she whispers, her breath against my mouth. "It would be easier to convince me that magic is real."

With my hands on her waist, I tug her closer. "Challenge accepted."

Epilogue

"How's that?"

"More to the left."

"No—to the right."

"I liked it more to the left."

"Yeah, there. That looks good."

"No, down a little. No, too much. Half an inch. No, no . . ."

"There! Perfect!"

"Eh, from this angle it looks a little crooked."

I groan. "I'm never hanging artwork by committee ever again."

"There, there!" says Pru. "Perfect."

When no one else objects, I affix the frame to the wall. I climb down the step stool, joining my parents, all four sisters, Quint, and Ari on the other side of the counter. I wrap my arm around Ari's shoulders, and together, we admire our newest decoration.

London Town by Paul McCartney and Wings, signed and matted and framed and hung in a place of honor behind the register.

"Looks great," says Pru. "Like Sir Paul is keeping watch over the place."

My dad grins. "It does feel good to have it back."

It's only been a week since our midnight run-in with Sadashiv, but what a week it has been. Not only did Sadashiv's assistant drop off the record first thing Monday morning, he also brought preliminary papers to start discussing the licensing rights to Ari's songs. She has a meeting with Sadashiv and some producers next month, and they've asked her to bring all her best songs for them to review, though it seems like Sadashiv is already determined to include "Downpour" on his next album.

On Tuesday, I submitted another piece of art to the *Dungeon*. I haven't heard back yet on whether or not it's been accepted, but honestly? It doesn't matter. Rejection never killed anyone, and if they don't like this piece, I'll just keep drawing and submitting more pieces. How else am I going to build up a portfolio to apply to art schools next fall?

On Wednesday . . . well, nothing really happened on Wednesday. Except that I got my grade back on the *Great Gatsby* paper—a B+—and only missed a few questions on our poli-sci test and heard from my art teacher that he really liked my figure sketches, though I could still use some work on my hands. (I mean, come on. Hands are *hard*.)

On Thursday, we finally received the shipment of exclusive Record Store Day merchandise, and while it was a little late, Pru was able to work her social media magic and bring in a hefty crowd that evening to get their special promo items.

Enough good things happened all week that there were times when I thought—maybe the magic is back. Maybe it found me again, even without the dice.

But then on Friday, Mrs. Andrews caught me texting with Ari in class and confiscated my phone for the rest of the day and I missed out on a surprise flash sale on my favorite D&D merch site. When Maya and the others told me about their amazing scores and felt awful that I missed out, I just laughed, thinking about what the fortune teller said.

Is it good luck? Is it bad?

Perhaps.

On Saturday, Ari and I had our first official date. We went to our favorite bookstore off Main Street, where Ari bought a book about licensing music rights and I got the newest title in a fantasy series I like, and then we went out for ice cream and sat in silence and read our new books together. Which was . . . perfect.

We also kissed from time to time.

Which was also perfect.

Ari beams up at me, still snuggled against my side. "I've been working on that ballad for your D&D campaign. The one for the adventurers that broke the curse."

"How's it coming?"

"Good. The comic book pages really helped. Gave me lots of ideas. But . . . I feel like the ending could use some work."

"Probably. It was giving me some problems when I tried to finish it before."

"Well, here's a tip." She stands on her tiptoes and whispers, "The bard should end up with the wizard."

"What?" I say, looking astonished. "Unexpected plot twist. Something like that requires some setup. Some . . . foreshadowing."

"Oh, there's foreshadowing." She gives me a meaningful look. "Trust me."

Sliding our fingers together, I lift her hand to my mouth and kiss her knuckles. "I guess I could make a few minor adjustments."

Acknowledgments

I am the luckiest of authors for being surrounded by so many incredible, supportive people who have helped bring this book to life. Let's roll the dice to determine who I should thank first! (The following order was in fact selected by a twenty-sided dice. Thanks for your help, Universe.)

(3) Thank you, Jill Grinberg: literary agent extraordinaire.

(10) Thank you, Jesse Taylor: songwriting assistant; broken-down car expert; fan club president; charming husband.

(1) Thank you, Liz Szabla: thoughtful, patient, wonderful editor.

(9) Thank you, Mary Weber: lovely author friend who helped with my California-specific research.

(19) Thank you, Sir Paul McCartney: Beatle; writer of "Hey Jude" and "With a Little Luck"; superstar.

(11) Thank you, Lish McBride: awesome author friend who helped me figure out high school schedules (among many other things).

(2) Thank you, the entire fantastic team at Macmillan Children's Publishing Group: Johanna Allen, Robby Brown, Mariel Dawson, Rich Deas, Sara Elroubi, Jean Feiwel, Carlee Maurier, Megan McDonald, Katie Quinn, Morgan Rath, Dawn Ryan, Helen Seachrist, Naheid Shahsamand, Jordin Streeter, Mary Van Akin, and Kim Waymer.

(20) Thank you, my beloved family: Jesse, Delaney, Sloane, and all the extended grandparents, aunts, and uncles. You really put up with a

lot—especially during deadline season—and I am beyond grateful to have you in my life. (Critical hit!)

(8) Thank you, Joanne Levy: outstanding author friend; podcast partner; eleventh-hour research assistant; comic book audio narration adapter.

(5) Thank you, Chuck Gonzalez: extraordinary artist who brought Jude's art to life in our gorgeous comic book pages. *(I love them so much!)*

(15) Thank you, Taylor Denali: graphic designer; business associate; many other things. You should get an award for your unfailing patience with me.

(4) Thank you, the amazing team at Jill Grinberg Literary Management—Katelyn Detweiler, Sam Farkas, Denise Page, and Sophia Seidner: cheerleaders, supporters, friends.

(6) Thank you, Ana Deboo: wonderful, keen-eyed copyeditor.

(16) Thank you, Jeff Ostberg: uber-talented cover illustrator.

(7) Thank you, Andrea Gomez, Alice Gorelick, and Basil Wright: thoughtful sensitivity readers who helped me write Ari, Maya, and Noah as authentically as I could.

(14) Thank you, Kendare Blake, Martha Brockenbrough, Arnée Flores, Tara Goedjen, Alison Kimble, Nova McBee, Lish McBride (again!), Margaret Owen, and Rori Shay: author friends; retreat partners; idea brainstormers; moral support.

(13) Thank you, Tamara Moss: magnificent author friend and best critique partner of all time.

(18) Thank you . . . You! I heart you, Reader.

(17) Thank you to the entire Macmillan Audio team, for bringing Jude and Fortuna Beach to life for listeners everywhere.

(12) Last but not at all least—thank you, Gryphon Aman, Althea Sandberg, and Dannin Zumwalt: panel of teen experts. Thanks for answering all my annoying, clueless-grown-up questions. I toast you with my Leonardo-as-Jay-Gatsby reaction gif.

Thank you for reading this Feiwel & Friends book. The friends who made *With a Little Luck* possible are:

Jean Feiwel, Publisher
Liz Szabla, VP, Associate Publisher
Rich Deas, Senior Creative Director
Anna Roberto, Executive Editor
Holly West, Senior Editor
Kat Brzozowski, Senior Editor
Dawn Ryan, Executive Managing Editor
Kim Waymer, Senior Production Manager
Jie Yang, Senior Production Manager
Foyinsi Adegbonmire, Editor
Rachel Diebel, Editor
Emily Settle, Editor
Brittany Groves, Assistant Editor
Michelle Gengaro-Kokmen, Designer
Helen Seachrist, Senior Production Editor

Follow us on Facebook or visit us online at mackids.com.
Our books are friends for life.